'A meditation on betrayal, nature, violence, and death. The unexplainable terrors of our lives haunt this **piercing** tale of revenge... rendered in precise and **exhilarating** language'
– *Washington Independent Review of Book*

'this novel gives a new definition to the word **'chilling''**
– *Dead Good Books*

'possesses a quiet, **haunting** elegance'
– *First Things*

'William Giraldi has gone over to the dark side with his Cormac McCarthy-like *Hold the Dark*, a **brutal** revenge tale... This novel casts an atmospheric, **noirish spell** that's hard to resist'
– *Shelf Awareness*

'One of the **best** novels I've read this year'
– *Commonweal*

'Written in a **galloping prose** embedded with a hard poetry'
– *Booklist*

'Giraldi's work is as cold and **merciless** as the Alaskan tundra in which it is set... [He] takes his readers deep into the darkness of the human heart'
– *The Absolute*

'Perfect for lovers of the works of **Cormac McCarthy** and **Donald Ray Pollock**'
– *American Booksellers Association*

ALSO BY WILLIAM GIRALDI

Busy Monsters

HOLD THE DARK

William Giraldi

NO EXIT PRESS

This edition published in 2015
by No Exit Press,
an imprint of Oldcastle Books
P.O.Box 394, Harpenden,
Herts, AL5 1XJ, UK

noexit.co.uk
@NoExitPress

A CIP catalogue record for this book is available from the
British Library.

ISBN
978-1-84344-575-3 (print)
978-1-84344-576-0 (epub)
978-1-84344-577-7 (kindle)
978-1-84344-578-4 (pdf)

Typeset by Avocet Typeset, Somerton, Somerset TA11 6RT
in 11pt Sabon
Printed in Great Britain by Clays Ltd, St Ives plc

For more information about Crime Fiction go to @CrimeTimeUK

For Aiden Xavier, may your dark always be on hold

O unteachably after evil, but uttering truth.

– Gerard Manley Hopkins

We fear the cold and the things we do not understand. But most of all we fear the doings of the heedless ones among ourselves.

– Eskimo shaman to explorer Knud Rasmussen

1

THE WOLVES CAME DOWN from the hills and took the children of Keelut. First one child was stolen as he tugged his sled at the rim of the village, another the following week as she skirted the cabins near the ice-choked pond. Now, in the rolling snow whorls of the new winter, a third was dragged from their village, this one from his own doorstep. Noiseless – not a scream, not a howl to give witness.

The women were frantic, those who had lost their children inconsolable. Police arrived from town one afternoon. They scratched sentences into notepads. They looked helpful but never returned to the village. Both women and men patrolled the hills and borders with rifles. Even the elderly, armed with pistols, escorted children home from the schoolhouse and church. But no one would send a party past the valleys to hunt the wolves.

The six-year-old son of Medora Slone was the third to be taken. She told her fellow villagers how she had trekked over the hills and across the vale all that evening and night and into the blush of dawn with the rifle across her back and a ten-inch knife strapped to her thigh. The revenge she wanted tasted metallic. The tracks of the wolves became scattered and vague, then vanished in the flakes falling like feathers.

Several times she sank in snow to her knees and imagined her tears turning to pellets of ice that clinked on the hoar and the rocks of the crag.

In her letter to Russell Core just three days after her boy was taken, she wrote that she did not expect to find him alive. A jagged trail of the boy's blood had led from their back porch and through the patchy woods into the hills above. Still, she needed his body, or whatever remained, if only his bones. That's the reason she was writing Core, she said. She needed him to get her boy's bones and maybe slaughter the wolf that took him. No one in the village would hunt the wolves.

'My husband is due back from the war very soon,' she wrote in her letter to him. 'I must have something to show him. I can't do without Bailey's bones. I can't have just nothing.'

Core was not a man who easily frightened. He'd begun as a nature writer, and in search of a project went north where the gray wolves found him one fall, watched him for a week as he camped and fished there. They trailed him along the river, wanted something from him, though it was not his death, he knew. He imagined they wanted a story woven of truth, not myth, one not tilted by dread. The following winter he journeyed to Yellowstone. His second book chronicled that year of living among the grays – a narrative written in an alien era of youth, so long ago that Core scarcely believed in its reality.

For the afterword he offered an essay on the only recorded wolf attack on a human in the park. A female gray had crept into a campsite and stolen a toddler while the parents slept off champagne. He explained this killing as the result of food shortages, migrating herds of caribou confused by a late winter, heedless human invasion into the domain of the wolf: roads and campsites and oil-starved engines, all of it an affront to the majesty of what once had been. Even his own presence among them was an indignity. He felt that daily. This girl's death was no mystery, no myth. Only elemental. Only hunger.

He was asked to help in the stabbing cold of that morning – the nature writer who had been tent-living among the clan of this killer. He could not say no. His daughter was the same age as the taken girl and his love for her then felt already like loss. The guilt of a father whose work takes him from home. He and the others, the rangers and biologists and camouflaged men, tracked the wolf across twenty square miles over the Northern Range, through Lamar Valley. He rode on a borrowed four-wheeler and was in radio contact with the sniping copters he hated. He sent them false information so they would not find her. Then he rode across the line into Montana where, alone and sickened, he found her and shot her from forty yards on a cattle farmer's ranch. The rifle they'd given him had no kick – it was nothing like the guns he'd fired as a boy, at the range with his father before his father slumped from life.

That morning Core thought his own land-borne bullet more respectful than those from rangers impersonating gods. Through the scope he could see the wolf's white muzzle still sprayed pink with the child's innards. Pieces of yellow pajamas were glued to the dried purple blood just over her flews. Her eyes were golden. Not the glow of red or green as in picture-book terror-wolves, but a dullish, perversely dignified human gold.

You don't see yourself full, Core knew, until you see yourself reflected in the eye of a beast. This task was a test of human dignity, and he had failed.

No one can deceive the eyes of a wolf. They always know. And in this way he came to know her too. He left just after he killed her. This was his book. It began in tribute and ended in slaughter. He'd studied that female gray for a year. He'd named her the name of his daughter.

Examiners found much of the girl mashed inside the digestive tract. 'A goddamn murderer,' the dead child's parents said of the wolf that robbed her. 'A goddamn demon.' But Core knew otherwise. The raider, this marauder, thief in the night – she dared to intrude not because it was her wish but because it was her need. Who was the transgressor here? He wanted to scold these parents, insist on a fine for their wanton camping in a restricted dale, for the plastic trash dumped beside their tent, but he could not.

Then he watched over the next decade as the gray wolf was hunted to near-extinction. Those cowards sniping from their copters. He recoiled each time he remembered squeezing the trigger on that adult female with the strands of cloth stuck to the hinge of her mouth. He became a help to Yellowstone reintroduction, penned newspaper editorials about man's hubris, spoke at college symposiums where khaki-clad alumni nodded in agreement, asked him to sign his book and then quickly forgot.

In her letter Medora Slone wrote of Core's book: 'You have sympathy for this animal. Please don't. Come and kill it to help me. My son's bones are in the snow.'

———•◆•———

He had Medora Slone's letter folded into the pocket of his denim jacket when he arrived at the nursing home, a sprawling one-level building that used to be an elementary school, classrooms converted into bedrooms but the hallways still school-like. A column of lockers still at one end, the fire alarms plate-sized red bells he remembered from his own youth. His wife of thirty-five years lay sleeping where she'd lain for the past thirteen months, only part lucid in a bed after a stroke had cleaved one half of her head. He stood looking at this woman who needed a power no man or god was able to give.

He went to the sink and drank. In the mirror he saw his white mane spilling to his shoulders from beneath a baseball cap, the ruff of white sprouting from his jawline, a chin that seemed elongated. He could not guess when he had gone so wintry, so wolfish. Thirteen months ago, perhaps. Microwave meals twice a day. The uneven sleep of the sick, all the hours of quiet he counted. The wind in winter an almost dulcet guest for the wail it made. Boredom daily morphed to despair and back. Sixty years old this year and he knew he looked eighty. Unable to summon the will even to see a barber.

How many more paintings could he produce of the wolf he'd slain? The walls of his library were already covered with such creations. Always, it seemed, of the same wolf. Always the yellow strands of cloth pasted into her bloodied mouth. He could not paint her back to the living. He could not will his own living back.

Thousands of titles stood in his library, gathered and read over a lifetime. Each morning he'd stand in that space, bracketed by books. Touching, fanning through volumes, smelling the poems in their pages, but without the urge anymore to read. A random stanza or paragraph was all he could manage. That pine desk, where he'd written his own books, had once belonged to his father. The chestnut leather armchair was a gift from his wife after they were married. In the foyer of their house an undusted crucifix kept watch upon galoshes and gloves, a parka and cowl hooked where she had hooked them a winter ago. A WELCOME mat worn down to COME. His painting studio in the attic, once so organized, was now a havoc of canvases and paint tubes, of brushes and easels and drop cloths. The washing machine broke last winter and he left it that way.

Through the cotton blanket he felt for his wife's foot and grasped it in some unsure gesture of goodbye. He thought of his estranged daughter, far off in Anchorage, a college history professor, what she would say when she saw him, when he arrived unbidden. He took his duffel bag and went. In the hallway a female attendant in a red sweater wished him a merry Christmas, handed him a candy cane broken at its curve. Core looked at his watch: Christmas was still three weeks away. He'd forgotten about Thanksgiving. In the parking lot of the nursing home, in the day's gaunt sun, sat idling the same white cab that had delivered him.

Outside the desert city an urgent wind whisked up sand. Dark mustard gusts passed before a buffed sun and looked like blots of insects sent to swarm. Their vehicle made plumes of tawny dust as they sped after a pickup rusted red and packed with men. Perched at the .50-caliber gun, Vernon Slone heard the sand pepper his face mask. This late in the day and the temperature stayed fixed at one hundred.

Back home he knew it was snowing – a winter he would not see. Behind him the city smoldered. If he turned he could behold the smoke and flames of this Gomorrah they'd made. But before him he could see just the windswept sand and the twirling dust of the truck fifty yards ahead. No one was shooting now. No one could see. Every few seconds, between horizontal gusts of sand, Slone spotted the truck's tailgate.

He watched the truck catch the gulley and overturn four times in near silence, in a storm of sand and dust. He'd seen pickups and snow machines flip in fluffed snow the same way: no sound. The men – what faction were they from? what region? – were tossed from the truck's bed like bags of leaves. The truck slid, smashed to a halt on top of them. Some limped from the tinfoil wreck and shot at Slone's vehicle. The lead dinged against the armor.

When the .50-caliber rounds hit them they tore off limbs or else left dark blue holes the size of plums. He fired into those on the fuel-damp sand and those still crammed inside the truck's flattened cab. Their blood burst in the wind as wisps of orange and red. Curious how orange, how radiant blood looks beneath a desert noon, in the dull even tinge of its light.

The truck ignited but did not explode. They let it burn there for fifteen, twenty minutes and then finally approached with extinguishers.

The boy inside was Bailey's age. The unburned skin of his face shone of caramel. Shirtless, without shoes, his feet so singed they seemed melted and remolded – feet fashioned from candle wax. Spalls of rock made piercings in his neck and chin, the jugular ripped unevenly by broken glass, below it a gown of blood to his kneecaps. Slone looked into the liquid gray eyes of the man beside him – a man whose simple name, Phil, did not seem to fit the darkness Slone knew he had within.

Who issues orders here? What foul game's pieces are we? They sat smoking on their vehicle. Slone watched the others search pockets and packs. Some clicked shots of the wreck, showed each other, and laughed. Phil bent to knife out the eyes and tongues of the dead – these would be his keepsake.

———◆———

Core arrived in Alaska in the faint hold of early dusk. He'd slept on the flight, was winched down deep into the vagueness of dreams where he saw the bleared faces of his wife and daughter, and of someone else in shadows, someone he suspected was his mother. At the airport he asked a man the way to the rental car counter and the man simply pointed to the sign directly in front of them, the company's name shouting inside a yellow arrow. In a shop he stood before a magazine rack, made-up faces grinning on covers but he could not name a single one. Alaska papers proclaiming weather. He bought a candy bar.

He rented a four-wheel-drive truck to go the one hundred miles inland to the village of Keelut. The truck had a GPS suctioned to the windshield but he'd never used one before, and the attendant told him that where he was going could not be found on GPS. He gave Core a road map, 'one of the more accurate ones,' he said, and in red marker traced Core's path from the airport to Keelut. But Core was lost immediately upon leaving the terminal, on a road that brought him to the hub of this odd city. He saw bungalows hunkered beside towers, Cessna seaplanes parked in driveways, cordwood piled in front of a computer store. Filthy vagrants loping along with backpacks, groomed suits on cell phones.

When he found the right road the city shrank behind him, the December-scape unseen beyond the green glow of the dashboard. He saw old and new snow plowed into half-rounded wharves along the roadside. The red and white pinpricks of light that passed overhead were either airplanes or space vessels. He felt the possibility of a close encounter with discoid airships, with gunmetal trolls from a far-off realm descending to ask him questions he'd not be able to answer. Half an hour of careful driving and the snow came quick in two coned lanes the headlamps carved from darkness. What would he tell Medora Slone about the wolf that had stolen her child? That hunger is no enigma? That the natural order did not warrant revenge?

He'd seen his daughter only once in the last three years, when she came home the morning after her mother's stroke. Three crawling years. Life was not short, as people insisted on saying. He'd quit cigarettes and whiskey just before she was born. He wanted to be in health for her and knew then that ten years clipped from his life by drink and smoke were ten years too many. Now he knew those were the worthless years anyway, the silver decade of life, a once-wide vista shrunk to a keyhole. Not all silver shines. As of this morning he had plans to return to cigarettes and whiskey both. He regretted not buying them at the airport.

Highways to roads to paths, towns to wilderness, the wider and wider dispersion of man-made light. One lost hour in the opposite direction, in a deepening dark of forest that seemed eager to ingest him. Then a trucker at a fuel station who gave him a better map, who pointed the way, although he wasn't certain, he said. An eagle was tattooed in black above his eye. 'I'm just looking for the easiest roads,' Core told him, and the trucker said, 'Roads? This place doesn't have roads.' He laughed then, only three teeth in a mouth obscured by an unruly beard. Core could not understand what he meant. The snow stopped and he drove on.

Hours later, Core made it to an unpaved pass without a mark to name it. This was the pass to Keelut, a right turn where the hills began to rise close to the road, just past a rotted shanty the trucker had told him to watch for. In four-wheel drive he bumped along this pass until he came to the village. He could count the cabins, arranged in two distinct rows. Most were one-level with only a single room. Some were two-level with sharply slanted roofs and radio antennae stretching into the cold. The hills beyond loomed in protection or else threatened to clamp.

He parked and walked in drifts to his shins. Sled dogs lay leashed beside cabins, huskies huddled together and harnessed, white-gray and cinnamon in sudden moonlight, the snow about them flattened, blotched pink and bestrewn with the bones of their supper. Muscled and wolfish, indifferent to this cold, uncaring of him. He was surprised by a child standing alone in the dark. He stopped to look, unsure if she was real, then asked her for the way to the Slones' cabin. This child's cordate face was part Yup'ik, lovely in its unwelcome look. She simply pointed to the cabin before turning, before fleeing into snow-heavy spruce squat in the shadowed dark. He watched her disappear between branches, wondered where she could be going in such chill of night. Why was she not fearful of wolves, of being taken as the others had been taken?

The moon on the snow tricked the eye into seeing the snow itself emanate light. To his left, silhouetted against a sky almost neon blue, stood a totem pole keeping sinister watch at the rim of the village – twenty feet high, it bore the multicolored faces of bears, of wolves, of humanoid creatures he could not name, at the top a monstrous owl with reaching wings and massive beak. He turned to look down the center stretch of the village – not a road but a plowed and shoveled path between two banks of cabins, at the end what seemed a town square with a circular stone structure, half hidden now in hillocks of snow. To his right a wooden water tower with a red-brick base, useless in winter. Behind it a grumbling generator shack giving power to this place. In the orange glow of cabin windows he could spot round faces peering out at him. The air now nearly too cold to breathe.

He walked on to the Slones' cabin. A set of caribou antlers jabbed out from above the door – in welcome or warning, he could not be sure.

———◆———

Medora Slone had tea ready when he finally entered. He was surprised by her white-blond youth. He'd expected the dark raiment of mourning and messed black hair. Her face did not fit, seemed not of this place at all. Hers was the pale unmarked face of a plump teenage softball player, not a woman with a dead boy and a husband at war. Her eyes were pale too. In a certain angle of lamplight they looked the sparest sheen of maize, almost gold.

Her cabin at the edge of the village was built better than most. Two rooms, tight at the edges, moss chinking between logs. Half a kitchen squeezed into a corner, a cord of wood stacked by the rear door, fireplace and granite hearth at one end, cast-iron stove at the other. Bucket of kindling near the stove, radio suspended from a nail in a log. He could brush the ceiling with a fingertip. Easier to heat with low ceilings, he knew. Plastic sheeting stapled and duct-taped over windows to keep out cold. A rifle in the umbrella stand, a child's BB gun in a corner. Compound bow and quiver of arrows hung above the hearth. His book on wolves was partially stuffed between two cushions of the sofa, pages folded over and under, the cover torn. He asked to use her bathroom and ignored himself in the glass.

They sat across from one another – she on a sofa whose cushions were worn to the foam, he sunk low in an armchair – and they sipped tea in the quiet welcomed by their exhaustion. She offered him the food that others from the village had been bringing to her since her son's disappearance – caribou soup, fry bread, moose stew, wheat berries, pie baked with canned peaches. But he had no appetite now. The tea warmed his limbs, a lone orange coal or glowing hive pulsing from the center of him. He rolled the sleeves of his flannel shirt. On the pine arm of the chair were the ring stains of a coffee mug – an Olympic logo warped and brown.

'*Canis lupus*,' she said.

'Yes, ma'am.'

'Apex predator.' She moved his book to the coffee table between them. 'Ice age survivor from the Late Pleistocene. What's that mean?'

'It means they've been around a long time and know how to hunt better than we do.'

'You sound... happy by that.'

'I'm sorry about your son, Mrs Slone.'

'You've come to kill it, then? To kill that animal that took him?'

He looked but did not answer.

'So why'd you come, then? I was a little surprised you replied to the letter I sent.'

The crushing quiet of his house.

'I came to help if I can,' he said. 'To explain this if I can.'

'The explanation is that we're cursed here. The only help is to kill it.'

'You know, ma'am, I'm just a writer.'

'You've hunted and killed one of them before. I read that in your book.'

'Where'd you find the book?'

'It found me. I don't know how. It was just here one day.'

She looked to the room around them, trying to recognize it, trying to remember.

'You mentioned getting the boy's bones, but... I don't know.'

'Yes,' she said. 'I was thinking that his bones would show during breakup.'

'Breakup?'

'You know, in spring. After the thaw.'

He did not tell her this was impossible. The boy's yellow snow boots stood like sentinels on the mat near the door, his pillowed coat on a hook, but there was no framed school photo grinning at Core gap-toothed from the mantel, no plastic trucks or toy guns on a carpet. If not for the boots and coat, this woman before him was just another story among the many he'd been told. Sixty years old, he was half sure he'd heard every tale worth hearing. That morning at the airport, sitting at a window in a boulevard of sunlight, in spring's cruel tease, he tried to remember his parents' faces and could not.

'I would have killed the thing myself,' she said. 'If I could have found it. I tried to find it. I tried to do it.'

'No, their territory could be up to two hundred square kilometers. It's good you didn't find it. The pack is probably eight or ten members. No more than twelve, I'd guess. You don't want to find that.'

'Can I ask you a personal question, Mr Core?'

He nodded.

'Do you have a child?'

'Yes, a daughter, but she's grown now. In Anchorage, she teaches at the university. I'll see her when I leave here.'

'A teacher like her father.'

'I'm no teacher. I maybe could have been, but... She's good at it, I hear. She wanted to be an Alaskan.'

'That city's not Alaska. Where you are right now, Alaska starts here. We're on the edge of the interior here.'

He said nothing.

'Mr Core, do you have any idea what's out those windows? Just how deep it goes? How black it gets? How that black gets into you. Let me tell you, Mr Core, you're not on Earth here.' She looked into the steam of her mug, then paused as if to drink. 'None of us ever have been.'

He watched her drink. 'I've felt that in certain places over the years.'

'Certain places. I mean what you feel here won't be the same as anything you've ever felt before.'

He waited for an explanation.

She gave him none.

'But this is your home,' he finally said.

'I'm not from here originally. I was brought here when I was a child, and that makes me not from here.'

'Brought here from where?'

'I don't remember that. I've never been told where and I never asked. But I know this place is different.'

He imagined her in the snow standing naked, almost translucent, a vision caught for only a second before blinking her gone. 'Yes, ma'am,' he said.

Her eyes flicked about the room in anxiety, in expectation. She lifted his book from the table and fanned through the pages. 'I don't understand what they're doing here,' she said.

'Who?'

'Wolves.'

'They've been here for half a million years, Mrs Slone. They walked over the Bering land bridge. They live here.'

They live here. And Core knew they helped rule this continent until four hundred years ago. Inuit hunters learned to encircle caribou by watching wolves. Hunting-man revered another hunter. Farming-man wanted its existence purged. Some set live wolves ablaze and cheered as they burned. *Wolf and man are so alike we've mistaken one for the other*: Lupus est homo homini. *This land has hosted horrors most don't care to count. Wolfsbane. But we are the hemlock, the bane of the wolf.* Core said nothing.

'I don't understand what they're doing here,' and she gestured feebly in front of her, at the very space on the rug where her son had no doubt pieced together a puzzle of the solar system. Or else scribbled a drawing of the very monster that would one day come for him, stick-figure mother and father looking on, unable to help.

'Why is this happening to me, Mr Core? What myth has come true in my house?'

'They're just hungry wolves, Mrs Slone. It's no myth. It's just hunger. No one's cursed. Wolves will take kids if they need to. This is simple biology here. Simple nature.'

He wanted to say: *All myths are true. Every one is the only truth we have.*

She laughed then, laughed with her tear-wet face pressed into her hands. He saw her fingernails were gnawed down to nubs. He knew she was laughing at him, at his outsized task here before her.

'I'm sorry,' he said, and looked at his boots. 'I don't know why this is happening to you, Mrs Slone.'

He could name no comfort for this. His face warmed with the foolishness of his being here.

More quiet. And then: 'Does your husband know?'

She seemed startled by the word, unready to recall her husband. 'Men were supposed to call him there, to call the ones who could tell him. But I said I would do it, that I should be the one to do it. I never did, though. I can't tell him while he's there. He'll see for himself.' She paused and considered her gnawed fingertips. 'He'll see what has happened. What we've done. What no one here was able to stop.'

'They're hungry and desperate,' he said. 'They don't leave for the fringes of their territory unless they're desperate. They avoid contact with humans if they can. If we'll let them. The wolves that came to this village must be rabid. Only a rabid or starved wolf does what happened here.'

He looked beyond her, looked for the language but it was not there. 'The caribou must have left early,' he said. 'For some reason.'

He could have told her more. That wolves have a social sophistication to make many an American town look lagging. That the earliest human tribes were identical to wolf packs. That a healthy gray wolf's yearly requirement of meat can reach two tons, that they'll cannibalize each other, kill their own if the hunger hones to a tip. He'd seen this in the wild. A six-year-old boy would have shredded like paper in the teeth of any adult male. It killed the boy at his throat and then rent through the clothing to get at the belly, its muzzle up beneath the ribs to eat the organs it wanted.

'If I can ask,' he said, 'why wouldn't anyone here hunt the wolves after what happened?'

'They're afraid. And the ones who don't have fear have respect. They respect the thing. They probably think we deserve it, we deserve what happened here.'

'I don't understand, Mrs Slone.'

'Stay here long enough and you might. Can I refill your tea?'

He indicated no. His tea was finished now and he felt the first shadows of sleep drop across his shoulders. Somewhere in the village a brace of sled dogs barked up at constellations stretched across a bowl of black. Both he and Medora Slone turned to look at the sheeted window. Where were the sled dogs when the wolves came? He remembered a Russian proverb: *Do not call the dogs to help you against the wolves.*

He remembered a story he'd been told and could never say if it was parable or fact but he told it to her anyway: 'In Russia, during a winter of the Second World War, a food shortage was on. No meat, no grain. The fighting decimated the land. The wolves rampaged into villages and mauled at random. Like they were their own invading army. They killed hundreds of people that winter, and not just women and children. Drunk old men or crippled men too weak to defend themselves. Even dogs. There was nobody left to hunt the wolves. All the able men were at the war or dead. Somehow aware of that imbalance, the wolves came and left scenes of carnage almost as bad as the bombs. Doctors said they were rabid, but the villagers said they were possessed by demons hell-bent on revenge. Their howls, they said, sounded like hurt demons. It was revenge, the old people thought. Revenge for something, for their past, maybe, I don't know.'

She stared at him – she didn't understand. She looked insulted.

'I mean you're not alone,' he said.

24

'Yes, I am. What's done can't be undone, can it? Just look what we're capable of, Mr Core,' and she held up her palm for him to see. But he did not know why and was too frightened to ask.

She lowered her hand and said, 'Come, I'll show you outside where the children were taken. Are those your boots?'

He looked at his feet. 'These are my boots.'

'You'll need better boots.'

This stolid village remained gripped in snow and stillness, and over the hills lay a breadth without end, an echoing cold with a mind that won't be known. Yellow-orange squares burned in the sides of log and frame homes, stone spires exhaling wood smoke. From the hook on a cabin hung a fish chain with two silver salmon. Core saw overturned dogsleds and toboggans, canoes and aluminum boats, ricks of exposed wood, pickup trucks with tire chains. Adjacent to some cabins were plywood kennels for sled dogs. Unlabeled fifty-five-gallon drums, rust-colored, most with tops torched off. Shovels and chain saws and snow machines, Coleman lanterns dented and broken. Gas-powered auger to drill lake ice. Blue tarp bungeed around a truck's engine on sawhorses. Vehicles mugged by snow and stranded. The church an unpainted A-frame beside the schoolhouse. And all around, those hills with howls hidden within.

He'd been deep into the reaches of Montana, Minnesota, Wyoming, Saskatchewan, but no place he could remember matched the oddness, the otherness he felt in this place. A settlement at the edge of the wild that both welcomed and resisted the wild.

'It's beautiful here,' he said, his words in a cloud. It was a lie, and he knew she heard it as a lie.

She looked to him. 'You don't understand.'

'What don't I understand, Mrs Slone?'

She neither tensed against the cold nor appeared to feel the freeze on her naked face and hands.

'This wildness here is inside us,' she said. 'Inside everything.'

She pointed out beyond the hills at an expanse vaster than either of them knew.

'You're happy here?' he asked.

'Happy? That's not a question I ask myself. I see pictures in magazines, vacation pictures of islands, such green water and sand, girls in bathing suits, and I wonder about it. Seems so strange to me, being there. There's a hot spring not so far from here, a three-hour walk, a special place for me, hidden at the far end of the valley. That's as close as I get to warmth and water.'

'A hot spring sounds good right now,' he said.

'Good to get clean,' she said, and he did not ask what she meant by that.

'I've come to help you if I can, Mrs Slone. Nothing's a novelty to me here.'

She wouldn't look at him now. 'Mr Core, my husband left me alone here with a sick child.'

'You met in this village?'

'We never met anywhere. I knew him my whole life. Since before my life. I don't have a memory he isn't in. And he left me here.'

'But the war.'

'I heard on the radio it's not a real war. Someone said that.'

'It's real enough, Mrs Slone. People are dying real deaths. On both sides.'

'He said he'd never leave me. That's what men say. Words can't be worthless, just thrown away like some trash. There's punishment for the wrong words.'

'But I've found that sometimes life interferes with words. Or changes what you meant by them.'

She turned from him and walked on. He followed. From a copse of birch a Yup'ik man and his boy, both with rifles, dragged a lank moose calf, barely meat enough for a family's meal. Medora Slone and Core watched them pull it through the snow to their cabin beyond the copse.

They walked again in silence.

'That's the pond where the first was taken.' She pointed.

He wiped his wet nostrils with a glove.

'Didn't you bring some warmer clothes?'

'I didn't expect this kind of cold,' he said.

'It's not even cold yet, Mr Core. I have some warmer clothes for you. And Vernon's good boots.'

'You said before your son was sick.'

'He wasn't the right one.'

'I'm sorry?'

'He stopped going to school after his father left.'

'That's normal enough, I think. Children usually don't like school at first. My daughter went through that.'

His daughter was of course grown, very much alive, a lifetime of school in her past. He wanted to blame his exhaustion, this ungodly cold for his carelessness, his stumbling words.

'I'm sorry,' he said, 'I only meant –'

'Stop apologizing to me.' She pointed again. 'The wolf came from that dip in the hill, at the far side of the pond there. I found its tracks. I followed them. And there was nothing normal about our son.'

He saw at the pond the snow-covered rectangle he guessed was a dock. Children leapt from that dock in summer, but imagining the sounds of their splashes was not possible now. This village tableau repelled every thought of summer and light. He wanted to understand what warmth, what newness and growth was possible here, but he could not.

'The second was taken over here. The girl,' she said, and they moved around the pond, behind a row of cabins to where the low front hills split to form an icy alcove. 'The children sled in here, down that hill there.'

He remembered: *Take warning hence, ye children fair; of wolves' insidious arts beware.*

'Bailey too?'

'Bailey didn't sled.' She paused here, hand on her womb as if the womb held memory the hand could feel. 'He just wasn't the right one.'

'I'm not sure what you mean by that, ma'am.'

'He didn't sled.'

They stood staring into the alcove; he tried to imagine the animal charging down the slope. A startled child's visage of terror. A gust lifted from their left, carried blurs of snow and yanked at their clothes. Medora Slone moved through wind and snow as others move through sun.

'How did it feel to shoot that female wolf?' she asked.

'I was there to study them.'

'And you really believe what you wrote? That a wolf taking a child is part of the order of things out there?' She gestured to the hills, past the hills.

'Yes, I do, Mrs Slone.'

'How did it feel to shoot it?'

'I didn't have much of a choice that day. It felt bad.'

'But not so rare?'

'Very rare,' he said. 'They aren't what you think, Mrs Slone. What happened here does not happen.'

She stared – her eyeballs looked frozen. 'What happened here happened to *me*.'

He closed his eyes and kept them closed in the cold, loathing the words that might come from him. He said nothing.

'I suppose you're hungry now,' she said. 'I have some soup for you.'

When they arrived back at the Slones' front door, he asked, 'Where was your son taken?'

'Around back,' she said, and gestured feebly with her chin at the corner of the cabin.

'May I see?'

'I'd rather you didn't now,' she said, and took his gloved hand to lead him inside, a lover's gesture he could not make sense of.

She heated caribou soup in a small dented pot on the burner. In the armchair he ate from the pot and let the broth transform him, quash his ability to fend off this insistent sleep. She traded him a mug of black coffee for the pot. He saw on a shelf a half-gone bottle of whiskey and asked if she might add some to his coffee. She poured into his mug and when he drank the heat of it filled the hollowness in him.

He asked then if she might have a cigarette and chocolate. From a cupboard she retrieved them, an unopened bag of chocolate he knew must have belonged to the boy, and a brand of filterless cigarettes he did not recognize. They sat and smoked together but they did not speak. His chest and lungs felt aflame at first, but after several pulls they remembered. He smoked smoothly with the chocolate smeared to the roof of his mouth and was thankful for this pleasure among so much sting.

She rose to answer a knock on the rear door. It was the boy of the Yup'ik hunter they'd seen earlier; he handed her an unwrapped slab of the moose calf, no larger than her palm, and she thanked him.

When she returned to the sofa Core said, 'The others here love you.'

'No,' she said. 'It's not love. It's just what we do. Everyone shares with everyone.'

'It's not common where I'm from.'

'I left a quilt and pillow here for you, Mr Core. I see you're tired.' She rose from the sofa and placed her mug on the counter-top. 'Thank you for coming here. I can't pay you anything.'

'It's all right,' he assured her.

'Is your daughter expecting you?'

'I'm not sure what she expects, actually. I might call when I'm done here. Or just go. Thank you for the soup and coffee.'

She fed the fire wedges of axed wood. 'You'll get cold in the night when this fire dies. That heater there works, when the electric works. You're free to use it, just roll it to you. Or I can start up the stove for you.'

'I'm all set,' he said.

'Good night, Mr Core.'

She clicked off the lamp before turning into the back room. 'To bed, to bed,' he heard her say, and the door clicked shut.

———◆———

In the dark beneath the quilt he felt the fissure filling in him, sleep his sole respite against the strafing day. He was still disoriented in this place; he wanted badly to remember where he came from, and why he had come.

He heard the howl of a wolf seconds before sleep would drag him down into darkness. It was mournful through the iced black of night – an uncommon howl, an appeal he could not identify: part fury, part fear, part puzzlement. The female gray he had tracked and killed so long ago howled at him – he knew the howl was at him – from across three miles of flat expanse, from the center of that stripped abundance.

Many nights he expected to be jarred awake by dreams of the wolf he'd killed, by the sharp crack of the rifle round. And when he slept soundly through till dawn, he woke feeling remorseful that his rest had not been disrupted.

With sleep wafting in now he thought he heard the mutters of Medora Slone from the back room, the incantations of a witch, songs whispered through sobs. He knew what haunted meant. The dead don't haunt the living. The living haunt themselves.

An hour into sleep, somewhere at the heart of an errant dream, he woke to light knifing out from around the bathroom door, to the sound of water running into the tub. He sat up on the sofa and listened. She had not closed the door completely, and in his wool socks, slick on the wood floor, he crept to look, terrified by what he was doing, by the chance of being seen by her, but helpless to ignore this. He could hear her muttering, and when he crouched by the door and looked into the crack of light, he saw her sitting in the steam of the tub, scrubbing herself raw with a bath brush, her expression one of pained resolve. Ashamed, he returned to the sofa and raised the quilt to his chin.

But soon he woke again, and he saw the naked figure of Medora Slone silhouetted before the window. She'd pulled away the plastic sheeting and stood now motionless with her hand on the glass opaque with rime, moon-haunted, it seemed to Core, but there was no moon anymore. The firelight had died and the blue-white night was unnaturally intense around her. He saw the folds of her waist, the weighted breasts falling to either side of her rib cage, the tiny cup of flesh at her elbow. He lay unmoving in a kind of fear looking at her over his cosseted body, his breath stifled lest she hear him watching, lest he disrupt this midnight vigil.

'Is he up there? Or down there?' Her voice, no more than a murmur, came to him as if from across an empty chamber.

'Mrs Slone? It's late, Mrs Slone. Are you all right?'

She turned to see him lying on the sofa. He could make out only half her face. If he sat up he could reach over the cushioned arm and stroke her hip, her breast, no more than a yard away.

He rose to stack more wood in the hearth, then wheeled

the electric heater near the sofa. When she moved toward him, he instinctively peeled back the quilt and shifted to make room. She fit into him imperfectly, the sofa sank more, then he covered them in the quilt and clutched her quaking body.

With her back to him, she took his hand and brought it to her throat, folding it hard around her windpipe, trying to will his grip to squeeze. He tried to retrieve his hand but she held tighter, then slid it down and placed it between her thighs, on a woolly patch of yellow hair. Arms around her again, he held her till she passed into the twitch of a nightmared sleep.

2

ON PATROL THROUGH THE western sector of the city Vernon Slone saw pyramids of tires flaming on street corners in their own weather of black smoke. A market bombed and abandoned, fruit on the stones like vivisected bellies, the buildings behind the market reduced to irregular mounds of rubble, some of them unrecognizable as former houses or places of ware. Another afternoon's creep, the cool of dusk an impossibility only dreamed of.

Their vehicle crawled and stopped and crawled again, not knowing where it wanted to be in a spread-out train of trucks snaking through these streets. First his wishes of being in the snowed-over scape he knew, then his teary-eyed vision from the fires. He searched for movement, for men among the wreckage, anything with life left to end. On the road the top half of a man's charred body, snipped through at the waist, entrails in a fly-feasting pile, his one arm outstretched as if trying to swim the torso back to his bottom part.

And then the rapid snaps from rifles on a rooftop. Or from the maw in a bombed building. He knew that one round had entered his right shoulder, had just missed his vest. He could feel the blood, the heated honey in his armpit hair. An explosion from under the vehicle in front of his. It lifted sideways from force of flame and burned there in front of him. A soldier on fire limped from the wreck, one arm missing like the jagged end of driftwood, his other waving somebody to come near, to extinguish this new thing upon him. But no one came and he dropped to burn in the road.

Slone scattered the .50-caliber rounds into bricks, into doors, into a disabled pickup with a missing front axle. Movement on a roof and he fired there. A face-wrapped man with a rifle darted from behind the abandoned pickup and tried to make the alleyway. Slone hit him before he reached it. The rounds punched his back and split his head, strewed the beige building with a flare of red. For an instant it looked to Slone almost like a painting, the lustrous spray of it something he once saw in an art book.

The other gunners in his line of trucks were unloading now in a din of machine gun fire. To his right behind a mound of rubble, another face-wrapped man. Slone trained on him as he moved, the rounds hacking off pieces of him as if from axe blows.

The burst in his neck then felt like the release of steam or gas – not even a spark of pain. When he slumped down expecting the mantle of black, he thought of Bailey in front of a television: *Dad, look at this, look*, and on the screen were trapeze artists breaking free of gravity, soaring, their bodies unnaturally elastic but strong. And then the trapeze artists were gone, the tent's top blew off, dispensed in smoke, and the boy's face turned an iced-over blue, mouthing slow words to Slone he could neither hear nor lip-read. But he imagined his son saying *Remember me* and he tried to reach out for the boy but could not.

Some time later – he couldn't tell how long, each minute a grain of sand dropping in an hourglass – he awoke on a gurney, worked on by others, rough hands mending his shoulder and neck, a corporal grinning down, 'You lucky fucker, you're going home.' His said his son's name and the corporal told him, 'Soon, you lucky fucker, you'll see him soon.' The small-caliber round had missed both his pharynx and spine.

'Nothing but a hickey, man,' someone said, and he felt the pinch of a syringe and sleep then lowered him into a grateful dark where he could not dream.

———◆———

Core woke in this winter dark before a belated dawn, Medora Slone still asleep and nude beside him on the sofa, the electric heater and their bodies an able source of warmth, the quilt a caul he wanted to remain in. Soon he built a fire, started the woodstove. She dressed and cooked and watched him depart with the AR-15 rifle and a pack of provisions and snowshoes. He wore her husband's boots and one-piece of caribou hide – a winter suit she'd crafted herself for the unholiest cold. She covered the end of the rifle barrel with masking tape. Core asked her why.

'To keep snow out of the gun,' she said.

'I won't get snow in the gun.'

'You will when you fall.'

'I'm not planning to fall.'

'Everyone falls in the snow, Mr Core. If you feel yourself starting to sweat, rest until you're dry.'

'What's wrong with sweat?'

'Nothing till you're wet through. Wet and it freezes to your skin when you stop moving.'

'I've been in the cold before,' Core said.

'Not like the cold that's coming here.'

She opened the door for him and he stepped outside, his face angled up into the flakes falling slant the size of quarters. She remained against the doorframe and tied her robe closed.

'I thought it might be too cold to snow,' he said.

'What's that mean?' she asked.

'Too cold to snow. I've heard that. Though I've never understood it.'

'Maybe where you come from. But here it's never too cold to snow. There's something off, something wrong with the sky here.'

Core looked up into the dark, looked for whatever it was she might have meant.

'Do you know if the snow is coming heavy today?'

'I don't tell the weather, Mr Core. It will tell me.'

Core thanked her, left her framed in a soft glow at the door of her cabin.

He saw the lightening sky through a splayed reach of trees. At the perimeter of the village, in the copse near the hill where the path wound up and around, he suddenly spotted a back-bent Yup'ik woman with a circular face burning items in a rusted drum.

He glimpsed her through the spiderweb of tree limbs and twigs. He stopped on the path to see if she would notice him. When she did she waved him over to the fire. He saw the red-orange radiance on her jowls, her creature garment thick and soiled, pungent-looking in the firelight, an anorak a century old. Her feet and shins were sheathed in moose-hide mukluks. He could not tell what blazed in the drum. He guessed she was burning household trash, but why at this dead hour? Seniors the world over woke before first light as if to win some contest with the sun.

She said, 'I thought you were something wicked coming my way.'

'No, ma'am,' he said. 'I'm heading into the hills.'

She had a man's voice, teeth missing. 'To get a wolf's tooth, I've been told.'

'Yes,' he said. 'How do you know?'

'We're a small village. We've had trouble enough here.'

'The wolves. I know, ma'am. I'm sorry.'

'Ah, you know? No, you think you do. I mean trouble since the start. Trouble before any of us was here. You would bar the door against the wolf, why not more against beasts with the souls of damned men, against men who would damn themselves to beasts? Answer that.'

'I'm sorry, ma'am?'

'I read the books they bring me. What else to do here through nights like these? I read the books. The Christians came when I was a child. The missionaries. They taught me the books. They came with books and they came with the plague.'

'I'm sorry?'

'The influenza plague.'

The flame widened in the barrel and Core could feel its broad heat from six feet away.

'Do you know the name of this village?' she asked.

'Keelut.'

'Say its meaning.'

'I don't know its meaning.'

'Its meaning is an evil spirit disguised as a dog. Or a wolf.'

'Why would they name it that?' he asked.

Her gums glowed part orange, part pink. 'Why indeed. You are the wolf expert, I hear.'

'My name is Core.'

'That girl knows this place is cursed.'

'The girl? Medora Slone?'

'Her.'

'She just lost her child. What she knows is grief.'

'Will the wolves come again for us tonight?'

'Wolves should not be coming here at all. Tonight or ever.'

'I did not say *should*. I said *will*.' She stared. 'They have the spirits of the damned.'

'They're hungry wolves, hungry animals. Nothing more.'

'I don't mean wolves.'

'I'll go now,' he said.

'Beware of false prophets, which come to you in sheep's clothing, but inwardly they are ravening wolves.'

'That's the Gospel of Matthew.'

'I told you, I can read the books. They taught me how.'

'Why did you say that?'

'Are you a Christian?'

'Ma'am, I know some things about nature and wolves. I write about them. I don't pretend to know about anything else.'

'We all pretend. And they know about you too.'

'I'll go now,' he said. He made to move up the trailhead. 'Have a good day, ma'am.'

'You're going the wrong way,' she said, not turning her face from the heat of the drum. 'Go back the way you came,' and she pointed a bent finger to the snow-blown center of the village.

Core ignored her and continued up the path, over chokes of rock and lightning-struck spruce.

***

He expected to find a wolf pack in the valley on the other side of these hills, a den tucked away, hidden on a bouldered ridge above the plain. He'd meet them just after daybreak at the den, if he could find it, meet them after their long night hunting afield. If there was a famine on this land, they'd have to seek their prey at the edges of the land they knew.

He remembered telling his daughter this when she was a girl: the Apache hunted the wolf as a rite from boy to man. A wolf kill turned a teen into a leader and earned him favor with the spirits of his ancestors. He remembered being outraged when she brought home from grade school the children's book *Peter and the Wolf*, how it painted the animal a hellish fiend. And now Core was hunting one for a reason and a woman he did not know.

The boy's bones would not be in the den; it had been twelve days since he was taken. His bones were spread throughout this wilderness by scavengers, blanketed by mantles of new snowfall. There would be no burial, no coming to terms for the woman and her husband. But he would kill an already half-dead wolf if he could. He would carry it back for Medora Slone, tell her it was the monster that had seized her son. The monster she wanted to believe in, to explain this away. A wolf's corpse meant relief to her – but only the illusion of relief, he knew. Perhaps she'd be able to quit the midnight vigils knowing that one wolf had been removed from the world. Perhaps not. Her every day was a midnight now.

He trundled through drifts to his shins despite these snowshoes. The sack of food and ammunition hung heavy on his shoulders. The snow ceased briefly beneath a clearing sky to the east. The coming dawn cast a half halo of light on the horizon, then clouds like great coats hurled in to cloak it. Year's end at this latitude the sun rose and set in such a truncated arch it seemed it might not find the will to bring the day.

He felt again the weight in his legs. Beyond the snowed-in trees, just over these hills, lay an unknowable compass of tundra, a tapestry of whites and grays. Everywhere the living cold. Like grief, cold is an absence that takes up space. Winter wants the soul and bores into the body to get it. What were the possibilities of this place? There were patterns hidden here beneath the snow, patterns knowable but he did not know them.

He walked on from one bluff to the next, knoll to knoll, snowshoeing over nonexistent paths and seeking tracks. The horizon kept losing its line, mixing down with up. Hours into his trek over the hills he stopped under a rock face, alongside what seemed an ancient esker. A minor sun drained of color blinked on and off behind clouds. The uniform white on the land pained his eyes until he remembered the tinted goggles in his bag. While drinking from snow and eating an egg sandwich she'd made for him, he heard the first howls down in the valley, half a mile over the tallest crest in the hills. He had seen no caribou tracks, no coyotes, no lynx, not a moose or hare.

What plague had invaded these vast silences? The virid earth, his memories of fruit breathing hotly in summer fields – all obliterated by this moonscape.

He felt the food warm in him and walked onto the snow-steamed plain. The wind flogged him, rushed around his hood, pushed against the padded contours of his clothes, made chalk dust of air. He adjusted the goggles on his face and tugged his chin low into the ruff of Vernon Slone's caribou suit. It seemed he'd have to walk a long while more. He looked to the sky but could not tell time from a sun this sick. The bluff ahead was at two hundred yards, or three hundred, or three-quarters of a mile – this land made measurement obsolete. Only a fool counted steps and yet he counted. The goggles kept clouding and he stopped to wipe them dry.

Where the plain began to rise again into an escarpment he found the first lupine tracks, a male, nearly six inches around, a three-foot stride, a hundred and twenty pounds, he guessed. He climbed the bank, over half boulders on the talus, and mounted the ridge from a narrow pass, all bluff face below him now, clouds gone north again. To his right he saw steam escaping from a copper-colored mouth in the crag, perhaps the hot spring she had told him about the night before. The sun sat low and wide; snow gave the glimmer of rattled foil. He crouched at the ridgeline and watched the valley beyond, and there he spotted the pack against the facing hills, a frenzy of ten gray wolves.

Through the field glasses he could see an infant wolf or coyote at the core of this ruck, teeth hooked into its flesh, the two largest wolves rending, angling for leverage, their hackles raised, the bounty shorn between them, snow mottled in purple and red. Core crouched there a long while looking.

He stepped sideways down the escarpment and lost his footing in the snow, then slid several meters until he stopped against a boulder. He sidestepped again the rest of the way until he again met the talus at the plain. There he crouched again and watched through the glasses as the rout of wolves consumed the last of the carcass. He checked to make certain the rifle's magazine was full, then loaded the first round into the chamber, the safety switch still engaged. He set off slowly across the valley floor, the crimped surface hoar crunching underfoot as if it were in pain. He lost sight of the wolves for a time but knew when the wind shifted west his scent would lift and reach them. He was afraid with every step in this snow, aware of the loaded rifle on his shoulder.

On a healthy day in a healthy land the wolf will run from man, turn at first sniff or glimpse – they want nothing of men. But he'd witnessed them prey on bison and caribou, a brigade of only four grays defeating five hundred pounds of beast with a lethal rack of talons. This was what he wanted for himself, he guessed. Unmanning, dismantling. *A body for a body.* Why come all this way for a bereaved woman he'd never met? Why then this futile hunt? He thought of the cigarettes and chocolate, of her scent on the sofa.

He could have ended himself at home. A pistol or rope. A razor. Or pills if he lost all nerve. Or his truck running in the shut garage, garden hose duct-taped to the tailpipe. But the almost pleasant nightmare that had played through his mind the night before he received Medora Slone's letter showed his lax body rent by wolves in an ice-blue scape he could not name. Her letter was the summons he wanted, the sentence that should have come long before. And his daughter in the city here? She was only the daylight reason. He'd never seen a daylight detail that could compete with midnight's verity. The predawn dark never learned to lie.

He walked on and topped the last small crest in the plain. The wind lifted his scent and in minutes the pack knew he was there. From a quarter mile off the wolves stared, their snouts to the air. Core stopped to stare back. He took several steps and stopped again. They looked stymied by confusion, bereft of their instinct to flee. Still they stared, tails raised. He walked toward them.

And they began their charge then, half head-on, the other half split on each flank. They'd surround him, he knew – he'd seen them do it. He dropped to one knee, pulled off a glove with his teeth, and stayed there in wait with the rifle aimed at the alpha out front, a male no more than six, a hundred and twenty-five pounds – it should have been heavier. Take it down, he knew, and the others would lose their will.

The white dust of trampled snow rose among the pack, glittered in broad frames of sun through an open stitch of cloud. Was this the wolf that took the children of Keelut, this deep silver gray with a gloss of cinnamon and that faultless stride?

He centered the wolf 's skull in the crosshairs of the scope. In a minute or less the pack would be at him, the alpha ripping his throat, the others threshing at his limbs. Laudable teamwork. They knew his disease of spirit, his want of this. Or else in their own disease mistook him for something other than a man.

He imagined slow-motion and no sound. He knew they must be mad to charge him this way, must be only days away from starving. He unsquinted and lowered the rifle, then let them come to him. This was penance, he knew. The silence of his living room, the thought of painting another oil portrait of the female gray he'd shot, the nightly whirring of his microwave – all an anguish he could not abide, already a death. Most of him wanted this reckoning. Some of him didn't. And he let them come.

When at the last instant he raised the rifle again and fired at the air above the alpha's skull, the pack halted at the crack of the round and glanced to one another. They knew the sound. When they neither advanced nor retreated, another shot above their skulls scattered them west from where they had come at the far end of the valley. He watched them go. He felt nearly surprised at his lack of tears. For the last year he'd imagined this moment a tearful one.

He stood and watched until they were gone. He'd return to Keelut now. He would tell Medora Slone that the wolves were fled from here. Remind her that what was done could not be undone, that blood does not wash blood. She'd have to live on with her lot. He knew no other way.

He trekked back through the late morning and afternoon, the day stiffened and already falling toward dark. He rested when he could, a long spell on the talus after the plain. He packed snow into an aluminum thermos and slipped it inside the caribou one-piece – the clothing of Vernon Slone, he could not forget. Then he sat in a crack in a ridge, safe from the wind. He ate the mixed nuts and ribbons of dried meat Medora Slone had also prepared for him. He thought of sleep. When the snow melted in the thermos he drank it, and then he packed more.

The walking began to feel automatic after that, his legs propelled by an engine wholly apart from him. He thought not of warmth or meal, wife or daughter, only of each step and then the next until he forgot to think about even those. And he walked on like that through the scanting light of day.

When he arrived back at the cabin his lungs felt weighted with rime. Medora Slone did not answer his knock. When he entered he saw her bedroom door ajar, clothes spilling from a closet and strung along the carpet – jeans, sweaters, a negligee of green lace. A suitcase with a cracked handle lying on its side. He called her name. The cold still infused his face; fatigue moved in surges through his limbs.

Weak light knifed through from beneath the narrow door that last night he had thought was a closet. When he opened it a chill hastened up from a never-finished root cellar. The rounded steps had been fashioned from available rock, the sharply slanted ceiling so low he had to duck to clear his head – a stairwell designed for storybook dwarves. A bare lightbulb lit this cramped space. The scent of soil and rock. Crates on an earthen floor. Mason jars of dried food he could not identify. Lumber and visqueen stacked in a corner. Rodent droppings on the dirt.

His breath hung before him as he moved beneath the bulb. Stones had long ago been dislodged from this wall beside the steps. A nook had been carved into the earth with a shovel or pickaxe.

The bulb's weak light did not reach here. He removed a glove to dig free his lighter from a pocket. He moved nearer. Inside this space he saw the boy – the frozen body of the six-year-old Bailey Slone leaning against the earth, cocooned in plastic, his open eyes iced over, mouth ajar as if exhaling – as if attempting a final word of protest.

He would rest here now for some time, sitting in the corner on an overturned Spackle bucket, his legs and back already sore from the hunt. At the airport the day before he'd read in an article that the cosmos consisted mostly of what we cannot see, energy and matter averse to light. He believed this though it sounded insane. He remembered then his hand around the throat of Medora Slone, how she had begged for a punishment, a purifying she could not grant herself.

3

RUSSELL CORE HOLLERED DOWN the center stretch of Keelut, his legs wasted from the day's long trek. He pounded madly on doors at dinnertime, shouted his breath onto the frosted glass of windows. The villagers came slowly, warily from their cabins, out into the road, some with rifles, others with lanterns in hand. Some still chewing food, evening fires at their backs. Some holding toddlers who looked upon him with dull suspicion, their ochre skin lovely in the lantern light. All emerged to see this wolf-man messenger Medora Slone had hailed, to confront the sudden roar he'd brought to their night.

'The boy,' he yelled. 'The boy. Bailey Slone.' He pointed behind him toward the dark, told them all the boy was dead, frozen in the root cellar. Most seemed not to understand, or not to want to.

A man they called Cheeon – Vernon Slone's lifelong friend, he'd later learn – rushed past him with a rifle, in untied snow boots and a flannel shirt, in dungarees that had been mended with myriad patches from other denim. Others followed him. Core stayed, bent and panting with hands on knees, attempting to recall the exact age his father fell from cardiac arrest.

46

When he regained half his breath and straightened in the road, he saw her there at the edge of a cabin less house than hut – the shrunken Yup'ik woman he'd encountered before dawn that morning. He limped to her, his left leg tingling from fatigue, his bared hands beginning to numb. Where were his gloves? He'd left them in the root cellar by the corpse of the boy.

'You knew this morning,' he said. 'You knew. When we spoke this morning. You knew what she did to the boy.'

She only stared.

'You knew,' he said.

'What can an old woman know?'

'How could you not say something?'

Above them a makeshift streetlamp throbbed with weakened light, fangs of ice hanging from its shade. The old woman smelled of wood smoke and something foul.

'Go back,' she said. 'Leave this village to the devils. Leave us be.'

Core thought to grab her arm, to lead her to the Slones' cabin to see the boy, to make her understand. But she turned, and on a shoveled path through snow she wobbled behind her hut and dissolved into darkness.

He remained beneath the lamp wearing the one-piece caribou suit and boots that belonged to Vernon Slone. More villagers hurried past him, some saying words he did not know. A snow machine screamed by, its one headlamp coning into the black. He could smell its gasoline fumes in the cold. He tried to follow but his legs wouldn't work and he sat in the road hearing himself breathe. Beguiled by this climate. Terrified of the facts he'd found and fearing already that he could not explain them.

When he reached the Slones' cabin he wedged through the villagers amassed at the door. The whispers he heard had no tone he could name and he wondered if they were accusations against him. In the root cellar, Cheeon had taken the boy from his tomb, untangled the cellophane from him, laid him on the earth floor. He and others were kneeling by the body, afraid, Core thought, to look at one another. A washed-out bruise coursed across the boy's throat and Core knew then he'd been strangled.

In the stagnant cold of that cramped space he heard himself say, 'Where is she?'

When no one responded, he asked again, 'Where is Medora Slone?'

Cheeon turned to him but would not answer. A brailled scar made a backslash from the corner of his mouth. His black hair was gripped at the nape by a length of clothesline rope. Core could not say what spoke in this man's face – it seemed some mix of boredom and rage. Cheeon said words in Yup'ik to the teen kneeling beside him, then took his rifle from the top of a crate and elbowed past others on the steps. Some remained kneeling by the body but then they too went.

Alone again with the boy, Core felt a kind of vertigo from the sight of him. Children are full of questions but they do not question their own being, are not troubled by their own living. Like animals, they cannot conceive of their mortality. Living seems to them the most natural state of things. But infants, he remembered, were repelled by the elderly, howled in the arms of the olden, as if they could sense, could smell the elderly's proximity to decay.

Core saw a woolen blanket inside a crate and used it to cover the boy. He remained there by him for many minutes, attempting to remember prayers he'd discarded long before this night.

Upstairs in the front room of the cabin again, he waited for someone to speak to him. Perhaps to comfort him. But the villagers only whispered among themselves. Most were Yup'ik, some were white, some mixed. All regarded him with an anxiety that felt both personal and old. Their clothing clashed; one woman wore animal-hide pants and a red jacket with the embossed name of a football team. Core somehow understood that police had been summoned from town, an hour's drive, longer in this snow and dark.

He looked to the whiskey on the shelf, then drank to let it tamp the dread in him. Where were the cigarettes Medora Slone had given him last night? He sank into the same armchair he'd sat in when he arrived the night before. Still no one would speak to him.

He'd never had trouble comprehending how people are what they are. If you live long enough, he knew, you see that the natural world matches the human one. Most are pushed on by appetites no more complicated than a wolf's. A wolf expelled from its pack will travel hard distances to find another – to be accepted, to have kin. It wants to stanch hunger, sleep off fatigue, make itself anew. He understood that. But Medora Slone. How could he explain this? Why did these people refuse to acknowledge him? They began leaving the cabin by twos and did not come back.

He creaked from the armchair to take another pull of whiskey, alone now in the Slones' cabin. At the open front door he squinted out into a mass of ebon silence and could not fathom where these people had gone. Shouts came from somewhere in the village. The barking of sled dogs. Another snow machine screaming through trees. When the wind lifted it carried clouds of snow into the cabin and Core closed the door. He built a hasty fire in the hearth, half surprised he could do it with hands so shaky.

He unpeeled the caribou suit from himself and returned to the armchair, woozy from two pulls of whiskey. From the day's long hunt. He thought of water and food but couldn't move. The heat of the fire flared against his face and he thought then of the husband, of Vernon Slone. Of how these facts would reach him. Of how a husband and father is ravaged by this.

And what he remembered before he blinked into sleep was his own father just after his mother had left the family for reasons no one knew. Ten years old, Core had thought his father would retreat into drink or Jesus. But instead he went to the cinema every night, that one-screen theater with the neon marquee in their nothing Nebraska town. Oftentimes he stayed in the theater to watch the same movie twice – *Spartacus, Exodus, Psycho.* Core would walk down to Main and Willow to search for him after dark. He'd steal into the exit door of the theater and find his father there – alone before those colossal talking faces, snoring in the chair with an empty bucket of popcorn aslant on his lap.

Police were in the Slones' cabin now, three white men wearing civilian clothes, winter hunting garb. Upright in the armchair, Core woke to the sound of their wet boots grating against the wood floor. He'd been asleep nearly two hours, he thought, maybe more. He wiped the spittle that had run into his beard, then stood to speak to the man who looked in command, the one with the crew cut, the russet beard, the cigarette behind his ear.

Donald Marium introduced himself to Core; he had the soft hand of a barber and beneath his beard a creaseless face. Core spoke too quickly – who he was, why he'd come, what he'd found – and Marium told him to sit, to breathe. He went with the two others into the root cellar to see the boy, and minutes later came back to Core, told him to begin his story, to begin where it began. They sat at the table and smoked.

When Core finished his telling, Marium said, 'Tell me again, please, why she asked you here.'

'I don't know that. She'd read my book on wolves.' He glanced about the room for his book but could not see it. From the pocket of his flannel shirt he took the letter Medora Slone had written him and passed it across the table to Marium, who read it in silence.

'And you decided to come here why?'

'To help,' Core told him. 'She said wolves had taken children from this village. It's in the letter. See for yourself. She said no one would help. I came here to help.'

'Wolves did take two kids from here last month. They weren't found. We came here to try and help these people, but I'm not sure how anybody can help that. You can't just walk onto the tundra looking for wolves.'

'But no wolf took Bailey Slone,' Core said.

Marium flattened his filter into an ashtray, then stood back from the table. Core did the same.

'We'll have to get it all figured out.'

'Are the others on their way?' Core asked.

'The others who?'

'The others. The police to find Medora Slone. Shouldn't there be more men here? Investigators? The TV shows have investigators.'

'Investigators? Mr Core, things don't happen here the way they happen anywhere else. And definitely not on TV.'

'No investigators? Just you?'

'For now. You have to understand where you are. We don't have full membership to the rest of the world. And we mostly like it that way. But let's take one thing at a time, please.'

'What time is it? Midnight?' His watch was missing from his wrist.

'It's six o'clock, Mr Core. You're not acclimated here. You said it was just dark when you arrived back here today? That was three-thirty, then.'

'That can't be. I left before dawn. I wasn't gone for so many hours.' He felt at his left wrist as if he could rub his watch back onto it.

'Dawn is at ten a.m. now, Mr Core. You're not acclimated here.'

'My watch is missing. I don't understand.'

'Apparently a woman is missing too.'

Core sat again. 'I tried to talk to these people but they wouldn't talk to me. Did they tell you anything?'

'Nothing much. Not yet,' Marium said. 'We spoke to some outside. As you saw, they don't talk much to anyone who isn't one of their own. Let's go back down to see the boy.'

In the root cellar the men clicked photos of the body on the floor, of the cavity clawed into the earth. The fat one scratched in a notepad; another with a mustache stood before a laptop on a crate. Core pointed, explained how he'd found the boy, that the man called Cheeon had removed him from the hole and unwrapped him from the plastic sheeting.

'He was upright in there?' Marium asked. 'Wedged in?'

Core nodded. 'Look at his throat,' he said. 'She strangled him.'

'Someone did.'

'It was her,' Core said.

'One thing at a time, please, Mr Core. When you came back here today after your hunt she was gone?'

'She was gone. Look at her bedroom, the back room up there. She packed. Her truck is gone. She's gone. She must have left me here to find the boy.'

'Left you here to find the boy. Why would she do that, Mr Core?'

'Why? Are you the police? You tell me why.'

'We'll find out why. We'll get everything figured out.'

'Someone has to tell the father,' Core said.

'Vernon Slone is at the war.'

'You know Vernon Slone?'

'If you live around here, you know of Vernon Slone.'

'Someone has to tell him,' Core said.

'Would you mind waiting upstairs please, Mr Core? I'm sorry to ask that. Would you mind?'

'I put that blanket on him,' he said, and did not move. 'I covered him.'

'We'll take care of this boy,' Marium said. 'Don't you worry. We'll take good care of this boy.'

Core made to leave.

'And, Mr Core?' Marium said. 'Please just have a seat up there. Please don't touch anything.'

Core went upstairs to the armchair and sat on his hands.

———◦•◦———

Hours later Marium and the men laid Bailey Slone in the bed of a police pickup. They walked cabin to cabin throughout the village, looking for the parents of Medora and Vernon Slone. Core remained by the police truck in the road and watched them, smoking from Marium's pack, taking sips of whiskey when the cold cut through him. Keeping solemn watch over the boy.

Retreating to the Slones' cabin to feed the fire when he could bear no more cold.

In the back room he looked at the messed bed of Medora Slone, the boy's tiny bed beside it, on the sheets superheroes faded from washing. He kept rubbing his wrist for the missing watch, kept feeling turned-around without knowing the time.

When Marium finally returned, Core was almost asleep again in the armchair.

'I'm going back to town,' he said. 'My guys are staying here. You should follow me back, to a motel there. It's way too easy to get lost in the night. And more snow's coming soon. You can't stay here.'

'Why not?'

'It's better you don't.'

'But why?' Core said. 'These people think I have something to do with this?'

'I didn't say that. But you can't stay here.'

'What'd you find?'

'Nothing yet.'

'Her parents? Or the husband's parents?'

'Nothing yet. Follow me back.'

'No one knows anything?' Core said.

'We'll know something soon.'

Core started his truck, let the engine warm, saw his breath frozen on the windshield from the day before. For sixty slow miles he stayed trained on the taillights of Marium's truck, two eyes ashine on a face of unbroken black. He fought to keep his own vehicle from slipping across unplowed roads, fought to stop sleep from slamming onto him. The window half open to let the frozen air slap him awake. The radio loud, an upset singer complaining of heart pain. Hard to tell how close the hills and trees came to the road. Impossible to know if there were humans in that darkness. He remembered nothing of this route from the day before.

At this hour of night he could have no accurate notion of the town. He'd expected some lesser oasis at the center of this dead world but the town seemed barely that. In its sickly fluorescent light the motel beckoned from the road without a sign to welcome. He followed Marium into the parking lot, then went to his driver's window to cadge a cigarette.

'How long you staying?'

'I don't know,' Core said. 'How long should I?'

'A few days, I'd say. At least. Until we get this figured. You can't remember anything she said to you about where she might go to?'

'She didn't say anything to me about leaving. We talked about wolves and we talked about this place. That's all.'

'You're sure she did this, but tell me how.'

'With a rope. I don't know.'

'I don't mean what'd she do it with. I mean *how*.'

'I'm not prepared for this, Mr Marium. You have to talk to the people of that village.'

'A tiny old woman came to me when I arrived tonight, as soon as I got out of my truck. She was just standing there. She told me Medora Slone was possessed by a wolf demon. She called it a *tornuaq*. That's what you get when you talk to the people there.'

'I'm not prepared for this.'

'You see this main road out here?' He pointed with his cigarette. 'Our station is at the end of it, on the left down there. Across from the market. Come talk tomorrow please. You should go catch some sleep now.'

But sleep would not come. He stretched on the bed in this dank room, hungry without the energy to eat. And he imagined Medora Slone's face in the dark above him. He remembered the flesh of her from the night before, her naked form quaking against his own body.

He could name the facts of nature.

A quarter of all lion deaths are the result of infanticide. A male bass will eat his offspring if they don't swim away in time.

Female swine and rabbits will stifle their young if the young are sick or weak, if resources run low. It's called 'savaging.'

Prairie dogs kill so many of their own young it's practically a sport for them.

Rats eat their own young if they are hurt or deformed. But they are rats.

Wasps. Sand sharks. Sea lions. Tree swallows.

Those dolphins we so admire for their intelligence: they've been recorded ramming calves to death, nose-first, like football players.

Over forty species of primates kill their own young. Our ancestors? Darwin doubted they participated in such barbarity: they weren't that 'perverted,' he wrote. Goodall observed female chimps killing and eating baby chimps.

Thirty percent of infant deaths among certain baboons are the result of infanticide.

Postpartum depression will cause a human mother to murder her child. But scientists have said that most human infanticide is caused by social or economic woe. The mothers are almost always very young. If there's a choice between children, a boy and a girl? The girl goes.

An Aborigine tribe has been documented killing a child to feed it to another. In the New Guinea Highlands, mothers kill their daughters and then try again for sons. !Kung mothers will walk into the forest with an unwell newborn and then walk back alone.

There is not a culture on earth in which a parent has not killed a child.

What was in Medora Slone's nature that day when she twisted a rope around the throat of her own boy in a root cellar? Look to the woods, he knew, not the books. The annals of human wisdom fall silent when faced with the feral in us.

On this motel bed at the rim of the world, Core could feel himself forgetting how to know, how to believe.

4

VERNON SLONE LANDED IN Alaska after dark, not in uniform but in dungarees fitted around combat boots, a baseball cap without a logo, a wool parka from a dead man at the military hospital in Germany. A patch on his neck, another on his shoulder. His sandy mane gone long and a blondish beard of weeks, lips hidden by mustache.

He'd been days in Germany, or a week, he couldn't know for sure – the pills, blue and pink. Surgery to remove the lead in his shoulder and neck, some of it lodged in bone. Then the unclear flight to a base back home. Kentucky, he was told. News about his boy. News about his wife.

An Army doctor spoke at him. *No one contacted you? Someone was supposed to contact you.* Slone couldn't bring his face into focus; his voice came as if from underwater. *It's been two weeks –* He looked at papers in a folder. *It's been nearly two weeks. You should have been told this.*

A shock wave softened by science, by more blue and pink. Another distorted voice from underwater. A woman this time, in civilian clothes. A counselor. Gold crucifix nestled in her jugular notch. She sat in a chair opposite him, at a table in his room, by a window. Her individual words were English, he knew, but her sentences seemed something else altogether.

She kept asking if he wanted to pray. Slumped in a chair, Slone looked out the window at the uniforms passing on the walkway. In another minute he was asleep with his forehead on the table.

Pulse felt everywhere in his body, in ears clotted with blood or clogged shut with cotton. Mention of a Purple Heart by a pock-faced officer he'd never seen before. Mention of a ceremony to honor him. Still more pills and the weighted sleep of the sick. He fell into some netherland of shade and vapor where faces are more creature than person, blurred screams stretched across silence. His son's name in his mouth.

In the sun outside. Someone pushed him in a wheelchair, though there was nothing wrong with his legs and the pain in his shoulder and neck had gone. A redheaded teenager dressed as a candy striper handed him a bundle of yellow roses, still in green cellophane – her breasts too large for her age, a face splattered with freckles, a mouth grotesque with metal, braces refracting sunlight that stung his eyes. She spoke a tongue he didn't know and nobody explained. He needed to weep but could not find the strength to do it.

Beams of sunlight segmented the room in cryptic patterns, from windows both west and east, it seemed. He could not understand this abeyance of order. Shadows from branches and twigs brushed the wall like bone arms. At evening the lamplight covered the corners in malign misshapes he tried to decode but could not. His son spoke to him in dreams and when he woke he found he'd been sobbing as he slept.

The waking world had an awkward way with time now. Alaskans, he'd been told, had the skewed circadian rhythm of arctic things, tuned in to a half year of dark and ice. In those nebulous corridors between wake and sleep he saw his father, that chapped man, skin like shale, fractured by tobacco and cold. Each time he woke he remembered the facts anew.

Days ago someone had given him printed pages of the news

article, black-and-white photos of Medora and Bailey. Photos that were three years old, he saw, partial and faded from the printer's low ink. Only the top halves of the sentences were visible, so that it seemed as if they were only half true – seemed as if he himself might be in charge of making those sentences whole, of completing the details of this story.

By the time he boarded the plane home he had flushed the blue and pink pills. He was beginning now to emerge from that gauzy lair.

His boyhood companion Cheeon met him at the gate. Slone saw him there among the colorful others eager to greet family – six feet tall, half Yup'ik, a fixed expression of grief and resolve. He recognized his drab winter clothes, his boots, the strong tobacco scent of him. Black hair pouring from beneath a camouflaged hunter's cap. His five-year-old daughter was the second child taken from the village by wolves, but he said nothing of this to Slone.

The men did not speak a word, did not clasp hands or embrace, only met each other's eyes and nodded. Cheeon took Slone's duffel bag, then handed him a cigarette and Zippo, a bowie knife in a black leather sheath. Slone moved briskly through the airport with Cheeon beside him keeping pace. Once through the double doors he lit the cigarette, fit the knife into his belt at the small of his back, and looked to Cheeon, who nodded the way to the truck across the road in the parking deck.

The temperature was two degrees now and would drop toward twenty below by dawn. His visible breath and the sharp scent of winter – Vernon Slone knew he was home.

For the eighty minutes it took them to arrive at the town's morgue the men did not speak. Cheeon drove and smoked and smoked again, his window cracked an inch for vent. The raised white scar jutting from the corner of his mouth told of the autumn morning when fishing on the lake in the valley. Fourteen years old, Slone cast his lure, not looking, and hooked him clean through the mouth. A quick yelp and Cheeon grabbed for the line so Slone wouldn't cast. Slone snipped off the barb with side cutters and threaded out the hook, holding down his laughter as the blood leaked onto their boots and Cheeon cursed him with his eyes and teeth.

This reticence between them, both instinct and ritual, was a lifetime old. Squalling babes the same age, they'd become instantly quiet when brought together, each a balm for the other in some way no one could explain. Bow-hunting elk or deer from adjacent stands in spruce, they'd pass twelve hours in uncut quiet, hand signals between them a superior tongue.

The winter hunt required an uncommon silence when the cold killed the sounds of summer, when ice muffled the earth and caribou a mile off could hear a man move through snow. They passed whole weekends of fishing for king salmon and trout without a single sentence on the river for fear that the fish could hear. All through November nights in their tent they wrapped around one another for warmth and never thought to wonder about an affection this natural.

On the rubber floor mats of Cheeon's truck: a hammer, a crushed coffee cup, a torn-open box of condoms, cigarette filters fallen from the ashtray, .22 rounds that rolled when the truck turned. His head back against the seat, Slone looked at the roads he knew so well, and as they approached town he searched for changes in storefront windows, in street signs, in front yards, every few minutes sipping from a water bottle Cheeon had handed him. A mother walking along a shoveled sidewalk with her boy – Slone sat quickly forward, turned his head to look at them as they passed. Electricity was everywhere outside the truck window tonight – the illumination of lives. Slone thought about protons, electrons, electrocution.

They were met in the dim hallway of the town morgue by two detectives, a lab-coated coroner, and by Russell Core, the wolf writer who had discovered his boy two weeks earlier, the one who had last seen Medora Slone. Core and the detectives tried to offer handshakes, attempt a feeble form of condolence, but Cheeon raised a finger to his lips, shook his head for them to remain quiet, to keep back, and he unlatched the steel door to the coldroom for Slone to enter.

He entered alone. He saw his son in an extended corpse drawer, the sheet folded to his waist, toe tag nearly the size of the boy's whole foot and attached like a price. His cobalt boy had grown in the year he was gone, the boy's face bones altered from either time or death. Hair longer than he'd ever seen it. Burgundy stain beneath the paper skin of his throat. Dark bulbs beneath slitted lids. He looked unfed and Slone wondered if this was a trick of death.

He breathed through sobs as a woman breathes through birth – solar plexus sobs, and he gave in to them, knowing this was his only time, his only chance for tears. He let them come and pass. For long minutes they rippled over him. Then he placed his palm on the boy's pale chest, his birdlike ribs. He bent – his skull tight from weeping, a pressure through his neck and face. He touched his lips to the boy's and whispered, 'Remember me.'

In the break room at the morgue, dense with the scent of coffee, the detectives sat in craters on the sofa. Across from them Slone and Cheeon smoked at a table. Russell Core sat in an armchair to their left, staring into his cup. Donald Marium had asked him here; he said Core was the only link to what had happened in the village. On the wall in this room a painting of a moose in scarlet wig and lipstick. When they'd first entered, Cheeon considered this picture closely, as if it were a calculus equation.

The cop with the mustache said, 'Do you have any idea where on earth that wife might've fled to, Vern? Any idea at all where she went to?'

'We'll get her,' the fat one said. 'She'll pay for it, Vernon. We've got leads, a few of them.' He held a file folder, a sheaf of documents on Medora Slone: photos and maps and Slone could not guess what else.

The other with the mustache said, 'We got her picture out all over the state. All over, Vern. Troopers looking high and low for the wife's truck. But it'd be real good if you could give us some idea of where that woman might've fled to. Into Canada, maybe? We been in touch with the Mounties there. Dumb asses, all of 'em, but we been in touch.'

This cop drank from a miniature Styrofoam cup and seemed irked by the morgue's coffee. 'I know it's a damn hard time for you, Vern, what that woman did.'

Most of the people in this town weren't from here – they were willful refugees from the lower forty-eight. Slone and Cheeon both could instantly spot a forty-eighter. The fat one, Slone guessed, was northern California, maybe Oregon. The mustached one was most likely from Texas. Migrated here to dabble in policelike work when not cutting down moose out of season. This wolf man was a midwesterner. They felt needed now, Slone guessed. Important. Useful in this dark.

Slone's left eyelid twitched as it often did when he went without sleep. He'd tried to nap on the plane but could not. He smashed out his cigarette and turned to see Core, his white wolf face and regal beard. He was sitting oppressed and silent in the armchair.

'You found my boy?' Slone said.

Core met his eyes, nodded yes, and glanced away. Slone half nodded in return, in his gratitude, his version of thanks said with the face. Core looked down at his feet, at the salt-stained boots that belonged to Vernon Slone, the boots Medora had let him borrow two weeks ago when he arrived. When Core realized he was wearing them his head lightened with embarrassment and he tried to cover one boot with the other but knew it was useless.

'Mr Core was called here by your wife,' the fat cop said. 'Damn woman told him a wolf took your boy. Can you imagine that, such a thing?'

At twelve Slone had shot dead a wolf in the hills above Keelut. For a live target to practice on, for fear and for fun. When his father found out, he took Slone's rifle and slapped the spittle from the boy's mouth. He could recall the old man's sandpapered palm on the skin of his cheek.

Then his father gave him a just-born husky to care for, 'to fix that hardness in you,' he said. And Slone cared for the animal for a decade until it lost vigor and grew lumps. At his father's demand Slone put it down himself with the .22 rifle, then buried it in the hills of Keelut beside the ravine. He felt certain – he was twenty – that he'd not again in this life undergo such gutting grief. He saw the dog everywhere, smelled it on clothing, heard it in the cabin, dreamed of it. Haunted and bereft, he learned then, were an unforgiving pair.

The mustached one said, 'We thought you'd have some questions for Mr Core, Vern, since he was there, since he saw that woman last. He's been a help to us so far.'

Slone turned again to Core in the armchair, sipped from his own coffee. He examined his knuckles, his wedding band, and under a thumbnail a blood blister that puzzled him. Each finger seemed a marvel of movement.

'Can you raise the dead?' he asked finally.

'No, sir, I cannot,' Core said.

'Then I've got no questions for you.'

'I'd like a cigarette, please,' Core said.

Slone looked. He did not understand.

'Can I get a cigarette from you?' Core asked again.

Slone passed the pack to him then, and Core, nodding thanks, fingered one free from the box – the same unknown brand Medora had shared with him when he first arrived in Keelut, a black dagger for a logo. He reclined again and lit it from Slone's lighter and sat staring at its glow.

'You can't think of where the wife's gone to, Vernon? Anywhere at all?' the fat one asked. 'A relative or friend, maybe? That woman have friends, any friends at all?'

Slone rose from the table then, bored by this, and Cheeon followed. Core stayed seated with the cigarette, his body still aching and warm from a flu that would not leave. The fizzing medicine he'd drunk an hour earlier had done nothing to quell the fever.

The detectives stood. The fat one said, 'We need a statement when you could, Vernon, and a bunch of damn papers that need signing. At the station would be best, if you're all set to go. Don Marium is there, you know Don? He asked us to meet you here and then bring you over to the station, if you wouldn't mind it. Sooner would be better than later, most likely.'

Slone stared at the cop and said nothing.

'Shit, we know you just got back, Vern. We're sorry as shit about all this. The more time we wait, the farther that woman gets, is what I'd say. We got them leads, a few we wanna go over with you, if you don't mind coming on back now. I know it's late. We got a map set up on the board there.'

Cheeon stood before the painting, once again inspecting the moose in wig and lipstick, somebody's idea of a gag in a morgue, this abomination he could not comprehend. When Russell Core began snoring in the armchair all four men turned to look at him.

In the lampless parking lot behind the morgue, Slone and Cheeon stood at the detectives' truck and watched the wolf man drive off into whatever night awaited him, whatever fate was ready to claim him. His headlights showed sideswept flurries that by first light would thicken into a scrim of snow.

They turned to piss shoulder to shoulder in the plowed berms at the edge of the dark lot, streams of yellow slapping into hardened snow. Slone could see the white and orange lights of town, the blinking red eye of the radio tower beyond the rails.

The fat one spoke behind them. 'You boys wanna follow us on over? We have coffee waiting there, good coffee, warm you right up. Put a splash of bourbon in there and you're all set.'

Slone zipped his fly and took the .45 from Cheeon in the dark. He turned and shot the fat one through the face from a yard away.

He shot the other through his forehead.

They dropped near their car and Slone stood above them and shot each again through his earhole, then braced the handgun in his belt. Cheeon passed him a flashlight and Slone saw fragments of skull and brain stuck frozen to the side door of their car. He bent with the light to gather the fallen papers on Medora – a black-andwhite photo of her face drizzled with blood and specked wet with snow – and slipped them back into the file folder. He looked again at the bodies, hardened blood like rubies scattered across a canvas of white.

Cheeon took the flashlight and folder from him and started the truck. Slone reentered the morgue through its rear loading door – inside an unlit hallway and the red glow of an exit sign. Minutes later he emerged with a body bag in his arms like a bride. At the back of the pickup, tailgate lowered, Cheeon held one end of the boy. They set him lovingly into the bed of the truck, where he sank several inches into a one-foot pad of snow.

An hour's drive to Keelut and the men did not speak. Cheeon smoked and drove as Slone reclined, his head turned to the bleached world he knew: houses, cabins, buildings, outside of town the numberless acres of land, not even the pledge of light in miles of such sable stillness.

The memory of alien sand, that slamming sun, the sheer exhaustion of those memories. Slone slept, the truck's tires a lullaby on asphalt.

Those first days towns or sectors of the city were always in smolder. Planes gave ruin. After, teams wheeled in block by block to find what still had breath. They crept door to door while buildings burned, smoke like night that made moon of sun. The men they sought seemed never to be where they should. Most were not in uniform. It was hard to know who should be shot, who would shoot. Families huddled in basements. Street dogs deafened and concussed, their ribs hunger-sharp. Gunfire on the next block, east or north, impossible to know.

Slone turned and found himself separated. Ducked into a doorway, squatted there for air. He swilled from a canteen, wiped sweat and filth from his brow. Voices, American, in a rubble-packed alley. Smoke like walls in the street.

When he stood in that entranceway he saw into the glassless window, through one rounded room into another: a soldier with a scalp of honey down, wearing Slone's own colors, his flag, from his company or not – his eyes still burned from sweat and smoke. A girl beneath this man's weight on a table, her bottom garb twisted aside. Slone watched him, a tattooed piston between her legs.

He entered the house with a voyeur's crawl. And he watched. The girl was very young, he saw now, sixteen or seventeen. Umber skin aglint with both her sweat and his. She did not struggle. She did not yell. She could not look away. She studied the soldier's face as if needing to remember it for some future use. Or else stunned by this adder, astonished that this shaitan could have honey-colored hair and such straight teeth. But for the quiet drip of tears she seemed almost partner to this.

More gunfire on the street. Rapid explosions nearby that sent a tremor through the floor of this house. The hissing of steam he could not guess the source of.

And then Slone was behind them. He saw nonsense hieroglyphs etched into the soldier's biceps. A medieval cross inked into his nape, and inside the cross a question: *Why hast thou forsaken me?*

He unsheathed the knife from his belt. The hand, the forearm, the shoulder – they can know their aim independent of mind. He stabbed this soldier through the right ear. A centimeter of the knife's tip poked through his left temple and Slone felt the body go limp on the blade. He held the man's drooped form upright with the knife so he would not topple onto the girl. He then thrust him quickly back and yanked free the blade in the same even motion. The serrated side of the knife was crammed now with bone and brain. On the dusty stone floor the man's blood puddled about his head more in black than red. His tattoo's useless question died with him.

Why has he forsaken you? Ask him yourself.

The girl sat up, leaking blood from her center. She covered her bottom half, crossed her legs on the table, wide-eyed at Slone not two feet from her. The bleeding blade still tight in his grip. He hadn't thought light-colored eyes a possibility among these people, but the girl regarded him now with a teal astonishment. Unsure what else that blade would thirst for. Unsure if another yellow-haired man would pry into her now too.

I can't hurt you, he thought. *I won't. Do not fear me.* And she seemed able to read these thoughts, to find in his face something she could not find in the other's. She did not tremble or flee – her tears had abated – and she could not look away from him. On the inner thigh of his pants Slone wiped the matter from the blade and held out the knife hilt first.

She was ready to read his expression: *Use this next time. Kill any man, any person who tries to bring you harm.* And she took the knife from him then. This gift. For a reason known only to her, she brought it to her nose to sniff its metal and hilt. She stood from the table and tucked the knife into her unclean garb. She looked to the body at her feet and spat onto it. She reached for Slone's right hand, tarry with the soldier's blood, and turned it over to inspect his palm. With her index finger she traced an invisible letter or sign no one but she would ever know.

Then she limped barefoot from the rear of the house and disappeared into roving smoke.

———◆———

Russell Core's motel room smelled of two weeks of sickness, a do not disturb tag warning away eager maids from the doorknob. Take-out food plastic from the one Chinese restaurant in town. Damp towels over chairs, a bed disrupted. Newspapers fallen on a floor more concrete than carpet, crinkled bottles of springwater in the trash. Torn packages of flu medicine, balled tissues, mugs of tea for the burn in his throat. On the dresser a chipped ceramic figure of a grinning Hawaiian girl in grass skirt and lei – Core could not decide if this was a joke or not.

For three days after the hunt his legs and back had ached, painful even to step to the toilet – an insistent reminder of his unfitness and age. His sleep was long and hazy with sickness. He'd wake not knowing the day, fight to recall which month this was. After several minutes not moving he'd remember: the dead boy, Medora Slone, his own wife no longer herself. A daughter he needed to see.

Since finding the boy he'd waited for two weeks for the return of Vernon Slone. He waited for a call that would finally tell of his wife's death. But no one knew where he was. He slept away those shortened days, mildly frightened of a sky that gray, of whatever impulse had led him to this place.

Back from the morgue now, he understood that he had waited for nothing. His daughter's phone number and address were folded in his wallet like an invitation sent to the wrong man. There was nothing Vernon Slone wanted from him, not another fact he could feed this family's horror.

And if Slone had asked him for an explanation? Would he have accepted the facts Core had to tell, the facts he knew of the wild? Those facts he had learned were no help here – no help to Slone and no help to himself. Awake in the night, the memory of Medora Slone's scent strong in him, he studied starlight from the window. What Medora had done was observable in nature. He'd seen it himself among starved wolves in the north. It was a fact he knew. But a fact that could do nothing to describe this.

The stale motel room around him, and the end or start of something else now, a new direction he couldn't gauge. Core unlatched the window, an eight-paned iron relic he had thought long extinct, ferns of frost on its glass. He swung it open into the outer black to let the cold clean this room. He knelt before the dark, his tears consumed now by a chaotic beard. He attempted his prayer but the words would not come to him, so completely had he lost them, so surely was he numbered among the damned. He stayed there at the open window until the night's cold turned to novocaine, until he found exhaustion enough to sleep again.

—◆—

Behind the hills of Keelut, Slone and Cheeon dug at the rear of a graveyard hidden in a clearing between two expanses of wood. A wolf keened from deep in the valley beyond, and from low branches of cedar, owls watched this midnight's work. They dug sideways into the embankment of snow with shovels and pickaxes, clearing a temporary tomb. Without equipment the ground was impossible to pierce now. Their labor was illuminated by the truck's headlights, snow swirling in the beams as if insects at a lamp in summer. The dark beyond seemed more than night, seemed a deliberate negation of day.

As boys they'd hunted here in autumn and winter, lynx and grouse, even though they'd been forbidden by their fathers to take game where the dead lay. Proper burial for the boy would have to wait till after breakup when the ground softened. For now Slone's son belonged in this ancient earth of the village with his forebears. The boy's grandfather, Slone's own father, was buried just yards from here, in a hole chiseled down into the earth by these same two men. All the graves and gravestones concealed now by drifts of new fall.

They swung the pickaxes into the bank of snow. Side by side they seemed railway workers who have absorbed each other's rhythm. They did not stop for water or smoke. Slone's neck and shoulder wounds ached with each swing. The boy lay on the snow in his bag, in hushed witness to his father's work.

Halfway through the thickest layer, Cheeon left the grave to Slone and went to the truck's bed to carpenter the boy's coffin. Three sheets of plywood, a handsaw and hammer, a tape measure and a score of tenpenny nails, pencil behind his ear, lantern perched on a toolbox giving some light. What he fashioned so quickly was just a box. But it was even and tight and all they could offer till they had more light and time, till the thaw came.

Slone stopped five feet into the bank. Out of the hole, he drank from the thermos Cheeon had taken from the cab and tossed to him.

They unzipped the boy from the bag and placed him in the box. Slone touched his face, turned away, and could not resist a second time. He then hammered on the lid, twenty-two nails. Over the coffin Cheeon grabbed for Slone's left arm, rolled the sleeves to the elbow, and slid a pocketknife blade diagonal across his forearm. He squeezed until globs of blood pooled like wax at the head of the box, then with a naked finger inscribed a glyph that looked part wolf, part raven – a symbol taught to him by his Yup'ik mother. Slone did not ask what the marking was meant to ward off or welcome, but trusted his boy was protected beneath it.

They carried and slid the box into the cubby they'd made, then took up shovels again to conceal what lay within.

His home, the cabin he'd built, was girdled in police tape. Slone stood at the front door and looked. The boy's sneakers by the portable heater, his tiny snow boots. Winter coat on a hook. The lightbulb above him blinked and dimmed. He stepped in, the bones of the cabin made taut by cold, by the absence of human warmth. They creaked beneath his feet. He clicked on the electric heater, pulled wood from under the tarp on the rear porch, stacked it thick and high in the hearth. Then he started kindling in the stove, blew the flame to life until he could no longer see his breath.

He stepped toward the sofa still in his coat. A whirling, a rocking on feet half numb. The black snap of the bulb above him. Then Slone was falling, asleep before he could feel the sofa catch his weight.

Awake before dawn, he poured boiling water on freeze-dried coffee. He knew that at first light the dead men behind the morgue would be found, and then he'd have scant time before police arrived here for him. Three or four hours in this weather, five tops. He stood in the root cellar to see the hole where the wolf writer had found his boy. He moved near to touch it, to smell the cold of it.

A meal of old eggs and hardened bread – he tasted nothing – and at the table he opened the folder of documents on Medora. A police report in faded ink. Photographs of his boy on the floor of the cellar. Where the Chevy Blazer might have been seen. Map of the highway between cities and east toward Yukon, a single blacktop artery with paved and unpaved roads branching off like capillaries.

On the map red dots indicating a possible direction. Many roads, he saw, were not marked, were unknown to townsfolk and cops, most no more than paths trimmed through a hide of birch and alder, unseen from the air. Both he and Medora had been on those hidden paths since childhood, since they'd first learned to ride snow machines, four-wheelers, dirt bikes. Wherever she'd fled, she'd fled, he knew, on those paths. He lit the folder at a corner, blew on the flame till it rose, then dropped it in the hearth to burn.

Aspirin for the ache in his shoulder, then more coffee. He stood at his wife's bureau and turned over each sheet of paper, each envelope. Unwashed laundry in a wicker basket by his foot: he brought her socks and underthings to his nose and mouth and inhaled the dank scent of her. At the bottom of the basket was the boy's T-shirt, a red race car with a bumper face that smiled – it still held his child's smell. Slone slipped it into his jacket pocket. In the bedroom he emptied her dresser and stripped the bed. Beneath her pillow an Inuit shaman's mask made of driftwood and pelt – the face of a wolf.

He sat on his son's bed. He looked and looked more and did not blink. Outside, the morning moved without him.

He began filling duffel bags. Socks and gloves, thermal leggings and insulated overalls. A hunting knife, ammunition, clips, cartridges. Compound bow and quiver. Maglite and rope. Field glasses. From the bathroom: ibuprofen, antibiotics, aspirin, bandages, peroxide, razor blades, stool softener. In the hollow floor of the closet a compartment of firearms: 9mm handgun, twelve-gauge autoloader, Remington rifle that had belonged to his father. The AR-15 semiautomatic he found near the back door: what the wolf man had taken on his hunt.

Cheeon had disentombed his Bronco from snowfall, changed the battery and fluids, filled the tank, draped the engine with an electric blanket to warm it back from death. Into the back hatch Slone loaded the duffels and guns. Blankets, a pillow, two containers of gas, snow boots. Pickaxe, shovel, chain saw. A sack of nonperishables with peanut butter, crackers, chocolate. The truck turned over with the first crank of the key and Slone let the engine rev and warm, the windshield and rear defrosters droning on high. He loaded the pistol and tucked it into his belt, then the shotgun and placed it beneath the seat.

Then he made for the old woman.

———◦•◦———

The village's main road was vacant this soon after dawn. In the year he'd been gone nothing he could see had changed here. The men and boys had left already for hunting, or to check their lines in the holes they'd drilled at the lake. Women tended to children and chores inside their cabins. A team of sled dogs staked beside a home stood in silence when they saw him and lay down again as he passed. The old woman's hut sloped beside the generator shack.

It had been there since long before he was a boy, behind the well house – a place they'd all avoided as children.

When he entered she was upright in a chair at the mouth of the fire, rocking among distaff and debris, among cordwood, pelts, stacks of leather-bound books arrayed as furniture. In this single-room hut the heavy stench of wood smoke, of boiled moose, unwashed flesh. On the back wall an old wrinkled poster of a soccer player in mid-kick. No appliances, just that woodstove, a teakettle and pot on top of it. Slone closed out the mass of cold behind him and slid the serrated blade from his boot.

'Vernon Slone,' she said. 'You came home, Vernon.' She looked to the blade in his hand. 'You come now to punish the old witch. But I am no witch. I knew you'd come. You're home now, Vernon Slone.'

He stepped toward her and considered her pleated neck, the fire's light in her eyes, her jowls in divots from some childhood scourge.

She pointed to a crate overturned at her stumped feet. 'Sit,' she said, and he did – he sat close enough to smell the filth of her.

'You think I could have saved the boy, me an old woman? You think I knew? I've known things since before your father's birth. But nothing I know has mattered. Go to your father's grave, ask him yourself. Ask the spirits. Take your wrath to the gods, to the wolves, not an old woman. Take it to yourself if you want to be rid of this, Vernon Slone.'

In her hands a fabric doll, without nose or mouth – something meant to hex or help.

'It was foretold in the ice, that boy's fate. Hers as well, from the start. There was nothing an old woman could do. Punish yourself. The both of you. You left this place for war, Vernon Slone. You should have died there. There in the sand. That was your fate. You chose not to accept it. So this, this is what you come home to.'

She shook the doll at him, then placed it on a mound of books beside her. Wood snapped in the hearth and the fire flared against the polish of Slone's blade. She pointed to a table near him. 'My pills,' she said, and he passed her the prescription bottle, medicine brought once a month by a doctor in town. Her hands trembled as she uncapped the bottle, as she placed a pill on her tongue and swallowed without water.

'This wasn't the first time the wolves came to Keelut. The elders here remember it as I do. We were children. What came before the wolves, the white man called it Spanish flu. We called it *peelak*. Half this village died in it. Half, I tell you. The sickness got the brain, the lungs, the belly. No one has told you this history, Vernon Slone, your own history here?'

He sat and said nothing.

'It was winter and some, like my father, those who held memories from the coast, they made snow igloos behind the hill. We kept the bodies there, protected there. A hundred bodies. Two hundred. No one would come here to help us. No one would dare come here to help. Each morning we'd wake to new death in the huts of this village. People drowned. Drowned in their own fluid. Their lungs filled with the sickness. Or their brains burned from the fever. They leaked from the bowels. They leaked day and night and were too weak to move.'

She leaned forward in the rocker.

'We could smell them. My father told me to stay away but I could see, see him carry a man, almost dead, this man, carry

75

him to a sled. Pull the sled around the hill to the snow igloos they made there. This man I saw wasn't dead. He looked at me shivering, his eyes very alive. My father and others, they stacked him in the igloo with the dead. He died there very soon. He died there with the dead, moaning in the cold with the dead. I could hear him over the hill.'

When she motioned for the jug of water on the floor, Slone passed it to her handle-first.

'The moans in the night were very bad. We stayed awake in bed listening, my sister and me, cuddled in the same bed, we listened. The blanket over our heads to keep the sickness out. And we listened, we did. Once when my father was trying to save a woman, he sent my sister and me, sent us to the creek to cut the ice for water. We hurried to do this. In dark and cold we hurried and chopped the ice for him. You know what we heard?'

Slone watched her face, the pencil-thin and chapped pale lips folded in on themselves.

'We heard them howling. Howling beyond the valley that night. We hurried and melted ice for my father as he told us. He stayed with this woman. He stayed until morning, giving her the water. He told us the water would save her. If she kept drinking it would save her. But she slept finally at the dawn and didn't wake. She never woke. My father stacked her on the dogsled with the other dead and brought them to the igloos behind the hill.'

Slone, still intent on the old woman's face, passed the blade slowly back and forth in callused hands.

'The next morning my father and others found what happened in the snow igloos. The wolves got in, they tore apart the bodies of the dead in the night. They feasted in gore on those many corpses, a hundred bodies. Their frozen blood and bones were all over the hillside, strewn. Scattered everywhere. Not a single body was spared by the animals.

From the tracks my father saw the size of this pack. Over twenty wolves had come, had feasted that night. It seemed a fate worse than the influenza. Everybody then gathered the bones, all the bones they could find, gathered them in baskets for proper burial when breakup came. But there is no proper burial after such a thing.'

She took up the doll again and caressed its head as if it had life.

'That is the history here, our history, Vernon Slone. You cannot blame an old woman for that.'

Minutes later, his wrist and hand gluey with the old woman's blood, Slone walked back into the brimming day. He stood breathing in the cold. If the villagers knew he was back they did not come from their cabins, neither to welcome nor damn him. Across the road he saw curtains part and close. He returned to his truck and looked over his home a final time.

Then he was gone from that place, fled down icy passageways that could not be called roads – paths through a wilderness forged long before his birth.

5

AT THIS DECEMBER DAWN behind the town morgue Donald Marium saw ice crystals shine atop the newest snowfall, drifts rolling to a dun-hued horizon. He took in the men's faces as they gazed upon the killed – shot dead, they lay frozen and twisted by the wheel of their truck. Snow had been dusted from their corpses to reveal splashes, rivulets of glassy blood. Across the open compass behind town, north toward the range, he saw snow-burdened trees bowed like penitents. The morning seemed made of muslin, the sun less than a smudge. The wind came in soughs and shook free a pine scent from trees, then sent snow aloft as mist.

Every one of these cops had seen deer and caribou and wolves like this, marten and muskrat, Dall sheep turned from white to red. A few had witnessed men dead of cold and wet in swollen rivers, or of long plunges from headwalls. Some had tried to rescue children yanked underwater, lost beneath capsized canoes, yoked to the bottom. But Marium understood that most here had never witnessed fellow men like this. He himself had seen such a mess only once before, and not in this town.

He spoke to the cop standing behind him. 'What's in the building?'

'Another one dead. Frank the coroner, we think.'

'You think?'

'Shit, Don, we can't get near enough him to see. He's in a whole lake of blood, in his office.'

'Dead how?'

'Dead all the way through, it looks to me.'

'You find the casings here?' he asked.

'The what?'

'Shell casings. How do you think these men were killed? With some tickling? Dig up that spot for the casings, please.'

'How do you know it's this spot?'

'Those wounds are nearly point-blank. You see the faint star pattern of that wound? On that man's face there? You're standing on the shell casings.'

'Something from here did this?'

'I'd say a someone did it. Dig up the casings, please.'

'Feels like a something to me. First that village kid, and now this. What a goddamn shitty way to end the year. That kid's gone, you know.'

'Gone how?'

'His body, it's gone. They took the kid's body. You ever see anything like this?'

'Not quite like this, no. Please find the casings.'

Marium stood smoking a cigarette in the cold as men continued this work. The ambulance sat silent and without use, its lights pointlessly in twirl. His dreams in the night had offered him no sign of what this day held.

The morgue's waxed hallways squeaked beneath a racket of wet boots. A half-moon of cops stood at the cusp of the coroner's blood. He lay facedown and Marium could see the stab wound was in the side of his head, through the ear and out the other side.

'You boys waiting for Frank to sit up and tell you who did

79

it? Mop right up to him, please, and look for boot marks as you go.'

'What about forensics, Don?'

'About what?'

'The guys from the city.'

'You photograph this room?'

'Took a hundred shots.'

'Then you and a mop are as forensic as it'll get right now. Look for a goddamn boot mark, please, and stop if you see it.'

'I thought the city guys were coming. Or troopers, something. How in the hell we supposed to handle this?'

Marium smiled at him. 'Troopers. That's a good one. I didn't realize troopers even knew we were here, this town. Let's think of this as our own mess for now. Stop touching things, please.'

His salmon-and-eggs breakfast sat half eaten on his kitchen table. He thought of coffee, Susan, his wife, in her bathrobe and nothing underneath, toenails the pink he liked. Twelve years younger, redheaded and lithe, she was a former dancer of ballet. Her breath stayed sweet even at waking. She was his promise of thaw in this place. She wanted children and kept Marium engaged in the task, early-hours coupling with an erotic unclean scent on her. He was prepared for kids, willing now at forty-eight.

At the rear of the hall he stepped into the break room. He could smell the cigarette smoke stuck on curtains and patted a jacket pocket for his own pack. He saw dents in the sofa cushions where heavy men had sat. Other rooms, offices down a second hallway, and the metallic coldroom at the end. He'd been to this morgue dozens of times over the years – to sign papers for old people dead from sickness, or young people dead from being dumb – but he'd never entered this coldroom. Never wanted to.

He grabbed the handle with a latex glove, pulled to open the door, then entered in the kind of caution born of superstition. The extended corpse drawer was empty, the sheet thrown aside. On the floor beneath it lay a toe tag in blue ink. He crouched to get it and read the name, read the numbers telling all of Bailey Slone.

Looks like your daddy's home, boy.

———◆◆◆———

Cheeon answered the knock, opened his front door and kept it open, a cigarette glowing to its stub, the heat from a cast-iron stove pushing at the cold. Marium's coat was unzipped to show no weapon in his underarm holster. When he saw Cheeon's cigarette he retrieved one of his own from a coat pocket. The men leaned against the doorframe smoking, looking fifty yards out in front of Cheeon's two-level cabin where police vehicles sat arranged on the snow front to back, four of them. The men behind wore flak jackets and helmets, their rifles lowered, some sipping from cups of coffee hastily got.

'Was wondering when you'd show up here.'

'I told them I'd try talking to you, Cheeon. See if I could get you to come without any goddamn mess here. I'm not claiming to be a friend. I wouldn't claim that.'

'If you say.'

'But we've talked over the years, when you were in town. Had coffee a few times, if memory serves. We've been friendly, anyway. Our fathers knew each other, I think. Your wife and girl were friendly with me. With Susan too, my wife. Would you agree with that?'

'If you say.'

'And that has to mean something.'

Cheeon spat, half in the snow, half on his boot.

'If you say. But I don't think it means what you want it to mean right now, guy. Not even close.'

A scud of wind lifted loose snow from roofs and moved across open space in a white swirl. The late morning sun was just a peach smear.

'I'm from this place just like you.'

'You ain't from this village.'

'No, not from here, but not that far from here.'

'You come to tell me your life story, guy?'

'We've got two cops killed out back of the morgue in town, Cheeon. Also the coroner inside with a knife wound through his head. And then there's a missing dead boy. That's what we've got here, Cheeon.'

He nodded and smoked but did not look at Marium.

'You list those dead in order of importance? Because a couple of dead cops is cause for a party around here.'

'No, I did not. I'm not saying that dead cops are something special, more special than anyone else dead. Dead all around is not a good thing, you ask me.'

'I can think of some sons of bitches that might do the world a bunch of good dead.'

'That's fine. I ain't disagreeing. I just don't want anyone else dying here today if we could help it, please.'

'Looks like you came expecting it, though. All these cops out here.'

'Like I said, I told them I'd try talking to you first. See if we could prevent a mess here.'

'Come quietly, you mean. That's the cop phrase, right? Come quietly.'

More silence while they smoked.

'Cheeon, most of these cops out here aren't our redneck guys from town. They're Feds, city boys, and they've got a fair amount of firepower they're ready to use today.'

'I've got a fair amount of my own I'm ready to use.'

82

'I know it. That's why we're talking here, Cheeon. Your father was busted a few times for illegal firearms. You know what they say about that apple not falling far.'

'Nope. I don't know nothing about that apple. But it'd be real smart of you, guy, not to mention my father again.'

'Okay. I won't. It was either you or Slone who killed those men and took that child. Maybe it was the both of you. I know you boys have been tight since way back.'

'Vernon's gone to the desert. There's a war there. You got a radio?'

'Vernon Slone is home. You know that. And you helped him. I was just at his cabin. Looks like I missed him by five or six hours.'

'If you say.'

'Listen, Cheeon. Whatever happened, we've got to get it figured. The cops were shot with a .45 Springfield. You've got one of those registered.'

'I've got others not registered.'

'I figured that. Frank, the coroner, was retiring this year, moving to San Diego, I believe. Hell, he wasn't even a real coroner. Just a doctor who did the job for us because no one else could do it.'

'San Diego, huh? Never heard of it.'

'He was stabbed straight through his head. Clear through, from one side to the other. Who'd do a thing like that?'

'You tell me.'

'You can probably guess he had some family who won't be the same.'

Cheeon nodded more, smoked more, nearly smiled. His fingernails were piss-tinted from tobacco.

'Yeah,' he said. 'There's a bunch of that going around here lately.'

'Where is Vernon Slone, Cheeon?'

Cheeon turned to him, smoke funneling from his nostrils.

His face – a crimped brow, the start of a smirk – said, *You're dumber than you look if you think I'll tell you that*.

'Yeah, okay,' Marium said. 'Maybe you'll tell me where that boy's body is, then. It's state evidence.'

'It's what?'

'Evidence.'

'That boy's body is nothing to you and your like. It's not of this earth anymore. Put that boy out of your mind or he just might haunt you, guy.'

'Where's Medora Slone?'

'She'll be found. Not by you or them, though.'

'What happened to her? How does that happen to a woman?'

'How in the goddamn hell should I know? I ain't a woman.'

A span of silence now. Cheeon pressed out the filter into ice with a boot toe, then lit another.

'What's the temp today?' he asked. 'Feels like a February cold is coming on and it ain't even January yet.'

Marium pointed. 'Thermometer says zero right there.'

Cheeon looked at the thermometer screwed into the outside sill of the kitchen window.

'That's broken. It's been stuck on zero all year, even last summer.' He stopped to pull in the smoke. 'Maybe it's not broken. I don't know.'

'Is that why those cops were shot?' Marium said. 'So no one but Slone would find Medora? So no one would interfere in his business? His revenge, whatever he wants. And Frank because the big galoot just got in the way?'

'What do I look like, like I enjoy all these fucking questions from you, guy?'

'I know your little girl was taken from here by a wolf. I know you don't have a body to bury and that there's nothing on earth worse than that.'

'You know that, huh? A lot of help you were for a guy who

84

knows that. You come an hour across the goddamn snow for my sorry ass but you wouldn't come for some kids dead in the hills.'

'We came.'

'You came and you left and you didn't come back. Worthless as shit, you city boys. Though even shit can fertilize, right? What can you do?'

'We ain't city boys, Cheeon, you know that.'

'You sure as hell are. I've been going there my whole life, I know what the goddamn city is.'

'We're an hour closer to Anchorage than you. That don't make us the city. Five thousand people is hardly a city, I'd say.'

Cheeon bent with laughter, coughed on his smoke. Laughed more, his teeth as stained as his fingers.

'You come here today to argue with me about the definition of a city, guy? You must have goddamn nothing else in the whole world to do.'

'I'm not arguing, Cheeon. No one's arguing. I'm just talking. And I'm saying: we're not that different from all of you here.'

'That's where you're wrong. That's one of the places you're wrong. You went to college and you're dumber than dog shit.'

'Okay, then. I'm wrong and dumb, I don't deny that. I'm just saying. We're not all bad. We helped get the plumbing set up in this village five or six years back. Helped put this place on the grid.'

'And now you want a goddamn trophy for letting these people take a shit in their own house. Ain't you something.'

'I don't want anything, Cheeon. I'm just saying.'

They looked at each other then, held one another's eyes for half a minute until Marium glanced away. What he saw in Cheeon's face just then was more than a mingling of rage and grief. It was a fundamental otherness that frightened him.

'Some of these cabins are still dry.'

'Some old-timers didn't want electric and plumbing. That's not our fault, Cheeon.'

'Feels good when you say that, don't it? *It's not our fault.* You really are goddamn something.'

'Okay. I know it's bad here right now. I'm not disagreeing with that.'

'You know a lot of stuff, I gotta hand it to you. But it's way past bad. There a word for way past bad? You learn that word in college?'

'There might be one for let's not make it worse. You've got a wife who probably needs you, I'd say.'

'She's gone from here.'

'She'll be back. It's her home, ain't it?'

'She won't be back. No one wants to come back to what happened here. This village will be a ghost town in a year, just watch.'

More quiet, a cigarette lighter shared, more smoke between them, thick white in the cold.

'I'm sorry for all this, Cheeon. I really am.'

'I've been thinking about it. Them dead sons of bitches at the morgue? Bastards like you and me? When we're killed the past is killed, and the past is dead already, so no big deal. But when kids are killed? That's different. When kids are killed the future dies, and there ain't no life without a future. Is there?'

'We have futures.'

A look now, more smirk than smile. 'You're wrong again there, guy. Our futures end today. The raven follows the wolf, and the wolf has come for you and me. Look there.' He pointed to a snowed-in spruce, a raven in a branch like an ink blotch with eyes.

'You can blame starved wolves for what happened to your little girl but you can't blame a person.'

'You can always blame a person. The world ain't nothing but

persons, every goddamn one of them starved for something.'

From behind the bulwark of vehicles police spied through field glasses. One on a satellite phone. A sniper in white camouflage on the ground beneath hanging slats of snow-heavy pine. Minutes more of quiet and smoke.

'Those boys look like they're not sure whether to shit or piss.'

'I won't lie to you, Cheeon. Most haven't taken part in anything like this before, not that I know of anyway. But that's bad for you, not good. Because when you're scared you're stupid. And stupid doesn't go too well with guns.'

'I'd bet they're stupid no matter what. What'd you all expect? Me to walk on out with my hands in the air? Some shit like that?'

'I'm just trying to prevent as much stupidity as I can here. If you come with me today I'll make sure everything's fair. I'll assure you of that.'

'Everything's what?'

'Everything's fair.'

His laugh was a nasal sound caught between a chuckle and a snort. He looked at his cigarette to find it sucked down to the filter.

When he was a boy he told his father he'd grow to become a doctor. He could recall the doctors from town who came to Keelut when called, bright and hale, their forehead mirrors like coronets. He recalled the command, the godliness of them. At fourteen he was beset by the migraines of viral meningitis – some sickness from the white world. The doctor, a white man with the braided mane of an Indian, sank a tall syringe into his spine and pulled the milky fluid. He returned daily for a week to shoot him full of medication and nutrients, a liquid red B_{12} that made a body-wide inner burn and high.

'I ain't going with you, guy. You can forget that.'

'It'll be a long dragged-out day, Cheeon. Into the night

and morning, maybe. Phone call after phone call. Right now police are clearing these cabins behind yours, and those across the way there.'

'Police can't clear these homes. These people won't move an inch for you sons of bitches.'

'Well, we're trying. And there's police in the trees, and behind the house. I don't know about you, but I'm goddamn tired today, slept like shit last night. The wife had me up all hours trying for this baby she wants pretty bad. I'm not complaining of it, just saying.'

'Well. I sleep like shit every night. Then sleep half the day gone.'

'What about work?'

'Shit, there ain't been work. Every mine for fifty miles around is closing, you know that. We trawled the gulf for two straight weeks a while back and couldn't catch a goddamned halibut. Caught a sneaker.'

'Things should improve.'

'Hauled some cords of wood into town last month. Just once, though. There's a famine here. Some kind of famine I never heard of before.'

'I never understood why you didn't join the service with Slone. You've done everything else together since birth.'

'Do I look like someone who takes orders?'

'It's a paycheck.'

'Do I look like a desert suits me? Because if you joined up these last ten years, you were going to the desert, guy.'

'Slone didn't mind it.'

'Well. Vernon's not like you or me. He has a... I don't know what to call it. A cunning on him. A way of making you think he's taking your orders when really he's doing exactly what he set out to do. But that takes a kind of cunning I don't got.'

From inside his jacket pocket he took a flask and drank from it, then handed it over to Marium, who despite this morning hour drank too and passed it back to Cheeon.

'Where's your wife, Cheeon?'

'It don't matter. Not no more.'

Marium lit another cigarette and shifted his body against the doorframe.

'I was on a raid one time, down in glacier country, outside Juneau. Before I came back up here for good, when my first marriage went to shit. A guy shot dead his wife in their hunting cabin. He wouldn't come out. A rich city fucker. Owned a company, cell phone towers, I think. After we were out there two straight days around the cabin he finally started shooting at us, shooting like crazy. We had to burn the place. We shot back for a while and then just burned it. Both of the bodies were nothing but charcoal stains when we went in.'

'A rich fucker and his rich bitch wife, both of them dead. And the world is a better place.'

'You know what bothered me the whole time? The goddamn boredom of it. Standing out there for two whole days. I can deal with bloodshed when I have to, but boredom I just can't stand.'

'Don't worry,' Cheeon said. 'I'll give you the bloodshed long before the boredom.'

Marium dropped the unfinished cigarette into the snow. He zipped his coat to the neck and stretched on gloves, then pulled the wool hat over ears flush from cold. 'I'm sorry it has to be this way, Cheeon.'

'I'm not.'

'Think about what I offered you, please.'

'And you think about that phone call your wife will get today. Imagine her there on the line when she hears it, hand on her belly. There's nothing on earth will stop that phone call now. You think about that, guy.'

He walked back into the heat of his cabin, leaving the door unlatched behind him.

6

Slone entered an old mining camp that had morphed into a shadow town without name, a commune pushpinned into the base of a bluff, mostly inaccessible by road. Beyond this place lay so many miles of tundra whole states could fit on its frozen breadth.

All the day before he had crawled through wilderness, on paths beneath canopies of cottonwood and birch that held most of the snow from recent fall. Only a six-inch pad of snow on these paths, but even in four-wheel drive with tire chains he had to crawl. He could tell that others from the village had recently crossed these trails: in trucks, on snow machines, on four-wheelers. Hours after nightfall he'd parked off the path and let the engine idle through the night for warmth. He ate from the food he'd taken from home, drank melted snow and wished he'd remembered to bring whiskey. Podded in a quilt across the back seat, he pressed his boy's T-shirt to his face and, inhaling its scent, he slept till light.

When he entered the mining camp the following day it was already near dark, the snow coming slantwise in sheets. The bluff above blocked the sinking sun and brought on early night. A memory stabbed at him then: he and his father here for a purpose he didn't know, nor could he know if the memory was even real. He left the truck between a bulldozer and a thousand-gallon fuel tank on four squat legs like a white rhino. In the onset dark, firelight began to burn in rude cabins and wood-frame buildings.

He walked along the unplowed center road, on snow waffled by truck tires. He saw snow machines in various states of dismantle, drays with wheels deformed by rust, truck tires in a heap. Empty pallets stacked for firewood. Lynx pelts splayed on racks, a pyramid of car batteries, sleds of birch, the well house to his right. fifty-five-gallon drums everywhere, a slouched wanigan. Across the road a Quonset hut collapsed at its center, and beside it a full-sized school bus, its morning yellow gone beige, the windows shattered, gaping like kicked-out teeth.

He found a two-story inn with steel kerosene cans piled under the porch awning next to pole wood. Inside, an inky shadow spilled through rooms. With a fingernail he tapped the door's glass pane, then tapped again. The woman waved him in without turning to see what illness had just walked out of this winter night.

She was bent before a woodstove. 'Very late in the season for travelers,' she said, and turned then to look at Slone.

She wore men's snow boots and clothing of odd design, a project of marmot, caribou, and wolf. A storm of brittle hair to her waist, eyeglasses missing a lens. She jabbed into the flame with a brass poker. Halfway up the wall were drums of condensed milk, fifty-kilogram sacks of sugar, flour, rice, cans of apple butter and spinach in shrink-wrap. Against the opposite wall stacks of ammunition, .22- and .223-caliber, bird shot and buckshot. On a nail hung a model human skeleton from some school's anatomy class – it wore a red Santa's hat, a cigarette crammed between its teeth.

'I was here once,' Slone said. 'As a child.'

The woman moved from the stove to the corkboard behind

the front counter, a collage of photos tacked to it, most dulled sepia by the decades, some more recent with robust color.

'Well, then your picture might be here. We take every traveler's picture who comes through. What year was it, you say?'

'I was a kid here with my father. Why were we here?'

'He might've had a gold or silver claim. Most all of us came for that, unless you were scientists from the college or else hunters or trappers. Them scientists have been coming steady for the past decade, I'd say, on their way north. Every week there's something on the radio about glaciers melting and the world heating up. I told them scientists: last year it was fifty below and the year before that fifty-eight below and you can take my word, fellas, they feel the same in the lungs.'

'That's my father,' and he pointed into the mix of photos at a bearded man whose features told of neither place nor age, his eyes with no trace of the blue Slone recalled from youth. His father had long ago left off appearing in his dreams. He'd catch himself going weeks or months without remembering the man. Without wanting or needing to.

She removed the partially concealed photo from the board. 'If this is your father, then this must be you here next to him. Handsome little fella.'

She handed the photo to Slone. 'That's probably twenty-five years ago,' she said. 'Judging from the film. They don't make that kind anymore, haven't for a while now, or at least I haven't been able to order any of it from the catalog. I miss that kind of film.'

It had been so long since he'd looked upon his father's face, and upon his own as a child, that the somber pair in the photo seemed holograms, ghost-town twins of themselves. His stomach tore at the top. He could make out Bailey just barely in his own boyhood stare.

'I can keep this?'

'It's more yours than mine,' she said. 'I only click a button. Your face belongs to you, fella. It's a good-lookin' face.'

'That one too?' He pointed to the newest photo, pinned to the far right corner of the corkboard.

'You know this one? She was just here. You missed her by a week and a half. She stayed a few nights. Strange thing is she shrieked a little when I took that picture. That was something new to me, I'd say. Who's she to you?'

'My family.'

'That's an odd family traveling apart this far out, if I can say so. But you're welcome to the picture. I make duplicates. I was a photographer before I came into the country. Where're you in from?'

'Keelut.'

'There's no road from there to here. Not directly.'

'Not directly.'

'Been here thirty years or more and I can say there's no easy road from there to here. My husband and me came up into this country from the lower forty-eight, to stake our claims. And here we still are. Most others are gone except for the twenty-odd of us. We like it, though. The others left for oil, when they were saying oil was the new silver and gold. Nothing quite matches precious metals, you ask me. We did mine this place bare, but it was good while it lasted, you bet.'

'Why was she here?'

'No place else to be if you're in these parts, I suppose. She wanted to see our Indian hunter for some reason. We call him that, our Indian hunter, as a joke, you know, but he's just John, he's been around here forever. He's not a forty-eighter like the rest of us. He was raised on the Yukon, in a river tribe. He was here in this spot before a single miner showed up. And he's still here.'

'Where'd she go?'

'Your girl there? Heck if I know. If she knew, she wasn't

saying it to me. I like to talk, as you might imagine, living in the country, but she didn't want to hear any of it. This one stayed in the room, mostly. I cooked her food but she just stared out that window there, like she was waiting for something to come in and grab her. A pretty girl, too. But a bit odd, if I can say so, no offense. She had your same color hair. And nose, too, I think. Real pretty, but odd, like I say.'

This photo in his fingers – her face just a week ago, a look of longing in it and something else not nameable, her irises all pupil. That green wool turtleneck was knitted by her two winters ago. She'd chopped her hair to her chin – it was waist-length when Slone had left. When he looked up he looked into the flashbulb of the woman's camera and it sent bolts through his eyes.

'You're a handsome fella,' she said, trying to fix her hair. She rubbed lip balm across her mouth. Her lips were so thin they were barely there, eyebrow like an underline, whiskers in half sprout from her chin.

'Another storm's coming late tonight,' she said. 'Or else by morning, the radio says. You staying with us?'

Slone nodded, blinked the flashes from his eyes.

'I don't have any more bread, I have to warn you. Plane hasn't been back in two weeks. We're expecting Hank again any day now, if the storms slow. Last time he tried to land that ski plane in weather, he missed the runway and hit the bluff. We call it a runway, you know, but it's just a bulldozed road tamped down.'

He looked again at the photo of Medora.

'Of course, there are some roads from the city to here, but you can't get a big enough truck along most of them, and anyway it takes more than a day. Plus you better know how to drive in snow because if you get stuck in a storm on one of those little roads you can forget being found till breakup.

94

So we don't mind waiting for Hank and his plane. He takes supplies way beyond us even, where no roads go. Hank's a real good man, you bet.'

'I want to stay in the same room she stayed in.'

'There's only two rooms up there. You can have your choice, fella. No one's fighting over those rooms. Honestly, I haven't changed the sheets in there, if you don't mind it.'

Slone stayed fixed on the photo and said nothing.

'Not sure what sort of battery you have in your vehicle but you might wanna pull it inside the garage there across the way. We call it the garage, you know, it's just a big corrugated metal hangar on a concrete slab. But there's a gas heater in there to keep the trucks from freezing up and it stays warm as the devil in fifty below. What're you driving?'

She bent to the window and with a sleeve wiped away the moisture to look out.

'That a Ford? Hard to see. I used to have a Ford, owned nothing but American, and then my husband said to me one day, he said, *We're not American anymore, we're Alaskan.* Last year after breakup he drove off to the city in the Ford and a week later drove back in a Jap model, a Nissan truck, or one of those SUV thingies. It's real roomy, better than the Ford, I have to say, what little I do drive of it.'

'What's the room price?'

'Do you have any magazines?'

Slone stared.

'Magazines,' she said. 'No magazines? You didn't bring any with you to look at while you're traveling?'

'What magazines?'

'I'm not real picky about them,' she said. 'Any kind with pictures. I like them all. I usually just get paid in magazines.'

Upstairs in the guest room – a compressed rectangle of wooded slats with the cold scent of stagnation – he looked in drawers, checked the closet, then beneath the bed. He peeled back the military-issue blanket and on his knees pressed his face into the sheet where Medora had slept. The vaguest outline of a fluid stain midway on the twin mattress – she slept nude no matter the month – and he thought he could smell her there. He breathed that way with his face to the sheet, then licked the stain.

He ignited the kerosene heater beneath the window, dimmed the lantern to a slow burn. Despite his hunger he stripped bare and reclined on the creaking bed as if his body could fit into the mold her own body had made. As if he could enter the morass of her dreams and learn her destination. He spent himself beneath the blanket, the first release in weeks, and fell asleep before he had the chance to clean his hand.

———◆———

An ungodly night in some sere village east of the capital, the heat at ninety still, hours after the drape of dark. He'd been in the desert ten months and two days. A roundup of men now, shoulder to shoulder against the wall of a building chafed by sand and time. A score of bearded ghouls, hands zip-tied behind them, filthy bare feet, toenails like impacted corn. Molesting lights from the vehicles made their shadows on the wall as black as macadam.

Wet through with sweat and fighting to keep awake, Slone sat on a low porch step while others kept howling women at bay, ransacked more homes, guarded men at gunpoint. An inept translator spat gibber to these seized ones who shook their heads in ire and spat back. Shoddy rifles collected and stacked in a mound. Chickens in cluck on the road, a goat roped to a pole. Somewhere the skirl of an infant, and beyond the slap of spotlights a perplexing desert murk.

Now a chaos of conflicting reports, unabsorbed information. A corporal on the radio sucking on a clot of gum, getting no answer, none they wanted to hear. The man they sought was either among the seized or not, guilty or not. Eyes shut, Slone leaned back against the mud-brick wall of the house and sweated some more.

This undermanned platoon of twenty-two was from the start an errant brotherhood counting corpses and days. Half were drug and battery felons who'd been given waivers to enlist. They daily mocked those frayed others, those men in the news they heard so much about, men soothed by doctors in the States. Men who returned home cracked, only part of what they were before coming here. Ten months in now and Slone had not come close to the sunder, to the nightmares and the morning shakes. And he understood that he never would. That the eclipse in him had been there since his start. His was the nightly sleep of the exhausted sane.

His warped brethren could smell in Slone all he was capable of – a calmness masking an urge for carnage – and they feared him in a way they'd feared few before. His mere presence among these men seemed to turn them more lunatic, seemed to increase their will to ruin.

On the ground by his boot, partially hidden in rocks, lay a metallic object. A harmonica, nicked and dented. Slone blew bits of gravel from the air chambers and brought it to his lips. At the mounted .50-caliber gun behind the spotlight the gunner unloaded on the line of seized men, red-stained the wall behind them as they jolted from the impact, as women shrieked on soiled knees. Blood enough to course through dirt, holes in them to fit a fist.

Slone wanted to breathe a song into the harmonica but it

made a clogged, rasping sound. He dropped it back into the yellow dirt and tried to sleep upright through the wail.

⸺ ⸱◆⸱ ⸺

In the frozen night Slone woke to the hue of flame in the window, alight at the other end of the mining camp, something burning along the bluff. He dressed in the dark and descended the stairs by feel – the chatty woman nowhere seen or heard – and outside through the deepfreeze he made his way along the center road, huts and cabins now in arrant darkness. Some homes were no more than caves hewed into the base of the bluff, one with an oven door for a window, others with oval entrances wrapped in moose hide.

Slone saw the hunter, fifty or fifty-five years old, hardened by decades of walking and mining – he could see it in his stance. The hunter stood in the wide glow of the blaze: pallets, crates, boxes, pieces of tree. Donned wholly in gray wolf pelt, with white man's skin and untrimmed hair still dark despite his age, he seemed a make-believe shaman. The wolf's tail was still attached to his guise, its fanged head pulled low over his own for a hood.

When he saw Slone approach he turned to grin and welcome him to the heat. His teeth looked like stream-bottom pebbles beneath the still gallant fangs of the wolf he'd killed.

'I thought this would get your attention. Maud said we had a young traveler tonight. I knew it was you.'

'You're not an Indian.'

'Not officially.'

'You're not a priest.'

'In my own way I am, same as you and everyone.'

'I'm no priest.'

'Have it your way, then.'

Long laminated scars embossed his forehead and face – the

admonition of a grizzly. The beast had taken a piece of his nose and upper lip as token.

'Why did she come to you?'

'Step closer here. It won't hurt you, this fire. I like a big fire all after freeze-up. As reminder, you know. Breakup is still a long way off.'

Fixed to a vertical spit in the blaze was a haunch of lynx or wolf he rotated with a ski pole. Above, the firmament was masked by its floor of cloud. A new storm was coming by daylight. This fire augmented with dark the surrounding night. The lard of the haunch cracked in the flame and Slone's airy gut yawned. The wind raised the bonfire and sent sparks in flight like insects aglow.

'I knew you'd be starved, traveling up from Keelut. Maud said you didn't eat. We're out of bread here, you know. Hank ain't been in with the plane. But we got meat to go 'round. For now.' He paused to turn the spit. 'Prey is real scarce this winter. Nothing I've seen before. You hungry?'

Slone looked at the meat in the blaze but said nothing.

'I got some potatoes too. I cooked them for us. You're welcome to one.'

The roasting fatty scent of meat nearly stumbled Slone with hunger. With a hay pick the hunter unloaded the haunch onto a grease-stained square of plywood.

'Come eat,' he said.

His cave had been burrowed into the rock bluff by machine. It stayed lit with kerosene lamps that cast demonic shapes about the concave space, the air dense with the smell of wood smoke. His crude kiln was a steel drum torched open on one side, twelve feet of stovepipe snaking over to the entrance – Slone had to duck to enter – and fastened with wire and galvanized concrete nails hammered into the rock. It threw a dry sauna heat that engulfed the cave.

The hunter dwelled among the heaped and hanging bones

of every beast born here, brown and black hides stacked like carpets at a market. A row of *National Geographic* and *Playboy* magazines, decades old, sat piled by a mattress gnawed on by rodents. A Ken doll in a string noose, hanging from a hook. On a wall the chasmal jaws of a bear trap. Wolf skulls by the score. Dozens of wolfish masks made of driftwood and dyed in ochre – they scowled from the wall and rounded vault. The masks were identical to what he'd found beneath Medora's pillow.

The hunter stripped from his costume to socks and briefs, his bare body muscled and scarred. He had the torso and limbs of a swimmer, though his face proclaimed every day of five decades. Slone sweated fast in the rolling heat of the fire and removed his parka. He sat opposite the hunter, cross-legged on a grizzly skin, eating burned potato and lynx meat from an earthen plate.

There beside the bed of pelts were Medora's boots, leather and fur, size eight, ordered from a catalog before freeze-up last season. The hunter saw Slone looking at the boots.

'I fixed her a new pair, mukluks with moose and wolf, waterproof lining, knee-high, real good ones. Those ones there are no good where she's going.'

Slone chewed and nodded. The hunter's two bolt-action rifles and a single-barrel shotgun poked out from a crate, hunting knives piled on a tree-stump table.

'She knows you're coming for her. She told me that. She told me too what she did. That's why she came to me, to answer your question. Counsel, you can call it. She had one of my masks. I don't know how. I give them away to whoever comes through here and they seem to find who needs them. One way or another. You're welcome to one. It releases the wolf in you, boy. The wolf we all have in us.'

They ate more in silence.

'How are you from this region, I wonder, with all that

yellow hair? You look like a Nordic to me. The woman too. She has your same hair, but a whiter yellow, and she has your face too, I'd say. Ever notice how people who live together for a long while start to resemble each other? That's why I live alone. I don't want to look like nobody but me.'

'You let her go from here.'

'It's not my business what she did. There's no decree in the country. It don't reach here. I help who comes asking me. What brings them here and where they go to is nothing to me. I've seen plenty of mothers kill their young. You see it out here a lot.'

He passed Slone a wooden jug of water with no handle, chill despite the warmth in the room. Slone drank it half gone and passed it back.

'I remember you, traveler. I remember your father too, when he came here with you. You were a little tyke then, maybe five or six. Don't you remember that?'

'Why did we come here?'

'To see me. Your father wanted a wolf's oil. He wouldn't shoot one himself. So he came to me for the oil. It was for you, this oil. Did you know that? Your father said you were unnatural. Said you had unnatural ways about you. That was his word, *unnatural*. An Indian witch from your village told him a wolf's oil could cure you, make you normal. Did it work? Are you normal now? I gave him the oil.'

He sliced off another portion of lynx and laid it on Slone's plate.

'What'd your father mean, you were unnatural? What's unnatural about you, boy? You look wholesome enough to me.'

'My father is dead. I am alive.'

'Me too. My ancestors on the Yukon worshipped the wolf as a god, you know.'

'Your ancestors are white like mine.'

'On the outside, that's true.'

101

'It's an odd people who will butcher their god.'

'Kill your god and you become your god. For survival, not sport, of course. Look at where you are.'

'I see sport here.'

'I trade them pelts with Hank. He can sell them at the city, mostly marten and lynx he wants. They fetch a good price for him, more than wolverine or wolf. He trades me provisions, brings whatever I might need for the season. That's called a living, not a sport, I'd say.'

'Tell me where she is.'

'It's not for me to tell. I'll feed and clothe a traveler but I don't meddle. Meddle is for others. There's no meddle here. The animals and weather have their rules and I obey those.'

They finished their meal without words. The hunter pressed tobacco into a pipe and passed it to Slone. From a flagon he poured moonshine the color and scent of gasoline. When Slone drank from it the liquid hollowed his sternum, sprawled in flame across his stomach. They smoked in quiet. Slone looked to the large hide hanging behind him, a shape and texture and tint he'd never seen before, neither bear nor moose nor caribou. He asked about its origin.

The hunter grinned, flecks of meat packed between his teeth. 'Do you like a story, traveler?'

'I like the truth.'

'The truth. Every story is the truth,' and he laughed the smoke loose from his nose. 'Okay. I'll tell you. It was '85 when I shot it. Early winter just before freeze-up. About a mile west of here, coming down a ridge into a ravine. Everything dusted with snow but not that hard cold of January yet. The ravine still running. It looked like a brown bear from the crest of the ridge. They'll stand on their hind legs, you know, to reach up a tree. And I saw it that way, standing. But then the path dipped down and around and when I had a clear view again, maybe eight minutes later, it was still standing. No brown bear stands that long. And through the glasses I saw it, its face gorilla, but not. A sagittal crest like one of them Neanderthals in the *National Geographic* pictures. Overall, I'd say, it was six hundred pounds easy but with the body shape of a human. You can see from that skin there behind you it was over seven feet in height.'

Slone turned to look, then handed the pipe back to the hunter.

'But it was the eyes that got me. They were human eyes. Larger, of course, but human in every way. Its gaze, I mean. It was aware, *self*-aware. It was the Kushtaka. I heard about it all through my youth and there it was, clear as the day around me. It had a young one with it. With her, it was a female, I could see the teats. Young one about five feet, less hairy. Its face like any child's you'd see. A little monkey nose. But already muscular. Round with muscles, and it just a little thing. They were at the water drinking and it seemed she was teaching the young one something. About fish, I thought. And then pointing up into the tree at birds but I couldn't see what kind. The son of a bitch had speech. The damnedest thing.'

He raised the pipe, took the smoke down deep into himself.

'This was a once-in-a-lifetime, as you can guess. I was a good eighty feet away but on my belly in thin snow and camouflaged real good in wolf down. Any wind there was in that ravine was against me, so they couldn't smell a thing. I had a .308 Winchester then, you know, the finest rifle ever made. It took that young one's head half off. The mother saw it before she heard it. Then she howled. Some sound, I have to tell you. Not like a wolf but a man's howl. It was the damnedest thing: half in the water, she tried to hold the young one's head together, where it was split, as if she could undo what been done. Of course she couldn't. And she just howled, looking up and around like it was lightning that did it. I dropped her right there, with the young one in her arms, right through the heart. You can't get a better shot than that.'

He paused to finger more tobacco from a pouch.

'I had a sled with me on the ridge top but I couldn't fit them both on it. I mean, I couldn't tote all that weight, heavy bastards. I tried going back that night for the young one but the wolves had their dinner of it. And I ate all winter of the mother. A pork taste, I'd say, not like moose or bear. Not gamy like wolf. The strength that meat gave me, the spirit of the Kushtaka in me… I can't explain it. I had orgasms just standing here, not stroking myself, nothing like that at all. Just standing. I saved the eyes too, those amazing eyes. They're around here somewhere.'

Slone drank again from the mug and they finished the last of the tobacco. Soon he rose and went slowly over to Medora's boots. He squatted and brought one to his face and inhaled the sweat-strong fur.

'You're welcome to the woman's boots. They're yours, really. I don't meddle.'

Slone returned the boot and stood. On a low table there among bullets and tools was the key to Medora's truck fastened to a key ring Bailey had made at school: a smiley-faced heart of fired clay painted over in scarlet gloss. Slone held up the key, dangled it in the jumping firelight for the hunter to see.

'Yes. I traded her trucks. She took my Ford. I got the better of the deal, I'd say, for that Chevy. But the Ford is a damn good truck too. She didn't want her vehicle spotted on roads, I'm guessing. I don't like to meddle. Told her just take mine, I'd trade her, an even swap. Plus the boots I made her.'

Slone removed the key ring, felt its polished flat weight in his palm, ran a thumb over its surface, then slid it down into a pocket. He said nothing.

Inching along the ribbed wall of the cave, he examined the wolf masks in museum display, each one crafted to look hellish and rabid.

'You're welcome to any of them masks there. Have your pick of them. It's not my business but I can see you need to let your wolf out a little. When's the last time you showed the monster in you, boy?'

Slone chose the black mask with elongated snout and overlarge fangs. With the leather straps he fastened it to his face through his yellow wreath of hair.

The hunter was bent now over the stove, adding a wedge of wood, and when he turned he seemed ready to say something. But Slone was in the mask with a knife gripped by the blade, handle aimed at the hunter.

They stood that way regarding one another, their fire-thrown shadows towering about the cave. Seconds later the blade pierced the hunter's chest to the handle, just above the aorta. Midway between them in the air the blade had caught the quick glint of firelight. In a gasp the hunter looked at the handle stuck to his chest, then at the upright animal across the cave. It seemed he wanted to ask yet another question he'd just lost the language for.

He needed both hands to yank out the blade. The coin-slot wound was black and withholding blood. He stood inspecting the knife almost in admiration of its design and the blood began seeping from the slot. Still gasping, he glanced at the monster in the mask. He stepped to the grizzly skin and collapsed on his back, waiting for what more would come.

Then Slone was above him, handgun aimed at the hunter's hairline, his own breath wet within the wolf face. Through the eyeholes of the mask he could see the hunter blinking and breathing, asthmatic, his lips trying to speak to whatever god he claimed for his own. Slone put the bullet in the hunter's forehead and watched the hole ooze a blackish blood.

He walked back into the polar night with Medora's boots beneath his arm, the mask still fastened to his face.

7

CHEEON STARTED SHOOTING AS soon as Marium reached the line of vehicles in front of his cabin. He didn't know the make of rifle Cheeon had in the attic but it was without stop, ripping cup-sized holes through the trucks. He could not fathom why a man would have a weapon like that, how he'd even go about getting one. He looked over to a cop to tell him to duck, duck lower, then saw a piece of his face and skull tear off in sherbet under his helmet. He ducked then and fell dead.

The rounds came faster than he'd ever seen or heard. He could see the flame from the long barrel in the attic window. It pivoted smoothly up and down, right and left, attached to a tripod. Cheeon wasn't quitting to reload. He didn't need to. The windshields and windows of the trucks were shattering, spraying over Marium, the men, the ground. Air hissing from shot tires. Rounds clunking into engine blocks, dull but loud like hammer hits.

When Cheeon turned the gun to the nearby pines the rounds trimmed off branches, hacked the bark through. The snow showered down in great mist. The men in those trees fell dead to the ground with branches and snow. He couldn't hear any men returning even a single round. They were crouched close to the earth, hands over their heads despite their helmets. Those who weren't shot dead looked amazed that this was happening to them. Or that such a thing was even possible at this place.

He crawled over to the end of the nearest truck, beneath the back bumper. He waited there with the carbine for a break in the fire, for Cheeon to reload. But it'd been a minute or more and the lead would not stop. He thought that soon one of the trucks would catch fire and blow, that they'd all be burnt or worse. He could aim at the attic window from beneath the bumper. He fired there, splintering the wood of the cabin. Maybe getting a round or two inside at him. He just couldn't tell.

Cheeon's fire broke for several seconds, then started again at the truck Marium was under. The lead piercing the truck sounded again like quick hits with a hammer. He didn't know what they were doing to the fuel tanks. He could see the rounds erupting in snow beneath the truck, hear them against the chassis. And once more he just could not understand why this man would have that weapon here. What purpose it was supposed to serve other than this one upon them.

He crawled back around, crouched behind a wheel, saw a man try to dash to a spruce where another flailed, yelling. This man was hit halfway there, his blood flaring bright against the white before he fell sideways. His insides spilled, steamed there pink in the snow.

A minute more of this and Cheeon quit. Whether to reload or just watch all he'd done, Marium could not know. At the left flank of the cabin a man shielded by spruce began firing at the alcove. It must have been his service pistol – the pop-pop discharge sounded pitiful after the barrage they'd just heard. Marium hollered for him to hold his fire. He knew as soon as Cheeon saw where the rounds were coming from he'd mow down those trees and that man along with them.

The trucks were perforated, made of tinfoil. He yelled again for everyone to stay low. A man was facedown near him, by the exhaust pipe, in an oval of his own blood. Marium turned him over and saw that the rounds had gone through his flak jacket, into his throat. This man hadn't had even a second for a last tally. Marium heard himself yelling again – for someone to get on the radio, the satellite phone, something, to call in backup. But no one responded to him.

He could tell they didn't want to move at all. Someone he couldn't see, whose voice he didn't recognize, yelled for a doctor. It was an odd request, he thought, since there wasn't a doctor among them or coming. No doctor who could undo what was being done here. Then Cheeon's fire hit where this man lay and the voice abruptly quit calling.

He saw Arnie there on the ground with his carbine. He crawled near him and said his name. Arnie looked at him as if trying to remember who Marium was. Or what Marium might have to do with this alien thing now pressed upon him. He said Arnie's name again, could see the shock in his eyes. Shock always looks the same, he knew – a cross between surprised and sleepy.

Arnie wouldn't respond. Marium slapped him then, hard on the face, and was ashamed at the force of his hand. The snot flew slant from Arnie's nostrils and he seemed embarrassed by this. He wiped his nose with a glove and the snot froze there in a white streak. He began blinking, swallowing, and Marium knew then that he'd come around.

'Are you hearing me now, Arnie? Arnie, goddamn it, please look at me.'

'I hear you.'

'You see those rocks there?'

He pointed behind them at the uneven row of boulders beside a snowed-in patch of spruce. Arnie looked to the boulders and nodded.

'You're gonna go to them, get behind them. I'll cover you as you go. Are you hearing me?'

'I am. I'm hearing you, Don.'

'Don't run till I start unloading, but when I do, run quick, please. As soon you get there stay low between that dip there, between those two big ones, you see there? You see where I mean, Arnie? Please look, goddamn it.'

'I'm looking. I see it.'

'Then I'll let up, and as soon as you hear me stop I want you to train that rifle on the window and don't let off the trigger till you see me reach the cabin, the right side of it. The right side. Am I clear?'

'It's clear, boss.'

'Is that magazine full?'

'It's full.'

'Please check. Check right now.'

'It's full.'

'You have others in that vest?'

Arnie felt his vest as you might feel for your wallet. 'I have them,' he said. 'They're right here.'

Marium saw that the lap of his pants was soaked through with urine. On the hood of the truck sat an unshot cup of coffee, smoking there with the lid off, waiting for someone to come sip from it.

'You ready, Arnie? Are you ready now?'

'Yes. Yes, I am.'

'You haul ass to those boulders as soon as I start, and when you get there unload on the son of a bitch and please don't stop till you see me reach the cabin. Do not let off on that window but for Christ's sake watch me too, okay, to make sure I've reached the cabin before you stop. Tell me you understand.'

'I understand. I'll do it, boss.'

'You do it, Arnie. His weapon can't go through boulders,

you understand that? Stay behind the rocks.'

'I'll do it.'

Marium motioned to the others, to those who were left, those looking at him. Motioned to hold their fire. He crawled beneath the back bumper of the second vehicle in their line. He began unloading on the upstairs window full auto. He hoped the rounds would last in time for Arnie to make the row of rocks. Arnie couldn't spare those few seconds it'd take Marium to load in another magazine. The rounds dislodged snow from the cabin roof, which slid down and off in a powdered sheet.

In a minute he was empty. Cheeon knew it and trained fire on him then. The rounds filled the wheel well, loud near Marium's face. They hit the rear axle as he crawled backward from beneath the truck. When he was clear he looked himself over for blood.

From the boulders Arnie began shooting hard at the cabin. Cheeon waited it out. When he did, Marium sprinted, out of view of the attic window. Slipping, falling in ice and snow. Crashing heavy onto both elbows, his stomach onto the stock of the carbine, the wind kicked from him. He struggled to breathe. Between a gap in their trucks he saw Arnie's fire stop. Marium showed him a thumbs-up but didn't know if Arnie saw or not. And then Cheeon started in on him, the rounds sparking against the boulders, chipping off shards in a thin cloud of snow and rock dust.

From this side of Cheeon's cabin he could see up the central road of the village. Sled dogs everywhere howled madly in their kennels. People stood in front of their doors and vehicles. He motioned for them to get back inside. They didn't move at all. He thought for some reason that one of them might start shooting at him with a hunting rifle.

Cheeon's rear door was locked. Marium waited for Cheeon's gun to start again before elbowing through a pane of glass. One step in and his boot screeched wet on the pine flooring. He stopped, looked down to lever off the boots onto the mat. And he saw there in the weak gray light what looked like a fishing line strung taut across the room, a foot off the floor. It passed through an eye screw in the baseboard, up the wall and through another eye screw in the crown molding. Over to a pistol-grip twelve-gauge fixed into the corner above the door, behind him, angled down at his head. The trip line girded to its trigger.

The sight of that shotgun, knowing how close he'd just come, felt less like relief than loss. He snipped the line with scissors in a Swiss army knife and felt sure then that he'd be carried from this cabin in a bag.

He squatted there and tried to breathe but his breath would not come. He could hear and feel the gun above in the attic. It vibrated through the walls and floor beams – a buzz that came into his bones. He didn't know if more men were being hit outside. He thought of the phone call to Susan that Cheeon assured him of when they'd spoken at his door. For many seconds he considered fleeing. Considered waiting for backup. Or else trying to burn this goddamn place to cinders.

There wasn't anything else to be thought. He'd talked to guys about moments like these. Guys with him on the special unit down in Juneau. Guys from the service who knew. And everyone said the same thing to him: for all we pride ourselves on thinking, at a crossroads with the devil, thinking falls to feeling and feeling starts you moving.

As he squatted there he tried to stay the shakes in his limbs. Then crept in, quiet in his socks, to see where the stairs were. His coat made a nylon scratch beneath the arms when he moved. He peeled it off, let it drop. And there on a hook was a little girl's pink-hooded jacket, some girlish cartoon thing grinning at him.

Out the front window he could see snow exploding where

the rounds smashed the ground, could hear the thunking of lead on metal. Ten steps led up to the attic. Each one took him more time than he needed or wanted. He felt odd in his socks, as if a man had to be wearing boots in order to do this. He knew he couldn't make the stairs creak. Cheeon had quit shooting – there wasn't a sound anywhere in the cabin or out.

Three steps from the top he could see Cheeon through the spindles of the railing. He was there smoking at the window of this sharply angled space. The ceiling low enough to touch. The weapon fastened to a tripod bolted into the floor – an M60 machine gun, Marium thought, used in helicopters, on Humvees. Next to it a five-foot heap of ammunition, enough to shoot nonstop all day, into the night if he wanted. Hanging all through the room was the strong scent of the gun. A smell close to the clean oil on new engines, almost pleasant. Hundreds of spent shells scattered the floor, and many rolled to the stairs. Again he could not comprehend where this gun had come from or why.

Marium was level with Cheeon now, over the top step, the carbine trained on his back. He said Cheeon's name. Cheeon did not tense with surprise, did not turn around right away. He stood there smoking, nodding, surveying all he'd done. He took his time with it.

'They didn't do so well down there, guy.'

'Turn, Cheeon. Let me see your hands. Let me see 'em now.'

'My hands? Your voice sounds strange, guy. You okay?'

'Turn, Cheeon. Arms out.'

Marium thought: *I will shoot you through the back, you son of a bitch.* Honor, some code of conflict – they did not apply here now.

Cheeon turned then, still smoking, his hands not out. One held the cigarette, the other in a back jeans pocket. Marium had expected a crazed, sweaty face. But Cheeon looked just as he had earlier when they'd talked at his door. He looked like a man resigned to things. A man who had just ended ten or more lives and was okay with wherever that truth placed him on the spectrum before his unsaving god.

Marium knew Cheeon wasn't walking out of this cabin. His legs quit quaking then because he understood that he himself wasn't going to die here.

'You stopped that phone call for today,' Cheeon said. 'That phone call to your wife. But it's coming, ain't it? That phone call's always coming.'

'Your hands, Cheeon. Put them out. Now.'

When Cheeon took his right hand slowly from his back pocket, Marium saw the nickel of the handgun. Cheeon didn't raise it at him. Just let Marium see it. Let it hang there at his side against his jeans, tapping it as if to a tune of his own making. The other hand still busy with that cigarette in his lips. His eyes squinting at Marium through smoke.

Marium shot at him full auto. It thrust him back into the open window. The handgun and cigarette dropped to Cheeon's feet. Marium shot at him more until he fell through and landed on the snow in front of his door. He went to the window and looked down at Cheeon on his back. His eyes were open still and it seemed he was looking. Looking at a wan sky that would not receive him.

—◆—

More men arrived – men he knew, some he did not. They searched the village for Slone, for hint of him, but the villagers told them nothing. They found an old woman in her hut, dead in a rocker, a knife wound clean through her throat. No one in Keelut would tell them anything about this old woman. They found no papers, no verification of her name or age, of who she was or had been.

They moved on through the village and found nothing.

When they returned to the old woman's hut to retrieve her she'd been stolen, spirited away for concealment. Or for what else Marium could not know. They checked the village again but could not find her or those who had taken her. He remembered Cheeon telling him, just one hour earlier, that they weren't alike – not the two men, not this village and the town. Marium knew then that Cheeon was right and wondered what else he was right about.

Hours later, after dark, at the small hospital in town – confusion because nobody there had seen anything close to this before. Wounds they could not make sense of. To Marium it seemed a good thing there was nothing to be done because the staff wouldn't have been able to do it. Those who died, died in a mess. Those who didn't walked away unscratched on the outside. The dead had been frozen, stuck to the ground by their blood and entrails. They had to be scraped off the earth with shovels, or else pried up with pickaxes. Marium and the men loaded the bodies in bags into two pickup trucks. Half had been brought here to the hospital and the other half to the morgue, a mix-up he tried to explain.

Not all were back yet from Keelut. Family members of police paced the hospital hallways, unsure who was living and who not. Some spouses wailed, wolflike, when news reached them. Siblings saw Marium come through the emergency entrance in squeaking boots. They clung to him with questions.

'Christ, Don,' someone said, 'they told us you were killed.'

He couldn't guess what *they* he meant but showed this man he was alive by standing there and simply pointing to himself.

Arnie's wife was there too. Marium reassured her and she thanked him, grabbed his hand hard, as if he had been the one who'd kept her husband living. Marium had to tell some of these family members to go to the morgue because that was where their husbands and brothers now were. Others he told to go to the station to wait because their guys would be there, alive, before long.

In the men's room of the hospital he knelt and wept, holding the sink for balance. Bent over a water fountain, he drank hungrily for more than a minute, the water too cold over his throat. He could see the snow melting pink beneath his boots, ice pellets of blood crammed in the soles.

Through a clutch of nurses, of doctors, he saw her auburn hair on a bench. When the clutch dispersed he saw her sitting, not blinking at the wall opposite, her face licked by grief, faint mascara trails over her cheekbones. It was only the two of them at that end of the hallway now. She seemed to sense him standing there because she turned. And what came from her then was a quick snort and a smile, almost a laugh, a quick shake of her head before she turned away again and sobbed.

He sat beside her and held her. She didn't say anything. He buried his face into her hair while she pounded his chest and shoulders. And she kept pounding as they sat there.

'I tried calling. I couldn't get you.'

'Goddamn it, we need you, goddamn it.'

He knew then the *we* she meant, and he held her again and said, 'I'm here.'

Later that night as she lay sleeping, he sat in his chair and smoked by the cracked window, watched her in the quarter light. He could not know if she was dreaming or how she felt to have such life inside her. But it seemed also the only possible cure for what had happened this day. He'd heard others talk of the numbness after such things, but he felt no numbness now. What he felt was tired through to the marrow, thick through the head as if a cold were coming on. But not numb.

Numb would have let him sleep, but sleep just then seemed a peace he'd not soon have again. It was a rare kind of torture, he knew, to be so tired and unable to sleep. He smoked for an hour, waiting for yawns that never came.

That old woman in the village, upright in her rocking chair: Slone had cut her throat straight through to the spine. And that was Marium's dread as he looked at his sleeping wife and the child inside her. The dread that there are forces in this world you cannot digest or ever hope to have hints of.

There was somebody's whispered voice in his head, in the quiet of their bedroom, keeping him awake. He thought it was Cheeon's voice. He had not wanted to do what Cheeon made him do. Killing a man can mean more for the killer than it does for the man killed.

Cheeon had let his pistol dangle there in his hand, in the attic of the cabin he'd built with that hand. He let Marium see it, didn't even have to raise it at him – he just knew. He'd prepared, waited for this, with that machine gun, the tripod bolted to the floor. And it all played out as he had wished. Marium gave him what he'd wanted. And for that he felt shame.

8

A STRONG LATE SUMMER rain seemed to signal the end of morning. Slone and Bailey were barefoot, shirtless in the cooling shower, single file on narrow hill paths, side by side on wider ones. They wound up and down the trail to stand on shaded boulders at the banks of the storm-gorged creek. The risen current rushed, its surface in full boil. Mosquitoes chased away by storm. They sat on the rock overhang, dangled their legs knee-deep in the creek. In minutes the downpour softened through the sheaved tops of trees and the dripping world grew silent again.

'Mama said you're going away,' the boy said.

'In a few months. Not so soon.'

'Mama said a long time.'

'A year, maybe a little less. Deployment is that long. You remember deployment?' 'No.' 'It means work. It means money for us.' 'We need money?' 'Yes.' 'Mama said money doesn't matter.'

'We don't need much. But we need it.'

'She said you can get money here.'

'Not lately I can't. No one can. It's my duty to go there.'

'What's duty?'

'It means when you're good at something, and something

117

needs to be done, you have to go do it.'

'For my birthday I'll be seven.'

'I know. It seems a long time. It's not so long. I'll be back when you're seven and a half.'

Normally clear to its sand bottom, this water had turned dark, dense in its quick swell downstream. A tree limb bobbed closely by like an arm reaching out for rescue. Bailey reached forth his own arm to touch it and Slone held the boy's belt loop.

'I can swim.'

'I know you can swim. It's moving fast today.'

'Mama said men kill people in war.'

'You have to, yes.'

'You killed a person before. When I was in mama's belly.'

'Who told you that?'

'Somebody.'

'Okay, somebody. Somebody who?'

'Somebody.'

Clamor of thunder and then the shuffling of it behind them, so muted it might be above the Yukon or else far into the core of Canada.

'It's bad to kill people but not bad to kill the caribou.'

'Yes. The caribou keep us alive. Sometimes it's necessary to kill a person too, if you have to keep alive.'

'What's necessary?'

'If you have no other choice.'

'You had no other choice.'

'No.'

'You did it to keep us alive?'

'To keep us safe, yes.'

'Who did you kill?'

'A man who would hurt Mama and you.'

'But he didn't hurt us?'

'No. I hurt him first.'

'And no one missed him?'

'I don't know that. It wasn't my job to ask that. Only to protect you and Mama.'

'No one told on you?'

'No one told on me. No one would dare. The village is our family. Do you understand what that means?'

'Yes.'

'Do you?'

'Yes.'

'It means you can count on them. If something's wrong, or if you have a secret to keep, you count on them to help. That's what it means.'

'Who?'

'Who what?'

'Who did you hurt?'

'A man who came into our village. He was a drifter.'

'What's drifter?'

'Like driftwood. See there? That driftwood? It means a wanderer without a home.'

The current's cool swiftness on their calves came close to massage. The whey sky seemed to sharpen all the green around them.

'How?'

'How did I hurt him, you mean?'

'Yes.'

'With a knife.'

'You like your knife,' and he turned to smile up at his father. He then smacked the water with a stick and Slone held tight to the boy's belt loop.

'Mama said Cheeon helped you.'

'Cheeon helped me.'

'He's my family?'

'Yes.'

'He's my friend?'

'Always. You're full of questions today.'

Across the creek a buck and its doe moved through alders dripping in the storm's stay. Slone pointed for the boy to look and, not speaking, they looked until the deer ducked from view.

'It felt good to kill my first deer,' the boy said.

'You're a good shot with the Remington.'

'It felt good and bad at the same time.'

'Don't feel bad. You fed two whole families that night.'

'My teacher said people aren't deer because people are equal. She said to kill any people is bad.'

'You'll hear that a lot.'

'My teacher said that.'

'I know. It's what they say. It's a lie.'

'It's not a lie.'

'There are good people who won't hurt you and there are bad people who will. Ask your teacher if those are equal, if good equals bad.'

'It's good to kill bad people?'

'If you have to.'

'Like that man who wanted to hurt Mama?'

'Like him, yes. The creek is cold today.'

'My feet are cold.'

This spot on the rock at the water was where the boy would come to think of his father.

'I'll be with you while I'm gone. Do you know what that means?'

'Yes.'

'Do you really?'

'No.'

'It means that even when we're not together I'll still be with you. I'll be right here with you.'

He placed two fingers on the boy's pale bird chest, his skin a see-through sheath.

'When you're away you'll still be with me?'

'Yes.'

'No you won't,' the boy said. 'Don't lie.'

And soon the hard shower began again.

The wastrel, another vagabond, appeared in Keelut one winter afternoon from where no one could know. Refugee from the pipeline, from a boarded-up mine or bust highway plan. Scrounger who still dreamt of gold in some missed gulch of this land. Backpack and blanket an earthen hue from the earth itself. Wind-lashed skin and a mane part mullet, hands coarse from the weather this wild place gave. Footwear fashioned from a hide no one recognized and tied down with twine.

The loamed-over face was creased from winter toil but his eyes beneath thatched brows kept the burn of youth, an unnamed liquid shade on pause from blue to green. Impossible to guess age in such a patchwork face. He carried with him a lever-action relic with a duct-taped leather strap and scope. Some of his clawed-at clothes looked sewn shut with dental floss.

At the hem of the village before the first snowfall he stood at the line of spruce and could barely be seen but for his breath. At night his campfire shone through the boles and at the first glow of day he could be seen loitering in the village as if waiting to be asked an inquiry or else handed meat.

On the second afternoon the vagrant sat against a boulder twenty yards in front of the Slones' cabin and watched the door. Slone and Medora studied him from a window, Medora eight months round and long past ready to have their child out. Each morning she woke with knowledge of her body's new districts. Knowledge of what she soon must do and the doubt of whether or not she could do it. The terror of what it would do to her.

'Another drifter,' she said. 'On his way west, probably.'

'He ain't west enough yet.'

'He looks hungry too.'

'That look on him is more than hunger.'

'Bring him something, Vernon. It won't hurt to give him bread and maybe some cheese.'

'He's got that rifle. He looks able to hunt for himself.'

They stood looking for many minutes, the child heeling against the walls of her womb.

'Bring him something so he'll go.'

Slone approached the vagrant with slices of cheese and bread in a bag. This close he could see the discolored sections of skin on his fingers and nose, the scars of frequent frostbite – they looked part bruise, part burn. Hands slightly swollen from constant freeze and thaw. The smell on him was pungent campfire, something charred. His pants were sealskin, made on the coast in another time, worn through in places as testament to a thousand miles of amble. The loose ruff of wolf hair at the top of a ragged parka drooped from his throat to show a necklace, a white stone rune of a horse.

'This home interest you, guy?' Slone crouched to him eye-level and passed the bag of food. The man placed it onto his lap without looking inside.

'A new boy arrives next month,' he said.

His teeth looked like cubes of shattered plate glass, ill-fit as if each tooth had come from a different skull.

'Someone tell you it's a boy? No one told us.'

'Feels like a boy to me.'

'You and whatever you feel need to move on from here. There's bread and cheese for you. It's dropping low tonight and the first snows are coming.'

'Termination dust won't come on tonight. We got a night or two more before that.'

'You're a weatherman too?'

'You could say I know a little something about weather and what's coming. Do you have a name?'

'My name's got no meaning to you.'

'Not yours. Do you have a name for the boy?'

'That's got no meaning to you either.' He leaned in toward the man. 'You eat that bread and cheese and then you and that rifle are gone from here. I don't care where you go, but you go there. If you're needing a ride to town or beyond to the city you wait on the road. Someone will be going that way before long. Stick out your thumb and someone will stop for you.'

'It looks warm inside,' he said, not looking at Slone.

'You should think about a home for yourself, then.'

'I mean your woman. Looks warm inside her. Makes me miss the womb.'

Slone turned to see Medora half veiled by a curtain at the window, her belly protruding, and he turned back to the vagrant.

'I want you to look into my face now. Look good. I want you to believe me when I say this: I will end your every day. Do you believe me? Do you believe me when I say that to you?'

Above them a passel of ravens erupted from the keep of trees like black memories freed, their wings in wild applause.

'I believe that boy has got a short life.'

'Mention my child again and you'll see how short your own is.'

The vagabond took a toothpick from a pocket and began working it between his cuspids.

'My granddad was on the Skagway trail,' he said. 'Up in the White Pass, back in 1897. He was fourteen, trying to get to the Klondike. Trying to pass over to the Yukon before freeze-up.'

'They were after gold,' Slone said.

'You bet they were. Sweet gold. They all were greedy with it. Thousands of men were on the trail at once, just a narrow footpath, with thousands of horses and mules too. More than fifty miles of narrow switchbacks, over rivers and them mean summits, through some godforsaken mires. And that trail was just clogged right up. No one could move, all those horses and people. They sat there for days at a time, not moving, some freezing to death, some starving. Disease too.'

He pressed one nostril shut and fired a nub of snot from the other. It landed on his knee and he picked it off and scraped it into his mouth.

'Place there called Devil's Hill,' he said. 'The trail on the cliffs was just a few feet wide. Wide enough for a man only. Them bastards tried to bring the horses and they just dropped straight down, fell real fast from all the pack weight. Hundreds of feet down, crashed dead onto the rocks. Fifteen, twenty at a time. What do you think about that?'

Slone said nothing.

'You know how many of them thousands of horses survived the Skagway trail that year?' the wastrel said. 'Zero. Granddad told me about piles of dead horses, huge stinking heaps of them, all their eyes pecked out by ravens. Fell into crevasses, worked right to death. Broke legs or drowned in them rivers. And they rotted there among them people. Just rotted right in front of them. A god-awful stink.'

With a black fingernail he picked at his nostril for another nub of snot.

'You know what Granddad said to me? Said most of them horses were committing suicide. Imagine that. Them horses were throwing themselves off cliffs two hundred feet high, hurling themselves over to end their torture from that trail. He could see it in their eyes, their will for death, for self-destruction. Now, can you believe something such as that?'

Slone studied his face a final time and stood. 'You've got till night to be gone from here. Remember my words.'

'You remember too,' the wastrel said.

In from the clamp of cold, Slone bolted the door. He went to Medora at the window.

'He'll leave soon,' he said.

'He was staring at me. What does he want?'

'Just food. He'll eat and leave.'

'He's not eating,' she said. 'He's staring.'

At dusk they saw the shine of the vagrant's campfire through trees. Medora stayed at the window as if held by hypnosis, summoned by the spell of a mage, her child low in her and still heeling for exit.

Hours later in bed Slone waited for her to pass over into sleep. He left soundlessly through the rear door and moved through the timber toward the vagrant's camp. In the clearing a World War II Army tent canted sharply at the sides. The hide of a hare splayed across sticks to dry before the crackling blaze. From the black of the woods he watched for movement, steadied his breath, watched more. He crept toward the tent and for minutes listened low to the ground. He could see or hear nothing of this man.

Avoiding shadows, he peeled the back side of the tent just enough, the hunting knife cocked to spear. But the tent was empty, the rank sleeping bag thrown open. He entered on his knees. The vagrant's rifle lay atop a blanket. Painted crudely on the inner fabric of the tent like Paleolithic cave art were horses disemboweled and eyeless. He felt the pictures with a finger and when he squinted closer saw that they had been limned in some prey's blood.

He dumped the vagrant's shoulder bag. Fouled socks and sweater. Jackknife, sardines, coffee. Ammunition, wooden matches, candles. Gun oil, compass, fishhooks. The mummified head of a marmot. A Mickey Mouse key chain without a single key. No paper or card telling of this man, of how he knew about Medora and their coming child. There beside the sleeping bag he found a figurine whittled expertly from driftwood – a woman gravid with child, breast-heavy and fanged. It was the fertility symbol of some predatory she-beast. It was, he somehow knew, meant to be Medora. And the nausea of dread lifted from his guts to his throat.

He sprinted then back to their cabin, bounding over fallen trees through a moonless night.

She lay half asleep, a dream mostly recollection:

The women of the village called her fortunate to be eight months at the start of winter instead of in the ninety-six degrees of last summer's heat, an August stifle they'd never known before in Keelut – a heat whose source seemed intent to maim them. Mosquitoes came in clouds and the villagers greased themselves in oils from wolf organs or beaver fat to keep the hordes of them at bay. They stood in the shade of poplars and simply looked at one another astonished, sweating as if some blight had been unleashed upon them. They went into the hills and down into the flume beneath canopies of cottonwood and sat in the cooling streambed for refuge from the heat and bugs. They didn't have memory, language, or myth for this heat, had never heard hint of it. The elderly whispered of curse, of punishment sent for the sins of the village.

Her eyes opened now and saw Slone's silhouette there

in the bedroom doorway. She smelled campfire on him and something else, something raw, she could not say. She wondered why he had gone out in the cold at this witching hour of night. She said his name but he did not respond. The fear started then in her upper chest. She leaned for the lamp and as sudden as gunshot its light found the vagrant there, steady there in the room.

What unlatched in her just then was not terror, but an awareness of a riddle, or of cause and effect – of how the dawn cannot possibly know the plot of day's coming dark. Instinctively she put a hand on her belly, as if drawing his attention to two lives would rally his will to preserve them both. She questioned the protocol here, who should speak first or else if words had become altogether useless.

'There's food,' she said. 'There's money. In a jar. By the stove. There's fifty dollars in the jar.'

'This boy can't live. Someone sent me to warn you.'

She heard her odd words – mere creaks in the floor beams – asking who he was, what he wanted.

'The hag sent me to warn you,' he said, his voice womanlike, almost calming. 'This boy can't live. Stop his life and go back to the place you came from.'

The questions she had for him would not find sound. Who had sent him? How did he know of them and their coming child? She looked to the window, thought of how quickly she'd have to move, to tear aside the curtains. To raise the pane and climb out. It wasn't cold enough yet for plastic sheeting on the windows but soon it would be.

His complexion was reddish in the orange shine of lamplight. He looked part Inuit: the straight bridge of nose, eyes pinched at their ends, mane a silken black. And because he did not advance, because he held no weapon, she had the smallest understanding that he had not come to harm her.

'What do you know about us?'

'I know what I need to know to warn you,' he said.

From inside his parka he retrieved a painted object carved of driftwood. He turned it toward the lamplight for her to see – a shaman's wolf mask painted with red ochre. He advanced by careful steps and reached the mask to her but she would not take it, would not remove her hands from her belly. He placed the mask on the bed beside her and returned to the doorway.

'That mask is yours,' he said. 'Someone made it for you.'

She looked to the mask rimmed with real wolf hair. When she was a girl her father told her that to kill a wolf was to kill a messenger from the gods who protected them.

'Wear the mask,' the wastrel said, 'and then you'll know what you have to do. That's what I was sent to tell you.'

She felt the wood of the mask, traced the teeth with a finger. When she looked again to the vagrant she saw the flash of blade rise from behind him. It spiked up beneath his chin at an angle deep into his head. His eyes strained but stayed fixed on her, stubbornly alive. Slone twisted the blade and a gout of blackish blood broke from the vagrant's throat and mouth. It dumped onto the rug in wet clumps. His whole weight went limp on the hilt of the knife, then Slone pulled it sideways and severed his throat through to the spine.

Slone dropped him then. Medora felt the vagrant's body thump against the floor. She looked at Slone rained-on with blood and heaving with breath from the run. She knew then that more trouble could not be stopped.

Slone and Cheeon mopped the mess. She watched from the bed. Before they drove the wastrel into the valley Slone gave her a handgun – it was the same gun he'd taught her to shoot with when they were ten years old, firing at pumpkins on a fallen tree. He instructed her to shoot the next person who came through their door. 'If that person isn't me,' he added. All the while she sat up in bed with the wolf mask in her hands, on her belly, feeling the points of its whittled teeth.

When the men left, she raised the mask to her face and tied it on.

———◆◆◆———

The boy was born at noon in their cabin, Medora assisted by her mother and village midwives, one of them Yup'ik. Her given name, long and guttural, had been truncated to Lu. She ordered Slone and Cheeon and the other men outdoors, where they smoked and paced, wordless and put-upon, hours yet from celebration, heavy from the fatigue of cold and waiting.

Twenty-two below zero and Lu instructed Medora's mother to open the windows and doors for the release of black spirits snared within these walls, to provide free passage for their ancestors, for them to enter, to bless, to aid in the arrival. In a corner, the hag rocked in a chair eating crackers, white crumbs stuck to her shawl, in one hand an amulet she'd fashioned from bone.

In front of the fire, on a woven circular rug covered with bedsheets, the six women knelt, crouched about Medora with white towels and basins of water, a sterilized straight razor and shears. They gripped her limbs. Lu knelt bare-handed at the center in the leakage, singing her language no one could sing but still seemed to comprehend. The hag said nothing through this long torment, only crunched her crackers, rubbed her amulet and rocked.

Medora's mother had made a bone-colored paste of aloe and oils from a wolf's organs. Lu daubed it now thickly on Medora's center as the others talked her through this with directions to breathe and blow, the pressure in her anus like a phantom defecation.

The hearth heat and stink of fluid hung strong even with the open windows and doors. The women sweated prodding out the boy. Medora wept and yelled and looked to her mother as the bottom pressure built and would not abate. She thrashed her hair in their laps, crying she could not do it – it had been hours and she could not.

Lu motioned for two women to stand and each took a leg behind the knee and pressed it back toward Medora. The pressure in her rent, Lu's naked fingers pulling her wide and shouting the same word no one but the hag knew. When the child crowned, Medora's cries cut through the village and the men outside knew it was soon.

The boy's oblong head was exposed now, turtle-like, slimed in silent squall. The birth cord was noosed about the neck, his body lodged there, bloodied in partial freedom despite Medora's pushing. Still crooning, Lu motioned for the razor while Medora bucked with her head back in her mother's lap, her eyes crimped closed. Another woman readied the morphine needle and plunged it fast into her hip.

Lu lifted, pulled at the child's head. With the razor she opened Medora one inch more. A rush of bright blood and Medora dropped limp into blackness while Lu pried a finger beneath the looped cord and stretched it away enough to cut through.

The child was unstuck now and with a pinkie Lu hooked into his mouth, trying to clear his airway. She then rinsed him there in the basin – his first cry a pule – as the others stanched Medora's bleeding with car-wash sponges and tied off the cord. When the placenta slid loose, Lu instructed a woman to place it in the hearth to burn as an offering to ancestors. The others sewed Medora closed.

'This child is cursed already,' her mother said, and she and Lu looked to the hag in the corner but she was gone.

Lu attempted to latch the boy to Medora but his cries came wild now for lack of milk. On the sofa Lu sat and put the child to her own full breast – wet nurse and mother of eight, she was never dry – and the boy fed weakly first and then in greed.

At the front door a constellation of men's faces, Slone's uncertain between joy and dread. Lu waved him in, only him, and he stood over his son and could not believe his ample hair – he'd always thought babies bald. He went to Medora, unconscious on the rug. The women mending her looked up and waved him away in a gesture indicating all was well or would soon be. Medora's mother would not look at him.

When they finished, Slone carefully lifted Medora and carried her to their bedroom, where two women wrapped her in towels and down covers, then stayed with her through the day and night. Her mother stood at the window as if waiting, wanting something, some force to fly in and halt her daughter's woe. In the main room on the sofa Slone held his slumbering boy, this wrinkled elf he'd made, intoxicated by the taintless scent of his head, his breathing in the swaddle no different from that of a newborn pup.

'It almost killed her,' her mother said to Slone. 'Almost killed the both of them.'

'She's alive,' he said. 'We're all alive.'

An immense fire raged in a stone pit at the center of the village, revelers dancing around its forked girth. Yup'ik supplicants chanted, drummed in celebration, pleaded to gods and ancestors for this boy's weal. They tossed bags of tobacco into the flame for sacrifice, drinking from carafes of gin and joyous in the freeze. Sled dogs yelped at the noise. The crouching clouds promised more snow but the villagers danced undeterred. Women brought frozen char and bricks of caribou sawed from a meat pole. They cooked over barrels and soon everyone ate with blessings and thanks.

Slone would hold his boy daily, at daybreak and after twelve-hour toil in the mine, while Medora slept recovering, indifferent to the child who spurned her breast. Lu remained there in their cabin during daylight; Medora's mother and a Yup'ik woman stayed till dawn. Slone whispered to his wife but she would not whisper back. Some sinister force had seized her, a sorrow fed by fear – it responded to no balm he knew. Her appetite was gone, her voice distorted, and at night came the inscrutable mumbling of the half possessed, even as the child wailed from his room till the wet nurse fed him.

On his monthly rounds a young white doctor arrived from town to see Medora and the boy, to inspect the suture, take notes on a clipboard. With his good haircut and teeth, his city-bought clothes and boots, he was clearly not of this village. He left blue pain pills, syringes, more vials of morphine. He told Slone to give her one week more to rebound – some women, he said, spiral inside themselves postpartum.

'It will pass,' Medora heard him say to Slone. She did not have the voice to tell this doctor that some afflictions can't pass.

What infected her was beyond all ransom, some warp in the fabric of things. As she lay for weeks in bed, turned to the ashen winter light at the window, she could not know what had been loosed within her, how her covenant with the world had been cut. Her mother and Slone and others seemed just dark streaks streaming in and out of rooms.

What she saw, she saw with fogged eyes – eyes somehow clouded over in distortion of all she knew. She saw peculiar eddies of dark and day. Sitting on the toilet was an agonizing effort, brushing her teeth and changing clothes impossible, the baby's pules very far from her, this new prison without clues of any kind.

Morphine plugged the rip in her, blocked all visions of the vagrant who had come to her in warning. Slone refused to give the morphine at night but Lu gave it twice daily while the baby slept. It was the only time Medora could stop staring at such pain. Her entire past seemed to point at this fray.

The vagrant failed to go away. She constructed false memories of him in her girlhood, could see him there in pockets of her past. Every wanderer who'd ever come through Keelut now had his gaze, his gait, his reek of wood smoke. Every one of them was now a harbinger of this day. In her opiate dreams she could see herself – at five with pigtails, at eight with a ponytail, at ten with hair pruned to her chin – see herself in the hills above the village. Rushing through green and white, fleeing or pursuing, she could not be sure.

She knew she didn't want sleep to stop. Waking brought a dullness, a deadening she grated against. The baby's howl and Slone's voice too seemed to emanate from some other cabin, from some other season in her mind.

The midnight impulses began then: standing naked at the window, motionless before a winter dark punctured by moon. Her hand on the glass as if trying to press through it.

Months tarried on in this manner before she began a partial exit from this place, that suspension between living and something else. The first day she was alone with her child she fought an urge to toss him into the fire. She was convinced that his birth meant the death of her.

9

IN THE HEATED HANGAR at the mining camp, Slone packed his gear into the innkeeper's truck. He checked to make sure the tire chains were tight, filled the tank with fuel from a can, then loaded the can into the hatch.

Medora's red Blazer sat beside it, pocked and dulled beneath a solitary bulb dangling from a chain. Slone searched her truck, under the seats and floor mats, in the ashtray and glove box. Both back seats were folded down. He knew she'd slept here on her way to the mining camp and he ran his nose along the carpet, trying to smell hint of her.

Leaning against the truck, he smoked and watched the gray pall waft up and cohere inside the bowl of the bulb's metal shade. The hunter's blood remained flecked across the toe of his boot. He slid open the hangar's entrance and stood looking beyond his breath at this castaway place, then got in the truck to leave.

In the headlamps just outside the hangar he saw her, the innkeeper in untied boots and eyeglasses, in a nightgown under a woolen overcoat with no hood. Her hair wild, rifle aimed at the windshield, her face like a starved convict. The first shot punctured the glass to the left of his head. He swerved to miss her, instinctively ducked over the gearshift, the night a dark mass beyond the reach of the truck's high beams.

The shots came fast now into the truck, into the side windows and doors. He stretched for the pistol grip of the shotgun in the passenger's footwell but could not grasp it. The front axle scraped over a drift of hardened snow and the grille scraped against a mound of cinder block beneath a tarpaulin tied by rope.

When he righted the truck and spun she was no longer there, but he did not slow. The shot entered from the left dark, just behind him, through the window and seat and into his shoulder blade. A spasm jagged into his neck. The singe of lead, the sudden pressure in his abdomen, the need to urinate.

Lamps were beginning to burn again inside these shoddy homes, a floodlight now in glare from the high gable of the inn. The silhouettes of men and barrels, their hollers at him. More rifle rounds into the rear of the truck. He sped slipping on the rutted street to the access road at the far end of the camp, and in the dark he found the path back toward Keelut.

———◆———

Hours later he halted at a junction in the wilderness. To his right was a snow-canopied path like a portal, one that would in several more miles open to the road north of town. He knew where he was now. At thirteen years old he and Cheeon had stolen his father's raised pickup and four-wheeled down this hidden byway, so muddied from spring's thaw. The mud sprayed out from the tires in billows, spattered the truck end to end, the wipers waving on high, two boys high-fiving in glee.

He paused now and lifted his clothes to see the blood pooled at the waistband of his thermals and pants. His shirt was fused to the skin of his back. He stood in snow to his shins and relieved himself there, his face aimed at a sky unseen and speckled with flakes, his mouth open for the gelid air. The wind wheezed through skeletal boles and branches with snow atop like icing. Then the wind fled west and there came a heavy quiet.

He scooped a plastic jug through untouched snow and set it on the dashboard heater to melt. After he drank he scooped more snow, every bit as thirsty as he'd been in the desert. And he listened to the quiet. In this land everything listened. The wilderness within and without. His father had told him that wolves can hear one another across three miles.

They can hear each other howl? he asked.

And his father said, *No, they can hear each other breathe.*

———◦·◦·———

Shan Martin's place was south toward Keelut, twenty miles outside town, a fuel station, garage, and motel, nothing more. South the road connected to town and the highways, and north it led loggers, hunters, and fishermen farther into the bush. Shan and his father had left Keelut eleven years ago to run this business, for three hundred miles the last access to a bed or fixed transmission.

Slone arrived near ten p.m. and saw the two-bay garage lit inside, heard a radio singing. Through pulled drapes the motel rooms flickered with television light. In the lot sat a Mack semi, pickups salt-stained from highways, disabled cars cloaked in snow, a camouflaged four-wheeler with a frozen deer roped to a rack, its tongue in loll, eyes still looking.

Through a fogged window of the bay door he saw Shan smoking beneath the hood of a Jeep with knobby tires. He entered through the side door, entered into the wall of warmth, and said Shan's name. When Shan turned it took him several seconds to say anything, and then 'Jesus Christ' was all he could utter.

Slone smelled grease and oil, the rubber of new tires. The radio gurgled an awful noise, an anthem for cowhands. Eviscerated trucks, orphaned engine parts everywhere. A new Polaris snow machine strapped to a trailer, plastic gas cans strapped behind it. The orange warmth came from a radiant heater overhead. Hung crookedly above the workbench was a year-old calendar with a half-nude model astride a motorcycle.

Shan was rounder, shorter now than when Slone had last seen him, years ago. A shaved head, tattoo of something behind his ear – a spider. Silver rings on every finger.

'Jesus Christ,' Shan said, clicking off the radio. 'Vernon Slone.'

'One of those is right. I need your help.'

'Christ, Vern. You're hurt?'

'I need you to get Cheeon for me.'

'Cheeon? Jesus, where've you been, Vern?' He crushed his filter into a can full of them, then took up a stained newspaper from the workbench. 'A trucker brought this paper through this morning.'

He showed Slone the headline, Cheeon's photo there beneath it. Slone could remember the afternoon this photo was taken by Cheeon's wife. The afternoon they'd returned from the first big caribou hunt, August three years ago. Cheeon wearing a full beard then, his hair short and spiked, the rifle strapped aslant his torso. Flannel shirt damp with caribou blood, knife in his belt. In the original photo Slone was standing right there beside Cheeon but the newspaper had cropped him out of existence.

'Good ole Cheeon caused a real bloodbath back home,' Shan told him. 'I'm real sorry, man, I know you boys were tight.'

Slone skimmed the sentences. He could not focus on them but understood the story they told.

'Them cops came looking for him and he just wasn't having

any of it,' Shan said. 'Cheeon never did like them cops.'

Slone needed to sit, but there was nowhere. He squatted with elbows on his knees, and between his boots examined a shape greased into the concrete floor – the shape of a running wolf. He stood then and took the cigarette and mug of coffee from Shan. For many minutes neither spoke, Shan shifting from foot to foot, suddenly interested in the grime stuck under his fingernails.

'You're shot?' Shan said.

Slone nodded with the coffee.

'Christ, Vern. Your upper back there?'

He was beginning not to feel the lead in his shoulder blade. He knew this was the start of not feeling his arm. A bullet aims to make a man aware of his body and then it aims to make him forget.

'Who shot you?'

'A woman.'

'Shit, who ain't been shot by a woman?'

They finished their cigarettes in silence.

'They're looking for you, Vern. Medora too. They got rewards. Cops were here a week ago, I guess, or ten days ago, asking if she'd been through, for gas or anything else. What-all in the name of Jesus happened to that village?'

'Nothing in his name. Some things in the name of the other. I need your help.'

Shan felt his shaved scalp, scratched at his ears. His forearm tattoo was now just a splotch of purple melanoma.

'Help how?' he said. 'Because, shit, man, you're in this mess pretty deep, far as I can see it.'

'I need this bullet out.'

'Yeah, well, I thought that's what you were gonna say.'

Slone did not move his eyes from him.

'Well, Christ, Vern. We grew up together, I haven't forgot it. I'm sorry as shit about your boy, I am. But I've got trouble

138

enough my own self, with the cops too. And with my ex-wife. You remember Darcy?'

'You're gonna help me, Shan. That's what's happening now. That and nothing else.'

'Jesus, Vernon.'

Slone moved the handgun from the small of his back to the front of his pants, behind the belt buckle.

'I'd hate to remind you,' he said. 'Remind you that Cheeon and me were the ones who dug your mother's grave that summer. When your pop and you were too bad off to do it.'

'Shit, man, I haven't forgot that. My pop's dead now, ya know. He died last year.'

'Lots of people are dead now. And lots more will join them. Do you understand what I'm saying to you, Shan?'

They left the garage then and hauled Slone's duffel bags from the truck to a vacant room. Shan turned the heat high, then with scissors cut the shirt from Slone's back.

'Jesus, Vernon. What round made this hole, a .223, someone's Bushmaster? What's a nice lady doing with this rifle?'

'She ain't so nice.'

'Must've gone through some shit before it found you, or else the thing'd be in your lung or heart right about now.'

'The window and the seat.'

'Damn lucky. Don't look like it hit anything important. It's not that deep, far as I can see.'

'It's in the bone. You have to pull it.'

'We gotta clean it first. We need vodka for this. Wait here.'

'I don't need vodka.'

'For me, man, I need it. Shit.'

Slone checked the shotgun and slid it beneath a pillow, then put a rifle in the bathroom, another behind the door. He filled the pistol's clip and watched for Shan through a tweed curtain. Shan soon returned with a bag of clean clothes and a prescription of painkillers, rattling them in the bottle for Slone to see.

'These babies are why I'm in trouble with the cops, man, these here. You can't get this shit anymore. They're practically heroin pills. Here, take one now, because this ain't gonna feel too pretty at all.'

He downed a pill with vodka as Shan stood at the sink and scrubbed the engine filth from his hands with a wire sponge and turpentine. Slone emptied his bags onto the bed for the peroxide, the needle-nose pliers, the razors, sewing kit, bandages, fishing line. Hunched at the edge of the bed, he held the pliers in the flame of a barbecue lighter. Shan unscrewed the shade from the lamp for better light, then laved Slone's upper back, the peroxide like an ember on the wound.

'Christ, sons of bitches sure like shooting at you, Vernon. What're these two scabs here, in your neck and shoulder here? You get these over there, where you were?'

Slone said nothing. They both drank again from the bottle and Slone winced against the burn of booze. Through the wafer wall he could hear the TV in the next room – a laugh track, a man's words about someone's wife not satisfying her husband, more laughter.

'I used to look for you on the news,' Shan said. 'Whenever there was a news report from there, about soldiers or whatever. But I never saw you. I thought I did one time, but it wasn't you.'

'We used to look for you too. Cheeon and me. Whenever we were in town. But we never saw you either. After you left, we never saw you again.'

'I never got into town much,' Shan said. 'Still don't.'

'Nor back home much either.'

Slone kept the pliers in the flame until they began to shift color and he felt the heat in the rubber handle.

'Those things gonna be long enough, man? I got longer ones in the garage, good ones.'

'The longer you wait, the sooner it's infected. Pull it,' and he handed him the pliers over his shoulder.

'You feel that pill yet?'

'I feel the bullet.'

'Yeah, I would too. You want something to bite on? A belt maybe? Isn't that what they always use? A belt or a bullet? Though I'm guessing you don't even wanna look at another bullet right now.'

'Pull it.'

Slone sweated from his armpits and forehead as the pain knifed up to his neck, into his eyes, then a wider pain lashed down through his intestines and groin. His tears dripped onto the knees of his jeans. Shan grunted, trying to grasp the lead. 'Stubborn son of a bitch,' he said, and Slone could feel the blood spilling fast now along his back, could hear the grind of pliers on lead and bone. Saliva seeped, then spilled from his lips and chin. Twice he fought back the migraines of a fainting blackness.

'Jesus, stop bleeding, Vern, would ya? I can't see shit in all this mess you're making.'

He poured vodka to rinse away the blood and then drank from the bottle. Slone's pants were pink in places, damp red in others. Shan handed him the bottle for his own gulp and then began grasping again. His mumbling sounded to Slone like the mocking prayers of a comic.

'You gotta move closer into this light, Vernon. I simply cannot see shit here, man.'

Shan dragged heavily on a cigarette as he leaned on the wall and mopped sweat from his face with a towel. Slone moved down the mattress and bent to hug his knees, to curve his upper back, the wound ripping, bleeding more. Shan put his cigarette into Slone's mouth and doused the wound with peroxide this time. He gave Slone a minute to smoke, to breathe again. To find some brace against this. Slone focused on the boot-stained carpet and felt the liquid spill from his shoulders and nape.

'Pull it,' he said.

He was only half conscious when minutes later Shan withdrew the lead and showed it to him in the teeth of the pliers, grinning as if he'd hooked a halibut. From the pill and drink and pain Slone fell sideways onto the bed in a shallow dark as Shan worked fast to sluice the wound once more, to cross-stitch it closed with a beading needle and fishing line. Slone woke fully and asked if the round had fragmented.

'Negative,' Shan said. 'I got it all.'

'You have to sew down through all seven skin layers.'

'I'm way ahead of ya, Vernon, just lay there. Jesus, you act like this is the first bullet I ever pulled from a man. I had to pull that .22 round from Cheeon's calf when we were nine or ten. You shot your good buddy aiming for a rabbit. You started off a pretty bad shot, Vern. I been told you got better, though. Lay still.'

The TV in the adjacent room was off now. They heard the couple there, the unoiled bedframe, uneven squeals that sounded half animal.

'How about that?' Shan said. 'Good ole Roger is having a time with a rent-a-gal from town. Sorry for the walls. My pop cut corners where he could. They're nothing but a sheet of plasterboard on each side, no insulation even. Just enough studs to hold them up. You want another pill, Vern?'

But he was gone again in that depthless dark. Aware of the room and the hurt. But unmoored, skimming somewhere without human sound or any verge he could see. Just the purl of a streamlet somewhere beneath him.

Shan bandaged the spot, trussed it tight, then wedged off Slone's boots, helped to clothe him anew, wrap him in quilts that smelled of stale cold. He left with Slone's bloodied clothes to burn them in the furnace. In his partial darkness Slone felt for the shotgun on the pillow, felt into his coat pocket for the T-shirt that still held the scent of his son.

Shan returned minutes later holding a spoon and steaming tin pot. He sat on the bed near Slone.

'Sit up, man. You gotta have soup, Vernon. I'll help ya.'

'Soup.'

'Hell yes, soup. You know of anything soup can't fix? You need to eat some soup.'

'What kind is it?'

'Vernon Slone. I just pulled a bullet from your back and every cop around is hunting you and you wanna know what *kind* of god-damn soup it is? It's Campbell's chicken soup. You know of a better soup than that?'

'I like tomato.'

'*I like tomato.* Jesus Christ, you are something. Eat this soup, man.'

———◦◦◦———

In his sleep, inhaling his boy's T-shirt, Slone remembered it:

A tardy cold that autumn, the mornings finally below freezing in late October. Slone and Medora sixteen years old, setting out at six a.m. hand in hand through the hills outside Keelut. Plodding over footpaths they've known since childhood, miles down into the dale, across it to where the screes and crags slope up sharply from the plain. Avenues through cities of rock, scattered pine, and tufts of short spruce seen by only a dozen eyes before.

They wear packs with sandwiches and water, towels and candles. Every twenty minutes they rest to see the scape beyond. They kiss there against cliffs, soft at first and then harder. They touch conifer cones like infant pineapples that have shaken off rain. Two hours in and the temp has risen enough for them to remove their coats, to trek in sweaters and hats. At last they squeeze through crevices in the shadow-stroked crags, then track around to the cave, the steam exhaling from its entrance.

'Is that the one?' he asks her.

'Yes, that's it, hurry,' she says, and smiling she pulls him along, up and around the rock-ribbed path to the cave.

Standing at the entrance on the slanted table of shale, with the sun strong at their backs now, they can see down into the hot spring. Steam in a steady hover on the surface of lucent water. She bounds smoothly over rocks into the heat of the cave, down to the rim of the pool. He follows her in. They erect candles in cracks around the pool, the steam aglow in a dozen small flames.

Their bodies are damp with sweat beneath their clothes. They strip bare, smiling at one another, Slone stiff already at the sight of her breasts in full weight, her blond patch of hair. Her velvet tongue tastes scantly of sugar. An inner writhing of excitement and need, at her touch a threshing all through him.

Her hand pumps him slowly there in the steam at the edge of the pool as they sit with their shins submerged. His fingers are gentle in her wet, his mouth on her breast, the skin of it almost liquid in its softness.

They enter the spring, its heat a whip on them at first, she in his arms as they spin laughing through the pool, as they go under together and hold, hold their breath, holding one another. When the heat swells they ascend to the mouth of the cave for October air to cool them. In the sun her blond nakedness seems the source of light, for an instant a halo about her matted crown.

This is a vision he will die with. The jolts and twitches deep within him, his arms around her in this morning chill, her breasts cradled in his hands. Soon they return to the warmth of the steam.

On a tabletop of rock above the pool they unroll towels. They lie enlaced and sweating. He's far inside her now and she claws a fistful of his hair and draws his face down to hers so she can breathe into his mouth, whisper her love into his throat. His left hand is pinched in her right, fingers linked, locked. Her white skin has turned rose from this twofold heat, a rash fanning from her breasts to neck. He waits for her to quiver and tense and when he empties inside her they both go limp.

And when Slone woke at Shan Martin's place, he knew where Medora was.

10

FROM HIS MOTEL ROOM'S window Core saw the weak sun between a dip in the range, its warmth nothing to the ferns of frost smeared on the glass. His sickness had finally gone during a medicated sleep of eighteen hours. He was hungry now for chocolate and cigarettes. With a mug of coffee from the motel's lobby, he smoked at the window of his room as the sun glumly ascended, ice particles suspended in the air like mists of glitter, the cold a living thing – a willful thing with mind and lungs. He spat gobs of hardened phlegm into the bushes of snow beneath him. The engine above was a Cessna with skis cutting its way eastward and north to taxi men to their hunt. He planned to shower and leave this place, leave for the city to see his daughter.

But on the television a local news program, a female reporter in the village of Keelut, the microphone clouded by her breath. Core could not find the remote to unmute the sound but he read in blue ribbons at the bottom of the screen all that Cheeon had done there. Photos of the men he'd gunned down, a panning shot of Keelut – the water tower, generator shack, sled dogs, rows of cabins, those hills looming above. Another reporter at the morgue in town, shots of the parking lot behind it, Donald Marium being interviewed, looking bothered by the microphone so close to his mouth. More photos, the two cops Core remembered from the morgue, the coroner, the words 'Vernon Slone,' and Core felt an unsnapping just below his chest.

In the shower he leaned against the tiled wall, the overhot stream on his scalp, hair long enough to touch his mouth. He felt filthy from days of illness, filthier still after seeing all Cheeon and Slone had done. He'd packed a towel in the space under the door of the bathroom and the steam swelled there around him. The water off now, he sat holding himself in the tub, addled by a dread he fought to understand, newly disgusted by his body hair. He could recall Medora Slone scrubbing herself in the tub, how he'd peeked on the night he arrived in Keelut. He reached for the razor in his bag, ran the faucet, and with a circle of motel soap he spent the next hour shaving his body, unbothered by the many nicks that dripped blood in the water.

When he finally rose he wiped the mirror clear, and with scissors he clipped away his beard and hair, sweating still. Soon the sink filled with wet clumps of white. He shaved his face, his throat. The exposed skin felt bloomed, seemed to exhale after decades of held breath. He stood studying himself for a long while and for a moment he recognized the new father he'd been at twenty-five.

A red square flashed on the telephone but he was hesitant to hear whatever news this message brought. Perhaps his daughter, his wife, someone calling him to return home. But no one knew he was here. He sat on the unmade bed and looked at the pulse of light. It was Marium's voice saying he needed to meet, his office number, his cell. When Core dressed, his newly shaven body was cool and naked-feeling beneath his clothes, sensitive, strangely alive against flannel and denim. The sensation felt like a secret.

When he opened the door to get more coffee, a cop in a

snowsuit was standing there. 'Don Marium sent me to get you, Mr Core.'

'I just got his message, yes.'

'He's in Keelut now. He wants us there.'

'Yes,' Core said, 'I'll go to the village.'

'I can drive you.'

'I know the way,' Core said. 'I've been there before.'

'Let me drive you,' the cop said. 'I know Don's looking to talk with you,' and Core was irked by the way he'd said it.

An eighty-minute crawl to Keelut, half that time behind a weather-wrecked snowplow fanning salt and sand across the blacktop, the cop not eager to speak and Core glad for the quiet. He read the paper, articles about the Slones, about Cheeon, this village. A foot of new snow mantled the land, undulating up into the hills, into granite rock faces. Marium was there at the entrance to Keelut, his truck pointed at the Slones' cabin.

He waved through the windshield for Core, the cop walked off into the village, and Core joined Marium in the cab of the truck, the air burdened with the scent of coffee and smoke.

'Took me a sec to recognize you without the beard,' Marium said.

Core stomped snow from his boots and shut the door.

'You got my message?'

'I did,' Core said.

'I was surprised to see your truck still at the motel this morning. I thought you'd've got the hell out of here already. It's been over two weeks. Not had your fill of us yet?'

'I guess not. I've been sick. I'm two days behind on everything, I'm sorry.'

Marium poured coffee from a bulletlike metallic thermos

and passed a paper cup to Core. From beneath his seat he retrieved a fifth of whiskey and added a shot to his own coffee. Core reached over his cup for the same. He bit from a chocolate bar and started a cigarette with Marium's lighter.

'What did you need to speak with me about?' Core asked.

'Just trying to get all this figured out, Mr Core. This mess we have here.'

'I just saw what happened. I saw you on the news. You killed that man? Cheeon?'

Marium said nothing. His face did not change.

'How's a person do that?' Core said. 'What Cheeon did here?'

'I was hoping you'd tell me that.'

'Me? How would I know that?'

Marium looked at him through the steam of his coffee.

'If you corner an animal he'll try to claw his way out,' Core said. 'But that's not what happened here.'

No animal, Core knew, does what Cheeon did. What Slone did at the morgue.

'I read some of your book last night,' Marium said. 'The one about wolves that Medora Slone had? I forget the title. Good book, though, the part I read.'

'Why'd you want to read that?'

'I was hoping to learn something about Medora Slone.' He paused. 'Was hoping to learn something about you too, Mr Core.'

'Learn what?'

'Why she asked you to come here.'

'And did you learn that?'

'Nope. Didn't learn a thing. Zip. I saw that wolves remind me of some bastards I know.'

'That's unfair to wolves,' Core said. 'They have a logic some of us could use more of.'

Marium looked at him over the top of his cup. 'So I need to jog your memory, Mr Core.'

'How so?'

'You're the last one to see Medora Slone. Last one to talk to her. You found that boy. And right now I'm wondering why you're still here.'

Core looked away to consider the hills, knowing he had no believable answer as to why he had not left this place. Because he'd been dreaming of Medora Slone. Because he'd been ruptured since finding the boy. Because he had little to return to. Because he was beginning to fear that man belongs neither in civilization nor nature – because we are aberrations between two states of being.

'I told you everything I know,' Core said.

'Why are you still here?'

'You suspect me?'

'I'm just asking. It's my job to ask.'

'I told you everything I know.'

'I'm hoping you can tell me just a little more. That woman contacted you because she thought you'd understand her.'

'That woman contacted me because she wanted me to find the boy,' Core said.

'And that's my question, Mr Core. Why you? Why a total stranger?'

'I don't know why me. She found my book on wolves. What are you implying here?'

'I'm not implying anything. I'm just stating what happened. A woman kills her boy and writes a complete stranger to come go on a wild wolf chase and then find the boy in a root cellar. Explain that, please.'

'You asked me these questions two weeks ago.'

'And I'm asking them again, fourteen bodies later.'

Core felt grateful for the smoke hanging there between them like a curtain. He recalled Medora's body next to his on the sofa, the vision of her in the tub.

'Nothing happens here in a way that makes any sense,' Core said. 'You told me that yourself.'

'That's not exactly what I said. What I'm saying now, Mr Core, is that Medora Slone must have mentioned something to you, something that might tell me where she could be right now. Because if we want to get this thing figured out, we better find her before her husband does.'

'Is that why Slone killed those cops at the morgue?'

Marium stubbed out his cigarette in the ashtray, then looked at the Slones' cabin. 'He couldn't take the chance of us finding his wife before he did. That's my view of it. So they wouldn't take her to where he couldn't get at her.'

'And the coroner too, why?'

'To get the boy's body,' he said, pouring more coffee for himself and Core. 'Or else he's just evil. It's not as uncommon as you might think.'

Evil is a distortion of love – Core couldn't remember who said it or when, and didn't know how it helped explain what was upon them now.

'Slone let you drive away from the morgue that night,' Marium said, lighting a new cigarette. 'He let you go. Why would he do that? The wife calls you here, the husband lets you live. Why?'

Two village boys, eleven years old, padded in fur and face masks, blared by on a snow machine that sounded like a chain saw. Villagers shoveled pathways around their cabins. With their faces pressed deep into hoods, toddlers stood nearly immobile in moose-hide suits. Every few minutes someone stopped to stare at the men in the truck but did not raise a hand of welcome. The sun was nowhere. Core cracked the window another inch, felt the air move in his stomach.

'Are you gonna answer my question, please? Why did Slone let you drive away that night?'

WILLIAM GIRALDI

'He wants a witness,' Core said.

'A witness to what?'

'To this story he's telling.'

'This story he's telling, okay. And Medora, she wants a witness too? That makes you the chosen storyteller, Mr Core. Please explain that.'

'How can I explain this?'

'Vernon Slone is a man and every man is explainable.'

'What kind of man does this?' and he nodded out the window at the village, as if all of Keelut were the direful work of one person.

'The human kind,' Marium said. 'You should get a grip on that and you won't be so surprised all the time.'

The human kind, Core thought, distressed in his new wavering between words, between *animal* and *human*, in this place where one world grated against the other. They sipped their coffees through silence, the wind-roused snow like mist against the glass. Core felt hungry for the first time today. Marium pressed on the radio, turned through the stations, searching, Core thought, for a weather report, for some fact he could understand. He didn't find anything he wanted and pressed it off.

'You didn't answer my question, Mr Core.'

'Which?'

'Why are you still here?'

'Because I'm trying to understand this thing, just like you,' Core said. 'I'm telling you everything I know. I'm trying to help. You should be talking to the people of this village, not me.'

'These people will tell us nothing,' Marium said. 'They have their own laws. Or they think they do. They think the whole world is their enemy.'

'They're your people, aren't they?'

'They sure as hell don't think so. And they're probably

right. Just because you're from this region, that doesn't make you part of the blood of this village. Besides, as long as I have this job I'm their enemy.'

'Slone killed that old woman here?' Core asked.

'I think so. It wasn't Cheeon, not his style. These people took her body. That's what I mean. They have their own laws.'

'Did you find the boy's body?'

'Nope, not his either. You can't look anywhere now. Every eight hours new fall covers whatever there is to find.'

'What about Slone's parents? Or Medora's? Has anyone talked to them? I imagine they can help you more than I can.'

'Slone's father has been dead awhile,' Marium said. 'I'm not sure how. I don't know anything about his mother, never met her. I believe I've met Medora's mother in town, years ago. Very blond hair and white-white skin. Strange-looking woman, her mother. Her father disappeared on a fishing trip. Someone told me that. Went to sea and never came back. But I don't know that for sure.'

'You've got to find out more about them.'

'It's damn near impossible to know anything about these people, Mr Core. That's the way they want it. Why they live here. Why they stay. Everything you hear, you hear second- or third-hand and you never know how much of it is true. These people don't come into town all that often. And when they do, they keep to themselves.'

'Still, someone should talk to the parents.'

'We tried. The Feds tried. I just tried again half an hour ago. I have a man out there trying again. No one here will tell you a damn thing. These homes you see' – he pointed with his cigarette – 'they aren't listed in any phone book. These people don't have a paper trail like you and me.'

'There have to be records somewhere,' Core said.

'You still haven't figured out where you are, have you?'

It occurred to Core then that his inability to comprehend this place and its people – their refusal to be known – was part of the reason he'd remained. He flicked his filter from the window, lit another, then aimed two dashboard vents at his body. He shook against a chill and reclined with his cup.

'So I'm on my own here, Mr Core. I just went through their cabin again, looking for whatever I missed the first two times.'

'You've got to check the hills,' Core said.

'We've had planes looking from here to the border and they haven't seen a goddamn thing. I took up my own plane yesterday before dark and there's nothing to see except white. East, west, north, south – nothing but white.'

'You fly?'

'You better fly or know someone who does if you live out here or you won't be able to get anywhere when you need to. We don't have roads like you have roads.'

'They didn't go west,' Core said.

'And you know that how?'

'West is the city and then the sea, right?'

'Eventually. So?'

'So watch wolves long enough and you'll see what their territory means to them. The Slones have been in these hills since they were old enough to walk. They won't flee somewhere they don't know.'

'Keep going.'

'I've seen some of what's out there past those hills,' Core said. 'I know you have too. I could see that tundra. She could hide forever in her own backyard and none of you would ever find her.'

'Slone would find her. Unless he's thinking that she'd never run to the most obvious place there is. But that's what I need to know, Mr Core, if I'm wasting my damn time here, if these people are long gone by now, deep into Canada or getting a suntan on a beach somewhere.'

'No, they're still here,' Core said.

A topo map of the region lay on the seat between them. Core unfolded it and tried to study its multiple lines and shades, but the vastness it showed would not be breached.

'If the people of this village came across Medora, hiding out there, like you say, they wouldn't turn her in,' Marium said. 'Even as what she's become, she's still one of their own. All the blood here is bonded.'

'What has she become?' Core said.

'I should be asking you that.'

Core looked away again and reached for the chocolate in his coat.

'What has that woman become, Mr Core?'

We are the most unnatural of all, he thought.

'A child is the mother's,' he said. 'Not the father's and not anybody else's. Always the mother's in a way we'll never understand. It's the same wherever you look out there, in nature. She was trying to fix something. Something was broken and she thought she was fixing it. Or saving him from something. Trying to, anyway. I don't know.'

'Who destroys something to fix it? Tell me who does that please.'

'It happens in medicine,' Core said. 'Chemotherapy does just that.'

'Are we talking about medicine or people here?'

'What Medora did is the same as chemotherapy. Kill the boy in order to save him.'

'Save him from what?'

'I don't know that,' Core told him. 'Don't you think I'd say it if I knew? I'm trying to know.' He lit another cigarette, studied Marium's lighter, a Zippo made of mock snakeskin. 'Saving him from Slone, maybe. From becoming what his father is. I don't know.'

'Well, I'll agree with you on one thing, Mr Core. What happened here is a cancer of some kind. And believe me, when this is all done, I'm going on vacation, taking my wife to the Caribbean or someplace, nothing but green water and hot sand.'

'The Caribbean?'

'Hell yes the Caribbean. But right now we're in this snow, Mr Core. So I need you to replay your conversation with Medora Slone. Start from the start and tell me everything she said to you.'

A young girl trudged before them in snow past her knees with a .22 rifle strapped slant across her caribou coat, face and hair lost in a hood and ruff, an unleashed husky before her exploding a path in great clouds of powder. Core knew she was a girl by her gait. How could it feel to be from this place, to have your every molecule formed by its rhythms? Medora Slone had told him that Keelut wasn't of the earth, and he'd puzzled over those words since then.

But no place is of the earth – every place is of itself, knows only itself. The Caribbean? A child there is as peculiar, as particular as this child before him trudging through snow. Medora Slone, he recalled, had told him that she looked at magazine pictures of green water and island sand and wondered about those places, about their reality – their reality that seemed to her like mystery. She told him this right there on the road in front of him, between those rows of cabins, when she showed him where the wolves had invaded this village. She told him that the only warmth and water she had now was the hot spring hidden in the crags past the valley. Her special place, she said. And again he thought of her in the tub that night as she scoured her skin with a brush, as she tried to get clean and could not. He felt his own clean-shaven body against his clothing.

'She said something to me,' Core told Marium. 'The night I

got here. She mentioned a hot spring to me. And I think I saw what she was talking about, that morning when I looked for the wolves. I saw a spring out there.'

'Why a hot spring? I'm not following.'

'If she's out there,' Core said, 'she'd need water. She'd need to get warm. Maybe she couldn't build a fire, couldn't risk being seen from the air, I don't know.'

'Okay. Lots of hidden springs out there, Mr Core. Where is this one you saw?'

'About a three-hour walk northeast from here.'

'What else?'

'She called it her special place,' Core said. 'That's all. I don't know what else.'

'Her special place. A hot spring.' He flattened the topo map on the seat between them. 'Show me,' he said. 'We're here,' and he uncapped a red pen with his teeth, marked a crooked X on Keelut.

'It would be here then,' Core said, pointing. 'Although I can't make sense of this map. How old is this thing?'

'That's okay,' Marium said, refolding the map. 'You don't have to make sense of it. You can show me yourself at sunup.'

'I'm sorry?'

'You're gonna show me where this spring is, Mr Core. We'll fly over at sunup. We can't take off now. It'll be dark in two hours, and we're still an hour drive from town.'

'It was just something she mentioned to me. I'm not saying she's there. How would I know?'

'If I had better leads than that, I'd follow them, believe me. But I don't. So you're gonna show me.'

'Shouldn't you take men with you?' Core asked. 'Other cops, I mean? I can't help you out there.'

'How many men you think fit in a Cessna? You and me will go, you'll show me this spring, and if we find anything, we'll come back for more men. You can stay at our place tonight.'

'I have a motel,' Core said.

'Stay with us, I insist,' he said, smiling. 'We have a spare room. And you'll like my wife. We'll have a home-cooked meal.'

'Because you'd rather keep an eye on me, you mean.'

'You're free to leave, Mr Core, you probably know that. But you haven't left yet, you're still right here talking to me. You can be a witness, whatever you want to call it, but you're gonna show me this spring.'

Through the windshield, through blurs of blown snow, they watched the young girl and husky get swallowed by hulking cones of covered spruce. Marium swigged from whiskey again and passed the bottle to Core.

In his double-bay garage, at six a.m., the sun still loath to bring its light, Shan Martin dialed Marium's office – he had the number memorized – and tried to get him on the phone. 'You tell Marium to call me, tell him I have information about Vernon Slone. I saw which way he's going and I believe that reward money is mine. You tell Marium to call me.'

He returned the phone above the workbench to a cradle blackened by years of oil and grease. On the radio a weather report complaining of more storms, snow from the north. He flattened a cigarette filter into a can and moved a truck's carburetor aside. On a square of aluminum he crushed a pain pill with a hammer, then with a putty knife scraped the residue from the head and chopped, plowed the powder into a line. With a rolled one-dollar bill he snorted half into one nostril and half into the other.

When Shan turned, he saw him there by the door in a wolf mask, the pistol-grip shotgun at his side like a cane. The sight of Slone in his garage made it suddenly hard to breathe.

'Jesus, Vernon? What are you doing? The hell you wearing, man? I thought you left.' His peculiar new voice was a choked wobble.

Slone stepped toward him slowly. Shan inched back against the workbench.

'Is this Halloween, man? The fuck you wearing?'

Slone's boots made not a sound on the concrete floor.

'I thought you left. You come back for some pills? That wound must be killing you. I can get you more.'

Just the breathing inside the mask.

'You all right, man? I was just talking to Darcy on the phone, she wants more money from me, you know women, it's always that way with them.'

Slone stepped nearer still and Shan looked to the gun. 'The hell you doing, Vernon?' Slone raised it to pump the first slug into the chamber – a sound metallic and final in the cuboid cold of the garage.

Cornered where the workbench met the cinder-block wall, his face a welter of anguish, Shan pitched wrenches and screwdrivers that bounced from the padding of Slone's coat and clanged to the floor. He shrank more into the corner, his face now coiled in a noiseless sob. When Slone reached him, he pressed the barrel up hard beneath Shan's sternum. In the muzzle of the mask a hollow wet breathing, those familiar eyes embedded above a lupine snarl.

Sniveled pleas, an appeal to their past. Excuses – what the divorce had done to him, his abysmal debt. An apology for this betrayal, a prayer with tears. The radio sound behind them, the weather report foretelling of this winter's reign.

The blast ripped up through Shan Martin's chest and out his throat and face in a vermillion flare, thrust him back into the cinder block before he slumped dead to Slone's feet, his face leaking teeth and pieces from where his mouth had been. Slone lifted a garage door, backed up his truck to the new snow machine strapped to a trailer, then attached the trailer to the truck's hitch... on the radio behind him the weatherman trying to explain arctic air, still in calm drone about what was coming.

11

A SNOWPLOW SCRAPED AGAINST asphalt at eight in the morning, shook the house when it hit the curb. Core woke to its headlamps and racket – woke in the spare bedroom in Marium's home, the room that in eight months would belong to Marium's child. Nothing in this room now but a single bed and an ironing board, the iron unplugged on a green carpet. No dresser, not a chair. Walls bare, a washed-out cream. Before sleep he'd felt that familiar sense of being afield in an unfamiliar bed, a welcome trespass among the scent of strange laundry soap. Lying wrapped in the dark and straining to hear the sounds of the house and not to make a sound himself.

The night before, Marium's wife, Susan, had cooked a meal of burbot and rice in a kitchen with appliances much older than her. All evening at the table she observed Core with barely veiled suspicion. He tried to diffuse such discomfort with talk of children.

'What's it like to have a daughter?' Susan said.

'It's good, though I'm not the best man to ask about kids. I haven't been the father I planned on being.' 'I hear no one is,' she said.

'I was away a lot, more than I wanted to be.' *And I'm still away now*, he thought.

'You were away to work, I'm guessing,' Marium said. 'To make money. That was for her.'

'There are ways to make money that don't involve being apart from your family. I was younger than you by a bit. What are you, forty-three? You're wanting a boy, I'd bet.'

'Sure I do.' He looked to Susan. 'But a girl is good too. And I'm forty-eight. A fogey like me having my first kid.'

'Fogey?' Core said. 'I'll trade with you.'

Now in the dark of the morning Marium knocked twice on the door to the spare bedroom. Core was already dressed, trying to unearth his toothbrush from the bottom of a duffel bag.

'Sunup is ten-fourteen,' Marium said. 'We gotta get to the plane. You're right that Slone is still here. We got a call in last night from a mining camp north of here. Slone was there yesterday and there's a dead man to prove it. Plus a call in early this morning from one of Slone's old buddies. We gotta get to the plane.'

'Shouldn't you go talk to those people? I can wait here.'

'There aren't any clear roads to that mining camp now, but I got a guy going to interview Slone's buddy. We're going to find that hot spring behind Keelut, Mr Core.'

As they drove through town, Core saw shops alight in dull fluorescence, their storefront windows thick with frost, slow shapes inside like fishes beneath lake ice. Bags of sand and salt stacked on a pallet in front of the hardware store. Someone had long forgotten to take down a wind chime and it hung now before the grocer's like a birdcage of ice. Stray citizens passed on a sanded sidewalk, sacks of larder slung across their shoulders. The hands of the clock tower frozen to the wrong time. The temperature was twenty below.

Marium rushed into a diner and returned with egg sandwiches and coffee.

'We won't have more than two hours' air time after sunup,' he said. 'You get caught in a blizzard this time of year and

162

you lose the horizon. Then you hit a mountain or the ground and never even know it. You know what day it is?'

'Friday,' Core told him.

'It's the winter solstice. Longest night of the year.'

'All the nights here feel pretty long to me,' Core said.

'Tonight is eighteen hours and thirty-three minutes of darkness.'

'What's that mean?'

'It means we have to get back before that dark begins to fall. Slone's buddy left a message at the station at six this morning, and if he's right that he just saw Slone heading somewhere, that means Slone's got a four-hour lead time on us.'

'Do you think this friend is right about seeing Slone? I doubt the man would let himself be seen.'

'Shan Martin is a thief and I never met a thief that wasn't a liar too, so I don't know. But if Slone came out of the bush then he must have needed something. Food or ammo, or maybe he's hurt. The woman at the mining camp told us she shot the shit out of his truck.'

'Call him, then, this Shan Martin,' Core said.

'I tried, he's not picking up. I got a guy going there.'

The sun broke then over the range, orange-pink and frigid-looking.

'What's the weather say?' Core asked.

'Says clear for now. But this place doesn't play by weather rules. Denali makes its own weather.'

'Mount McKinley, you're talking about?'

'Denali, please, Mr Core. You forty-eighters should quit calling it McKinley. Denali is the weathermaker. I've seen six feet of snow fall from a sky that two hours before was all baby blue with a smiley-face sun. There're more lost planes in this state than there're lost kittens in a city.'

When they approached the lake, the sky was beginning to bruise in maroon and blue, a dim amber east through trees. At the shoreline the ski plane was dressed in insulated covers on its engine, tail, and wings – a lava-colored Cessna incongruous against this vast white. Core helped Marium unfasten the covers, then with brooms they swept snow from the flanks of the plane, the air so stinging he wondered how machinery could be coaxed into motion. How metal didn't fracture, crack from so much cold.

Core took the caribou one-piece suit from his duffel bag and began dressing at the door of the plane.

'Fancy outfit you got there,' Marium said, still sweeping snow from the wing. 'Where does a guy get one of those?'

'This belongs to Vernon Slone,' Core told him. 'The boots too.'

Marium stopped sweeping then. He watched Core button the suit. He looked either appalled or superstitious but said nothing.

The engine belched twice before catching, before the propeller would consent to a throaty fan. Core had expected the leather and metal odor of a vehicle but he smelled only the cold, an odor that was no odor at all. A cold that forced him to breathe through the nose. When he breathed through his mouth his throat seized up into a coughing fit.

'How's any engine start in this cold?'

'It shouldn't be this cold so soon in the season. And I don't know where all this snow's coming from in such cold. Snow needs moisture and there's no moisture now. Something's wrong with the weather, I don't know what. But overall this isn't really cold, Mr Core. Wait till February. That'll be cold.'

'As long as this plane stays up.'

'This plane doesn't quit till forty below. Guys working up in the arctic? They leave their Cats running day and night, never shut them off 'cause they won't ever start again. But us here: twenty below is a lark.'

'Some lark.'

'Thirty below, you gotta be a little more careful. Forty below and you better make sure a fire is five minutes away. And fifty below, don't even leave the house. People on the outskirts of town, living in dry cabins? They'll walk out in fifty below, walk down to a creek bed to cut ice for water, thinking they'll be gone maybe twenty minutes, so they don't dress right, and they never come back. Freeze solid right where they stand.'

They waited for the engine to warm. The crown of sun crested distant trees, and all along the lakeshore wooded acreage breathed in snow. Through a break in the wood Core saw a large home, too many windows for a day this cold, its chimney awake with smoke. A kind of madness to live here, in this land that merged weather and flesh, that didn't let you forget.

He recalled reading accounts of those almost frozen to death in the arctic: first the lassitude, then the slurring of thoughts, memories in confusion, and then just before death you forget the freeze, a warmth spreads through the blood before your organs quit. As long as you feel the cold you're not about to die. Core could not remember being colder.

The last time he'd been in a plane this small he was twenty years old, being flown to pass twelve days in the remotest north of Minnesota. That was a winterscape like this one, limned with snow and ice, in the sun a crush of bright. The weather, he remembered, was like this – it had its own language, its own grammar of invigoration and hurt, but he was young then and welcomed it.

A plane floats on air as a boat floats on water. A friend from high school who became a Navy pilot had once told him this, but he could not understand the sense of it, the physics that performed the feat. Many tons of metal midair always seemed to him a supernatural act.

The cockpit warmed quickly. In the headset Marium's voice sounded less severe. The anticipation of flight lent it a lightness it lacked elsewhere. The skis upset snow in trailing mists as the plane sped to takeoff – white birch in easy blur along the lakeshore – and when they lifted it was not with thrust but a seamlessness he did not expect. The skis were so waxen along the snow of the lake that at first he did not even realize they were airborne, not until he turned to see the sinking spruce and birch, the lake falling away from them by feet.

Eastward from the lake he saw the sun fleshing pink all the white below it. Denali loomed to their left and looked not of this world. Beyond town were scattered homes, then broad fields etched with the day-old harrows of snow machines, mostly covered by new fall. Behind them slate clouds like fungus, storms hidden within. Minutes later a rolling whiteness, drifts of snow like waves from this height, ripples across a plain that then erupted into hills, into swells of snow. The marvel of this land cloyed with white. It seemed to Core a miracle it should ever have been discovered, ever have allowed itself to be trod on.

In twenty minutes Marium pointed as they came upon Keelut. 'Tell me what we're looking for now,' he said.

'Northeast,' Core told him. 'That valley there past the village, over those hills. You can tell the hot spring because it's the only spot down in the side of the rock that isn't covered in snow. Aim for those bluffs there off the plain.'

'You see those there below us? Those tracks in the plain where the trees stop? Those are new snow machine tracks.'

'Those could be anybody's,' Core said.

'They're somebody's, that's for sure.'

Soon they neared an oval of hills, uneven cliffs with a pan between, a rift inside a fort of crags. They passed low along hummocks, along corniced ridges. They looked for tracks in the snow of the escarpment. Core pointed to the steam exhaling thinly from a bald hollow in the brow of a crag, brassy rock sprouted from snow.

'That's it there,' Core said. 'See it? I don't see a truck or tracks. You can't be down there without making tracks to show it.'

'It snowed last night. Not much, but enough to cover whatever tracks were there.'

'I don't see anything,' Core said.

'Let's look closer. I can set her down there between those hills. We've got a bit before those clouds catch us.'

'You're landing here?'

'I'm a smooth lander, Mr Core, don't worry.'

They set down on a suede drag and circled back closer to the cliffs. Marium strapped the scoped Remington across his jacket and gave the field glasses to Core. Leaning against the aircraft they smoked and ate chocolate. In quiet they considered the crags, this rock forged epochs ago. The wind came in raspy blows and chafed snow from the wide face of the cliff. The day was gaunt, already half gone, and to the west of them the land looked laced to sky.

Marium passed Core charcoal heating pads. 'Slip two of those into your bunny boots,' he said. 'And save two for your hands. Fingers and toes are the first to go out here. It's probably twenty degrees colder than it was when you were last out here. Probably more. Do you recognize where we are?'

'I came that way, through that break in the hills there. But I was on the other side of these crags. I can try to get us there.'

Kicking through new snowfall on the talus, trudging over landslips and scree, they sought entrance through this rise of cliffs. They had to breathe sideways when the wind swiped from the plain. Core touched great polyps and pikes of ice on the rock walls, some clear as shellac, others opaque as bone,

one like a waterfall on pause. For fifteen minutes they labored along the sloped perimeter of cliffs. Core stopped when he came to the wolf tracks stamped in the shallow felt of snow, tracks that padded from view around the bluff.

'How fresh are they?' Marium said.

'An hour or two, I'd say. Four of them. Adults. A hundred pounds apiece, give or take.'

'Four of them. Where's the rest of the pack?' Marium unstrapped the rifle and bolted the first round, snow and beads of ice on his beard of mixed browns.

'Not far, I'd guess. Their den must be near here. Should we go back?'

'Let's look a little farther,' Marium said.

'We don't want to meet those wolves.'

'Let's look a bit farther. If we see sign of anything we'll turn back.'

More hard walking along the scree and gusts turned to gale, air of solid snow swept quick from the plain. Marium pointed to a cavity in the spur of the crag and they moved up into it. They sat on rocks free from the whited wind. They smoked, watching walls of snow blow by them.

'Can we take off in this?' Core said.

'Not in this. It'll pass soon. This isn't whiteout. You'll know whiteout when it comes because you won't believe it.'

And then: 'When I was a kid my mother told me about an Eskimo woman who had to make half a day's journey from one village to another and midway she got caught in a blizzard. A heavy, blinding whiteout. She was carrying a bearskin to bring to the other village, and she burrowed a hole down into the snow, four or five feet deep, curled up in the bearskin and went to sleep. The blizzard roared for two days straight, and when it stopped, she woke up, crawled out, and walked on to where she was going.'

'How's that possible?'

'She stayed dry. You get wet out here, you're dead. You ever read *Last of the Breed*, that book by Louis L'Amour?'

'No. But my father liked that one. It's one of the last things I remember about him. The paperback – I remember it was a thick blue paperback.'

'Yeah, the cover shows Joe Mack running through the snow. There's a scene where Mack swims across the river in below-zero weather in Siberia, and then just keeps going, like he was in Honolulu or some goddamn place. If you get wet like that, in that temperature, and don't make a fire in five, six minutes tops, you're dead. That Eskimo woman survived because she stayed dry.'

'And women are stronger than men,' Core said. 'You'll see how. You'll see in eight months.'

'We gotta move to keep warm. Those charcoal pads working in your boots?'

'They're working.'

The gale diminished and they walked on minutes more along the loins of the crag to a man-width slit, a path they squeezed into, free once more from wind, free to hear their breath. They coursed through to the rift inside the oval of cliffs, and across the pan they saw the spring exhaling its steam.

'How'd you spot this in here?' Marium said.

'I was up on the ridge at the far side, glassing the valley. It's an easy climb from that side. I should have taken us that way, I'm sorry.'

They walked along against the wall of rock and Core stopped to glass the ridgeline. 'There's movement up there.'

'What movement?'

'I'm not sure,' Core said. 'Wolves maybe.'

'Why would wolves be up on the ridge?'

'They can see better from there.'

'See what better?'

'See us better,' Core said.

'They climbed to the ridge to see us? Are you kidding?'

He passed the glasses to Marium. 'There is no smarter hunter. Not out here. Do you see movement?'

'Nothing now,' he said, and handed the glasses back to Core.

'Let's sit here until they move on.'

'We can't sit long. We gotta move.'

They sat on boulders and looked across the pan at steam rising from the spring and at the ridgeline above it. Core tried to start another cigarette but the lighter would not fire.

'It's too cold for that lighter to work right,' Marium said. 'The fluid is all gel. Take these,' and he dug into his parka for a box of wood matches. 'We can't sit long.'

Core lifted the glasses and looked again at the ridgeline. And as he did a figure hove into view, stepped slowly at the crest, forty yards from them across the rift. A wolf for certain, he thought, and he said Marium's name. Both men stood then. Core trained the glasses on the ridgeline and saw the figure rise now full over the crest and stand on two legs against an iron sky.

Core instinctively reached for Marium's arm and then focused the glasses. What he saw did not fit: a man with the face of a wolf – pointed ears and an elongated black face in front of yellow hair. His bow was already drawn and steady by the time Core could see him in focus.

The rifle dropped into the snow at his feet. When he turned, Marium was against the rock face with the arrow through his throat, the tip poking through his nape, hands around the shaft as if he could keep it from doing more harm. The noise coming from his neck was a gurgled sigh, his teeth red and dripping. Core dove, grabbed on to Marium's legs at the knees, and tugged him down behind a berm of fallen rock just as another arrow smashed, sparked against the crag.

Blood pulsed from the shaft thick and almost black but in

the snow made a shock of red. Core gnashed off a glove and drew the arrow from Marium's neck, but he was already still, his chest and throat already without sound, his lids closed and the front of his jacket stained through. Core lay on him, thinking to keep him from cold, his breath plugged in his breast. How odd that the groaning wind could breach the oval of crags, but then he listened again. The groaning was his.

12

CORE TOOK UP THE rifle from the bloodied snow near Donald Marium's feet. From the berm of rock he aimed through the scope to where Slone had stood on the ridgeline with the bow – he knew it was Slone – but he was not there now. He lay again, low behind the berm, half the air clipped from him, looking at Marium fast turning to frost, his cheeks and lips now an identical ash, a rivulet of red from his mouth, pebbles of blood frozen in his beard.

Christmas was four days away and he would have this gift for Susan, the wife with child who had glared at him last night over dinner in her home. He was the invader, he knew. Messenger from the other world, taker of her husband. He wondered at the anguish of this place, all those snowed-over acres accountable to nothing.

He retreated with the rifle back through the cleft in the rock, and from the sheltered path he emerged again into an onrush of wind and snow. The wind pushed at him, groped against him, the snow like stones on his face.

Beneath his hood he unrolled his hat down into its face mask and pulled on goggles. Just then he heard the chorus of wolves behind the crags, their plaintive howling borne on the gale. He rushed along the talus to the level strip where the plane sat in its cherry paint behind webs of snow. This blizzard had come again quickly and he trudged through it aslant to keep the gusts from stealing his breath. Every few seconds he looked above to the ridge of the tallest crag and expected to spot Slone there with his bow drawn.

The door of the plane flapped in the gale. When he approached he saw the left engine cowling thrust open, hoses and wires hacked through, spark plugs stolen. In the cockpit he forced the door shut against the wind and tried to breathe. He saw the knife wounds through the instrument panel and radios. Wind nudged the plane, wailed around the windows and wings. He wanted to weep from cold. Moisture froze inside his nostrils. When his left eye wouldn't open he knew it was sealed with ice. He rubbed it frantically for fear of blindness, then cupped a wood match in his palm. He brought the flame near enough his face to inhale its heat.

The mind is the great poem of winter. He recalled those words but could not name the poet and could only guess now at what it meant – this scape identical to the mind, in moments knowable to itself. It touches the past, foretells the future. He worried that the plates, the fault lines beneath his own mind were now starting to shift, to cause a quake he could not stop. The mind's mountains, those cliffs to fall from. At a certain point this place obliterated all imagination. Like the sun, it refused to let you impose yourself upon it.

Out the cockpit window he tried to imagine the tundra beyond these crags, a breadth so barren now even wolves sought reprieve. Primitive man must have looked with horror upon such foreboding land. What doctrine of the soul would have saved them? They died without souls. He knew that in the earth, under this veil of snow and ice, there flourished spores of life blown here from the vacuum of space. How far below him did the earth's lava like blood surge under crust?

But we were not born to survive. Only to live. He knew his thoughts were those of a dying man.

Marium's blood was stained like shards of glass on his jacket and gloves, droplets on his pants and in the laces of his boots. He imagined himself a mummy found in summer inside this plane, dead for two seasons, his gnarled body a warning to those who sought to trespass here. He thought of the phone call to his daughter, the news from an uncaring official, but when he summoned her face it was three years old, his daughter as a child before time took her from him.

In the cargo space behind the rear seat he found a canvas duffel bag, inside a first-aid kit, aerial map, hunting knife, rounds for the Remington rifle, a dog-eared paperback called *Prepare for Fatherhood*, and in a buttoned side pouch an unopened fifth of whiskey. He said Marium's name aloud and sat on the floor of the plane, between the seats, drinking from the bottle. Snow swarmed more against the windows. The whiskey heated him from within, reached all the way to his feet. He unearthed the chocolate from inside his overalls and lit his last cigarette, the cramped space of the plane filling with a smoke hued blue in the cold.

Winter solstice, he remembered then, Marium's words from that morning, eighteen hours of night. He could stay here, he knew. He could pass into a drunken sleep and simply stay. He could recline with this bottle and simply wait – wait for the cold to change to a deceiving warmth before the final dark.

He needed to move. A stiffness had begun spreading up his shins and into his hips, a creaking he could almost hear. A final sip from the whiskey bottle and he pocketed the hunting knife and rifle rounds, then stepped out from the plane. He made his hard way again into the gale, onto the rutted talus, around the bluff, the snow erected there in the air like walls, great windrows along the rock face. He fought through them to the spot where he and Marium had rested. The new footprints here were Slone's. At the spur of the crag the prints doubled back and Core turned with the rifle, terrified Slone was behind him.

And as he tried to reach the chasm on the east side of the crag, he turned every few seconds, expecting to spot Slone behind him along the rock face, blurred by snow. The footpath through the chasm was obscured by new fall atop crisps of hoar and snarled with loosed rock, but it was still and silent screened from the gale. He paused here at the head of the path to look back for Slone.

At the top of this path, canopied by rock, he knelt beneath a fluted cornice of snow with the rifle ready. Into this tall oval, away from the wind, snow floated as if part of a nativity. To his right fifty yards down lay Marium's brown boots jutting out from behind the berm.

He cross-shouldered the rifle and stepped out from the path onto boulders and flat shapes of shale, testing each foot down. At the bottom he hid behind a berm, and in the rifle's scope he saw the entrance of the spring, steam on black. Breathing, he waited. When he moved again he stayed close to the inner face of the cliff as he crept around to the rocks spilled like a bumped tongue from the mouth of the spring.

He ascended the ramp to the level swatch of shale at the mouth and crouched there with the rifle, aiming in as far as light would go. Beneath his boots the hardened dung of lynx or Dall sheep. To his right just inside, a fire pit circular and charred, beside it the toothpick bones of a ptarmigan, others from a snowshoe hare. The warmth of the spring wet his lungs and he rolled up his face mask and hunkered into the spring with hesitant steps.

By minutes his eyes adjusted to the weakling light and he saw down the slant of stone to the pool venting steam, beyond it crevices vanishing into earth. He squatted and watched with the rifle, listened to the cavern and inched in farther, glad for this hugging heat.

Ten yards from him in a corner of partial dark, atop the incline of flat rock, he saw her feet, new mukluks of moose hide where the light stopped stretching. Beside her against stone were a stack of blankets and cans of food, a rifle and lantern. He padded in farther toward the corner, the gun trained just above her feet, an anticipation in him like liquid that felt part fatal. She angled her shoulders and head from the shadows and then he saw her face. She was sitting on a sleeping bag leaned against the wall of stone, her cheeks sucked in from hunger, her eyes heavy in a way that spoke of either exhaustion or indifference.

Core said her name. His voice in this cave was an echoed noise he had not heard before. He kept the gun on her chest, squinted to see if she held a weapon, but her hands were folded at her waist. He asked if she was injured but she leaned her head back on the stone and considered him in what seemed boredom. Sweating now, he shed his gloves, peeled off the one-piece suit of caribou, and lay the rifle across it. He went to the paraffin lamp and lit the wick, her face warmed by the sheen of light. The girlish beauty he remembered, the white-blond hair. He asked again if she was injured and moved toward her with the lamp, stood before her, on the rounded stone walls and vault his lank shadow like ink.

'Medora,' he said. 'Medora Slone.'

She would not or could not speak, had seemed to arrive at some place past words, a limbo between worlds where language failed – movement or no movement but never words.

'We have to leave. He's coming. He's behind me. He's coming for you.'

176

She would not move and Core repeated, 'He's coming.'

Then in the lamplight her face changed, twisted, and from her neck and chest came a moan, a low caw of dread. Core turned and saw him there at the mouth of the cave, the silhouetted form of Vernon Slone in the wolf mask, standing before the flurried gray-white of day.

The arrow lanced through just beneath his collar, noiseless and smooth, no slap against the body, no impact on bone. The orange vanes of the arrow against his shirt, two feet of shaft jabbing out from his back. The sound he heard now was his own gasping as he leaned against stone, as he slid several feet to his side. He lay uneven on plates of shale, his mouth flushed with saliva that drooled over dry lips. A nausea now, this fear a vexed knowing of death.

For this he had come. For this he had remained.

Sideways on the stone, he sweated and bled watching Slone stalk into the cave with the bow. Core glanced to the rifle out of reach on the caribou suit, then listened to his own damp gasp and behind him to the muted whimpers of Medora Slone. A numbness was replacing the pain now, spreading from his neck and chest, down into his left arm and his fingers tipped with blood. He understood that he would be dead soon.

Slone stepped toward Medora. He dropped the bow and stood looking at her in the lamp-lit corner of the cave. She sobbed with no sound. Core thought he could hear Slone breathing inside the mask but the wheeze was the blood bubbled within his own breast.

Slone stopped at Medora's feet, his head tilted at her one way, then the other, as if trying to recognize her after thirteen months apart – after all she'd done. She wept and extended her arms to him, wanting end to this havoc. And he bent then with both hands clasped to her throat and hoisted her up, smashed her hard against the stone.

Core's voice, the shouts at Slone, would not come – they were pinned in his gullet beneath the blood. She gagged in Slone's grip, tried to kick free, then reached to lift the mask from his face. The mask dropped to the stone and she grabbed fistfuls of his hair and pulled his head to hers. When their faces hit he loosened his grip, loosened more, and found her lips. They breathed, groaned that way into one another's mouth, haled at one another's hair, their animal noises weaved with hurt, with the hunger born of separation.

They tore at their clothing with that hunger and Core saw them drop nude in a corner not breached by lamplight. He glimpsed her full breast and thigh before a shadow swallowed them. Heard a rapt keening he hadn't thought possible from a person. He almost recalled that splendor, almost remembered youth, his wife and daughter now crystal figurines in memory. He lay on stone fading, feeling himself rasp and wane and sweat, unable to summon the buried prayer he wanted.

In time a body emerged nude from the shadows and steam, into the lantern light, his blond beard stippled with dew, chin-length hair tangled and wet. He woke Core fully, startled him from his slow falling through layers of air. *You would not seek me if you had not found me.* He went to one knee to grab the shaft of the arrow at Core's upper back, then drew it through, yanked it clean, quick, but the pain spiked up from the wound and through Core's neck, into his teeth, the bones of his cheeks, reeling in ripples.

On the sleeve of Core's shirt Slone wiped the blood from the arrow and squatted there to consider him. Core could not make sense of Slone's face, could not ascertain the mysteries there. Behind him Medora stepped slowly from the dark, her matte flesh dappled with rash, an inch of semen slipping down her inner thigh. He shook from the cold of blood loss, the heat of this spring unable to warm him now. Medora draped the caribou suit over his torso and legs, tucked the hood around his throat, then knelt near Slone and reached for Core's hand. She seemed willing to comprehend Core's confusion and love. He nearly smiled.

Seeing their faces side by side, Core could notice the same dimpled chin and bumped nasal bridge, the identical ecru of their eyes. He knew his vision must be merging them, knew his mind was dying.

He looked at Slone. 'The boots,' he managed, though his throat and mouth were so dry with thirst he barely heard his own words.

Slone leaned in to him, squinted to show he didn't understand.

'The boots,' Core said again, nodding to his own feet. 'They're yours.'

Slone looked to the boots Medora had lent Core for his hunting of the wolves, then looked back to Core with a partial grin, an expression that told him to keep the boots. He rose to go, and when Medora released Core's hand he once more felt his long falling.

They dressed and packed their provisions, packed the rifles and bow, the blankets and lantern. Core watched them between lengthy blinks. Before they left him in the dark and steam of the cave, Slone came to him once more, crouched to place a lit cigarette in Core's lips. With his left hand numbed and gummy in blood, Core struggled to dig out the chocolate from the wide bib of his overalls and then unpeeled the foil with his teeth.

He smoked on the taste of chocolate spiced with blood, and listened to them leave the spring, descend out of earshot until he was alone in the hush and dark. Where the day's ill gray light grazed the rock above him he saw his smoke fuse with steam, cohere into shapes whose meaning he could not divine. Such shapes: he would have liked to paint them. He remembered he'd been a painter. And he would have painted them with purpose, with the grace not given to him now.

Sorry not to be dying from an excess of whiskey and tobacco, he wished he'd allowed himself more pleasure these last thirty-five years. Other people were defective wells of pleasure. They sought pleasure of their own. They ripened or rotted away from you, left you bumbling. He was a white-haired man who'd invested in a future that forgot him. He saw distinctly now the faces of his father and mother – their youthful faces as new parents – but could not see their deaths because he was not there. Most of us get the deaths we've earned. Not Bailey Slone.

And then he was crawling on arms he could not feel, leaving red-brown hand marks on the ribbed ground of rock. He dragged himself to the mouth of the cave, half his body in the snow and failing light. On his elbows and belly he looked down into the pan. The Slones were crossing to the cleft in the rock. He collapsed then and rolled, first to his shoulder and flank and then to his back, his arms outstretched.

He could feel the flakes on his forehead and mouth, the chill seeping into his clothes. This cream sky had no layers, no divisions of cloud – he stared into a gauze without knowable start or finish, flakes coming from a fuzzed heaven.

The silhouettes on the ridgeline to his right were the wolves heeding him with abnormal calm, six of them waiting. How he admired their patience, their wisdom to wait. Before he dropped heavy through strata of varied black, he felt, for an instant, honored to give them this sustenance. He felt honored to lose the confines of his flesh, to let it give them life. And before he slept, he saw the boy standing behind the wolves – Bailey Slone, looking just as Core had found him in the root cellar, the strangle mark on his throat, his complexion the white of the dead, his eyes telling Core there was much to fear.

The four men who woke him wore goggled faces pressed far into the hoods of wolf-ruff parkas. They did not speak. Terrifying angels without wings. Behind their heads the padded sky had started to darken in purple casts, and it darkened more now as the men passed before it. With mittens they brushed a film of fallen snow from the top half of his body. One man propped him upright at the waist, while two others stretched and pulled the one-piece caribou suit onto him. Without the body-wide burn of cold and the pain of the arrow wound he guessed this was his death.

They wrapped him in a blanket – a shrouded corpse, he thought – and lifted him by the shoulders and feet, placed him on a pelt. They carried him down from the spring, into the pan. They had no haste – a funeral procession. As they reached the wall of rock Core could see beneath him the spot where Marium's body had been, the teeth-torn clothes and bone, the pink mess his innards had made, paw prints of blood. Core knew the wolves had feasted, but had spared him, though being spared had not been his wish.

Two sled-dog teams rested or nipped at one another in the snow. When the men came through the gap in the crags the ready dogs stood mindful. The snow had ebbed. In the east the full yellow moon shone through a rip in clouds. The men laid him on the bed slats of a dogsled. He felt himself being encased in the pelt with a husky who lay beside him – the clean cold scent of its fur, its wet nose on his mouth and chin.

They packed him and the husky against the stanchions with more pelts, his head on the brush bow, his face in the animal's neck, his body slowly imbued by the eighty-pound heat of the dog. Under him he felt the rough skidding of the runners on crusted snow, and then the smooth riding in fresh fall as the sleds mushed on toward moonlight.

Each time he dipped into a shallow sleep he expected the abyss, expected not to wake, not to rise. When he did, he once again felt the sled's motion, smelled the dog, heard the canine yelps just ahead of him. Each time he woke he had to learn anew that he was not dead. A jagged passage – one hour or two, he could not be sure, time had turned into a back-and-forth slosh of sand, his memory leaping over decades. The sleds arrived in the village of Keelut.

The men carried him into a cabin and left, left him in front of the fire with a huddle of short-sleeved women who unwrapped the blanket from his body and stripped him to the waist. The arrow wound had ceased bleeding, had dried front and back in dark caps. A woman brought a basin of warm water and rags. They stripped him full and washed him there on the floor before the fire, on a blue tarpaulin, lifted his head so he could drink from a squeeze bottle, and when the wounds were clean they daubed them with a pungent ointment that chilled before it stung. He saw a blond woman take up the caribou suit. She looked it over, sniffed it for scent, and Core could not comprehend what was happening.

With car-wash sponges they rinsed his lap and legs where blood clung in clotted naps. He lay aware of the water and air on his shrunken genitals, but he was unashamed. They dried him gently and then dressed him in clothing soft and old with mothball scent. The tenderness of the female hands on his chest and limbs took him close to weeping.

When had such loving hands touched him last? He was just then willing to die, again and again, to experience such affection, such saving as this. Before apathy had claimed him how often had he gone to the barber for just that reason? Not because his hair needed trimming but because those hands on his head were a confirmation that he was still here, still capable of knowing touch. No body massage ever felt as fine as a barber's delicate fingers.

They gave him more water from the bottle and then brought a cast-iron pot warmed in the fire, an acrid broth gamy and sweet. The blond woman fed him with a birch ladle, a woman near his age, it seemed – the mother of either Medora or Vernon Slone, he was sure.

He drank the broth while others held him upright. He could not shift his eyes from this woman who fed him because he saw that her face, by some witch's trick, was a mix of both Medora and Vernon Slone – the fine blond hair, the nose and chin, the yellow-brown eyes and oval ears. In this woman's still-lovely face he could behold both of the Slones. She was the mother of both. He recalled the matching faces of her daughter and son as they'd knelt beside him in the steam of the cave.

And before he let sleep drag him down into a wide pasture of night, he understood that this one woman above him, this woman caring enough to save him, was not just the source of both faces, but also, perhaps, the reason for the wolves.

When he woke the following morning in a hospital in town his daughter was there, sitting beside him in a wooden chair, wearing glasses he'd never noticed, a red sweater as if to welcome the holiday. Her smile signaled only the smallest relief. In the medicated fog of waking he believed for a minute that she was his wife thirty years ago. He glanced to the blanket then and felt his hand in her own.

She'd want to know all he'd witnessed. She'd want to hear the truth of these events. But he would have for her only a story – one that seemed to have happened half in dream, rent from the regular world he knew – and that story would wear the clothes of truth. Propped up in bed, he prepared himself for this tale. He searched for the beginning, and for the will to believe it.

13

THEY SPENT THE REMAINING months of winter many miles from Keelut, in their father's sod igloo hidden in the taiga, an earthen grot he'd built when they were children for three-week hunting trips. They'd known about these crude outposts all their lives – many hunters in the village had built them for the winter hunt when the caribou migrated east. In the valley beyond the village their mother had left them backpacks of provisions, including a map with the location of their father's sod igloo circled in blue pen.

It had taken them an entire day to find it, in four-wheel drive on pathways until the truck was choked by snow, until they were forced to walk, carrying what they could. They dug for forty minutes through drifts to reach the entrance, the pine door that looked clawed at by grizzly. Once inside they found it dry, with a working stove, cut wood and kindling stacked beside it, steel drums packed with nonperishables made before their birth. That clean scent of frigid earth until Slone cleared the vent of snow and started the stove.

They saw at once that their father had stocked this lee with food for two seasons: Bisquick and beans, oatmeal and rice, noodles and raisins, powdered milk and coffee, dried peaches and apricots. In a different drum: medical kits, candles and matches, radio and batteries, tissue paper and snowshoe bindings, Coleman fuel and lantern wicks. The chocolate she'd devoured as a child and hadn't seen in years. Cartons of cigarettes. Sweaters, socks, long johns, overalls. Blankets, ammunition, books. A mattress hung by wire from the low ceiling to keep rodents away. With sugar and vanilla they could make ice cream of snow.

Perhaps, she thought, their father had prepared for this very day, the day when his twins would need this shelter – the day their otherness became known and they were forced to flee, to enact their exile from the world for sins they could not control. She hadn't seen their father's face in six years, since the evening before he slipped a shotgun barrel into his mouth and pressed the trigger with his toe, but she remembered it, could recall his cigarette scent, his voice always as rough, as stubbled as his appearance. This sod igloo meant that he'd loved her, she knew – meant that he'd loved them both, no matter their otherness.

They slept and ate and read, feasted on one another in the afternoon. She rebandaged the bullet wound in his upper back, applied ointment, pulled the stitching once it fully healed. For weeks they did little but lie naked beneath blankets as snow piled around them, exhausted in a way she'd never felt before, the stove too much heat for this small lee. He chopped more wood and hunted lynx, fox, rabbit, whatever he could find, but a famine was still on this land and he couldn't find much. He kept the rifles ready by the entrance, shotgun by the stove, handgun always in his belt. He told her what to do if ever he was out and she heard men coming through the thick. In six places around the perimeter he strung tripwire between trees, in front of the wire sharpened sticks in the snow to impale a man.

One afternoon, hunting before dusk, they came upon a single-engine propeller plane suspended, mangled in the treetops, camouflaged in snow – one of the countless lost planes in this country. Lighter than her brother, always the better climber, she let him hoist her into the branches and she made her careful way to the plane above. Through the shattered glass she saw the bush pilot seat-belted in a bank of snow, just a wool-clad skeleton now, the headset still fastened to its skull. The propeller was smashed back into the engine from the impact, on the door black streaks from fire. The tail cracked and dangling, one wing snapped off, bent beneath the fuselage. She brushed snow from the other wing, tested her weight on it, and entered through the missing glass. Behind the seats several wood-slat crates of mail. The year stamped on the letters was 1968. She dropped a bag down to Slone – there was nothing in the plane they needed – and for two weeks that winter she read these letters, forgotten messages from worlds she tried to imagine, amazed by the varied handwriting of people who had long since moved on to other lives.

She read these lines aloud to Slone, dulled blue ink on peach-colored paper that still held a ghostly whiff of perfume, lines from Mary to Joseph that began, 'Please don't you dare go to that jungle over there. There's no love in war and I have all this love for you waiting. You can dodge it, Joe. Just run, come here to me, stay with me, they'll never find you here.'

———◆———

Winter diminished and breakup came, spring a savior she thought hadn't remembered them. It was always that way, she knew. By the end of each March they always believed themselves forgotten by spring.

Slone dug a larger sod igloo into a wooded ridge near the rim of taiga, hidden from the ancient caribou trail and from the sky beneath the hemlock. Just ten feet from them in the forest no one could know they were there. She watched him work shirtless in moving shafts of sunlight, watched him dig high enough into the earth, above the water table, careful of proper drainage to keep them dry. She watched him frame the structure from spruce, make the notched posts and ridge beams, pound poles into the soil.

He built with tools others from the village had left for them in the valley – whipsaw and axe, hammer and mallet, shovel and pick, bag of nails and spikes, roll of plastic sheeting. She helped with saplings for the sod-block walls, with the pilings, helped cut and carry sod. She scraped clean the conifers for the roof. She learned how to fasten the beam joints with spikes. He taught her this with a patience that surprised her.

No windows. A rounded entrance of five feet. Together they carted the mattress and woodstove from their father's igloo, carted the goods their father had stored for them. They trekked to both of their vehicles, hidden in the hills two miles apart, and trekked back with the duffel bags of supplies they'd been unable to carry in winter.

They moved by starlight sometimes, whenever they'd noticed the same plane in their patch of sky two days in a row, unsure if that plane was searching for them. In the purple just before dusk they'd check their quarry, traps and snares in the forest, nets in the water – they'd check when they couldn't be spotted from the air. She wondered if the world really cared anymore about what they'd done in winter. She couldn't be sure.

Naked in the nearby lake or river under moonlight was a startling way to be, the water still chill in midspring. They gathered food, walked a black wood they felt their way through, paths they'd made and memorized, owls and bats sounding their way. They ate grayling, jackfish, bluebell shoots. Marten and fox and deer. Each night their eyes adjusted more to the dark. He could skin a deer by moon or fire. He knew which footfall was bear, which was moose. If ever they needed to be on paths in daylight he knew to stomp through the bush, hooting as he went, so as not to come suddenly upon a grizzly or brown bear. The scourge on this land, whatever curse had been here, fled when winter relented. The animals were back now after breakup.

She'd listen to him breathe, snore beside her. When his snores stopped she'd hold her own breath and try to hear the new morning outside through the sod walls. They'd sleep through the day and he'd wake her at the gloaming. After three days of hearing no planes they'd return once again to the daylight.

They relocated Bailey's grave once the ground was soft enough to pierce. They rescued him from the melting ice of the cemetery of Keelut and carried him in his plywood box deep into the taiga. Slone picked the spot beside the heather where they slept. He made her watch as he dug the hole, made her open the lid with a pry bar and look – not a glance but a look with two accepting eyes, and she did it because she knew that once she did, he'd never again mention what she'd done.

She possessed certain memories. She was a girl of five or six, summertime in the forest by the village, a forest of immense hemlock and oak. She could see rays of sun dispersed through the treetops, pollen suspended in the light like a galaxy of stars. Or those first years in the village schoolhouse, so long ago, their teacher a missionary from the States, a young man of beauty, she remembered. Dark hair and blue eyes – she was startled by the combination, had never seen it before. He had enough Bibles for all twelve children. He read verses as they sat rapt, not looking at their own text but at him, his lips, how they moved in such delight as if the words themselves were pleasure.

When she told Slone of her memories now, he said that memory is a trickster, the great deceiver. He couldn't recall half of what she could. They'd gone hand in hand everywhere together, surely he'd remember too if her memories had really happened, if the pollen in the shafts of sunlight had resembled stars that summer day, if the schoolteacher had given them Bibles. *He wants my memories too,* she thought. *He has my face and body, my every cell, and still he wants more, wants to steal my shadow too.*

As kids they'd come to this country for several days each summer with nothing but their bodies. She remembered they napped naked in the sun on beds of moss, on rocks of lichen, and later in the night they wrapped around each other for warmth. It was like that again now. Daily she grew round with another, with the new one he insisted on. Inside her she could hear already the sucking, sobbing, the pulse that led to a wailing for food, want of growth. And it was then she remembered she had other hopes.

At their spot in the valley they met their mother after breakup. She smacked him on the beard, held his chin firm in her hand, squeezed his lips. She told him, ordered him to make Medora pleased, and to make her pleased too. She said his teeth were filthy. He only nodded and looked away to the hills as Medora stifled a laugh.

In sunlight and moonlight both they walked far, and along the way she gathered salmonberries, bunchberries, mossberries, birch sap, and cottongrass stems. The fireweed she picked for its color. She could see it shine, really shine, in the first hour of daylight, and often she walked without him to collect the fireweed before they slept. The warm calm of the morning, these moments alone – she could not let them pass.

A late spring breeze came in through the entrance of their igloo and she woke with a knife in her hand, hovering above him as he slept. Their mother had given her a magazine a month earlier at their meeting place, and in it she'd read that dreams are useless. They mean nothing, hint at neither future nor past. They are the discard of the brain as the body slumbers. Why then, how did she see herself with the knife before she felt it in her hand, before she woke to find herself above him about to plunge a blade into his neck? Because, she knew, we call our wishes dreams, and she put down the knife to sleep again.

Acknowledgments

Feeling thanks to:

Bob Weil, torch in the night.

Steve Almond, rabbi, brother, friend.

John Stazinski, invaluable from inception.

Will Menaker, reader extraordinaire.

David Patterson, sapient 007.

The committed staff of W. W. Norton and Liveright, paragon in publishing.

Katie, Ethan, and Aiden, forgiving in this dark.

About Us

In addition to No Exit Press, Oldcastle Books has a number of other imprints, including Pulp! The Classics, Kamera Books, Creative Essentials, Pocket Essentials and High Stakes Publishing > oldcastlebooks.co.uk

For more information about Crime Books go to > crimetime.co.uk

Check out the kamera film salon for independent, arthouse and world cinema > kamera.co.uk

For more information, media enquiries and review copies please contact Frances > frances@oldcastlebooks.com

VIRAGO
MODERN CLASSICS
721

Antonia Barber (1932–2019) gained early recognition for *The Ghosts*, first published in 1969. It was shortlisted for the Carnegie Medal, an award she was later shortlisted for again in 1983 with *The Ring in the Rough Stuff*. *The Ghosts* has been adapted for film twice, in 1972 and 2021, released both times as *The Amazing Mr Blunden*.

Antonia's first picture book, *The Mousehole Cat*, was published to great acclaim in 1990, with beautiful illustrations by Nicola Bayley. It was awarded Illustrated Children's Book of the Year at the British Book Awards and won the Children's Choice in the Nestlé Smarties Book Prize. A perennial favourite, the story has been adapted as a play, a musical, a puppet show, a ballet and an animated film.

The Amazing
Mr Blunden

ANTONIA BARBER

virago

VIRAGO

This paperback edition published in 2021 by Virago Press
First published as *The Ghosts* in Great Britain in 1969 by Jonathan Cape

1 3 5 7 9 10 8 6 4 2

A CIP catalogue record for this book
is available from the British Library.

ISBN 978-0-349-01659-7

Typeset in Goudy by M Rules
Printed and bound in Great Britain by
Clays Ltd, Elcograf S.p.A.

Papers used by Virago are from well-managed forests
and other responsible sources.

MIX
Paper from
responsible sources
FSC® C104740

Virago Press
An imprint of
Little, Brown Book Group
Carmelite House
50 Victoria Embankment
London EC4Y 0DZ

An Hachette UK Company
www.hachette.co.uk

www.virago.co.uk

For Ken

PART ONE

Chapter 1

If it had not been such a rain-lashed, windy evening, the people who jostled the pavements of Camden Town might have noticed something a little odd about a white-haired elderly gentleman who made his way against the steady flow of the crowd. But they shivered as they left the warm brightness of the Underground station and, burying their chins deep in the lapels of their coats, butted their way out into the driving rain seeing nothing but the puddled pavements and a great multitude of hurrying feet.

Perhaps the strangest thing about the old man was that he walked upright, untroubled by the cold needles of the rain. And though he moved against the press of the crowd, he never once stepped aside, but passed through the groups of burly workmen, the thin-faced office boys, the breathless, scampering girls, without seeming to touch any of them.

He moved purposefully, past the neon-lit self-service laundry and the shuttered fish-shop, past the busy green-grocer's spilling its wooden boxes and pyramids of bright fruit across the pavement outside, until he reached a row of terraced houses which stood back from the road behind wilderness gardens. Here he paused uncertainly and stared at the first house which lay in a pool of shadow behind a stunted tree. A small light shone from the basement window, making a halo of brightness on the rain outside. The old man turned and, making his way along the path and down the steps, he tapped hesitantly upon the basement door.

The woman who opened it was still young and would have been pretty if she had not looked so tired.

'Mrs ... er ... Mrs Allen,' inquired the old man. He sounded strangely nervous.

The woman nodded cautiously and at once he launched into a little speech like a doorstep salesman uncertain of his reception. 'I represent a firm of solicitors, madam, the firm of Blunden, Blunden, Claverton and ...'

'I suppose it's about the rent?'

The woman's interruption seemed to throw the old man completely. He stopped his speech abruptly and looked deeply hurt at being suspected of so unwelcome a mission. He shook his head several times reproachfully and seemed to have difficulty in finding the broken thread of his thoughts.

'Indeed no!' he said at last. 'I am not a debt-collector. I am a senior partner in the firm of Blunden, Blunden, Claverton and ... dear me ... now what is that young fellow's name ... ?' He paused absent-mindedly and gazed up thoughtfully into the falling rain. 'Well, no matter' – he recollected himself – 'the important thing is that the news I bring will, I am sure, prove entirely welcome.'

The woman looked doubtful, as if she no longer believed in good news. Then she shivered: it was cold standing in the doorway. 'You'd better come in,' she said, 'out of the rain.'

The room was small and crowded and untidy. There was a pool of light over a table to one side where a boy and a girl sat eating their tea. The boy started to his feet as they came in but the old man stopped him. 'No, no!' he said with grave courtesy, 'pray continue. It is I who must apologize for disturbing your meal.'

'Do sit down,' said the woman, moving some knitting

from a chair by the fire, 'and perhaps you would like a cup of tea?'

'The chair I accept gratefully,' said the old man, 'but the tea I must decline. It is many years since I have been ... er ... allowed to drink it. But if you will pour some for yourself and sit with me for a moment, I will come straight to the purpose of my visit.'

The woman did as she was told. Clutching her cup in nervous hands, she perched herself on the edge of a chair and waited as if for another blow to fall.

The children ate steadily, watching their mother and their unexpected visitor with unmoving eyes. The boy thought: He's a weird old thing. His clothes are so old-fashioned and he talks like someone out of *David Copperfield*. The girl noticed that his clothes were not steaming in the heat of the fire. They seemed to be quite dry although he had not carried an umbrella. But it was only a small fire, she told herself, and as he was outside the circle of the overhead light, it was hard to be certain whether he was wet or not.

'I will not ... er ... stand upon ceremony,' the old man began. 'I shall come ... er ... straight to the point ...' But he seemed curiously reluctant to do so.

The boy wondered if he was an encyclopedia

salesman. If he is, he thought, he's wasting his time on us. We couldn't afford a Penguin between us.

But when the old man finally overcame his embarrassment enough to finish his sentence, it turned out that he was offering not twenty-eight matched volumes, but a job or rather, as he put it, 'a responsible position'.

Mrs Allen was so surprised that she could not answer at first, and misunderstanding her silence the old man said anxiously, 'I trust I have not offended you by making such a suggestion. I realize that a lady like yourself ...' He paused miserably and then added by way of apology, 'I had reason to believe that the ... er ... money might be useful to you.'

The woman took pity on him: she gave him a sad smile, half of gratitude and half of disappointment. 'Why should I be offended?' she asked. 'It is true that the money would be very useful and I have often thought of taking a job, but I have the baby to consider. He's not a year old yet and he has never been very strong. I couldn't leave him with strangers while I went out to work.'

'No, no, of course not!' said the old man soothingly. 'That is why the position I mention would be most suitable for you. Perhaps you would allow me to explain a little further?'

Mrs Allen nodded and he went on, 'My firm is seeking a reliable person to act as ... er ... as caretaker to a property which is in our charge. The last owner, a Mr Latimer, died some time ago without direct heirs and we are endeavouring to trace more distant relatives. So far, alas, we have met with little success and indeed it seems at times that there are none surviving. In the meantime, the house must be cared for, and for ... er ... various reasons we have had difficulty in finding anyone willing to take the post. It is the ... um ... the remoteness, you understand. It is a very fine house and pleasantly situated but it stands alone some way from the nearest village. There is a rent-free, caretaker's cottage attached to the house and your duties would be very light, nothing more than a regular inspection of the house to see that all is in order. A woman comes up from the village to do what cleaning is necessary and the local builder is at hand for any repairs that may be required, but we are anxious that there should be someone living on the premises at all times.'

The old man paused. The woman said nothing. She seemed almost unable to grasp what he was saying, unable to believe in an offer that so completely answered all her needs.

'The country air would be most beneficial to the children,' he continued, 'and the remoteness may, perhaps, encourage you to concentrate on your music.' He hesitated a moment and then added enticingly, 'There is a very fine piano in the music-room.'

The girl stopped eating and stared at the old man. How had he known that their mother had once . . . ?

Mrs Allen said abruptly, 'I don't play any more. I haven't played for a long time, not since . . . ' Her voice trailed away.

'Not since your husband's death,' prompted the old man gently and she nodded without speaking. 'It was a tragic accident . . . A tragic accident,' he repeated, 'and our loss as well as your own. It is rare to find a young man with such great talent.'

The widow's pride overcame her sadness. 'They had only just begun to realize how good he was,' she said. 'We were so thrilled when he was invited to conduct some of his own music in New York.'

'Ah, yes, indeed,' said the old man. 'It must have given him a particular satisfaction to know that his work was appreciated in his own country.'

'Yes, it did, especially since he had been away for so long. We met in Paris, you know, when we were both students' – she smiled as she remembered – 'and after we were married and the children were born, we decided to settle in London. Dick had no close relatives in the States and he was happy here. He used to say that he was a throw-back because he felt so much at home in England.'

Listening to the conversation, the boy had grown uneasy. He wondered how the old man came to know so much about them. He had obviously been snooping around asking questions, but why? and why had he chosen them? Perhaps he was looking for a family with no relatives to miss them. He would lure them all to this dark old house, and they would never be heard of again. He remembered a book he had once read about a mad old professor ...

The girl was watching her mother and she marvelled to see her talking so freely of the husband who was dead. She never talks to anyone about him, she thought, not even to us. The past is like a room with a locked door that we must never open. And yet she was talking away to the old man, almost as if she were talking to herself, almost as if he was not really there.

'He wanted to take us all with him, but of course we couldn't afford it and I was expecting the baby, so he went alone.' She was silent for a moment, then she began again in a rush of words. 'When the cable came we were all so excited. We thought it must be good news, you see, and then, when we saw ... a car-crash ...' She seemed to be on the point of tears and the girl rose quietly and went to put her arm round her mother's shoulders. The movement startled her, as if she had forgotten the children; she even glanced at the old man with some surprise as though she had indeed been talking to herself. 'Well,' she said awkwardly, 'I haven't felt like playing since then.'

The old man sighed. 'You have my deepest sympathy,' he said, 'but you must try to believe me when I say that time will heal your grief.'

The woman made no answer but almost unconsciously shook her head.

'You don't believe me now, but you will find that it is true. I am an old man ... a very old man ... and I have learned wisdom the hard way. It is not grief that scars, but guilt; not the blows we suffer, but the injuries we do to others ...' His words faded and there was a long silence. Then he seemed to recollect his mission. He leaned forward into the light of the fire. 'Come now,' he said earnestly, 'grasp this opportunity if only for the children's sakes, to take them away from this place.'

The woman reddened slightly, feeling the criticism that his words implied. She glanced around the room with its gloomy paintwork and damp-stained walls. 'It is awful, isn't it,' she said, 'but it was the best I could find. Housing is such a problem when you have children. There were so many debts and so little money. Dick wasn't one to plan ahead. He used to joke and say that musicians and artists are the lilies of the field and that God provides for them.'

'Perhaps he does,' said the old man, 'perhaps he does ...'

Suddenly the woman smiled and the boy, watching her from the table corner, saw again for a moment why he had always thought her beautiful. She glanced up at the old man and asked, 'Did he send you directly?'

But he seemed strangely flustered by the suggestion. 'No, no!' he said, 'I am only an old man anxious to help.' He seemed to withdraw into himself. 'But he moves in so mysterious a way,' he muttered, 'it is possible that even I, unworthy as I am, may serve some purpose.' A look of deep gloom spread over his face.

'I'm sorry,' said the woman gently. 'I didn't mean to distress you. But if you mean your offer of a house and a job, then to us you are a Godsend.'

Before the old man could answer, the sound of a baby's piercing cry came from the back room.

Mrs Allen rose to her feet anxiously. 'Oh, dear,' she said, 'he's had such a cold and I think he suffers from earache. Please excuse me while I do something for him,' and she hurried from the room.

Left behind, the children and their visitor sat in an uncomfortable silence.

After a while, the old man cleared his throat as if he were about to speak. Then he glanced anxiously at the children and cleared his throat again. But he said nothing.

The girl, feeling it her duty to put him at his ease, gathered up her courage and asked, 'Are you sure you wouldn't like a cup of tea?'

'Thank you ... um ... er ... Lucy, my dear. It doesn't agree with me, I fear. But I wonder,' he paused and seemed to search for the right words, 'now that we are alone I wonder if I might ask you both a question. I hesitate because it is rather an unusual question and hope that you will consider it seriously.'

'Of course,' said the boy cheerfully, 'you fire away,' but he thought: if he asks whether we have any surviving relatives, I shall know just what he's up to.

But the question took even him by surprise. 'Do you think you would be afraid,' asked the old man cautiously, 'if you saw ... um ... er, that is to say, if you saw ... a ghost?'

Lucy stopped trying to work out how he had known her name and shivered. But she considered the question seriously as he had asked. She decided that she would be absolutely terrified but she wasn't going to admit that in front of her brother so she said, 'I think I should be just a little bit scared.'

The boy thought her answer very dull. 'I think it would really depend on what kind of ghost it was,' he said. 'I mean if it was just wandering around in a white sheet moaning a bit, well, it would be all right wouldn't it? But I once read a story about a man who was going along a dark lane one night when he saw a figure in a long dark cloak and hood.' He warmed to his subject, never noticing the growing gloom on the old man's face. 'Well, just when he was passing it the ghost, because it was a ghost, of course, turned round and threw back the cloak and it had no head, just a sort of grinning emptiness and below it a grisly skeleton. He screamed and ran away but it came after him and he felt its bony hand on his shoulder and ... '

'I think that's a lot of nonsense!' interrupted Lucy. She could see that the old man didn't like the story and she wasn't keen herself. She knew that she would remember it if she woke up in the night. 'After all,' she said scornfully, 'how could it grin if it had no head?'

The boy looked annoyed and the old man intervened.

'It was not that sort of ghost that I had in mind, James, and indeed I do not believe that there are such visions. These ghosts would appear to you ... well, very much like ordinary people: children of about your own age, perhaps, or even' – he laughed creakily – 'an old man such as myself.'

'Oh, we wouldn't be frightened of a ghost like that.' Jamie was confident to the point of scorn. 'I mean you wouldn't know they were ghosts, would you? unless, of course, you could see through them and even that wouldn't be very scary if their heads were in the right place.'

Lucy said nothing. She was looking at the old man closely: his narrow trousers would not have looked out of place on a teenager but they seemed odd for a man of his age. And there was something about his collar and the high folded cravat ... He was gazing absently into the fire.

'Sometimes,' he began, 'ghosts are people who come

back seeking help. They are people who, during their lives, were not strong enough ... or wise enough ... or good enough to meet some challenge. They come seeking help because they cannot rest for the knowledge that they did harm and the longing to put it right ... ' His words were so soft they might have passed for an uneasy sighing but Lucy heard them. She dimly understood that he was talking about himself, but because he sounded so very sad, she was not afraid.

'We would help you if we could,' she said timidly.

The old man raised his head and she found herself gazing into dark, strangely transparent eyes. She shivered involuntarily and then smiled to make up for it.

The old man nodded. 'I think you understand,' he said. 'Children do sometimes, but as they grow older they become less sensitive. They lose the power to believe ... to believe ... in the unlikely.' He seemed to be murmuring to himself. 'Once the meaning of words ... have set rigidly in the mind, the incredible becomes the unbelievable ... the possible and the impossible are irremediably sundered by a brief prefix ... '

The children listened in silence, having only the vaguest idea of what he was talking about, but pleased to find that he seemed to approve of them.

The old man made a sudden effort and gathered his thoughts. 'When you come to the house,' he told them, 'you will hear strange tales. They will tell you in the village that it is haunted, but you must not be afraid. When the time comes ... you will know what to do.'

'We shan't be afraid,' said Jamie firmly, and Lucy added, 'We will do what we can.'

'Thank you,' said the old man solemnly and he rose to his feet. 'I must not stay,' he said. 'I fear I have already been too long.'

'Shall I fetch Mummy?' asked Lucy politely.

'No time,' said the old man nervously, 'no time! But if you will ask her to call at my chambers tomorrow ...' He moved in haste towards the door as though he might miss a train if he delayed.

'Where is it?' asked Jamie.

'Sensible child ...' The old man paused as Lucy opened the door. Fumbling in his pocket he produced a thin, yellowing card.

Jamie took it and read it and asked, 'Will you be there?'

The old man shook his head. 'I am ... er, that is I was ...' He seemed at a loss for words and Jamie suggested, 'Retired?'

'Retired!' The old man gave a sad, hollow laugh. 'Ah,

if it were only so, an honourable retirement ... But alas, the truth must be told: I am, or rather I was ... struck off!' He spoke the words in a whisper as if it was the most terrible thing in the world, but Jamie was quite relieved.

'Is that all?' he said. 'I thought for a moment that you were going to say that you were dead!'

'Dead!' exclaimed the old man mournfully. 'Why, death is nothing. To be dead is a mere detail, but to be struck off is the most shameful thing of all.' He stood in the doorway, shaking his head sadly, and all the time he seemed to grow more frail and insubstantial. 'Tomorrow,' he said and his voice was faint. 'Tell them ... I sent you ... Claverton will be there ... or young ... what's ... his ... name ...'

Then he moved out into the shadowy garden and the wind and rain seemed to blow him away.

Chapter 2

Lucy poked her finger into the baby's padded woollen tummy and watched him crow with delight. He thrust up his little thin arms at her and bubbled affection. She laughed and poked him again.

'You two sound very happy.'

At the sound of her mother's voice Lucy withdrew her finger hastily. I don't know why I should feel guilty, she thought; but she did, perhaps because her mother could not hide the undertone of reproach in her voice. It isn't that she doesn't want us to be happy, thought Lucy; she just can't understand how we can be, now that he is dead. It's not so bad for us because we are old enough to understand, but it's not fair to the baby. She loves him but she can't play with him or laugh at him and, after all, it's not his fault. She turned to look at her mother and seeing her lined face, went to put her arms around her.

'He's only a baby,' she said defensively, 'and I do love to hear him laugh.'

Her mother hugged her and looked down at her wriggling son. 'My poor darlings,' she said.

Lucy changed the subject. 'What did Mrs Ryan say?'

'Oh, she'll be glad to keep an eye on him but I still wish I didn't have to leave him. She's always so busy with all those children and she is a bit slap-dash. But it's too cold to take him out, so there's nothing else for it. I only hope he doesn't get one of those coughing fits; they wouldn't even hear him with all that noise going on.'

Lucy thought the baby would love the cheerful rough-and-tumble of the Ryan household but she could see that her mother would worry so she said, 'Why don't you let me stay with him?'

'Well, I don't know . . . ' Mrs Allen hesitated. 'A house in the country, it's such a chance for us, but I'm sure they'll turn me down when they find there are three children.'

'The old man seemed certain that you would get it.'

'I know, Lucy, but you tell me he won't even be there.

Suppose they didn't know when they sent him that there were three children?'

'He seemed to know an awful lot about us,' Lucy pointed out.

Mrs Allen frowned and considered. 'No,' she said, 'I think you and Jamie had better come with me. People never believe you when you say that your children are quiet and well-behaved, but perhaps if they see you . . . '

The door opened again and Jamie came in, loaded with shopping.

'Phew!' he said. 'This lot weighs a ton but it's mostly potatoes. I got everything on the list and there's one-and-threepence change. I've almost given up Carter's Stores, you know; there's always a penny more on everything.'

Shopping was Jamie's personal chore and he regarded it as a price war between himself and the local shopkeepers. He brought back the food like the spoils of battle and his change like a trophy.

'You'd better put a clean shirt on,' said his mother as she stacked the groceries in the corner cupboard. 'And we mustn't be long; I couldn't bear it if someone else got there first. You have got the card with the address on it, haven't you?'

Jamie fished in his pocket and brought out the small square of yellowed pasteboard. 'Blunden, Blunden and Claverton, 7 Old Square Chambers, Lincoln's Inn,' he read from the fine copperplate. He frowned, 'Now I wonder what could have happened to young whatsit?'

The sign on the polished brass plate said: Blunden, Claverton and Smith.

'I suppose it is the same firm?' said Mrs Allen doubtfully, already suspecting that the whole thing had been a dream.

'Of course it is,' said Lucy reassuringly. 'Smith is the one the old man couldn't remember.'

'Ah!' said Jamie solemnly, 'and what became of the second Mr Blunden, that's what I want to know?'

'It might have been the first Mr Blunden,' Lucy pointed out.

'Oh no, I'm sure our old man was the first Mr Blunden, and he seemed all right.'

'Yes, but he did say he had been ... '

'James, Lucy, please! I've brought you along to show them how sensible you are. Don't start one of your foolish arguments.'

The children's faces fell. They could tell from the

sharp edge on her voice how much the interview meant to their mother. Jamie took her hand and squeezed it.

'Sorry,' he said. 'We'll be absolute angels.'

She gave him a nervous smile. 'I know, Jamie, but we mustn't hope for too much.'

They made their way up a dark staircase until they found the names again on a glass door. After a moment's hesitation, Mrs Allen drew a deep breath and they went in.

The room was larger and grander than they had expected from the outside, with sombre panelling on the walls. A young clerk rose from a desk at one side and came smoothly to meet them.

Mrs Allen went momentarily to pieces. 'I've come about the job,' she began, 'a caretaker, Mr Blunden told us . . .'

The young man raised one eyebrow in a rather superior way and said, 'You have come about a job?'

Mrs Allen pulled herself together. 'I understand,' she said coolly, 'that you are looking for a caretaker for a rather remote country house.'

The young man looked surprised. 'The job has not yet been advertised,' he said disapprovingly, 'how did you come to . . .'

'Mr Blunden himself informed me of the vacancy and advised me to call on you. He gave me his card.'

Her mother's manner was, thought Lucy, a shade uppity, but it seemed to impress the young man. Or perhaps it was the sight of old Mr Blunden's card; he was staring hard enough at it.

Jamie wondered whether the young man was Smith and if he was upset at finding his name omitted.

The young man looked up from the card. 'I see,' he said, in the puzzled tones of one who obviously did not see. 'You must forgive me if I was a trifle abrupt. Mr Blunden has not been at the office recently and I did not realize that he had taken a hand in this matter. If you will let me have your name, I will inform Mr Claverton that you are here.'

'Well done, Mrs Allen!' hissed Jamie while they waited for his return, and was pleased to see his mother smile. Funny, he thought, when people are kind and sympathetic, she gets sadder and sadder, but as soon as someone treats her unkindly she comes back fighting.

Mr Claverton came out of his office to greet them. He was a round, smiling, rather pompous little man.

'Ah, Mrs Allen, this is a pleasure. And these are ... er, your two children?' He sounded as though he had not expected children and their hearts sank.

'This is Lucy and this is James, and I have another child, a baby, at home,' said Mrs Allen firmly. I might as well tell him the worst and have done with it, she thought.

'Indeed. Well, they do you credit, I'm sure. Now perhaps you will come through to my private office and we will talk about the house.'

When they were all seated, he began, 'I must confess that although Mr Blunden has been in contact with you about this matter, he unfortunately omitted to mention the fact to me.'

The children grew sick with disappointment, but he went on, 'He is an old man and in poor health; he is virtually retired. No doubt he got in touch with you feeling that you might accept the post and then . . . another bout of illness perhaps, and the matter slipped his mind. So you will bear with me, I hope, if I ask you a few questions and explain again some of the details of the position.'

They listened patiently while he told them again about the house and the caretaker's duties. Then he frowned and continued somewhat hesitantly, 'You understand, of course, that it is a rather remote house and . . . er, for that reason we have had difficulty in finding a caretaker. The last couple we employed stayed only a week . . .'

He glanced at the children. 'They found the isolation too . . . ' He eyed the children again. Then lowering his voice a tone he said confidentially, 'Mrs Allen, I wonder if I might speak with you alone?'

In the outer office Jamie and Lucy sat side by side on straight-backed, slippery leather chairs. Jamie began to kick his heels on the rail but remembered just in time and sighed. Lucy stared at the panelled walls and then turning her head sideways considered the dim portrait above the mantelpiece.

'It's Mr Blunden,' she said.

Jamie frowned at it. 'So it is,' he said, 'only he looks a bit younger.'

The clerk coughed and looked up with a supercilious smile.

'You are looking at Mr Blunden's portrait?' he asked, with a hint of suppressed amusement in his voice.

'Yes,' said Jamie. 'He does wear rather odd clothes, doesn't he?'

The young man fairly sniggered with pleasure.

'I'm afraid we've caught you out,' he said. 'The portrait is in fact of Mr Blunden's great-grandfather who died nearly a hundred years ago.'

Jamie and Lucy stared at the painting.

'Oh, but I'm sure that's the man we saw,' insisted James. 'I'd know him anywhere.'

The clerk smiled indulgently. 'An understandable mistake. There is a very strong family resemblance. The Blunden nose in particular has been handed down from generation to generation.'

Lucy stifled a desire to laugh.

'Yes, indeed,' continued the clerk, 'if it were not for the clothes, even I could believe that it was the present Mr Blunden.'

Jamie considered the clothes: the tight trousers, the waistcoat with lapels, the high old-fashioned collar ... He began to say, 'But that's just what he was wearing when ... ' but Lucy interrupted hastily.

'Is that the Mr Blunden who was "struck off"?' she asked, just to change the subject.

The effect on the young man was alarming. He turned very pale and glanced around nervously as if afraid that she might have been overheard.

'S-s-struck off!' he stammered. 'What an extraordinary notion. This is a most respectable firm, young lady, and none of its partners has ever been ... ' He seemed unable to repeat the terrible words and contented himself with repeating, 'a *most* respectable firm!'

'What does it mean anyway?' asked Jamie, who could not see what all the fuss was about.

'It means,' said the young man solemnly, 'that a lawyer's name is removed from the Roll of Solicitors, that he ceases to be a lawyer because of some offence he has committed. It is not the kind of thing that would happen in a firm like Blunden, Claverton and Smith!'

A likely story, thought Jamie. It's obviously the skeleton in their cupboard and they're afraid it'll get out. Bad for business, I suppose. But to spare the young man any further embarrassment, he only said, 'Are you Mr Smith?'

The clerk sighed. 'Oh, no,' he said, 'Mr Smith is the junior partner. I am Mr Clutterbuck.'

'You should be glad,' said Jamie comfortingly, and seeing the young man's surprise, he added, 'I mean to say, no one could forget a name like that.'

Fortunately the door of Mr Claverton's office opened at that moment and the solicitor came out smiling at Mrs Allen.

'Well, dear lady, I must say I am delighted to have a responsible person like yourself to take charge of the house. I shall write to confirm our arrangements and I will contact the estate agent to meet you on your arrival. He will give you the keys and show you everything.'

Mrs Allen thanked him and they prepared to leave. As he saw them to the door the lawyer said, 'And I feel certain that you will have no trouble from the little matter we spoke of . . . Mere country superstition, nothing more . . .'

Jamie pricked up his ears.

'Well,' said Mrs Allen, as they breathed deeply the cold winter air of the street outside, 'I think this calls for a celebration. What shall it be?'

Lucy hesitated, knowing what their father would have offered but unwilling to speak the traditional words.

But Jamie pitched straight in. 'Squashy cream cakes at Fortnum's!'

Lucy saw her mother catch her breath and thought, Don't let it all be spoilt.

Mrs Allen sighed. 'We haven't had them for a long time, have we?' she said wistfully. Then she smiled. 'Oh, well, come on. I've got so skinny lately I shan't even have to diet afterwards.'

'Good old Mr Blunden!' said Jamie as they set off along the street.

'Yes,' said his mother. 'I can't think why he should be so kind to us. An old sick man coming so far to visit us through all that rain.'

Lucy was about to say that she didn't think the weather made much difference to him now, but she thought better of it.

Jamie reached for another cream bun and asked, 'What was all that about country superstition?'

Mrs Allen, who was just raising her cup to her mouth, replaced it on the saucer with a clatter and said, 'Oh, nothing much.'

There was an uncomfortable silence and the children waited, knowing that she could never keep a secret.

'It was really nothing,' she repeated with even less conviction, 'just local gossip.'

The children waited.

'Oh, well, I suppose I ought to tell you,' she said at last; 'you're bound to hear about it in the village. But it was too good a chance to miss and I didn't want you to be frightened. It's just a lot of nonsense about the house being haunted.' She paused anxiously to see their reaction.

'Oh, is that all?' said Jamie, never pausing in the demolition of his bun.

'You don't mind? You don't think you'll be afraid? It's still not too late to change our minds, although it would be a shame. Lucy, dear, what do you think?'

'It's all right,' said Lucy calmly. 'Old Mr Blunden told us about the ghosts. He said they were nothing to be afraid of.' And to herself she added firmly, When the time comes, we shall know what to do.

She was glad that her mother turned away too soon to see her shiver.

PART TWO

PART TWO

Chapter 3

Lucy sat on the wide stone window-seat in the big drawing-room of the old house. Behind her in the wet April garden the sun was coming out and she felt its warmth touch the back of her neck through the small thick panes of the window.

For three weeks now they had lived in the little cottage that joined the back of the house, and in that space of time the peace and warmth of the old house had begun to heal them all. The baby's stick-like arms were growing fatter and his pale cheeks had coloured. She and Jamie had begun to lose the sense of some great disaster lurking round the corner, which had haunted them ever since their father's death with its awful legacy of debts and hardship. And their mother had taken the dust-sheets off the grand piano and polished it lovingly, though she had not yet found the courage to touch the silent keys.

Lucy smiled to herself remembering how frightened she had been when they first arrived. The strange way in which they had been brought to the house and the talk of restless ghosts, had preyed upon her mind all through the long journey and she had pictured with growing fear the dark-towered, owl-haunted pile that awaited them. And then to come at last upon this long, low house with the warm grey-brown of its stone walls and its roof patched with lichens in green and gold.

It stood against the sheltering flank of a small hill like a natural outcrop of rock, as if it had grown with the landscape. Beyond its neglected lawns and the weed-filled lake, the woods crowded in, a circle of springing green that seemed not so much to isolate the house as to enclose it in an enchanted circle. They had arrived towards sunset when the lengthening rays of the sun touched all the budding trees and the wide lawns and the warm stone walls with yellow and gold. It seemed the least likely house in all the world to be haunted.

And yet, she thought, there was something strange about it; something that drew her day after day to wander through its rooms. The furniture stood in place under its dust-sheets; the cupboards and drawers were full of old clothes; and little things, workbaskets and books, lay as if waiting patiently to be taken up and for life to begin again.

It was such an old house. It seemed to her sometimes that all the past was gathered up inside it as if in a great box; as though it had a life of its own that continued to exist just beyond the reach of her eyes and ears. And in that way, she thought, it was haunted, although its ghosts were unseen.

She had given up looking for visible ghosts. Once she had asked Mrs Tucker, who came up twice a week to dust and clean, what the stories were that were told in the village. But that stout lady had denied all knowledge of ghosts. 'Just a lot of rumours, dearie,' she had said firmly, 'the sort of tales they tell about any big house that lies empty for a while. Nothing to be afraid of. After all,' she added rather cryptically, 'they're only kiddies.'

Lucy had repeated this to Jamie.

'Who are?' he demanded.

'Who are what?'

'Only kiddies?'

Lucy considered. 'I suppose she means that it is only the village children who say the house is haunted.'

'Then it probably is,' said Jamie. 'Children know a lot more than adults about such things.'

But he was only trying to be clever, thought Lucy. As the uneventful weeks had passed, they had both stopped believing in the ghosts, but whereas Jamie was genuinely disappointed, Lucy was secretly relieved.

She had stopped glancing anxiously over her shoulder expecting to see a pale lady in an old-fashioned dress; she no longer started at the sight of a grandfather clock draped in its dust-sheet. She sometimes wondered if they had imagined old Mr Blunden's mysterious hints, or if the old man who was by all accounts ill, had been wandering in his mind.

And yet ... if the ghosts were not to be seen, she felt sometimes that she could almost hear them. Even now, as she sat in the April sunlight, her ears seemed to catch the faintest sighing of long-ago voices, a dim murmuring as though generations of people were all talking at once but very softly. As she sat listening, her mind drifted and the voices seemed to grow louder, with here and there a word that was clear ... or very nearly so. And then it seemed that the sounds reached her ears from inside, like a roaring in her head that frightened her so that she rose up from the window seat and hurried away, clattering along the stone passage and up the wide staircase until the noise of her feet drove the voices away.

She moved along the first-floor landing and opened the third door on the left. This was her favourite bedroom with a small four-poster bed hung with faded pink curtains. Lucy had always wanted a four-poster bed. She wished that she could sleep in it just once instead of in the little white bedstead in her room in the caretaker's cottage. She opened the dark wooden chest where blankets waited for the bed to be made up again. They still had the faint spicy smell of last year's lavender. I'll ask mother if I can, she thought, just once. But suppose she woke in the night and saw a lady in grey go gliding through the wall? Nonsense, she told herself, there are no such things ... But she closed the door gently as she went out.

She climbed the small twisting stairs where scores of housemaids had come and gone: yawning sleepily in the cold light of dawn as they went down to black the grates; yawning wearily by the light of their candlesticks as they went up again at the end of a long day. High under the roof were their little bedrooms with sloping ceilings, but these had not been used for a long time and they had a forlorn neglected air. Lucy longed to make curtains for the tiny windows, to paste back the wallpaper where it hung down from the walls. She hoped when they found the owners that they would have children to live and play in these little rooms at the top of the house. Whenever the murmuring voices filled her head, it was always the clear, high voices of children that she caught most distinctly.

She pressed her nose to the glass of a window at the back of the house, and beyond the old lead gutter, filled with green moss and the small bones of a long-dead bird, she could just see the courtyard in front of the caretaker's cottage. The red bricks had dried in the sun and Jamie was out there painting a kitchen chair bright blue. He had a lot of newspaper spread about and a large ancient pot of paint which he must have found somewhere. The baby's playpen had been put out in the sun and he bounced up and down calling to Jamie, who snatched his attention from the fascinating painting now and then to call back.

Their voices, echoing in the small room, seemed to Lucy to come from high up around her, sighing through the little attics under the sloping roofs. 'Lucy ... Lucy ... Lucy ...' It's the ghosts, she thought, they are calling to me; any moment now they will speak. She panicked as the voice grew louder. 'Lucy ... Lucy ...' Then it said, quite distinctly, 'Jamie, do you have any idea where Lucy has got to?'

The thudding of her heart died away as she saw her mother standing in the yard. She tapped on the window to draw her attention but it was too far away, so she turned and ran along the passage and down the back stairs, round and round the circling steps, down and down until she arrived, breathless and dizzy, on the ground floor. She plunged through the green-baize door that connected the old house with the cottage, and out panting into the yard.

'Lucy,' said her mother, 'where have you been?'

'I ... was in ... the attics ... I heard you ... calling.'

'Well, darling, it wasn't urgent. You'll break your neck one of these days, racing down those stairs.'

'I'm all right,' said Lucy, her breath back. 'What did you want?'

'I thought it would be nice to have some flowers for the house, to brighten up the place for Easter weekend. There are daffodils in the long grass by the lake, and over in the shrubbery I saw a rhododendron coming into bloom.'

'I'll pick some for you.'

'Would you, darling? There's an old trug in the back pantry and some kitchen scissors. Oh, and Lucy' – Lucy stopped impatiently in her tracks – 'put your wellingtons on; the long grass will be soaking wet after a week of rain.'

The wet daffodils shone in a golden heap in the grey trug as Lucy came up the path from the lake. The gravel that crunched beneath her feet was full of sprouting weeds and moss grew in the shady patches. The whole garden was badly neglected but it still had a wild beauty. Now that the summer is coming, thought Lucy, I'll get Jamie to help me tidy it up a bit.

She took a short cut through the overgrown ruins at the east end of the house and stopped to look up at the pointed window arches that stood out like bones against the sky. Like the bones of the bird in the gutter, she thought; all that is left of a long-dead building. She could see that it had once been a wing of the house, but the soaring arches seemed to be of some older style, perhaps some old abbey, destroyed by Henry the Eighth. Clumps of herbs had spread from the garden into the ruins: thyme and marjoram which gave off a sweet, wet scent underfoot. There were wallflowers too, high up on the stonework, and she added to her basket the few that were within reach.

Beyond the ruins, a gravel path wound its way into the shrubbery and she went on in search of the rhododendron. She smelt it before she saw it, a thick, honey scent filling the air, and then round a corner she found the big pale-pink blossoms against dark leaves.

She picked half-a-dozen and then stood idly, breathing in the rich perfume. The air was noisy with birds and she could see through a gap in the bushes the bright green of the lawns with the crowding trees beyond. The heat of the spring sunshine was drying up the heavy rainfall which rose in patches of mist above the grass.

Lucy began to feel strangely drowsy as though the scent of the rhododendron were a sweet, heavy drug. Her mind seemed to be growing still and empty almost as if it had stuck in a groove from which she was unable to move it. Her eyes seemed to focus somewhere short of the point she was looking at. She felt that she ought to make some movement, to break the growing sense of stillness that was creeping over her, but the effort was too great. A blackbird was calling, a single note repeated, a warning note; but she could not turn her head to look at him. It was as if she were concentrating all her mind upon one thing, but against her will and upon something that she did not understand.

Then she sensed that there was something moving through the mist on the lawn, just beyond the point at which her eyes were focused. She could not see very clearly, but it seemed to be two pale figures and they were moving towards her, slowly and with purpose.

Fear gripped her. She dropped the basket and her mind leaped from its groove. She looked wildly around her but there was nothing there. The columns of mist were dissolving above the lawn; the blackbird was singing, a full, bubbling song, as though he might burst at any moment.

Everything was perfectly normal and yet she was afraid. She felt convinced that she had narrowly escaped something. With swift, nervous movements, she gathered up the scattered flowers. Then she ran as fast as she could towards the house only to crash headlong into Jamie who was coming the other way.

'Now then,' said Jamie soothingly when he had regained his balance, 'what's the matter with you? You look as if you'd just seen a ghost.'

Lucy hesitated for a moment before she said, 'I thought I had, or rather, two ghosts.'

Jamie was delighted. 'Where?' he asked. 'What were they like? What were they doing?'

Lucy tried to explain but it sounded pretty feeble and Jamie was clearly disappointed.

'Is that all?' he said. 'Just the mist over the grass?'

'It wasn't only that ...' Lucy struggled for words. 'It wasn't so much what I saw as how I felt: as if something else had taken charge of me. Oh, I can't tell you what it was like but I was frightened. And somehow I was sure that they were ghosts.'

She shuddered and, watching her, Jamie was irritated. Why should something interesting like a ghost happen to Lucy, when she only got into a state and ran away? He had been looking for some sign of a white shadowy figure ever since they had come to the house and he hadn't seen a thing yet.

'Now look, Lucy,' he said firmly, 'if you did see some ghosts, it was a bit mean to run away. After all, we did tell the old man we wouldn't be afraid. He explained all about them needing help. Now let's go back and you can show me where it happened and I'll see if I can see anything.'

Lucy had already begun to feel foolish. So, after a moment's hesitation, she took Jamie back along the path until they stood beside the heavy, scented pink blossoms.

'It was just here,' she said. 'I thought I saw them over there on the lawn.'

But everything had changed. The sun was warm and bright and the mist had almost gone. Lucy stood by the bush and watched Jamie as he hunted around for any sign of footprints and grew increasingly scornful when he found none. As if ghosts would leave footprints anyway, she thought crossly.

And then it happened again.

A cloud passed in front of the sun and it was suddenly cold. Lucy became aware of the monotonous single note of the blackbird, the warning call, and again she sensed that her mind was slipping out of her grasp. She heard Jamie chattering as he hunted near by, but she could no longer make out what he was saying. She called his name suddenly, in fear, and reached out her hand to him.

Jamie jumped at her unexpected cry and turning saw his sister's pale frightened face and staring unfocused eyes. Suddenly the whole thing ceased to be a game and he ran to her and took hold of her hand. It was very cold and as he grasped it, he too seemed to be caught in the spell, like the people in the fairytale who touched the golden goose.

As they stood motionless, side by side, they became

aware of two figures which they sensed rather than saw, passing across the lawn just beyond the line of their vision. Lucy was afraid and clutched at her brother's hand. But Jamie, whose only fear was that she might break the spell, clasped her hand tighter to give her courage. Then they stood without moving until the figures passed into focus: a tall girl in an old-fashioned dress and a little boy, who came walking quite naturally along the path towards them.

Chapter 4

Jamie felt distinctly foolish when he saw the children at close quarters. Their clothes were a bit odd it was true: the girl's shabby brown dress was too long and she wore a rather dated straw hat; the boy had narrow white trousers and a blue jacket. But apart from that, he could hardly imagine any two children looking less like ghosts. They must live somewhere near by, he thought, and were dressed in this rather Victorian style by dotty parents. Even Lucy seemed to have lost all nervousness and her hand was quite warm again. He let go of it, feeling that their frozen attitude betrayed too much of their passing fear.

The tall girl looked straight at him with calm grey eyes. 'At last,' she said, 'we have found someone with a little good sense, who did not run away screaming at the sight of us.' She frowned briefly at Lucy.

Lucy lowered her eyes and said apologetically, 'I'm awfully sorry, but in the mist I thought for a moment that you were ... ghosts.' Then she added by way of justification, 'They do say this house is haunted, you know.'

The tall girl smiled as if at some private joke. 'Yes,' she said, 'we did know.' She looked thoughtful for a moment and then said, 'I suppose if I say we *are* ghosts, that you will run away again.'

Neither Jamie nor Lucy knew what to make of this. They were beginning to be aware that there was something not quite right about the newcomers, but they could not think what it was.

'I don't believe you are ghosts,' said Jamie boldly, 'but if you were, we should not be afraid. We know quite a lot about ghosts. They don't do you any harm, in fact they are often people in need of help.'

The little boy spoke for the first time. 'Who told you that?' he asked.

'An old man we know,' Jamie told him, 'a lawyer named Mr Blunden.'

The little boy kicked the gravel path. 'Blundering

Blunden,' he said contemptuously. 'He's a silly old fool!
If he had helped us when we asked him . . . '

'Oh, don't, Georgie! Please don't say it! It causes him
so much grief. You must remember that it's never too late
to right a wrong if you are truly sorry.'

The little boy snorted and kicked at the gravel again.

Lucy stared at his small foot as it sent the stones
flying and then at her own feet. She looked at the girl's
feet and then at Jamie's. And then she saw what was
wrong.

She said timidly, 'You are ghosts, aren't you?'

Jamie stared at her as if she had gone out of her mind.

The tall girl frowned and said, 'It all depends upon
your point of view. Seen from where you are, I suppose
we are in a way. But from where we are, we are not ghosts
at all.'

Jamie thought this sounded like a lot of rot; but he
could see that Lucy knew something.

'What makes you think they are ghosts?' he asked her.

She looked at him nervously and then at the boy and
girl. She stepped a little closer to Jamie and said, 'They
have no shadows.'

Jamie looked carefully. The sun was full out now and
Lucy's shadow and his own lay clear and black across

the pale gravel path. But the other two ... a shiver ran up his spine.

The tall girl was also surveying the ground with interest.

'You are quite right,' she said in a rather surprised voice. 'Look, Georgie, we have no shadows; we must have left them behind.'

Georgie looked. He capered about, glancing over his shoulder to see if his shadow was lying behind him. He jumped in the air to see whether it was under his feet. 'We haven't, have we Sara?' he said. He sounded rather pleased as if this put them in a superior position to ordinary people who must walk around with shadows shackled to their ankles.

'But if you are ghosts,' said Jamie, 'you must be dead, and you don't look very dead.'

'Of course we are not dead!' Georgie stopped his prancing and stared up at them. 'You do say some stupid things. We are no more dead than you are!'

Sara smiled. 'He's really too young to understand,' she apologized. 'Yet he is right in a way. No one is ever really dead, only dead to certain times and places. To you, the people who lived before you were born are now "dead", but you are also "dead" to the people born after you.'

'But they haven't been born *yet*,' Jamie protested, 'and we know we are still alive.'

Sara sighed. 'I fear it is very hard for you to understand,' she said, 'but Time is not as you think of it. You think it is a straight line along which you move, so that it is either ahead of you, when you call it the future, or behind you, when you call it the past. But really, it is more like a vast wheel turning and you two and Georgie and I are on different parts of the rim.'

Lucy nodded; she thought this sounded quite possible and she felt less afraid.

But to Jamie it sounded like typical girl's reasoning. He decided that there was only one way to find out whether they were ghosts or not, and that was to reach out and touch them. If his hand went right through them ... well, at least he would know where he was. When Georgie kicked his feet, the gravel flew, which seemed to suggest that he was pretty solid. And yet, a solid object standing in the way of the sun's rays ought surely to cast a shadow.

As he considered the vast implications of this offence against the laws of nature, Jamie began to be afraid. It was all very well for Lucy to accept a person without a shadow as though it were no more than an unexpected oddity of dress. Lucy lived in a world of books and fairy-tales and was conditioned to take such nonsense in her stride. But Jamie knew better and if the girl and boy had no shadows, then, however lifelike they might appear, there was something very wrong with them.

The story of the headless horror stole back into his mind and as he looked at the girl's hand, he seemed to see the bones inside the skin. If he reached out to touch it, he might find nothing there, which would be bad enough. But suppose his hand grasped a long-dead skeleton and the bones clung to him and the girl began to laugh, a high-pitched, blood-curdling laugh ... He shivered and raised his eyes to look at her face, half expecting a skull with glowing eyes in deep-set sockets. Instead he met only the calm, grey eyes which seemed strangely familiar, as though he saw himself in a glass.

Sara smiled. She had seen him shiver; seen his anxious eyes as he stared at her rather thin fingers, and she knew a little of what passed in his mind. She held out her hand to him, slowly and deliberately, like a challenge.

Jamie felt his face redden. His instinct was to grasp her hand, to prove that he was not afraid. And yet the very fact that she seemed to read his thoughts tended only to confirm his worst suspicions.

Lucy put her hand on his arm seeing what he meant to do. She was not afraid to stand and talk with these strangers, but it was another matter for Jamie to touch them. She had not forgotten the sense of helplessness, of being possessed in some way, that had filled her when they first appeared. The girl's face was undeniably pretty but a hundred fairytales had convinced Lucy that evil appears in fair disguises.

Sara and Jamie continued to stare at one another. She was no longer smiling, only waiting, willing him to accept her.

Jamie took a deep breath and summoning all his courage reached out his hand and grasped hers. It was warm and small and very normal.

A great wave of gratitude swept over Sara, and she clasped his hand in both of hers.

'You are the brave one,' she said. 'Your sister will understand what is beyond your reach, but you are the one with courage.' Her face seemed to grow very sad as she added, 'And it is your courage that we desperately need.'

In a strange way, once Jamie had taken Sara's hand, the children accepted each other as though their meeting had been perfectly normal. But there remained many questions buzzing in Jamie's mind.

'All this Wheel of Time business,' he said, a trifle crossly to hide his embarrassment, 'if you're on one bit of the edge and we're on a different bit, how can we possibly be standing here in the same garden at the same time?'

'It was the writing on the window,' said Georgie as though that explained everything. 'It was in the book,' he added, just to make it all crystal clear.

Sara smiled. 'It's really rather a long story,' she said, 'and someone may see us here. Could we not go to the round seat and sit down and I will tell you everything?'

'Where is "the round seat"?' asked Lucy, puzzled.

Sara looked about her as if to take her bearings. 'It used to be over here,' she said, and led them away through the dark rhododendrons which grew like trees above their heads. 'It has all become sadly overgrown,' she observed, 'I'm not certain ... ' But at that point she darted forward. 'Here it is,' she called, 'but, oh, the view is quite lost.'

The round seat was in fact only a semi-circle, a stone seat half-covered with moss in the gloomy shade. The ground about it was paved and a path had once led away from it through a gap in the bushes giving a view down the sloping hillside. Now the bushes had grown up obscuring the view but making a perfect corner for talking undisturbed.

'It all began,' Sara told them, 'one day when we were alone in the nursery. Georgie was breathing on the window panes and drawing pictures on the misted glass, when suddenly a word appeared already written. It said "Look", nothing more. We had almost forgotten about it when several days later it happened again, only this time we read "Look in the library". At least, that is what we thought it meant to say for the writing was very shaky and the last word ended in a smear as though all had been written with great difficulty. Naturally, we were very much intrigued and took to breathing upon the panes every day until little by little we made out a message that we were to look for a book hidden in the library.

'Unfortunately, this was not easy, for we are forbidden by Mrs Wickens to go into the library ... '

'Yes,' interrupted Georgie, 'and that awful Meakin is always spying on us and trying to get us into trouble.'

Lucy would have liked to ask who these people were, but Sara continued without regarding the interruption.

'However, we watched patiently for a chance and one

night, when they were all in bed, we went down to the library and hunted by candlelight until we found, on a high shelf and behind some other books, an old dusty volume. It was written by hand and was full of receipts, remedies and charms which seemed to have been copied from other books. Among them was one called "A Charm to Move the Wheel of Time".'

Jamie was fascinated. 'Did it work?' he asked eagerly. 'Oh, I suppose it must have done or you wouldn't be here. Can you teach us the words?'

Sara shook her head. 'It isn't as simple as that,' she told him. 'Be patient a little longer and I'll tell you everything. The book explained that Time is like a great wheel and that at the centre of every wheel, however fast it spins, there is always one point where it is still.' She paused for a moment and looked at them inquiringly to see if they would understand.

Jamie was quite good at mechanical problems.

'I suppose, if you accept this Wheel of Time business,' he said thoughtfully, 'then it would make sense. The two halves of a wheel are always going in opposite directions so where they meet in the centre there would have to be a bit that wasn't moving either way.'

'Then you will understand that to go from one part of

the Wheel to another, you must pass through the centre where Time is for ever still. To do this takes very great concentration. You must be able to separate your mind completely from the time you are in.'

'Well ... yes ... I see that,' said Jamie doubtfully, 'but I don't see how it can be done.'

Sara sighed. 'For some,' she said, 'it is simpler than for others. Little children find it quite easy to forget Time and to lose themselves in make-believe. But as we grow older, the real world takes a hold on us and we can never quite shake it off. But in the old book we found a receipt of herbs. It said that if they were brewed together and the liquid drunk, they would make the mind absolutely still. We hunted through the garden and found all the herbs and we brewed them together over the nursery fire.'

'But weren't you afraid to drink it?' asked Lucy. 'It might have been poisonous?'

'Oh, I thought of that,' said Georgie casually, 'so I put some in Mrs Wickens's gin to see if she would die or not.'

There was an awkward silence. Jamie and Lucy knew that their disapproval showed in their shocked faces, and Sara looked slightly embarrassed at her brother's bluntness.

'Suppose she had died?' said Lucy timidly.

'Jolly good thing if she did!' said the little boy cheerfully. 'She's absolutely beastly!'

'That's all very well,' said Jamie, 'but if she had died it would have been murder.'

'Oh, I don't think so,' said Sara quickly. 'You see, he didn't give it to her because he thought it was poison but only to make quite sure that it wasn't.'

Jamie couldn't help feeling that this argument was unsound.

'It was either Mrs Wickens or the cat,' said Sara defensively, 'and the cat had never done anyone any harm.'

Faced with this choice, Jamie and Lucy saw that any right-minded jury would acquit, and they felt relieved.

'Besides,' said Georgie gloomily, 'she didn't die at all. She just slept for a long time and woke up next day in a fearful temper saying that she had had terrible dreams. She gets like that from the gin most days,' he added.

'Yes,' agreed Sara, 'only this time she was twice as horrid as usual so we were the ones who suffered most.'

Lucy felt very sorry for them.

'The herbs didn't work then?' asked Jamie disappointedly. 'You must have been pretty fed up after going to all that trouble.'

'Oh, but it couldn't have worked for her,' explained

Sara patiently. 'Georgie only wanted to make sure that it was safe for us to take it. You see it said in the book that the charm will only work on two conditions; the first was "If the Need for Help is Great Enough" and the second "If the Will to Help is Strong Enough".'

'But it worked for you,' said Lucy, 'otherwise you wouldn't be here.'

The light faded from the other girl's eyes. 'Yes,' she said sadly, 'it worked for us.'

Lucy took hold of her hand as it lay on the cold stone bench.

'Tell us,' she said; 'tell us what is wrong.'

A cool breeze was moving among the dark bushes and the sun had moved so that its rays no longer reached through the tall branches.

Sara stared down at her small shoes.

'For us,' she said awkwardly, 'the need for help is very great indeed, for unless we can find someone to befriend us, Georgie and I may soon be dead.'

Chapter 5

It was not just the wind springing up and beginning to toss the high branches of the trees that made Jamie and Lucy shiver. It was the growing feeling that they were being drawn into events beyond their comprehension.

Ghosts who appeared from the past, provided that they came in such acceptable form, with no more frightening strangeness than a shadow more or less, had something of the fascination of men from Mars. Jamie had read stories of people who encountered beings from outer space and held conversations about life on other planets. But none of the unearthly visitors had ever talked about their personal problems.

Lucy had begun to feel that she was watching a play where the audience, in accordance with the rules of plays, could not intervene, but in which the characters were real.

She said anxiously, 'Surely you don't mean that someone is planning to harm you?'

'It's our uncle,' said Georgie angrily. 'He's plotting to get rid of us. But he won't get me! Why, I'd have finished him off long ago if Sara hadn't ...'

'Oh, Georgie,' said Sara patiently, 'you know there is nothing we can do. Besides, it isn't Uncle Bertie, he's not really bad ...'

Now there's a Wicked Uncle, thought Jamie; all the best stories have one. I've been eating rich food and reading too late at night: I shall wake up soon.

'Tell us from the beginning,' said Lucy, and Jamie half expected Sara to start 'Once upon a time'.

But she said, 'Our grandfather had two sons who were half-brothers. Our father was the elder but he and our mother died three years ago when their carriage overturned.'

A car-crash, thought Jamie, she means a Victorian car-crash; only they lost both parents. If Mother had gone with him to New York ... A wave of desolation swept over him and it no longer seemed like a dream or a story.

'After they died ...' Sara was trying to tell her story

matter-of-factly but the trembling of her voice gave her away. 'After they died,' she repeated more firmly, 'Uncle Albert became our guardian. We seldom saw him at first. He left us here with our governess because he found life in London much gayer. He was very young, you see, and was easily led once he fell into bad company.

'But his gay life lasted only as long as his share of our grandfather's money. It wasn't a great fortune for he was only a younger son. Most of the money had passed to Papa and then to Georgie, though it is held in trust until he is of age. After a while, Uncle Bertie began to fall into debt but he would not change his ways and his money melted until he had barely enough to live on.

'He started to come down and live with us for a few weeks at a time to save some money and escape his creditors. Then he would suddenly declare that he could not stand the dullness of the country a day longer, and he would hurry back to London.'

'And half the silver cutlery with him,' added Georgie.

'We cannot be certain,' said Sara. 'It could have been one of the servants. He is not bad, only foolish.' She seemed almost to plead for him, and Lucy saw that she had been very fond of her gay, young uncle.

'The trouble began on one of his trips to London. He

went to the music-hall one night and fell hopelessly in love with one of the ballet girls. Her name is Arabella and she is very pretty, but in her mind she is only a child. She cares for nothing but clothes and sweet things, although she is not really bad at heart.'

'Oh, really, Sara!' her brother wrinkled his nose in distaste. 'The way you tell it, absolutely everyone is good inside. Next you will find some hidden virtue in old Mrs Wickens.'

Sara's face clouded. 'Mrs Wickens is an evil old woman,' she said, 'and her husband is a brute. You see,' she explained, 'they are Arabella's parents and, with our uncle, they have all come to live at the house.

'The old lady used to run a gin-palace. She is coarse and mean and quite unscrupulous. Her husband was once a prize-fighter but the boxing damaged his brain, I fear, for he is little more than a mindless mountain, and does whatever his wife tells him.'

'When he is not too drunk to move,' put in Georgie crossly.

Lucy was appalled. 'But how can your uncle bear to have them in the house?' she exclaimed.

'Oh, he thinks of nothing but Bella,' Sara sighed. 'He wants to marry her, you see, but she is only seventeen and cannot marry without her parents' consent. Mrs Wickens is not going to waste her daughter on a penniless younger son and she pesters him all the time saying what a shame it is that the money must go to Georgie.

'One day we heard her remarking cheerfully upon how thin we were looking and it was true for she had taken over the housekeeping and we were getting very little to eat. But Georgie became very skilful at climbing through the pantry window ...'

'It's jolly difficult,' he interrupted, 'I doubt if anyone else could do it. I'll wager Tom could not!'

'I'm sure he couldn't,' said Sara soothingly; 'but you must let me finish my story, for time is short.'

Her brother tossed his head impatiently and she went on, 'Mrs Wickens found, much to her annoyance, that starving us was a slow business, so she took away most of our blankets and insisted that we sleep with all the windows wide open, even on the coldest nights. But Tom told us to put old newspapers between the blankets, which proved to be very warm. And somehow the fresh air, though it is said to be very unwholesome, seemed to keep us in excellent health while the others, who slept with roaring fires and the windows safely closed, fell victims to one ailment after another.'

Jamie and Lucy thought this hardly surprising but it did not seem the moment for a lecture on modern advances in hygiene.

'For a long time', continued Sara, 'we treated the whole affair as a battle of wits and did not truly think ourselves in danger. But then we overheard Mrs Wickens and her husband discussing the possibility of an accident befalling us. We were alarmed at this since an accident is hard to foresee and harder to guard against. We went to Uncle Bertie but he was sitting with Bella and he told us to be off and not to bother him. It was then that we decided to write to our other guardian for help.'

'Who is your other guardian?' asked Lucy, who had a strange feeling that she knew the answer.

'He is one of the family solicitors,' Sara told her, 'a man named Frederick Blunden.'

Lucy was about to point out that she and Jamie had met him, when she realized how foolish it would sound. Their Mr Blunden must surely be the grandson of Sara's guardian. And yet she wondered ... But she only said, 'Was he very shocked when he found out what was happening?'

Sara smiled sadly. 'Who can tell?' she said, 'for he never answered our letter.'

'Maybe it didn't reach him,' said Jamie. 'Did you post it yourself?'

'No,' she admitted, 'but Tom took it and he promised that it was safely dispatched.'

Before Lucy could ask who Tom was, Georgie burst in, 'Of course old Blunden got it, but he thinks only of his fees. He would not dare to challenge our uncle. Wait until I inherit,' he said darkly, 'I shall throw him out on his ear! I shan't forget the way he has treated us.'

The others were silent. They could see that his future vengeance counted for little unless he could survive the present danger.

'Couldn't you run away?' suggested Jamie at last.

'We did,' said Georgie gloomily, 'but they caught us in the village and we were taken back. Mrs Wickens shut us in the cellar for days and fed us on bread and water for a week.'

'But is there no one you can trust?' asked Lucy. 'You said you had a governess.'

'Oh, she went long ago, soon after the Wickenses arrived.' Sara sighed. 'She said she was a decent woman and would not stay in the house with them. I can't blame her, for they treated her with great disrespect. And when Mrs Wickens took over the housekeeping, the servants began to go. Some gave warning and left because they would not tolerate her rudeness; others, like cook and our old nanny, protested when she was harsh to us and were promptly dismissed. One by one, all the servants were replaced by others brought down from London, most of them creatures who would not get a post in any decent household.

'There is no one in the house we can trust and the estate is so vast that we rarely see anyone from outside. The only friend we have left is Tom, the gardener's boy, who lives in the lodge cottage a long way from the house. His father is a surly old man, but Tom would do anything he could to help us.'

'But what can he do?' said Georgie scornfully. 'Tom Fletcher is only a servant after all, and they are not very intelligent.'

Sara coloured angrily. 'Georgie! How can you be so mean! Tom is as clever as you or I.'

Georgie sulked. 'He can't even read,' he said stubbornly.

'Of course he cannot! He has never had the opportunity. But I am teaching him and he learns very quickly. If you had had to learn to read at the end of a long day's work in the garden, you would never have gone beyond "A"!'

'He is not cleverer than I am!' Georgie raised his voice and Lucy saw that he was jealous.

Sara seemed to see it too, for she smiled at him suddenly and said, 'George dear, of course he is not. But he is our friend, the only one we have, and I will not have you be unkind to him.'

For a moment the child continued to scowl as if bent on punishing his sister. But the desire to be friends with her was too strong so he stopped kicking the stone bench and grinned at her.

Lucy marvelled to herself that she could have mistaken him for a ghost. He was such an ordinary little boy with his moods and his tantrums. He might do for one of those spirits who throw china and play tricks, she thought, but they are always invisible and this child was very solid-looking.

'But surely,' Jamie was saying, 'surely there is something you can do?' but his voice lacked conviction.

'We have done the only thing we could,' said Sara. 'It was after we tried to run away that the writing began on the nursery window. It seemed to us that someone was trying to help us, so we sought out the book and made the potion. We resolved that if we could not run to another place for help, we would go to another time.'

At once Jamie understood everything, or thought he did.

'But of course!' he said eagerly. 'You can stay here, in our time, where they can never reach you.' He swung round to Lucy. 'They can live with us!' he exclaimed delightedly. 'I don't know quite how Mother will take it, she may find it hard to understand at first, but once she knows they are in danger . . . ' He turned back to Sara. 'I'm afraid we're pretty hard up,' he said apologetically, 'and with two more to feed you may find the meals a bit plain, but you can share Lucy's room and . . . ' His voice trailed away as he saw that she was trying not to cry. 'Oh Lord,' he said awkwardly, 'I didn't mean to upset you. Whatever did I say?'

'It is only because you are so kind.' Sara sniffed, and accepted Lucy's proffered handkerchief. 'I had forgotten that people could be kind. Oh, I wish we could just walk home with you as you say, and never, never see Mrs Wickens again. But it is not so simple. You see, after a time, we begin to feel thin and light-headed; then everything fades around us and we are back in our own time again.'

'And we always arrive back at exactly the same time as we left,' added Georgie, 'so that it is no use to take it to pass the time when we are shut in the cellar all day.'

'But if you can't stay in our time, what good was it to

come?' Jamie was at a loss, but Lucy was beginning to understand.

'You want us to help?' she asked Sara, knowing as she said it that they would be committed, that they were starting along a path from which there would be no turning back.

'It is our only hope.' Sara's voice was apologetic. 'We have tried several times before but either the gardens were deserted or, if we saw someone, they could not see us, or, if they could see us, they screamed and ran away.'

Lucy wished she had been braver.

'It was as though we were trapped,' the other girl continued, 'trapped behind a wall we could not see, through which we cried for help and were not heard. Until your brother came, and he was not afraid.'

'But what can we do?' asked Jamie, who could not bear to see anything in a cage.

'You want us to go back with you?' said Lucy. It was not really a question for she already knew and did not want to know.

Sara nodded.

'Go with you? You mean back to your time?' Jamie could hardly believe his good fortune. 'But is it possible? I mean, how can we?'

'I will help you to find the herbs,' said Sara. 'Most of them seem to be here still, growing wild about the garden. You can brew the potion as we did. After that, it depends upon whether "the Will to Help is Great Enough".'

'Well, it is,' said Jamie who found it a bit embarrassing when Sara was so solemn. 'You don't think we would stand around and let that awful old woman do you in. Why I'd ...'

'Sara! Sara!' Georgie's voice, high and anxious, cut across Jamie's words.

They all turned to look at him and saw that he had grown very pale, his skin almost transparent. 'I don't feel well,' he said miserably.

At once, Sara was on her knees beside him. 'Don't be afraid,' she said calmly. 'Remember that when you get back, I shall be there. You were very brave when it happened before. It is soon over and ...'

Even as she spoke, with her arm around him, he grew thin and faint and was suddenly gone.

Lucy felt sick. One minute he had been there, so real and solid, and the next ... only the empty air, the waving bushes behind him, the marks of his feet on the gravel path. All this would happen to her and to Jamie: and how could they be certain that they would ever return?

Even Jamie was startled.

Sara rose to her feet and dusted off her dress. 'It is because he is so young,' she said matter-of-factly. 'I am afraid to let him drink too much and so he returns before me. But since no time passes while we are away, we always arrive back together.'

Jamie swallowed hard. 'How can we be sure,' he asked, 'that, if we do drink the potion, we shall go back to your time? We might go forward as you do, or we might go back to a different time.'

'I must confess that I do not know for certain.' Sara frowned. 'It seems to me that if you are meant to help us ... and perhaps if we hold hands as we go ... But I cannot be sure. Perhaps you should not take the risk.'

'We'll chance it,' said Jamie firmly. 'I think you're probably right about holding hands.'

'I'll help you to find the herbs,' said Sara. 'Georgie is a warning to us that I may soon follow him, so I must search for them before I begin to grow weak.'

As she hurried away along the gravel path, her small feet in their white stockings seemed hardly to touch the ground.

'They will probably be near the old herb garden,' she called back over her shoulder. Her full skirts were flurried by the wind as she ran, and the ribbons on her flat straw hat streamed out behind her.

Jamie could not bear to see her go. He seized Lucy's hand and they hurried after her.

She paused by the old sundial and began to hunt about among the overgrown plants that surrounded it. They heard her say, 'Balm and hyssop, madwort and musk ... ' as she picked a sprig here, a few leaves there. She muttered to herself as she searched for others and found them with little cries of triumph. At one point she paused in her bird-like darting and, gazing at the bunch of herbs in her hand, said anxiously, 'Oh, I do hope I've got it right!'

Not half as much as I do, thought Lucy. I've got to drink the wretched brew. She particularly disliked the sound of 'madwort'.

'Toad flax ... and bergamot!' Sara made a last dive into a clump of russety-green leaves, and stood up looking very pleased with herself.

'Here,' she said, holding out her hand with a bunch of herbs. 'Put five leaves of each into a bowl, mind it is not metal, and pour on hot water but do not let it boil. Keep it warm for about an hour, and then strain off the liquid through a piece of woollen cloth.' She spoke quickly so that it was all they could do to follow, and even as they watched, she was growing pale.

'Bring the potion and meet me here at ten o'clock tomorrow morning.'

'All right,' said Jamie eagerly but Lucy, remembering just in time, said, 'It will be Good Friday: Mother will want us to go to church with her in the morning.'

'The evening then!' Sara's voice was anxious and her face had taken on that transparent lightness. 'Here ... by the sundial ... an hour before sunset ...'

She was growing wraithlike and then, at the last moment, she stretched out her hands in a pleading gesture and cried, 'Promise you will not fail us ...' Then she was gone.

Jamie stood staring at the place where she had been, and Lucy heard him say under his breath, 'I promise!'

Chapter 6

'We must not think of our Good Friday worship as a memorial service, but rather as the celebration of a great victory ...'

Lucy shifted uncomfortably in the straight-backed pew. The wooden seat had been polished to a high gloss by generations of fidgety worshippers, and as her feet did not quite reach the ground, she kept slipping forward. She wondered if it would help to edge the hassock towards her with her toe and use it as a footrest. But on reflection she decided that her shoes were too muddy from the walk across the fields and that it would be foolish to put mud on the dingy plush where she would shortly have to kneel.

She tried hard to concentrate upon what the vicar was saying, but to do this she needed to keep her eyes on his earnest face, and every time she slid slowly forward in her seat, he vanished out of sight behind a large pink hat with much veiling.

Lucy wondered about the potion. The brewing had been fairly simple. They had counted the right number of leaves into a small ovenglass jug, and Jamie had put on the kettle and added the hot water in the kitchen under cover of making everyone a nice cup of tea. But the brew, when it was finished, looked, in Jamie's phrase, 'a bit grotty', and Lucy didn't like the thought of drinking it.

'Let us resolve that in us this day shall die all the uncharitable thoughts, the corrosive indifference, the acts of selfishness, that come between us and the love of God ... '

Lucy heaved herself back in her seat and stared at the vicar. With his head emerging above the pink spotted tulle he seemed, ridiculously, to be wearing a lady's evening dress, and she stifled a desire to giggle. It was a kind face, though, she thought, and he looked as if he meant what he was saying. He was quite young and seemed the sort of person you could go to with your problems. Lucy felt tempted to ask him what they should do about Sara and Georgie. But she knew that once she had explained that it was all happening a hundred years ago, it would be hard to get anyone over the age of sixteen to consider the problem seriously.

There was something about the whole business that was worrying her, but she kept pulling her mind away when it tried to consider the matter. It was rather like having a bad tooth, she thought; your tongue keeps poking it to see if it hurts but not very hard for fear of starting a pain you can't stop. Gingerly, she let her mind drift into the problem: if something was happening a hundred years ago, then it had already happened, and however much you cared nothing could change it. So, if Sara and Georgie were going to die, then they were already ... The pain of thinking became too sharp and she swung her thoughts back to what the vicar was saying.

' ... and of the Holy Ghost, Amen.'

He had finished his sermon and was coming down from the pulpit.

Gratefully, Lucy sprang to her feet in the general surge of people and reached for her hymn-book.

> *Through the night of doubt and sorrow*
> *Onward goes the pilgrim band,'*

Jamie always enjoyed the hymns most of all. Lucy had accused him of being tone-deaf and out-of-tune, but he did not believe a word of it. To him it seemed that his voice rang clear as a bell, and he sang with great gusto. If the people in front turned round to stare at him, as they so often did, he assumed that they wanted to see who could be the owner of such a rich, tuneful voice, and he smiled so engagingly that even music-lovers had been known to smile back.

> *'Chasing far the gloom and terror,*
> *Brightening all the path we tread.'*

Today the hymns were particularly welcome. They took his mind off the nagging doubt which he dared not share with Lucy, but which had distracted him all through the service.

He knew he was not very bright in some ways. His

mind never made sudden, brilliant darts of understanding as Lucy's did. All that business about Time being circular, which Lucy found quite simple, seemed to him a picturesque piece of fantasy. As an explanation of how Sara and Georgie came to be walking around their garden a hundred years out of time, it sounded pretty thin. But he had held Sara's hand, so his common sense told him she was really there; and he had watched her vanish with his own eyes, so he believed that when he and Lucy drank it, they would end up in some other time, though he was not at all sure it would be Sara's.

The point at which his common sense baulked and refused to go along was at the suggestion that if he and Lucy did find themselves face to face with the formidable Mrs Wickens, they would be able to do anything to frustrate her schemes. After all, he thought, the past is the past and you can't get away from it. What's done is done. If only I knew what did happen.

He sighed and then, taking a deep breath, threw himself headlong into the last verse of the hymn.

> *'Soon shall come the great awakening,*
> *Soon the rending of the tomb . . . '*

He always liked the bit about the great awakening. He could see in his mind's eye the sleepers in the churchyard, sitting up and yawning and rubbing their eyes, with the green turf folded back like a blanket and the jars of daffodils overturned.

And then, as he listened admiringly to his own rich rendering of the familiar words, a light came on in Jamie's mind. 'The rending of the tomb'. Of course, it would all be there, written down for them to read, carved into solid stone. For once he would dazzle Lucy with his cleverness.

He raised his voice gratefully, and sang the 'Amen' louder than ever.

The vicar smiled politely at Mrs Monk-Burton with her heavily powdered face under her unsuitable pink net hat and tried not to think uncharitable thoughts. But it was not easy, for he knew her to be a selfish and vain old woman. He shook her hand and tried to look modest and grateful as she announced in her loud, patronizing voice, 'Such a splendid sermon, Vicar. Just what I am always saying myself, all that about sacrificing ourselves for others. Isn't that what I'm always saying, Horace?' and she poked her elbow into the thin nervous-looking man who stood beside her.

'Oh, always, dear, always,' he said eagerly. 'Yes, indeed, all the time.'

His wife frowned at him for a moment as though suspecting sarcasm, but seeing only anxious agreement, she turned back to the vicar.

'We must bear one another's burdens,' she said with a heavy sigh, 'how true, how true!'

The vicar smiled briefly and turned to greet his next parishioner.

But when he saw that it was the young widow who had taken the caretaker's cottage at the Old House, and that she had three children with her, including a rather fretful baby, he decided that Mrs Monk-Burton might be of use for once.

He guessed from their muddy shoes that the young family had come by the field path, but even by that route the Old House was two miles from the village. No buses ran in that direction, and it was a long way to walk carrying a child.

He smiled and greeted her, tried without success to make the baby laugh, and seeing that the Monk-Burtons had almost reached their glossy car, he called them back.

'Dear Mrs Monk-Burton,' he said, 'knowing how you

love to be of service, I have no hesitation in asking you to give Mrs Allen and her family a lift.'

She frowned. 'I'm afraid we're not going that way . . .' she began.

'Which way are you going?' asked the vicar sweetly.

'Well, we have to go by the Furniston road,' she said, choosing the only road that crossed the high heath and passed through no villages.

'Perfect! Then you could drop them all at the gates of the Old House.'

'The Old House? I didn't know there was anyone living there. Oh, very well!' She conceded defeat as ungraciously as possible, but Mr Monk-Burton seemed delighted as he shepherded his small party towards the big car.

The vicar smiled as he watched them go and, with a positively unchristian feeling of triumph, went off to have his lunch.

As they drew near the car Jamie, who saw the vicar's well-meant manoeuvres ruining his plan, said to his mother,

'I say, would you mind if Lucy and I walked back the way we came? I saw some nests I'd like to have a look at, and there wasn't time on the way here.'

Before she could answer, Mrs Monk-Burton, seeing a chance to reduce the number of muddy feet in her car by four, said quickly,

'But of course; so much healthier for the dear children to walk, and so pleasant to see the dear birds.'

Jamie smiled at his mother. 'May we,' he asked, 'if we promise not to be too long?'

'All right,' she said, 'and by the time you get back I'll have fed the baby and the lunch will be ready.'

He gave her a grateful peck of a kiss and seizing Lucy by the hand dragged her back across the churchyard towards the footpath gate on the far side.

Lucy protested crossly. 'I want to go with Mummy,' she said, 'I don't care a bit about the "dear birds"!' She had been quite taken with the idea of herself riding in the big, glossy car.

'Listen,' said Jamie, 'that wasn't really why I wanted to walk. While we were in church I had a brilliant idea. All we have to do is to hunt around in the churchyard and look at the names on the graves. If we find two graves with ...' he checked himself, sensing that Lucy would find the idea of the children's graves too ghoulish. He rephrased the sentence, 'I mean, once we have made sure that none of the gravestones has Sara and Georgie's names on, then we shall know that they didn't die.' He paused and looked at Lucy for encouragement, but her face was wary and thoughtful.

'Don't you see?' he persisted; 'we shall know in advance that we managed to save them, and then we can go off into the past knowing that it will be all right.'

Lucy, hearing his eager tones, felt a bit churlish that she could not share his enthusiasm. She did not like to pour cold water on his ideas because he did not have them very often, but there was something about the whole scheme that gave her the shivers.

'We couldn't be sure,' she said. 'They might have buried them secretly; people often do when they've murdered someone.' Even saying the words made her feel queer. She had accepted that Sara and Georgie, coming from a different time, were in a way already dead, but to think of someone actually ... She shook the thought out of her mind.

Jamie was saying cheerfully, 'But of course they wouldn't. If their uncle wants to inherit the money, it would be no use having them just disappear. What he would have to do would be to make it look like an accident. Then he would bury them in the churchyard and pretend to be very sad and all that.'

'I don't like it,' said Lucy abruptly. 'It's a silly idea. I don't think it's nice and I shan't look.'

'All right, don't!' Jamie went into a huff. It was just like Lucy: she was always the one who had the bright ideas and he had to help her carry them out. She seemed to think he was some kind of beast of burden. Now that he had come up with a brilliant idea, she called it silly just because she had not thought of it first. 'I can look by myself,' he said moving off along the line of gravestones. 'And I shan't tell you if it's there or not!' he called over his shoulder.

Lucy had gone off in the other direction and, with her back towards him, she was swinging gently on the kissing-gate that led to the footpath.

When she heard his sudden shocked cry of, 'Lucy, Lucy, come here!' her heart sank. She felt she had known all along that this would happen. She climbed down sadly and went to stand beside him.

He was staring down at the inscription on a small, grey, timeworn stone. Lucy read the names:

SARA CATHERINE LATIMER

GEORGE RICHARD LATIMER

and the date below.

'It's tomorrow,' said Jamie, his voice dull with disbelief. 'It's tomorrow, only a hundred years ago!'

Lucy could think of nothing comforting to say but she took hold of his hand.

They both started violently as a voice from behind them said,

'Ah, that's right, a hundred years ago, poor little things. 'Twas a real tragedy and 'tis no wonder if they wanders around the garden still, poor little lost souls!'

They turned, half expecting another ghost, only to find a short, sturdy old man, with a friendly face under a battered brown hat. He gave off a strong smell of tobacco and onions that was reassuringly human.

'Why, I'm sorry if I startled 'ee then, my dears,' he went on, seeing their pale faces. 'I thought 'ee'd 'ave 'eard me comin' on the gravel like. Just lookin' at the grave of them poor kiddies, eh? Sad business, very sad.'

'Do you know who they were, then?' asked James, half unwilling to pry any further but feeling that nothing could be worse than what they already knew.

'Ah,' the old man nodded, 'I reckon I could tell 'ee about every little grave in this churchyard. I bin sexton 'ere more than forty years afore the diggin' got too much for me. Not that I'm past a bit of diggin' mind yer; I still does me old garden single-'anded an' I sees the churchyard's kept tidy, but 'tis the depth as gets 'ee. Six feet deep, y'see,' he explained confidentially, 'an' when you'm gettin' to the bottom 'tis too far to throw the dirt up. Not to mention the trouble gettin' out when you'm finished. "One of these days you won't get out again, Benson," the vicar says to me. "Tha's true enough," I tells 'im, "for it comes to all of us, but I ain't ready for it quite yet!"'

He laughed cheerfully but Lucy was in no mood for graveyard humour. Horrid old man, she thought. She turned her eyes away and stared at the next gravestone. It seemed to be very old, with a carved death's head like a grinning monkey.

Jamie pointed to Sara and Georgie's grave. 'Tell us about them,' he said.

'About they poor children?' The old man's voice grew sentimental again. 'Ah, 'twas a dreadful thing! A fire it was, one night, an' them fast asleep in their little beds. By the time the flames was spotted, 'twas already burning like a furnace, for it started in the library, they say, an' the books burned like tinder. No one could get to them, poor little mites. Not that they didn't try, mind. Down in the corner of the churchyard there,' he pointed towards a clump of trees, 'you'll find a little grave with no stone, but 'tis always covered with violets an' forget-me-nots in season. They say 'twas the little gardener's boy as tried to save them. My old grandfather used to tell me the story when I was as young as you are now, about 'ow this little lad climbed up the drainpipe to their bedroom window. But somehow the pipe gave way, I suppose 'twas the heat on the lead, or mebbe it weren't properly fastened, an' just as 'ee reached the window, the poor little lad come plungin' down an' was killed.

'An' then there was their guardian too. 'Ee'd bin to the 'ouse that day an' was on 'is way back to London when 'is carriage broke down. When 'ee saw the flames in the distance, 'ee seized a 'orse an' come ridin' back as if the devil 'imself was at 'is 'eels. My grandad 'eard it all from the lodge-keeper at the 'ouse, and 'ee said as 'ow the old man took on somethin' cruel when 'ee knew they was dead. "Too late!" 'ee kept saying with the tears runnin' down 'is face, and then "My fault, all my fault!" though what could 'ee 'ave done, poor gentleman? An' then, all of a sudden, 'ee collapsed in a 'eap and they 'ad to carry 'im away. Some said as 'ow 'ee died of grief and others that 'ee was never right in 'is 'ead again. And there's some claims to 'ave seen 'is ghost too, wanderin' about the Old 'Ouse, besides them poor little ghosts of children that comes and goes in the gardens.'

'Have other people . . . I mean, have people really seen them?' asked Jamie.

'Oh, indeed they 'ave!' said the old man eagerly. 'Why, the couple as used to live in the caretaker's cottage, they saw 'em twice, little misty white figures, walkin' across the lawn. They wouldn' stay; packed their bags an' went back where they came from. Ah, 'tis 'aunted sure enough! You don't want to go near the Old 'Ouse, I'm tellin' 'ee. Why, none of the village folks . . . '

'We live there,' said Lucy rather frostily.

The old man's face registered surprise, regret, and false jollity, all in rapid succession.

'Why then, I was only kiddin' you,' he said with a wheezing chuckle. 'Ho-ho-ho! Made it all up I did. I knows 'ow kiddies loves to 'ear a story Mind you, there's no such things as ghosts!'

'That depends on your point of view,' said Lucy, 'but you needn't worry, we're not afraid of them.'

The old sexton gazed at her uncomfortably.

Jamie thought he was rather nice and that Lucy was being a bit acid. After all, the old man couldn't possibly know that he was talking about their friends. And it was best to know what had happened, however depressing it might be.

'Well, thanks for telling us the story,' he said. 'It was very interesting, but we have to hurry off home now, or we shall be late for lunch.'

He smiled at the sexton who said 'Good-bye' rather awkwardly, and then taking Lucy's arm, he hurried her out of the churchyard, through the kissing-gate, and along the path towards home.

They had gone quite a way before Jamie realized that Lucy was crying. There was no sound, but fat tears rolled in a steady stream down her cheeks.

'Oh, Lucy,' he said, 'Lucy, don't get upset.'

'I ... can't ... help ... it ...' she said between stifled sobs. 'I keep thinking about Sara and that little boy ...'

Jamie walked along in silence. He knew she was waiting for him to say something, but it was hard to think of anything comforting.

After a while, Lucy said, 'Do we have to go, Jamie? Do we have to drink that awful stuff and ...'

'We can't very well let them down,' he said.

'But I couldn't bear to be there and see it all happen

if there's nothing we can do to stop it. It would be too awful!'

'I know,' he agreed miserably, 'but ... well ... I don't think you should abandon a cause just because it's hopeless. We must go, Lucy, at least, I mean *I* must. You see I promised ...'

'But if there is no way?'

'I know, but I did promise. You didn't make any promises, Lucy; you needn't come if you don't want to.'

'Oh, of course I shall come if you are going.' Lucy said it crossly to hide her concern for him.

They walked on along the narrow path which led through a wood where brilliant leaves burst from tree-buds overhead and folded yellow daffodils opened in a bright carpet along the ground. It was very different from the grey littered pavements of Camden Town and, looking about her, Lucy felt her spirits rise in spite of everything. It is hard not to be hopeful in the woods in April.

'Don't you think it just might be possible to do something?' she asked wistfully.

'To save them? No, how could we? What is past is past. You can't undo it, you can only change the future.' Jamie would have liked to say 'Yes', but he knew that it was crueller to raise her hopes and then dash them, so he spoke bluntly.

'But Sara said that our future is the past to people who come after us, and we can change that. After all, this is the future for Sara and Georgie and if we are in their time ...'

'It isn't possible,' said Jamie doggedly. He could not make head or tail of Sara and Lucy when they started juggling with words, but his common sense told him what was possible and what was not.

Lucy said, 'If someone had asked you yesterday whether you could travel through time, would you have said that was impossible?'

Jamie saw that she was making a trap for him to fall into. 'I suppose I might have done,' he said cautiously, looking for a way round it.

'There you are then: anything is *possible*.'

But the trap was empty. 'I shan't believe it is possible,' said Jamie, 'until *we* have done it.'

'But Sara said ...'

'What Sara said is not evidence, it's hearsay,' said Jamie smugly. He remembered this from a court scene in a television series.

Lucy was furious at finding herself outwitted, and sulked the rest of the way home.

Jamie was sorry when the first flush of triumph had worn off and he thought he would butter her up a bit. But then he decided that she was better off sulking than weeping, and he watched her with a fond smile as she stalked along ahead of him. Good old Lucy. He knew that she would insist on going with him, whatever might lie ahead, and he was glad in a way. It would be bad enough as it was, but worse, somehow, to face it alone, the one helpless onlooker. He wished he did not have to go, but he felt bound by his promise. Besides, he couldn't leave them alone if there was anything he could do to help. And yet, what could he do? He turned his face up to the blue sky that shone through the green tracery of branches, and racked his brains for an answer. But the only possible answer came from his heart: I might comfort them, I suppose.

Chapter 7

Jamie heaved a deep sigh and asked, 'Lucy, are you quite sure you want to come?'

'Yes, yes, yes! I've told you a hundred times!' Lucy's voice was irritable with misery. 'I do wish you would stop asking.'

'Well, I wish you would stop grizzling!' said Jamie reasonably. 'You say you want to go on with it, and then you sit there sniffing and snuffling all the time. Sara and Georgie may be here at any minute' – he glanced at his watch – 'they should have been here twenty minutes ago, and what will they think if they see you crying? They'll want to know why, and I'm not going to tell them. I mean, how can you tell someone they are going to ...' He couldn't face the end of the sentence, but Lucy understood.

'I'm sorry.' She sniffed again and, fumbling out her handkerchief, blew her nose and tried to pull herself together.

There was a long silence and then she said, 'Maybe they won't come. Maybe we imagined the whole thing.' She began to sound hopeful. 'It could have been a sort of hallucination.'

Jamie considered the idea and found it half comforting and half disappointing. 'I hope it was,' he said. But he had taken Sara's hand and he knew that she had been real.

'Why do you hope I'm a hallucination?' Sara's voice was gentle and amused but both the children jumped, partly with surprise and partly with embarrassment. She was standing beside the sundial, looking down at them, and she was alone.

Jamie got to his feet awkwardly and tried to change the subject. 'Hello,' he said, 'we were just wondering where you had got to. Where is Georgie?'

'I'm afraid he is locked in the cellar. That is really why I am so late. He had a slight disagreement with Mrs Wickens and I fear he was very rude to her.' She smiled suddenly and went on, 'It was wrong, of course, but I cannot pretend I was not glad. She was so put out, I thought she would have a fit of some kind; but she just screamed at one of the servants to lock him in the cellar, and went off in search of her bottle.'

'But will he be all right?' asked Lucy anxiously. 'Do you think it was safe to leave him?'

'Well, I was afraid to do so at first,' Sara told her. 'I fetched Tom and we tried to get him out by the coal chute, but it wasn't possible. We talked to him and he sounded quite happy, but it seemed wrong to go until I remembered that no time would pass while I was away.

'So I left Tom on guard beside the cellar grating and drank the potion. But I have taken only a little for I am too anxious to stay here for long. I feel safer always when we are together. Georgie is reckless but he is only a child and I know they are plotting some evil thing against us.'

Lucy turned pale. It had been bad enough to think of the fire happening to someone far away in another time; but with Sara standing there, so close and so real, the breeze lifting the long, dark strands of hair ... However much she tried, the tears began again.

'Oh, Lucy, don't,' said Jamie, sitting down beside her, 'please don't, not *now*.'

Sara stood staring at them. Then she said, 'There is something you know. Please tell me.'

Lucy's tears flowed faster than ever and Jamie was in despair.

'It's nothing, nothing,' he repeated, feeling a terrible fool.

'You must tell me.' Sara's voice was kind but firm. 'Whatever it is, you *must* tell me.'

Jamie looked up and saw that she was very calm. 'Well,' he began, 'well, you see . . . ' but he couldn't find the words.

'Don't be afraid to say it. I know much more than you think I do. We did not want to tell you too much, in case you were afraid.'

'It was in the graveyard,' Jamie blurted out the truth, 'on the tombstone. We found your name and his. The sexton said it was a fire.' He glanced away. Even now, he could not say that it would be tomorrow.

There was a silence and when he looked up again, he was surprised to find that she did not look particularly distressed. Only her face was very sad.

The sun was setting and as it went, a few horizontal beams escaped from the clouds and lit up her face with a strange radiance.

'It is true,' she said, 'it was a fire.'

Lucy seemed to see the flames flickering across her face, but she could not look away.

'I know about the grave,' Sara went on, 'I too have walked in the churchyard, but Georgie doesn't know. He is brave but very young: we could not tell him everything. We could not tell him that it will be tomorrow.'

She hesitated for a moment and Jamie wondered whom she meant when she said 'we'.

But she continued, 'It is because of what happened that we need your help. You see, we are going to try to change the Pattern of the Wheel.'

As she spoke, the sun went down, and her face passed into the shadow. Behind her, the darkness began to thicken and take shape until it seemed to Jamie that he saw the figure of an old man standing there. Lucy gasped and he knew that she had seen it too, but Sara seemed unaware of the apparition behind her. The figure seemed not real, as she did, but insubstantial and grey. It reached out thin hands and placed them on her shoulder.

Lucy screamed. But Sara only raised one hand slowly and touched the thin fingers. 'Are you there?' she asked softly.

At her touch the grey figure grew more substantial and Jamie saw that it was the old solicitor, the same old man who had come to see them on a rainy night in Camden

Town: Mr Blunden of Blunden, Claverton and Smith. He moved slowly round to stand beside Sara. 'Yes, I am here,' he said.

Jamie could hardly recognize his voice, it seemed so full of sorrow. But Sara smiled at the old man and said, 'Then you must help me to explain. You are so much cleverer than I am; will you tell them how it is possible to change the Pattern of the Wheel?'

When they were all settled on the seat by the sundial, with Lucy feeling very sheepish at having been caught screaming for the second time, the old man began to explain.

'Sara has told you, I think, that time is not a straight line, endlessly passing, but more like a vast wheel, on the rim of which we stand at different points, except very rarely when we meet like this.'

The children nodded to show that this, at least, was clear to them and he went on.

'I want you now to picture an infinite number of wheels, all turning in different directions, but all having the same still point at the centre.'

He paused and Lucy thought hard. She felt that she had disgraced herself and she sought some way to regain their respect. So she struggled to grasp what he was saying and while Jamie was still scratching his head in perplexity, she said, 'It would be like a round ball: all the wheels together would make up a great sphere ... like the earth itself.'

The old man smiled and patted her hand and she did not flinch.

'A great sphere like the earth itself,' he repeated, 'but infinitely more vast. That great sphere is Time itself and Space and all Creation.'

He paused and looked at them closely.

'I think I understand,' said Lucy slowly, 'but it's a bit difficult.'

'Well, it's all Greek to me,' said Jamie cheerfully, 'but if you say that's how it is, I'll trust you!'

The old solicitor seemed strangely touched by this casual assertion. He said solemnly, 'For that I am grateful. It is far more than I deserve.' Then he fell silent.

Sara squeezed his hand. 'Please go on,' she said. 'I can't stay very long: I only drank a very little.'

'Forgive me,' said the old man, 'I was lost in thought.' He turned again to Jamie and Lucy.

'You must understand,' he told them, 'that all the wheels are constantly crossing one another and that each one represents a different course of action. For at any given moment in time, a man has many different futures open to him, and yet all those possibilities have existed since time began. Your science books will tell you that nothing is ever really created or destroyed, and your Bible will tell you that there is nothing new under the sun. So that at any time, a man can choose which course he will take, but once he has chosen, he cannot turn back and undo what he has already done.'

As he said this, he seemed quite overcome with gloom, and it was some time before he could continue.

'Once, long ago when I was alive, I made the wrong choice, not by chance, for that is easily forgiven, but through my own indifference, my own selfishness. I was guardian to Sara and George and I failed to guard them; I was their trustee but I was not worthy to be trusted. They came to me when they needed help, when no one else could help them, and I failed them. I would not listen to them, and as a result . . .'

His voice broke and Sara said comfortingly, 'It is all right, they know what happened; you need not say it.'

The old man shook his head mournfully. '"It were better for such a man", he said, "that a mill-stone were hanged about his neck and he were drowned in the depths of the sea!"'

Sara sighed. 'Oh, please don't take on so,' she said. 'It is all forgiven long ago.'

Old Mr Blunden turned back to Jamie and Lucy who were watching him with helpless embarrassment.

'For a hundred years I have suffered,' he told them. 'I have been disgraced in my profession and tormented by my own conscience and to me it has been like a thousand years. But now, I have been given the chance to put right the terrible wrong I have done, and to bring my punishment to an end. To do this, I had first to obtain forgiveness, and Sara has forgiven me, though Georgie, I fear . . .'

'He is too young to understand,' said Sara hastily. 'You must not mind him.'

'Ah, he is right to hate me,' said the old man sorrowfully. But he went on, 'Secondly, I must find someone who will trust me once again, someone who will trust me to guard him, even with his life. And lastly, I must go back to undo the harm I have caused and, with my own suffering, change the Pattern of the Wheel.'

Jamie began to see what he had to do, and it no longer seemed like a game. 'I am the one who has to trust you?' he said. 'That's why you brought us here, why you came to Camden Town?'

The old man nodded.

'And it was you who wrote on the window, to tell Georgie and Sara about the book?'

'Yes, indeed. In the beginning it was not easy to make contact.'

Jamie hesitated. He had an uneasy feeling that the old man was using them, as if he and the other children were all puppets and the old lawyer held the strings. And yet, if he was to be believed, he meant no harm, only to save Sara and Georgie from the dreadful fate he had once brought upon them. If he had just asked me to help him, he thought, it would have been easy, but do I really trust him . . . ?

'It is not an easy thing, I know.' The old man answered as if Jamie had spoken his thoughts aloud. 'I have done nothing to deserve your trust. But alas, I did not make the conditions and there is no other way for the pattern to be changed.'

'What shall I have to do?' asked Jamie, trying to sound matter-of-fact.

'It is not yet clear,' said the old man, 'but whatever it may be, nothing shall harm you. I promise that I shall guard you from all dangers however they may come. I know I am not worthy, but beg you to trust me for it is our only hope.'

Jamie could not face the pleading eyes. He rose to his feet abruptly and went to lean on the sundial with his back to them all. He hated to make a promise unless he was certain that he could keep it. He tried to imagine what might lie ahead, and he knew in his heart that he was afraid.

He turned and said to Sara, 'Have you forgiven him?'

She smiled and took the old man by the hand. 'I have forgiven him,' she said.

Impulsively, Jamie reached out his own hand. 'Then I will trust him.'

The old solicitor looked up at him as though he could not believe his good fortune. Then he reached out and grasped Jamie's hand in his own, which was cold and felt very fragile.

Jamie turned to Lucy who seemed rather left out. 'You must trust him too,' he said.

Lucy took his hand and said timidly, 'I will try.'

Sara took Lucy's other hand, and the circle was complete.

'It is time to go,' she said.

Now that the moment had come, Jamie and Lucy felt very nervous.

Lucy was clutching the little bottle which contained the brew of herbs. She uncorked it and looked at it anxiously. Suppose Sara had got the mixture wrong.

Jamie knew what she was thinking. He took the bottle from her and throwing back his head, gulped down half of it. It tasted bitter and he pulled a face but he seemed to feel the same as ever. He handed the bottle back to Lucy who raised it nervously to her lips. But though she was reluctant to drink it, she was even more unwilling to let Jamie go without her. As she began to drink, she comforted herself with the thought that no time would pass while they were away. She put down the bottle and stared at Jamie. She thought she saw something odd about his eyes, but it was hard to be sure. Her heart was beating very fast and she began to feel a strange stillness creeping through her limbs. She wanted to cry out, to call to Jamie, but her head began to spin faster and faster. She felt as if she were being sucked down into a vast whirlpool, deeper and deeper and deeper . . .

Then everything became black.

PART THREE

PART THREE

Chapter 8

Lucy's head cleared and for a moment she thought that nothing had changed.

The sundial was still there and the garden seat, and Jamie was still holding her hand. He was looking at her rather anxiously so she smiled to reassure him that the dizziness had passed. She heard Sara saying cheerfully, 'I felt like that the first time. I think it is more nervousness than anything, because I have never felt faint all the other times. Indeed, sometimes it is so easy, I hardly realize that I have changed.'

Have I changed? thought Lucy wonderingly. Has anything changed? She noticed that the old solicitor had gone, but he could simply have walked away. She fancied that the plants growing around the sundial looked neater, that the trees in the distance did not loom so high, but in the twilight, it was hard to judge size and shape.

'Where are we?' she asked Jamie. She meant 'When are we?', for she could see very well where she was, but it seemed a silly question and she knew that Jamie would understand.

He said, 'We are in Sara's time.' He tried to say it calmly so as not to alarm her, but it was impossible to keep the excitement out of his voice.

'It looks the same.'

'Only from where you are standing,' he said. 'Now turn around slowly and don't be frightened by what you see.'

Lucy gripped his hand as she turned around, but in spite of his warning her heart leaped into her mouth when she saw the great building that loomed up in the darkness with lights in the windows here and there.

'Where did it come from?' she gasped.

Jamie grinned. 'You remember the old ruins?' he said. 'Well, they couldn't have been as old as we thought. In Sara's time that building was still standing.'

It was hard to see the details in the dim light, but by concentrating Lucy made out that the soaring arches, which she had taken for some old chapel, formed the front of a quite ugly Victorian-Gothic wing which had been added to the old house. Really, she thought, it looks better as a ruin. She was just wondering what could have happened to it, when she heard a low voice calling, 'Sara, Miss Sara! Are you all right, miss?'

'Oh dear,' said Sara. 'Tom is growing anxious. He hates me to go into the garden alone at night, even for a moment, in case . . .' She paused, not wanting to frighten Lucy. 'We had better go and reassure him,' she said.

She hurried off along the path with Jamie and Lucy following. As they drew near the house, they could see in the light from one of the windows the tall figure of a boy who came quickly towards them.

'Oh, there you are, miss,' he began, 'I was just . . .' Then he gasped and drew back in fear, staring at Jamie and Lucy as they moved into the light. For a moment he hesitated, then rushing forward he seized Sara and dragged her away from them. He pushed her behind him and standing in front of her, faced the children with the air of a man confronting a savage bull.

'It's all right, miss!' he said. 'They shan't harm you.'

Sara stood on tiptoe and they saw her astonished eyes peeping over the boy's shoulder. 'Oh, Tom,' she said, 'I didn't realize . . . It is quite safe, I promise you. They are friends of mine.'

She came out from behind his back, and took Jamie and Lucy by the hand. The boy seemed horrified and Lucy wondered why he should be so put out. She glanced down at herself to see if she looked the same as usual, and realized with embarrassment that, compared with Sara's, her own skirt was very short indeed.

She had read that Victorians were very prim and proper, but could the sight of her bare knees be quite so terrible?

The boy swallowed hard. 'Friends of yours, miss?' he said incredulously. 'Then I'm sure I'm very glad to see them. You must have thought me very ill-mannered, miss, to seize ahold of you like that. But with them being so strange and misty like, I fancied I could see right through them and for a moment, well . . . ' he hesitated, 'I took them for ghosts, miss!'

'We are all ghosts in a way,' said Sara very gently. Jamie saw that she was teasing and he laughed, but Lucy was too busy peering at her fingers in the dim light, to see if anyone could possibly see right through her. She did not like the thought at all.

'My friends are as real as you or I, Tom,' went on Sara, 'and they have come a very long way to help us.'

'Then I welcome them, miss, for you are in need of friends,' and, impulsively, the boy held out his hand.

Jamie realized what an effort it had cost him, having once taken Sara's hand in the same gesture of good faith. He grasped the hand and shook it warmly, and saw a look of wonder and relief grow on the boy's face.

'Why, Miss Sara,' said Tom eagerly, 'I seem to see them quite clearly now.' He turned to Jamie. 'It was a trick of the light,' he explained; 'what a rare fool you must have thought me!'

'No,' said Jamie, 'I think you are very brave.'

'So do I,' said Sara, and the boy reddened awkwardly, seeing her smile at him.

As if to change the subject he said, 'I see from the way you dress that you don't come from hereabouts. I suppose you wouldn't have come from the New World?' he added hopefully.

'Well, yes, I suppose you could say we have,' said Jamie, feeling that the whole truth would be hard to explain.

The boy's face lit up. 'They say 'tis a wonderful place, the New World!'

'Er ... yes, it is,' agreed Jamie.

'Of course, 'tis a terrible long journey,' Tom went on earnestly, 'but 'tis one I plan to make myself one of these days. When I'm older, like, and Miss Sara has taught me to read and write, I mean to go there and try my fortune.

They say there's a fine future in America for a young man as can read and write and ain't afraid of a bit of hard work!'

He seemed quite carried away in his enthusiasm, until Sara interrupted him, saying quietly, 'How is my brother, Tom? Is he quite safe?'

Tom looked dismayed. 'Oh, whatever must you think of me, Miss Sara, rambling on about myself? But he's safe enough, I promise you, though he must be growing hungry for he declares he will not touch their dry bread. He told me ...'

But they never learned what Georgie had told him for at that point, a harsh, demanding voice cut across the conversation.

'Sara!' it screamed. 'Sara, where are you, you lazy slattern!'

Sara turned pale and Tom clenched his fists angrily. 'Oh, miss,' he said, 'if you'd only let me strike her down! I'm not a one to hit a woman, but she's a devil, miss, to say such things.'

'Oh, Tom, please don't! Please go before she comes and finds you here. Go home to your supper; I know you must be hungry too. I will try to persuade her to let Georgie out. She cannot remain angry for ever.'

As the boy hesitated, the voice came again, only closer now.

'Sara! You wait till I find her, you little hussy. 'Anging around in the bushes with that garden boy, I don't doubt. I know what you're up to, miss!'

Tom flamed with anger. 'Oh, let me stay and face her,' he begged. 'I'm not afraid of her. You know I'd die for you, Miss Sara!'

'I know, Tom,' said Sara, 'but she will only dismiss you and I shall lose the last friend I have. Now, go quickly, for my sake!'

Tom groaned with despair. 'Well, I shan't go far, miss,' he said. 'If you need me, you have only to call from the nursery window.' Then he turned and vanished into the darkness.

'Should we go with him?' asked Lucy nervously. 'We don't want her to know that we are here.' The truth was that she was afraid to face the woman whose heavy footsteps could be heard lurching towards them along the path.

But to her surprise, Sara said, 'No, keep still where you are. I think it will be all right.'

Lucy moved a little closer to Jamie, and they stood in the shadows behind Sara as a huge woman with a mean, ugly face and a wide flat nose came shuffling into the light of the window.

'So there you are,' she hissed when she saw Sara, 'and all alone, I see. But 'oo was 'ere with you a moment ago? One of them vulgar servants, I'll be bound. Not only 'ave you got no sense, miss; you ain't got no taste, neither. I don't know 'ow a gent like your dear uncle can abide 'avin' you in the same 'ouse. An' settin' such a bad example to my dear Bella an' all!'

'I'm very sorry,' said Sara meekly, 'but I only came out to speak a word to poor Georgie, through the grating there. Oh, Mrs Wickens, won't you please let him out? He's only a child and it is so dark in there!'

Jamie was furious. It made him sick to hear Sara speak so humbly to a coarse old woman who was not fit to polish her shoes. How can she do it? he thought; I'd rather die.

But Lucy understood. She knew that it took more courage for Sara to humble herself than for her to defy the old woman, and she saw that, for Georgie's sake, the older girl would sacrifice herself in any way.

'Don't talk to me about that brat!' roared the old woman. 'After the things 'ee said to me, 'ee'll be lucky if 'ee gets out before next week.'

'Oh, but please . . .'

'None of your cheek, miss!' and Mrs Wickens swung her fat fist at Sara.

It was more than Jamie could stand. He ran forward out of the shadows and pushed the old woman away. 'Leave her alone!' he shouted. 'You rotten old bully!'

Lucy was horrified. Now, she thought, Jamie would be locked in the cellar too.

But to her surprise, Mrs Wickens did not seem to see him. She felt the force as he pushed her, and she staggered drunkenly. 'What's that?' she muttered. "Oo did that? That murdering gardener's boy. I'll be bound.'

Jamie faced her. 'No, it wasn't,' he said, 'it was me, and what's more I'll do it again if you touch Sara.'

The old woman looked straight through him as though he were not there.

We are ghosts, thought Lucy as the truth struck her for the first time; Jamie and I are ghosts!

Mrs Wickens was still muttering angrily, "E'll have to go. I've seen 'im snoopin' around in the bushes . . . '

'I tell you it was me!' shouted Jamie angrily.

Lucy walked forward out of the shadows and touched his arm.

'You keep back, Lucy,' he said. 'I'll deal with her.'

'She can't see you,' said Lucy quietly. 'She doesn't even know you are there.'

Jamie faltered in his anger and looked uncertainly

from Lucy to the old woman and back again. Now that he paused to consider, he realized that there was something very odd about the way the woman ignored him. He waved one hand in front of her bloodshot eyes but there was not the slightest flicker of reaction.

'I do believe you're right,' he said. 'She doesn't seem to hear me either. Do you think she's had some kind of fit?'

'There's nothing wrong with her,' said Lucy, 'it's us. We are ghosts!' Now that she was growing used to the idea, she rather enjoyed the sight of Jamie's astonishment.

'But we can't ...' he began, then stopped, peered at his hand, and found it solid. 'We can't be!' he said incredulously.

'Ask Sara,' said Lucy.

Jamie turned to Sara. 'Are we?' he said.

Sara hesitated, glanced at the old woman who was beating around in the bushes for the elusive gardener's boy and, finding her busy, nodded violently.

'But Tom could see us; why can't she?' he demanded.

Sara glanced nervously at Mrs Wickens. 'Too old,' she hissed, 'too insensitive.'

'Remember what Sara told us?' said Lucy eagerly. 'When she and Georgie came to our time, they found that most people could not see them. She said that only children, or people who were very ...'

But she was interrupted by the old woman who had caught Sara's whispered words. 'Old!' she screamed. 'Insensitive!'

'No, no,' said Sara quickly, 'I said my hands were growing cold and insensitive. It is the night wind.'

It wasn't a very good lie, but Mrs Wickens was prepared to accept it rather than be called 'old'.

'And 'oo's fault is that, miss?' she sneered. 'If you will sneak out to keep your assignations ... Get inside now. Up to the schoolroom and be quick about it!'

'But Georgie ... ?' Sara tried once more.

'He stays where he is. Now be off with you.'

Sara's head dropped miserably as she made her way into the house, followed by the old woman.

Lucy glanced at Jamie. He shrugged his shoulders and then nodded, and they went after the others up the steps and through the front door.

It was strange to walk into the same house and to find it so different. Not only were the pale dust-sheets gone but also the simple pieces of old furniture beneath them. Gone were the old Persian carpets with their lovely faded patterns and the delicately coloured curtains. In their place there was massive ugly furniture in ox-blood mahogany, heavy folds of dusty plush and a terrible abundance of hideous ornaments. The walls were sombrely papered, the floors darkly carpeted, and the air smelt indescribably stale.

Jamie wrinkled his nose. 'Place wants a good clean,' he said loudly, as they made their way upstairs. His voice echoing and re-echoing around the high roof, reminded Lucy of the long-dead voices which had whispered in the empty house, like old family keepsakes in a great box.

Mrs Wickens had obviously set out to escort Sara to the schoolroom, but she was too fat for the stairs and she was already puffing. She called out and a thin-faced maid appeared from nowhere.

'Meakin,' she said, 'take Miss Sara up to the schoolroom and lock her in.' Then she collapsed panting on to an overstuffed sofa.

The maid, who seemed to have a thin line for a mouth, bobbed ingratiatingly. 'Yes, ma'am,' she said.

But as they turned to go, a high, childlike voice called, 'Mama, Mama! see my new pink silk!' and along the passageway came a girl of about seventeen. She was plump but pretty, with fair hair in a mass of ringlets and china-blue eyes. Her round cheeks too were like china, white with a faint touch of pink, and, like a china doll's, her expression was quite blank.

Mrs Wickens lolled back on the sofa fanning herself with one hand. A look of smug satisfaction spread over her face.

'Bella, me love, you are a picture,' she said, in a voice of oily sweetness. 'Turn around and let Mama see yer.'

Bella held out the skirt of the pink dress and revolved vacantly like a dancing doll on a music-box.

'Lovely, my pet, lovely. Bertie will be struck all of a 'eap when 'ee sees yer.'

Arabella smiled like a well-fed cat and turned to Sara. 'Ain't it pretty, Sal?' she said.

'Very pretty,' said Sara who, to Lucy's surprise, seemed quite to like this stupid-looking, doll-like girl. Lucy was not unkind but it irked her to see Sara in her threadbare dress, admiring this plump creature in her ridiculous flounces.

Safe in the knowledge that only Sara and Jamie could hear her, she remarked loudly and clearly, 'I think she looks like a stuffed, pink pig!'

The effect was startling.

Bella's jaw dropped and she swung round to stare

at Lucy. Then she opened her rose-bud mouth and screamed and screamed.

Confusion reigned. Meakin, the maid, and old Mrs Wickens ran to calm her.

'What is it?' Lucy turned nervously to Sara. 'Surely she can't see me.'

Sara frowned. 'I think perhaps she can,' she said softly. 'I should have realized. She looks very grown-up, but she has the mind of a child. She can probably just see you in a thin, transparent way.'

Bella's screaming died to a whimper. She pointed at Lucy with a shaking hand. 'What is it?' she said. 'It's a ghost, I swear it is! I can see right through it!'

Mrs Wickens stared at Lucy. ''Ush now,' she said, 'there ain't nothing there, you silly gel. 'Ere, let's smell yer breath. You ain't been at me gin again, 'ave yer? I told yer before, Bertie don't like it!'

'But I 'aven't, Ma, I 'aven't!' said Bella desperately.

Then Lucy had a brilliant idea. It would be cruel to tease the simple Bella, she thought, and yet it was crueller still to shut a little boy in a pitch-dark cellar. Perhaps Bella would have some influence on her mother.

Slowly she raised one arm and pointed at the quaking girl.

'Hear me, Bella,' she said, trying to sound as imposing as possible, 'I shall haunt you until little Georgie is released from the cellar.'

Sara flashed her a look of gratitude, and Jamie murmured, 'Oh, very cunning! Well done, Lucy.'

Bella clutched at her mother. 'Let Georgie out of the cellar, Ma,' she pleaded, 'then maybe it'll go away.'

'What'll go away?' The old woman looked impatient. 'I already told yer, there ain't nothin' there.'

'But there is, Ma, there is!'

Jamie felt perhaps he should increase the pressure. Besides, it looked like fun to act the ghost, and he wished he had thought of it first.

'Let Georgie g-o-o-o-o,' he moaned in a sepulchral voice, waving his arms in the air as he imagined a bona fide ghost would do.

But the appearance of a second, and even more frightening vision, was more than poor Bella could stand. With a piercing scream, she fainted clean away, falling to the floor like a crumpled rose.

Sara, Meakin, and old Mrs Wickens clustered anxiously around her.

Lucy glared at the crestfallen Jamie. 'Trust you to overdo it,' she said sourly.

There was a sound of footsteps hurrying along the corridor and a young man appeared. He was tall and thin, with dark hair parted in the centre and neat side-whiskers. He had a smooth round face with slightly protruding eyes.

'What is this?' he cried in a high-pitched, anxious voice. 'I heard someone screaming.'

Meakin stepped aside to reveal the pink heap of Bella lying on the floor. The young man turned pale.

'Bella, my love!' He knelt down beside her and clutched her hand.

Bella opened her round, blue eyes and gazed about her blankly. Then seeing the young man, she threw her arms round his neck.

'Oh, Bertie,' she said, 'I was that scared! Tell Ma to let 'im out, Bertie, or they'll be after me again.' And she began to wail at the very thought of it.

'Let who out? Who is after you, Bella dearest? What is all this about, Mrs Wickens?'

He turned on the old woman angrily, and at once she became flustered and apologetic as she tried to explain how Georgie came to be in the cellar.

'Go and release the child immediately,' snapped Bertie. 'I won't have Bella distressed. And Meakin, fetch the smelling salts from Miss Bella's room.'

The maid hurried off along the passage, but Mrs Wickens remained.

'Well,' said Bertie crossly, 'why are you waiting?'

The old woman simpered. 'Oh, Bertie, 'ow can I leave me precious child while she's like this?'

'Bella is perfectly all right with me,' said Bertie coldly. 'Now go and do as I say.'

'But Bertie, all them stairs ... Me 'eart won't stand it.'

'I'll go,' said Sara quickly.

Mrs Wickens grumbled but she parted with the key which hung from a chatelaine at her belt, and by the time Meakin had returned with the smelling salts, Sara's swift feet had taken her down to the cellar and back with a rather coal-dusty, angry Georgie.

'Take them to the schoolroom, Meakin, and lock them both in,' ordered the old woman. She lowered her voice to a hiss so that Bertie would not hear. 'I shall deal with them two later,' she said, and her mouth set into a grim hard line.

Chapter 9

'If only we knew just what they are planning to do,' said Lucy, 'it would make things a lot easier.'

'Yes, and what time they are planning to do it,' added Jamie.

The four children were sitting together in the school-room at the top of the house. It was a large, bleak room and at first Lucy could not place it, although she had explored the old house thoroughly and thought she knew every room. Then she realized that this was the top floor of the ugly Victorian wing which had been destroyed in the fire and which remained, in their own time, only as a creeper-covered ruin. The thought made her uneasy.

The room contained only a few battered oddments of furniture which had been thrown out of other parts of the house. The floor had a small, badly worn rug in front of the fireplace but otherwise the boards were bare. It was cold, too, for the thin warmth of the spring sunlight had gone and there was no fire to break the gathering chill of the night.

Jamie and Lucy had found no difficulty in getting into the schoolroom since Meakin, in the general confusion, had left the key in the lock of the door.

Jamie had been disappointed to find that he could not pass through walls. 'I can't understand it,' he said. 'In all the ghost stories I've ever read, the ghosts can go back and forwards through solid oak doors without any trouble. I mean, it's one way of telling that they are ghosts.'

'We had the same trouble,' agreed Sara sympathetically. 'When we first arrived in your time, Georgie got a nasty bruise trying to pass through a garden wall to save going round by the gate. It is my belief that it only happens when the "ghost" you see is someone still in his own time who passes through something built at a later period.'

Jamie considered the idea. 'I expect you're right,' he said, his voice tinged with admiration. Sara was clever, he thought, like Lucy but without Lucy's timid ways. He wished that they did not belong to different times. Most of the girls he had met were so silly and giggled all the time; but Sara was almost as good as a boy, better in some ways.

Not being able to pass through doors meant that Jamie and Lucy dared not risk being locked in with the Victorian children. So they had unlocked the door and hidden the key under the stair-carpet.

'Meakin will get the blame for losing it,' said Georgie gleefully, 'and it will serve her right, for she's a rotten spy.' And he went around shouting 'Sneakin' Meakin' with obvious delight.

Lucy thought he was a rather spiteful child, but she remembered that he had grown up with no parents and tried to make allowances. She saw that Sara, who knew him best, loved him dearly, so she told herself he must be good at heart. But sometimes she suspected that Sara, having no other family, was simply blind to his faults.

'It's like sitting on a time-bomb and waiting for it to go off,' complained Jamie, and then had to explain to Georgie what a time-bomb was. The little boy was delighted with this invention, and ran about the school-room shouting, 'A time-bomb under Mrs Wickens ... BOOM! A time-bomb under Uncle Bertie ... BOOM!'

'He makes a great deal of noise,' said Sara smiling,

'but it is easier to talk about what might happen, if he cannot hear us. He is so young, he should not have to think of death.'

He seems to enjoy thinking about everyone else's, thought Lucy, but she knew she was being unkind, and that all little boys pretended to kill people.

'Perhaps Lucy and I should go and eavesdrop,' said Jamie, 'and see if we can find what they are up to.'

'You will learn nothing now, however hard you listen,' Sara told him. 'They are all gone in to dinner and they will not dare to speak of such things while Mr Blunden is there. He is a foolish man but I am sure he is not bad. Besides, he thinks too highly of his profession to be a party to any unlawful plots.'

'Do you mean old Mr Blunden, the solicitor?' Lucy was surprised. 'What is he doing here in the house?'

'He has come to see Uncle Bertie on business. I think our uncle needs more money, and he is trying to persuade Mr Blunden to arrange a loan for him.'

'But surely he will help you,' said Lucy. 'We must tell him everything and persuade him to take you away from here.'

Sara sighed. 'You know we have already written to him,' she said. 'I fear he does not believe us.'

'But he would if you talked to him,' said Jamie. 'After all, your letter could have gone astray.' Sara seemed doubtful and he went on earnestly, 'Don't forget that he brought us here from Camden Town. If it wasn't for him, we shouldn't be here at all.'

'Yes,' said Lucy, 'and the sexton told us that Mr Blunden was terribly upset when he came back after the fire and found . . . ' she left the sentence unfinished.

Sara shook her head. 'It's not the same man,' she said. 'At least, it is the same, and yet it is not.' She frowned. 'It's very hard to explain, but the Mr Blunden who is downstairs now, just does not know how sorry he is going to be.'

'Then you must tell him,' said Jamie firmly. 'We must make him understand or at least we must try. You have nothing to lose now that time is so short. They can only lock you up again and then you will be no worse off than before.'

Sara thought of the beatings she had had from Mrs Wickens in the past, and she was about to argue the point. But it came to her clearly that a beating was nothing compared to the fire.

'Very well,' she said calmly. 'We will go down and hide in the bushes opposite the front door, and try to catch him as he leaves. Out there we shall have more chance of speaking to him before they can stop us.'

'Shall we leave Georgie up here?' asked Lucy hopefully. 'It's very damp out there.'

'Oh, no,' said Sara anxiously, 'I cannot feel safe unless he is near us.'

'Then he'd better leave his time-bombs behind,' said Jamie, putting his hands over his ears as a particularly loud one went off under his chair. He turned to Georgie sternly. 'Listen,' he said, 'we are going downstairs to hide and you'll have to be very quiet, do you hear?'

The little boy stuck out his chin. 'You are just a silly old ghost,' he said, 'and you can't tell me what to do!'

'Georgie,' said his sister quickly, 'we are going to play hunters in the African jungle. The one who is quietest will be the chief.'

Georgie froze into a mouselike stillness.

I just don't have the knack, thought Jamie.

It seemed to Lucy that they had been sitting on the rain-wet seat in the cold, damp shrubbery for hours. Georgie had been miserable and aggravating by turns and at last, to everyone's relief, he had fallen asleep wrapped about in Sara's old cloak and with his head on her shoulder.

I'm uncomfortable enough myself, thought Lucy, wriggling into a new position, but she must be cramped all over sitting still like that so as not to waken him. And yet she doesn't complain. She stared at Sara. Her eyes were closed and her pretty face looked thin and tired. Lucy thought how often she herself had wallowed in self-pity since her father had died, wondering again and again why it should have happened to her. Yet Sara had lost her father and mother; she had no older brother to lean upon, only a temperamental child to whom she must be everything. And in spite of all this, she had not once complained.

Lucy drifted into a day dream in which she herself was strong and brave, beautiful and uncomplaining, and in which boys like Tom and Jamie fell over each other to be of service to her. But her dream was rudely shattered by the sound of horses' hooves and by Jamie shaking her.

'Wake up, Lucy, they'll be coming out at any moment.'

'I wasn't asleep,' she said guiltily, and opening her eyes she saw that a carriage had drawn up at the door of the house. Sara was sitting upright now and staring nervously towards it.

'Shall I take Georgie?' Lucy offered, 'if you don't want to wake him?'

'I hate to disturb him,' Sara admitted, 'but I think the sight of him is more likely to soften the old man's heart.'

Georgie woke irritably, rubbing his eyes and beginning to grizzle. Jamie and Lucy both thought that Sara herself was far more likely to soften anyone's heart, but they did not like to say so.

'I know you are tired, Georgie dear,' she was saying, 'but we must ask Mr Blunden to help us, so do be patient.'

Georgie stuck out his lower lip. 'Blunden is an old fool,' he said, 'and I hate him.'

The door of the house swung open and the old solicitor appeared on the porch. But to their surprise, they saw that the children's uncle was beside him, dressed in travelling clothes. Bella clung to his arm and she was pouting miserably. Her high-pitched voice carried across to the shrubbery.

'Dearest Bertie, do you 'ave to go? Poor Bella will be so sad without you.'

'Oh, if he is going too, then we are really lost,' breathed Sara. 'It was some comfort to have him in the house, for though he is foolish, he is not really wicked.'

Bertie was consoling the clinging Bella. 'It will be only a night or two, my pet, but Mr Blunden thinks it advisable that I go with him to London. Now don't cry for it must be so, and you will only spoil your pretty eyes. There will be papers to sign and it will save a great deal of time, and I must get some money soon or, dash it, there will be no more silk dresses for you.'

The old solicitor came down the steps towards the carriage. Sara took a deep breath.

'Now, Georgie,' she said, 'or we shall be too late,' and she ran across the gravelled courtyard pulling him by the hand.

Lucy and Jamie watched anxiously as she approached the old man and began to speak to him.

The wind was growing stronger and her soft voice was blown away, but it was plain from her earnest face and pleading hands what she was saying.

'Oh, surely he will listen to her,' said Lucy. 'He is a kind man, I know he is.'

The old man seemed startled by the sudden appearance of his wards out of the dark night. He bent to hear what Sara was saying but as he listened his face grew embarrassed and then annoyed. He wagged a finger at the children and Jamie and Lucy caught the words 'mischievous children ...' and 'a kind and considerate guardian'.

Sara raised her voice. 'But it is Mrs Wickens, she means to harm us, I know. Oh, you must not leave us here alone with her.'

Mr Blunden looked shocked and for a moment Lucy thought he was convinced. But then he frowned and turned to the children's uncle who, in his efforts to escape the clinging Bella, had not noticed their arrival. As the old man spoke to him, Bertie's face fell and his eyes seemed to protrude more than ever. Bella looked most indignant and they heard her cry, 'She cannot mean to accuse Mama!'

Bertie patted her plump arm. 'Of course not, dearest,' he soothed. 'We all know that your mother is a splendid woman.'

This was more than Georgie could stand. They heard him shout, 'Her mother is a drunken old witch!' just as Mrs Wickens herself came sweeping out of the door to see what the noise was all about.

She nearly exploded. "Ow did them kids get out?' she shrieked. 'You wait till I see that there Meakin ... Lyin' little troublemakers, you are, the pair of you. You shall both go in the cellar, and I'll see to it myself ... '

Her voice was lost in the general confusion that followed. Georgie was shouting insults, Bella was bawling like a lost calf, Bertie was pleading with her, Mr Blunden was scolding the children, and through it all, Sara stood quietly weeping.

'Oh, I can't bear it,' said Lucy. 'How can they treat her so? She is so gentle. And that stupid old man: I thought he was so nice.'

'I shall go and speak to them myself,' said Jamie. 'Perhaps if he sees me, he will remember what is going to happen.'

'But it hasn't happened yet,' said Lucy, 'so how can he remember it?'

'Well, he must remember something. After all, he brought us here.'

But as he moved forward, he felt a hand upon his shoulder and turning he jumped at the sight of the old solicitor standing behind him. He stared incredulously for a moment then looked back at the figure of Mr Blunden on the steps.

'But ... there are two of you!' he said.

Lucy turned in surprise, hearing him speak, and though the apparition startled her at first, she found it strangely comforting.

'Yes, there are two of us,' said the old man sadly, 'though we are the same man. We are separated by a great gulf of time and knowledge. But he would not know you; it was I who brought you here.'

Jamie was growing hopelessly confused. 'But surely if I told him . . . ' he began.

The old man shook his head. 'He would not hear you, he would not even see you. He is a shallow, insensitive man, incapable of visions. If it were not so, I would plead with him myself.'

Jamie saw that there were tears running down his cheeks, and looking from one man to the other, so much alike and yet so different, he decided that it was all too much for him to understand. Lucy, who usually screamed and ran, seemed to accept this weird situation without difficulty; she seemed almost glad to have the wraithlike figure beside her. Jamie sighed in perplexity. There was only one thing he did understand, and that was that he was unlikely to be seen whatever he did. He turned and moved quietly away through the bushes.

Lucy stood beside the old man and watched the distressing scene on the porch.

'It's all so difficult,' she sighed. 'We have come here to help, but there seems to be so little we can do.'

'It is not yet time,' said the old man sadly. 'For the time being, everything will go on as before. You see, the others cannot change the past: they must fulfil the pattern they have already created. Only you and your brother, coming from another time, can change the Pattern of the Wheel. But not yet. Now you can only wait, and for a while be patient. When the time for action has come, I will return, never fear . . . ' His voice seemed to be fading. 'Tell your brother I shall come . . .'

The words were lost on the passing wind and turning to catch them, Lucy found that he had gone. She turned back towards the porch. Bertie and the old solicitor were in the carriage and the driver was gathering up the reins. Sara and Georgie were walking forlornly up the steps into the house with Mrs Wickens storming after them.

In a flurry of hooves and turning wheels, the carriage moved off along the drive. Bella waved until it was out of sight; then she too went back into the house. The door slammed shut and all was quiet.

Lucy turned to speak to Jamie but he was not there. She looked about her anxiously; he was nowhere to be seen. She called to him: there was no answer. Her heart began to hurry as she realized that she was alone.

She had always been afraid to be out in the dark by herself, even if it was only to go as far as the coalshed. But she had learned to keep her fear under control and not to give way to the shudders until she was safely back in the kitchen with the door closed. Now she found herself alone with no door against darkness, no safe, warm place to run to. It came to her suddenly that if she never found Jamie again, she would be utterly lost in time as well as space.

Panic seized her, and she began to run blindly through the dark bushes, calling his name over and over again. Her heart was pounding and she seemed unable to catch her breath. She paused gasping and in the windy quietness she heard footsteps coming along a path near by. She plunged towards the sound and saw a dark figure moving through the night.

'Oh, Jamie,' she sobbed, 'thank goodness I've found you ...' But as she almost collided with the looming figure, she saw that it was much too tall to be Jamie. Out of the shadow of the bushes came a huge, shambling man with a great bundle of wood in his arms. His lurching shape was so close that she could hear his animal-like breathing. Lucy screamed and ran desperately away through the high, wet bushes.

The moon had come out and threw a nightmare jigsaw of light and shadow over everything so that she could not see the ground and stumbled as she ran. To her horror, she heard the big man give a hoarse cry and come blundering after her.

Then, just when it seemed to Lucy that it was all a terrible dream and that she must either wake or die, she felt her arm seized roughly and she was pulled to one side. A hand went over her mouth and a voice said, 'For heaven's sake, Lucy, it's only me!' She stumbled and fell to the ground, crying with relief.

'Keep very still,' said Jamie. 'He can't see you, remember, and he can't hear your voice, but he can hear the bushes rustling as you move among them. Keep absolutely still, and he will go away.'

Now that she had found him again, Lucy would have obeyed if Jamie had told her to stand on her head, anything so long as she did not have to be alone in the hostile darkness.

'But who is it?' she hissed. 'He was more like a monster than a man.'

'I think it's Mr Wickens, the old prizefighter,' whispered Jamie. 'Sara said he was a mindless mountain.'

As they crouched motionless beneath the bush, Lucy became aware of a sweet, powerful perfume like a waterfall around them. It seemed mysteriously familiar and glancing upwards she saw great pale blossoms gleaming in the moonlight. It was an early rhododendron in full flower. Surely, she thought, they can't be the same flowers that I was picking for the house only . . . was it yesterday? She realized with a start that her yesterday was a hundred years away and she wondered whether a rhododendron could live that long.

Stumbling footsteps and a rough voice called, "Oo's there then . . . ? I can see yer!'

Jamie gripped Lucy's hand and they held their breath.

The big man snorted. 'Cats!' he said scornfully, 'or them blamed foxes.' And he shuffled away into the darkness.

When it seemed safe to talk again, Jamie said crossly, 'Whatever were you playing at: tearing around in the bushes, screaming your head off! It's a good thing that ugly great ox couldn't hear you.'

Lucy felt rather put out that he, not being so short of breath, had got his reproaches in first, when it was clearly she who had been wronged.

'You just disappeared,' she said indignantly. 'Why did you run off and leave me alone in the dark?'

'I left you with old Blunden.'

'Thanks a lot,' said Lucy bitterly; 'only he promptly dissolved into thin air which wasn't very reassuring.'

Jamie saw that she had a good case, so he changed his tactics.

'Well, anyway,' he said, 'I was doing something useful. You remember the old sexton said that Mr Blunden came back when he saw the fire, but he was too late?'

Lucy nodded.

'Well, I've made certain that they'll be back a lot sooner. I've cut the harness on the horses half through with my penknife. They won't get far before it snaps.'

Lucy sighed, 'I don't think it will make any difference,' she said. 'It's not time yet,' and she told him what the old lawyer had said.

'But if the traces break . . . ' protested Jamie.

'Perhaps it would have happened anyway: the old sexton said the carriage broke down.'

Jamie remembered that she was right and he felt very deflated. He had been rather proud of his exploit.

'Well, I think old Blunden is wrong,' he said crossly, 'but I'm not going to argue about it. We had better sneak back into the house and see what has happened to Sara and Georgie. We'll only get pneumonia if we sit out here.'

Chapter 10

Half-an-hour later, Lucy and Jamie were sitting on the stairs not far from the schoolroom door. It was warmer and drier than in the shrubbery outside, but their mood was, if anything, even gloomier.

It had taken them a little while to find Georgie and Sara. Jamie had expected to find them banished to the cellar again, and they had wasted some time blundering through the coal cellars and wine cellars in the dark, getting dirty and cross but finding no one.

And all the time the two Victorian children had been locked in the comparative safety of the night nursery next to the schoolroom. This time Mrs Wickens herself had been their jailor and she had chosen the nursery when she found the schoolroom key was missing.

Sara assured them through the keyhole that they were really quite happy. They were sitting on the bed, they had a stump of candle, and she was reading Georgie a story.

Lucy and Jamie had retired to the stairs to think things out.

'Of course, Sara is only putting on an act to stop Georgie being frightened,' said Lucy. 'She must be terrified really.'

'Sara's not the sort of girl who terrifies easily,' said Jamie admiringly.

Lucy, still smarting from the memory of her panic in the garden, took this as a personal reproach. She sniffed miserably. 'I should never have come,' she said. 'I can't help it if I get frightened in the dark.'

It took Jamie a moment or two to get to the bottom of this remark. When he did he said, 'Oh, don't be a ninny. I wasn't getting at you. After all, no one would expect you to be as brave as Sara; you've always had me around to look after you.'

He said it with a certain smugness but Lucy decided to let it pass.

'Why do you suppose Mrs Wickens changed her mind?' she asked. 'Locking them up here, I mean, instead of the cellar?'

'Maybe Bella put in a word for them,' said Jamie. 'She's really not too bad ... Bella, not her mother. I wonder how that old hag came to have such a pretty daughter.'

Lucy was not prepared to discuss Bella's charms.

'It's right over the library,' she said.

Jamie stopped thinking about Bella's blue eyes and considered the library. Lucy's remarks were so cryptic. Suddenly he saw what she was getting at. 'Oh, Lord,' he groaned, 'of course, that's where the fire started. They'd have been safer in the cellar.'

'It's all happening just as it did before,' said Lucy. 'Mr Blunden said it would.'

'Then what's the use of being here at all?' said Jamie angrily. 'The people we want to talk to can't see us or hear us, and if they can, like Bella, they promptly have hysterics.'

'It was the same for Sara when she came to our time,' agreed Lucy. 'It's really very frustrating being a ghost. No wonder poor Mr Blunden was reduced to writing on steamy windows.'

'When we *do* do something,' continued Jamie, who wasn't listening to her, 'we find we still haven't changed anything. We just seem to fit into some pattern which was always there.'

'The Pattern of the Wheel,' said Lucy thoughtfully.

'But it can be changed, Jamie, or why would he bring us here? It's only that the time hasn't come yet. Mr Blunden said that when . . .'

'Mr Blunden, Mr Blunden!' said Jamie irritably. 'Do you really think we can trust what he says?'

Lucy stared at him in dismay. 'Jamie, you *must* trust him,' she said. 'If you don't, nothing *can* be changed. You remember what he said: he could only change the pattern if Sara would forgive him and you would trust him.'

'There you go again,' said Jamie. 'It's always "He said this" and "He said that".' He was silent for a moment: then he growled, 'Look at the way he spoke to Sara; he actually made her cry and she's not the sort who cries easily.'

Lucy was too alarmed to care if this was a slight or not.

'Jamie, you must trust him!' she begged. 'You promised to trust him in spite of the bad things he had done. That was one of the conditions.'

'Maybe it was' – Jamie's jaw set stubbornly – 'but that was before I had seen him doing it. I don't think I could trust him now.'

'Oh, Jamie!' Lucy saw from his face that it was useless to argue with him and she began to be afraid. A terrible sense of disaster seemed to eat at the edges of her mind.

She knew, though she could not begin to explain it, that what was required of Jamie was an act of faith: he must give his trust to a man he knew to be unworthy of it, or there could not be a second chance. And if there was not . . .

'For Sara's sake,' she said desperately. 'You must trust him for Sara's sake.' Surely, she thought, this appeal would reach him.

'I can save her by myself,' said Jamie obstinately.

'But that's just what you can't do. You can't change the pattern single-handed. Mr Blunden said . . . '

'Mr Blunden said . . . ' Jamie did a very mean imitation of her voice, high-pitched with nervousness. 'I'm sick of hearing his name, Lucy. I tell you I can save them by myself. We know more or less what is going to happen and forewarned is forearmed. I shall get hold of the keys and when the fire starts I shall just unlock the door and let Sara and Georgie out.'

Lucy was too miserable to answer. She knew in her heart that it could not be that easy, and if anything happened to Jamie . . . Perhaps he would never get back; perhaps he would be altogether lost in Time. The silence lengthened as she struggled to find the words with which to convince him.

There were footsteps on the landing below.

'Quick!' said Jamie. 'We'd better get out of sight.'

'They can't see us,' said Lucy dully.

'Bella can, and it sounds like her step: light and a bit bouncy.'

They drew back into the shadows of the upper landing and it was indeed Bella. She came up the stairs to the nursery carrying a tray with two mugs of steaming milk and a plate of biscuits. She unlocked the door and went inside.

'Get the key,' hissed Lucy.

'It's no use,' said Jamie. 'If we take it now, so that she can't lock them in, she will tell her mother and the old battleaxe will move them to another room. We have to take the key without anyone noticing. When she comes out, we must follow her and see what she does with it.'

Five minutes later, Bella emerged with the empty mugs. She locked the door, put the key on the tray and went downstairs.

Jamie and Lucy tiptoed after her and reached the landing just in time to see her vanishing down the long corridor. As she arrived at the top of the main staircase, her mother joined her.

'Well, did they drink it all?' she demanded.

Bella nodded. 'They were real 'ungry,' she said, 'but Sara wouldn't eat the biscuits; she made Georgie 'ave them all.'

'Then let 'er go 'ungry, little fool,' said Mrs Wickens crossly, 'if that's all the thanks I get for me kindness.'

'It was more than they deserved after saying them awful things. I should 'ope they'd be very grateful to you.'

Mrs Wickens seized her arm. 'But you didn't say as I sent it?'

Bella squealed. 'Oh, Ma, you're 'urtin' me arm. I said as you told me, that I was doin' it secretly out of the kindness of me 'eart.'

A slow smile spread over the old woman's face. 'That's a good girl,' she said, 'only I don't want 'em to think I'm getting soft, see. Now be a good child and take that tray back to the kitchen.'

She took the key from the tray and, while Bella went on downstairs, fastened it to the great chatelaine of keys that hung from her belt. Then she smiled to herself. 'Me gettin' soft!' she repeated as if she found it amusing and she began to laugh.

'Quickly, now,' said Jamie who had been waiting his chance. 'We must get that key from her.'

'What do you think she meant ...' began Lucy, but

he was already away down the passage in pursuit of Mrs Wickens.

Lucy sighed and went after him.

It was a strange feeling to walk so close to the old woman knowing that she could neither see nor hear them.

Jamie turned to Lucy. 'Run ahead of her,' he said, 'and do something to make her stop.'

'But she can't see me.'

'Well knock something over, smash an ornament, anything so long as she stands still for a moment. If I try to undo the key while she's moving, she may feel it pulling.'

Lucy ran ahead of the old woman, almost brushing against her as she passed. She glanced back and it was rather unnerving to see that she really was invisible. It made her feel somehow less than human.

There was a vase on a side-table and she reached towards it. But it was an old vase of a lovely shade of blue and it looked strangely familiar. She realized suddenly that she had seen it before, that it stood in the drawing-room of the house in her own time. Does that mean that I can't break it, she thought, since it is still there a hundred years from now? Or if I do break it, will it be gone when I get back? Her hands were round it, but she hesitated.

'Oh, stop dithering!' Jamie's exasperated voice jerked her into action. She let go of the vase, then grabbing at a gilt-framed painting on the wall, swung it sideways so that it hung at a grotesque angle.

Mrs Wickens stopped dead and stared at the painting. 'Oh, my Gawd!' she exclaimed, 'that gave me a fright! Whatever made it move like that? Must be the wind, I s'pose.' She looked about her nervously, then reached up to straighten it.

Jamie took hold of the thin belt that held the chatelaine and cut through it with his penknife. But the heavy key-ring slipped from his grasp and fell to the floor with a crash.

The old woman swore and letting go of the painting, grabbed at her belt. 'Now me belt's broke,' she muttered crossly and she bent to pick up the key-ring just as James told hold of it. She saw it move in his hand and gave a frightened shriek. ''Elp, this place is 'aunted!' She made a sudden grab at the keys, taking Jamie by surprise, and tore them out of his hand. Then gathering up her skirts, she ran down the passage and into her room, slamming the door behind her.

Her ungainly figure with the fat legs and her awkward gait, made her look like a pantomime dame. Jamie thought that it would have been very funny if it had not been so serious. He ran to the door and tried to open it, but even as he turned the handle he heard her shriek again and the key grated in the lock.

Jamie stood and fumed at his own clumsiness.

Lucy tried to comfort him. 'It wasn't your fault,' she said. 'It just isn't time yet, so it's no use trying to change things.'

Jamie did not trust himself to answer. He snorted and stalked away towards the stairs.

'Where are you going?'

'I'm going to climb in through her window. We have to get those keys somehow.'

Lucy sighed. It was no use arguing with him. She wandered slowly after him. When she reached the blue vase, she stopped and touched it gently. I couldn't break it, she thought, because it still exists in our own time, just as the grave exists in the churchyard. She picked up the vase with a sudden urge to smash it, just to prove that she could change something. The light gleamed on the delicate blue glaze and she felt the wonderful shape in her hands. Carefully she set it down. But it is only because it is so beautiful, she told herself; I could do it if I wanted to. And she ran down the stairs after Jamie.

He was standing on the gravel outside, staring up at the house and trying to decide which was the right window. He calculated that it was the first room of the Victorian wing where fortunately the ivy had spread across from the old house. He tugged at the twisted stems to gauge their strength and then began to climb.

Lucy watched him anxiously. 'Oh, Jamie, do be careful,' she called. 'It won't help at all if you break a leg.'

But he reached the window without much difficulty and, peering in, found that he had indeed picked the right one.

Mrs Wickens, obviously in a state of shock, was lolling in a large armchair. There was a gin bottle on the table beside her and she had a full glass in her hand. Next to the bottle lay the ring of keys. If the window had been open, Jamie reckoned that he could have reached it, but as it was a chilly night and as the Victorians were not enthusiastic about fresh air, all the windows were tightly closed. Jamie felt desperate. He broke off a long twig of ivy and put it between his teeth in readiness. Then he reached in his pocket for his handkerchief and, winding it around his fist for protection, smashed the window pane.

He had guessed that the sound of breaking glass would

bring the old woman to her feet but he had banked on being too quick for her. He would poke the ivy twig through the window, pull the key-ring within reach and be away down the ivy with it before she could do anything.

But he had only the one free hand and when he picked the twig from between his teeth he was hampered by the handkerchief. He fumbled wildly and the twig slipped from his grasp. He pulled at another one, but by the time he had broken it off, it was too late. Mrs Wickens, alternately shrieking 'Ghosts!' and 'Burglars!', was already dragging the heavy inside shutters across the window.

Disconsolately, he climbed down to the ground where Lucy stood waiting.

'Maybe you're right,' he said. 'Maybe we can't change anything. We were fools ever to come.'

'Oh, don't say that.' Lucy could not bear to see him in despair. 'It's only because it isn't the right time. When it is, Mr Blunden will come.'

Even as Lucy spoke, there were footsteps on the gravel and they turned half expecting to see the old solicitor. But it was the big man and they stood very still, shrinking back instinctively into the shadow of the wall. As he passed by in the moonlight, they saw him glance furtively back over his shoulder.

'What do you think he gets up to?' whispered Lucy nervously. 'He's always shuffling around in the darkness. Last time I saw him, he was carrying a great bundle of wood.'

'I don't know.' Jamie was not really interested. 'I suppose Mrs Wickens makes him do all the dirty jobs around the place: fetch the coal and light the fires. He looks too stupid for anything else.'

'Light the fires . . . ' His casual words seemed to click in Lucy's mind with something else: something which she had been aware of ever since she came out of the house, but which she had not really registered. She sniffed and sniffed again. Then she grabbed Jamie's arm.

'What is it?' he said, sensing her sudden fear.

'Smoke!' she said and they stared at each other not wanting to believe it.

'Quickly,' said Jamie. He seized her hand and they ran along the gravel. As they reached the far end of the house, they saw that the library was already burning.

'I think the time has come,' said Jamie bitterly. 'Where is your Mr Blunden now?'

Chapter 11

Jamie's first reaction to the fire was a cold feeling of panic, a feeling that he would not be able to cope with what was happening. Ghosts he had found intriguing, moving out of his own time was an exciting adventure. But now, reality seemed to have overtaken him without warning and there were two lives at stake.

He stared at the dark windows of the nursery, high up on the second floor. There was no sound, no sign of movement, and he wondered if Sara and Georgie had fallen asleep. He picked up a handful of gravel and threw it up towards the window. Most of it fell short, but a few small stones pattered against the blank glass. There was no response: they were obviously sleeping. The stump of candle would have burnt out long ago leaving them in the dark, and it would be hard to keep awake then.

Lucy was staring at him expectantly. 'What can we do?' she asked anxiously. She felt somehow personally responsible for Mr Blunden's failure to appear.

Jamie considered the drainpipe. 'I might be able to climb it,' he began.

'Oh, no, you mustn't!' Lucy caught his arm. 'Remember what happened to Tom when he climbed it. The sexton said . . . '

'You mean, remember what *will* happen to Tom when he climbs it,' Jamie corrected her.

Lucy looked confused; then she saw what he meant. 'Of course,' she said, 'he is bound to come. You must stop him, Jamie.'

'No,' said Jamie gently but firmly, '*you* must stop him.' He put his hands on her shoulders and looked her in the eye, trying somehow to put courage into her timid heart. 'Listen,' he told her, 'we have got to separate for a while. I am going to the cellar to find an axe or something; since we can't get the keys I shall have to break down the nursery door. But someone must stay here to warn Tom and it has to be you. His life depends on it.'

Lucy swallowed hard; she was beginning to feel sick.

The whole thing was somehow going wrong. She had been so sure that Mr Blunden would come. She wondered if he could not come because Jamie had broken his promise to trust him. She felt certain that they could not do it alone. Jamie acted as though it was a simple matter of saving two children from a fire, forgetting that it had all happened a hundred years before. But Lucy knew that it was beyond their power to change the Pattern of the Wheel unaided.

She dreaded the thought of being alone again but she nodded and said, 'I'll stay here. I'll see that Tom is all right.'

'Good girl!' Jamie sighed with relief.

Lucy watched him go with a leaden heart. Suppose . . . suppose she should never see him again.

It was nightmarish when he had gone. The wind was high and clouds were blowing up over the moon. Within the library the fire had taken a firm hold, eating its way greedily through the books and bookshelves.

If only we could run to the telephone, thought Lucy, struggling to keep her mind on commonplace things, and call up a large friendly fire-engine with hoses and turntables and burly, reassuring firemen. It came to her with something of a shock that her life and Jamie's were full of everyday marvels that would make Sara and Georgie gape with astonished disbelief. She stared up at the darkened window, and thought of the instant miracle of electric light . . .

There were running footsteps in the night and out of nowhere Tom was suddenly beside her. His face was upturned towards the high window and he had not noticed Lucy.

'Miss Sara, Miss Sara!' he called frantically. 'Oh, Miss Sara, are you there?'

Lucy called his name but he was shouting too loudly to hear her. She ran forward and caught hold of his arm.

'Tom,' she said, 'it's me. Don't you remember? I'm Miss Sara's friend.'

Catching Sara's name, he paused and peered at her in the dim light.

'Why, 'tis you, miss,' he said. 'Is Miss Sara all right? Is she safe then?'

'Not yet, she and Georgie are still in the nursery. But Jamie has gone to find an axe to break down the door.'

'T'will be quicker by the drainpipe,' he said. 'I reckon they must be sleeping so I'll go on ahead and waken them.'

'Oh, but you mustn't,' Lucy told him, 'you see the drainpipe is dangerous, you are sure to fall.'

'Now don't you go fretting, miss,' he said reassuringly, "tis a new building and them pipes is as safe as houses.'

He moved away towards the wall.

Lucy ran after him. 'But, Tom, it isn't safe, really it isn't! You will fall and be killed; I know you will.'

Tom tried to be patient with her.

'Now, see here, miss,' he said and he thumped the big square drainpipe with his fist, 'don't that sound strong enough? Why, this part of the house weren't built above fifteen years back.'

Lucy had to admit that it did seem to be quite sound, but that only made her task harder. Tom had already taken hold of the pipe and was looking for a foothold.

She grew desperate. 'Oh, please don't, Tom. Really, you mustn't. I just know that you will be killed if you do. I can't explain how I know, but believe me, I do!'

He paused a moment and the moon lit up his face as he looked at her kindly. 'Happen I shall be killed,' he said simply, 'but there's some as a person would gladly die for. Miss Sara has been everything to me. There's not another soul in the world has a kind word for me, but Miss Sara ... she's so gentle, and she's teaching me to read and write. Oh, 'tis hard to explain, miss, but she's in danger now and if I knew as certain as tomorrow that I should break my neck, why, 'twouldn't stop me trying to save her.'

Lucy groaned and buried her face in her hands as he began to climb.

We can't change anything, she thought. I wish we had never, never, come. I don't want to see it all happen.

She forced herself to look up at Tom, stepping back to see him more clearly.

'It won't help Sara if you are killed!' she called angrily. 'You will only make things worse.'

She covered her eyes again, dreading to see him slip and fall.

If only that awful potion would wear off, she thought, and I could find myself back beside the sundial. If only Mr Blunden would come. If only there was something I could do!

A loud, harsh voice jerked her back to reality, and she saw the big man standing not six feet away from her.

'You come down, you sneaking brat!' he growled. 'I'll not 'ave you meddling.'

But Tom was out of reach, climbing steadily up the pipe which, to Lucy's relief, seemed steady enough.

'I'll 'ave you down off there, you little varmint!' The big man raised his hand and waved what looked like a heavy iron poker. He thrust it between the pipe and the wall and began to pull on it, grunting and groaning in the effort to force them apart.

It was a moment or two before Lucy realized what he was doing. She remembered with a gasp of dismay that the old sexton had only guessed that the pipe had been weak. No one could have known when the fire was over and the broken body was found, that the gardener's boy had not died accidentally.

Instinctively, she began to call for Jamie, but she soon realized that it was useless. For once she would have to act by herself.

Without pausing to consider the consequences, she rushed at the big man and, seizing the back of his jacket, began to worry at it like a determined terrier tackling an angry bull. She was too small to budge him but he was momentarily distracted. He turned with a roar and though he saw nothing, he struck out with his fist into the darkness. Lucy felt a blow that knocked her sideways and she fell heavily on to the gravel path.

When she staggered to her feet again, with her hands

and her knees bruised and sore, the big man had resumed his attack on the drainpipe, but Tom was almost at the top. Lucy saw him reach out, feeling for a hand-hold, but the window was shut.

Lucy shouted to Sara to open it but it remained dark and blank, the heavy curtains unmoving. She wondered how they could possibly sleep through so much noise and confusion.

With a hoarse grunt of triumph, the big man wrenched the bottom end of the pipe away from the wall, but Tom had grasped the window sill and was painfully hauling himself up.

'Sara, Miss Sara!' Lucy heard him call. 'For pity's sake, miss, open the window.'

The big man rocked the drainpipe from side to side but found it impossible to dislodge the gardener's boy. He paused, muttering angrily to himself, and seemed to consider what to do next. Then he snorted, picked up the poker again, and stepped back a little way. Lucy saw the gleam of broken teeth as he smiled and a look of cunning stole across his face.

Then his arm went back and, with a sudden lunge, he sent the heavy poker flying through the air towards the nursery window.

Lucy couldn't bear to see what followed.

She hid her face in her hands, but she could not keep out Tom's sudden cry of pain or the crashing thud in the bushes below the window.

Chapter 12

When Jamie left Lucy, it was not without misgivings.

He knew that she would be very nervous alone, that it would not be easy for her to wait patiently in the wind-moaning, owl-haunted night. But he also knew that she had her own sort of courage, not the kind that acts boldly, but the kind that endures. Lucy would not desert her post, of that he was certain, and, safe in the knowledge that Tom would be all right, he turned his full attention to the problem of Sara and Georgie.

Once inside the house, it took him a minute or two to get his bearings. But he found the cellar door unlocked and went down into the darkness, fumbling for a light switch until he remembered that there was none. What a fool I was not to bring a torch, he thought, I might have known

I should need one. He felt in his pockets and among the useful oddments without which he never felt dressed, he found a tattered book of matches. As he tore one out, his fingers told him that there were only two there.

I mustn't strike one, he thought, until I know what I'm looking for. I want the coal cellar, the one where Georgie was. There will be a chopper in there for splitting firewood.

He knew from the garden grating that this cellar would be by the outside wall, but he had lost his sense of direction on the winding stairs. He felt his way around the clammy walls, until he found a passage leading away. Then he struck his first match with care, and was rewarded with the glimpse of a door at the end of the passage. The brief light faded to a red glow between his fingers. He dropped the spent stub and hurrying through the darkness, pushed open the door.

A shaft of moonlight shone through the grating, and his heart leaped as he saw it gleam on a bright axe. The blade had been sunk deep into a log of wood by a strength far greater than his own. He seized it and pulled, but it was like trying to get the sword Excalibur out of the stone. In desperation he raised both axe and log high in the air and brought them down on to the floor with all his might. The axe rang clear on the cold stone as the split log fell apart.

Panting a little, he glanced around for anything else that might be useful. The moonlight caught the glass of a lamp hanging from the roof. He lifted it down carefully and opened it, and finding that the wick smelled of oil, he chanced his last match. The flame flared and then dulled to a soft yellow glow which lit up the dark corners of the cellar and showed him a coil of rope hanging behind the door.

There was no time to lose. Slinging the rope over his shoulder, he took the axe in one hand and the lamp in the other, and went back along the passage, but the axe was heavy, the lamp was awkward to hold, and the coil of rope kept slipping. He could see no further than the pool of light he carried, and he thought longingly of electric light and powerful, straight-beamed torches.

The sound of the fire grew louder as he reached the ground floor and made his way towards the stairs. It was a dull, gnawing noise with here and there a loud crack like the snapping of bones, as if the house were being swiftly devoured by some giant animal. As he walked resolutely towards it, he felt that he was walking into the animal's den.

If I read about this in a book, he thought it would seem like a bold, heroic exploit. But in fact, I'm only doing it because I can't think of any alternative. He could not even run to the rescue as people did in stories; he was too burdened by lamp and axe and rope to do more than plod doggedly up the stairs.

The smoke was growing thicker, and the bright circle of lamplight had contracted to a dim blur on the surrounding darkness. Worse than car headlamps in a fog, he thought gloomily.

There was something uncanny about the quietness of it all. A fire should be a scene of noise and confusion, bells ringing, people shouting, not this steady low roaring in the night. And why no sound from the nursery above? He was on the last flight of stairs now and had expected cries of alarm, fists pounding on the door, not this disturbing silence. A terrible suspicion seized him: he had read that most people in fires died of suffocation and the rising smoke grew thicker as he reached the top of the house ... The thought was unbearable and, reaching the landing, he broke into a run. Outside the nursery, he set down the lamp and, dropping the rope and the axe, hammered upon the door.

'Sara!' he called. 'Sara! Georgie! Are you all right?'

But there was only silence from the room beyond.

The door was stout and Jamie realized that he was wasting time. He gripped the axe in both hands and began to hack at the wood. It was not as easy as he had thought. Unlike the doors in films which are made of thin wood for the hero to destroy at a blow, this was of solid oak. If the axe came down with too much force, it bit deep into the wood and stuck there, so that he had to spend valuable seconds wiggling it up and down to loosen it.

A fit of coughing brought on by the dense smoke made him helpless for a minute or two, and he realized with a growing sense of urgency that he might well be overcome before the door was open. I ought to lie on the floor, he thought: the air is always clearer near the ground because the smoke rises. But what was the use of knowing all the sensible things to do in a fire, if you were too busy hacking down a door to bother with them?

He raised the axe angrily, and much to his relief, felt the wood splinter as it went through. But that was only the beginning. There was no key on the inside to be turned by stretching his hand through the hole. Before the door would open, he must cut out the lock completely.

He felt sick with the smoke he had swallowed and the fits of coughing that tore at his lungs. But the door was weakening. All at once, without warning, it gave way under a particularly heavy blow, so that he was caught off balance and stumbled forward into the room. The falling axe missed his foot by a fraction.

He turned back for the lamp and as the light fell inside the room, he saw with a rush of thankfulness that the well-fitted door had kept out the smoke. Now, however, it came billowing in, forming a blanket of darkness above his head. He turned hastily to slam the door and stood leaning against it, breathing the clearer air and trying to get some strength back.

In the corner of the room, just beyond the circle of the light, he could see Sara with her arm round Georgie, lying on the bed. Through all the splintering crashes of the axe on the door they had not stirred, and yet with no smoke, they could not have suffocated. He picked up the lamp and moved wearily across the room, half afraid to reach them. Suppose they were dead? Suppose the fire had been meant only to cover up a murder which had already taken place? And yet, they looked so peaceful as though they had simply fallen asleep.

He stood gazing down at them. He half stretched out

his hands to touch them, but he was afraid that he might find them cold.

I was wrong, he thought, I haven't changed anything. It wasn't possible for me alone, I should have trusted the old man, and now it is too late. However hard I try, there is always something I have not bargained for.

And then a tiny movement caught his eye. He held his breath, staring at the pillow where a strand of Sara's long, dark hair was moving gently. It lay an inch or two from Georgie's face and he realized with a surge of joy that the little boy was breathing. He reached out his hand and grasping Sara's arm, shook it roughly.

'Sara!' he said. 'Sara, wake up!'

But she lay quite still.

He put the lamp down on a nearby table and seizing her with both hands pulled her up into a sitting position. Her head fell forward and her steady breathing grew a little louder.

Jamie stared at her for a moment in disbelief. It was ridiculous that anyone should sleep so heavily, especially in a burning house. He shook her and called her name urgently, but she slept on. It was almost, he thought crossly, as though she had been drugged ... And then it all became clear to him: Bella and the mugs of hot milk,

Mrs Wickens alone in the passage, holding the empty tray and laughing. She had given the children something to make certain they did not wake during the fire and devise some means for their own escape.

He lowered Sara on to the pillow and stood for a moment baffled by this unexpected frustration.

But before he could think what to do, a sudden cry rang out.

'Sara! Miss Sara!'

It was very close at hand and coming, unlikely as it seemed, from just outside the window. In a moment he was across the room, pulling aside the heavy curtain. A tense, white face stared in from the darkness outside. Jamie struggled with the catch and threw up the window to find Tom staring up at him. His hands were strained to skin and bone as he clung to the window sill.

Without pausing to consider how or why he was there, Jamie leaned out and catching hold of him by the back of his jacket, hauled him inside. As he did so, Tom cried out and something struck the wall by the window with a clang and fell noisily into the bushes below. Glancing swiftly down, Jamie saw Lucy, her head buried in her hands, and the big man, snarling angrily as he stared up at them.

There was no time to speculate on what had happened. Tom lay in a heap on the floor trying to get his breath, and as Jamie crouched down beside him, he gasped, 'Miss Sara ... is she ... all right?'

'They're alive,' said Jamie, 'but they seem to have been drugged. It's a good thing you're here,' he went on, 'because we're going to have to carry them down the stairs.'

Tom scrambled to his feet and let out a yelp of pain.

'What is it?' asked Jamie anxiously.

'That Mr Wickens threw something at me. It caught my ankle and 'tis a bit damaged like.'

'Can you walk?'

'Oh, I'll walk all right if 'tis to get Miss Sara out.' His voice was bluff and confident but, seeing his face twist with pain, Jamie had his doubts.

He crossed to the door and opened it. As he did so there was a rush of wind and the flames leaped higher. He closed it again quickly and turned to Tom. 'It's the window,' he said, 'it's making a terrible draught. We must shut it or the stairwell will be like a giant chimney.'

The gardener's boy limped over to the window and wrestled with the sash. When it was safely closed, Jamie said, 'There's no point in opening the door again before we have to, it only lets the smoke in. Now the first thing is to find some water and damp a cloth.'

Tom looked bewildered. 'But 'tis wasting time . . . ' he began.

Jamie was tearing wide strips off one of the sheets. 'You haven't been through the smoke,' he said. 'It's suffocating out there; we'd never make it without something over our mouths.'

Tom found a copper water jug and turned it upside down. 'Not a drop,' he said mournfully.

Jamie cast around frantically. In one corner there was a small vase of wilted daffodils; he threw them out and with a mixed feeling of relief and repugnance, found a few inches of stale green water.

Damping the cloths, he tied one each over the faces of the sleeping children and showed Tom how to tie one over his own mouth and nose.

'Now,' he said, his voice muffled by the foul-smelling cloth, 'let's get them out of here as fast as we can.'

'I'll take Miss Sara,' said Tom.

It seemed sensible since the gardener's boy was bigger and stronger, but Jamie wondered about the weakened ankle. However there was no time to argue and he was about to hoist young Georgie across his shoulder when the door burst open behind them. It hit the wall with a shuddering crash, Tom gave a cry of dismay, and Jamie turned to see the big man. He stood in the doorway with the poker in one hand and an expression of scorn on his face.

'Did you think you 'ad me beat then?' he sneered at Tom. 'Did yer think I'd let yer play the 'ero, and spoil everything now?'

Tom was standing in front of Sara. 'You'll not touch her,' he said. 'You'll not lay a finger on either of them!' His eyes flickered from side to side as he searched for a weapon. Then he stooped suddenly beyond the ring of light and as he straightened up the lamplight gleamed on the edge of a blade. He faced the big man with the axe in his hands and his voice trembled a little; 'I'll kill you,' he said, 'before you shall touch her.'

Jamie's stomach turned over. He stared from one to the other, from the gardener's boy, cold with resolution and fear of what he might have to do, grasping the great axe with its icy blade, to the big man framed by the flames and the billowing smoke with the iron poker in his hand.

A momentary fear gleamed in the man's eyes as he saw the axe. He stepped backwards, taken by surprise, and lurched sideways against the doorpost. Jamie saw that he was drunk. He ran to Tom's side, 'You can't kill him!' he said. 'He doesn't know what he's doing.'

'I'm not minded to kill him if I can help it,' said Tom, 'though he well deserves it. But I'll keep his eyes off you while you drag Sara and Georgie out. Now get back into the shadows where he can't see you.'

It was hardly the moment, thought Jamie, to explain that the big man could not see him anywhere, but he was grateful for the freedom it gave him.

Tom moved forward into the circle of lamplight while Jamie edged round in the shadows behind him. He decided to take Sara first while he had most strength and, cautiously, he began to drag her towards the door. As he did so she stirred slightly and he saw a gleam of hope. He remembered that when people were drugged you had to walk them up and down to revive them. So he changed his hold on Sara, grasping her round the waist and throwing one of her arms across his shoulder. At first her feet dragged along the floor, but then he felt her take a few stumbling steps. As they reached the door, the big man lunged towards Tom and they were able to pass behind him unseen, out into the thick smoke on the stairs.

Jamie could hear the heavy trampling of feet and once the awful clash of steel on steel. But the shout that followed was more a grunt of frustration than a cry of pain and he dared not pause to look back.

Sara was now carrying some of her own weight and though her steps were uncontrolled, Jamie found that he could guide her without too much difficulty. As they reached the top of the stairs, she tried to speak but her voice was muffled by the wet cloth.

'It's all right,' he mumbled back, and his mouth was filled with the taste of wet daffodils.

She raised her head a little and he saw her eyes move searchingly above the white mask. Then he made out what she was saying. It was, 'Georgie?'

He had to lie. He hated it, but he knew that if he told her that her brother was still up there, she might fight to go back.

'He's safe,' he told her but his words were drowned by a crash from above, followed by a string of oaths. 'Safe!' he repeated. 'Now do come on!'

Sara seemed to accept his assurance without question, which made him feel worse in a way. But I will come back for him, he promised her silently. I'll see that he is safe. And he struggled on, step by step, keeping close to the wall for the flames were creeping up the well in the centre.

As they started on the last flight, he heard steps on the stairs above and glanced up anxiously, afraid that they might be pursued. But he could see only dark figures moving in the dense smoke and then a sudden gleam of flames on the axe blade as it struck the banister rail. He tore his eyes away. If he could only get Sara safely outside, he could go back and help Tom somehow. She was walking more easily now as they reached the bottom of the stairs. The fire was burning fiercely a little way along the passage that led to the library, but the smoke was less dense now that they were at ground level. Panting for breath, he half carried Sara the last few yards to the outer door and flung it open. With a roar the wind swept in and they stumbled through into the blessedly clean, damp coolness of the night.

He realized that the wind was a terrible threat to those still inside so he let Sara slip to the ground and turned to close the door. He knew that he had to go in again, but he also knew that unless he paused to fill his lungs with clean air, he might never make it.

He pulled the now blackened cloth from his mouth and drew a deep breath. Even as he did so, he heard a cry of joy through the dark night and Lucy came running.

'Oh, Jamie,' she said, 'I thought you'd never come!'

'I have ... to go ... back,' he gasped.

'Oh, Jamie, you can't.'

'It's Georgie,' he panted, 'and Tom ... got to help.'

'But Jamie ...'

'Look after Sara,' and before she could stop him, he had pulled the mask up over his face and plunged back into the building, closing the door behind him.

The first thing that met his eyes was the body of the big man. He lay at the bottom of the stairwell and it was obvious that he had fallen. It was equally obvious from the grotesque position in which he lay that he was dead.

Jamie ran up the stairs calling to Tom but there was no answer. He found him at the bottom of the second flight, his head and shoulders on the landing, his legs sprawling untidily upwards. He was quite still. Jamie uttered a silent prayer as he bent over him and could have shouted with joy when he found that the gardener's boy was still breathing.

I ought not to move him, he thought, in case there are broken bones, but I can't leave him here. As gently as he could, he grasped Tom under the arms and eased him along the landing to the lower stairs. He was much heavier than Sara, and Jamie could only drag him by moving backwards, feeling blindly for each step as he went.

He saw with dismay that the banisters were already burning. Fierce tongues of flame licked along them and the brown varnished wood first blazed and then blackened. His heart sank as he realized that he had yet another trip to make, that Georgie was still trapped in the nursery above.

I must not think of it, he told himself. I must concentrate on what I am doing.

They had reached the bottom of the stairs and now, at every step, they drew a little nearer to the door and the life-giving air beyond it. Three more steps ... two more ... one. He lowered Tom gently to the floor and turned the handle of the door. The sweet air roared in around them and the stairs seemed to explode into flames.

He found Lucy outside with Sara leaning against her. When she saw Tom, the older girl gave a cry and knelt down beside him.

'Oh, Tom!' She put out hand to touch him. 'Is he all right?'

'I think so. He's alive anyway.' Jamie straightened up

and rubbed his hand wearily over his blackened face. His eyes were sore from the heat, his eyeballs dry, his eyelids scratchy.

'But where is Georgie?' Sara seemed suddenly to remember him. She looked up at Jamie. 'Is he still up there?' Her eyes grew wild and she stared up at the nursery window. She rose to her feet but stumbled and Lucy had to steady her. 'I must get Georgie!' she protested.

'It's all right,' said Jamie, with a confidence he was far from feeling, 'I'm going to fetch him now.' Ignoring Lucy's cry of dismay, he turned and, taking one last gulp of cool air, he went back into the burning house.

Left behind in the garden where the leaping flames made monstrous shadows among the tossing branches of the trees, Lucy tried hard to be calm and strong. She drew a deep breath and fought down the urge to scream. She forced herself to turn her back on the house, to help Sara to drag Tom across the gravel on to the lawn.

And so it was that she did not see the dark figure of a horseman who came galloping up the drive, the broken carriage traces trailing behind him. The crunch of the children's feet on the gravel, and the roaring of the fire drowned the sound of the horse's hooves and the man's stifled cry of dismay. He slid to the ground and ran towards the burning building with the awkward gait of a man who is no longer young. In a moment he had passed into the house, and the heavy door slammed shut behind him.

The horse panicked at the sight of the flames and cantered away into the windy darkness.

Chapter 13

Jamie had known even as he closed the door behind him that it was impossible, and yet he had not turned back.

It's all my fault, he thought, for thinking I could do it alone. Lucy was right: I'm not just trying to save two children, I'm trying to change the Pattern of the Wheel. Mr Blunden said it could only be changed if he suffered instead, but now he is not here and there is only me.

He stared at the staircase; the carpet was blazing and the flames had begun to devour the wooden treads. I can't walk through it, he thought desperately, my shoes would bum and my clothes ... and coming back it would be even worse. He remembered the rope. The fire might not be so bad upstairs, it might be possible to lower Georgie from the window, he would not be so very heavy, not like Tom or Sara. If it was only possible to get up there.

He talked to himself reassuringly as if to a frightened horse; as if by persuading himself that he could do it, it would become possible. After all, he argued, I'm not even here really: this is all happening a hundred years ago. I'm not even born yet, so how can the fire hurt me?

Half-convinced, he took a deep breath and moved towards the inferno. But the heat met him like a glowing wall and beat him back before he even reached the flames.

I can't do it, he admitted at last, it isn't possible. Whether or not I have the courage, I just cannot walk into those flames and come out alive.

Desolation filled him, a terrible feeling of helplessness. Tears stung his eyes and involuntarily he cried out, 'I would if I could! Don't you see that it just isn't possible!' as if the sleeping child accused him.

A voice beside him said, 'Take my hand' and, turning incredulously, he saw the tall figure of Mr Blunden not thin and wraithlike but real and solid beside him.

'We will go together,' said the old man, 'and the fire will not touch you. It is not your fault, it is not your punishment, and it will not harm you. It will take all your courage for the flames will surround you and the floor will burn under your feet, but while you hold my hand, you will feel nothing.'

Jamie stared at him and fought against the doubt in his mind. If only I had not seen him that last time, he thought, if I could only think of him as good and kind . . .

' . . . it would be easier to trust him,' the old man finished the sentence which had been spoken only inside Jamie's head. 'That is what you were thinking?'

Jamie nodded miserably.

The old man sighed. 'Alas,' he said, 'it was not meant to be easy. To change the Pattern of the Wheel: it is not an easy thing. You must trust me not because of what I am, but in spite of it.'

'I think I understand now,' said Jamie.

Mr Blunden held out his hand. 'It is an act of faith,' he said gently. 'It is your trust that is necessary and your courage but not your suffering. Only you can act, but only I shall suffer.'

Jamie took the old man's hand and it was cold as spring water.

'It is time.' Mr Blunden's voice was strangely joyful. 'Look straight ahead of you,' he said, 'and do not be afraid.'

Jamie looked straight ahead of him and together they walked towards the fire. As they drew near the wall of heat, Jamie felt the edges of his mind shrivel in anticipation and yet he passed into the fire and felt nothing.

He lifted his feet and put them down on blazing carpet and crackling wood and his shoes, brown leather and rather muddy, remained unscorched. He grasped the burning stair-rail with his free hand but the skin stayed smooth and unblistered.

He realized that coolness was flowing into him from Mr Blunden's hand and a wild excitement filled him. Forgetting the old man's injunction to look straight ahead, he turned saying, 'It's incredible, I can't feel a thing,' but the words dried in his mouth at the sight of the old lawyer's face. Though the fire had not touched it, it was twisted with pain, and Jamie realized with a shudder that just as the coolness flowed into him from Mr Blunden's hand, so the pain that he could not feel flowed back into the old man.

'Look ... straight ... ahead!' The words came like a gasp and Jamie tore his eyes away. He stared upwards at the burning stairs and walked on, drained of feeling.

The flames were not so fierce on the second flight of stairs. Even the thick smoke seemed unreal. Jamie found that he could breathe in and out as easily as though he were in the garden outside, and he tried to close his ears to the sound of the old man coughing.

Georgie lay on the bed still sleeping soundly. Because he was much smaller than Sara, the drug had affected him more deeply and he made no movement as Jamie lifted him and slung him over his shoulder. To do this he needed both hands and he was forced to release Mr Blunden's hand for a moment. As soon as he did so, the choking smoke seemed to fill his lungs and the heat of the room brought him out in a sudden sweat.

He turned quickly and, taking hold again, moved with the old man towards the stairs. This time he knew better than to glance at his companion. He concentrated his attention on the problem of balancing Georgie over his shoulder. The strange immunity from harm seemed to envelop both of them, and as they reached the last flight of stairs where the fire was fiercest, Jamie moved into the flames without flinching. They roared and sucked about the woodwork, the carpet had quite vanished and the wooden steps were like glowing firewood, split and twisted and with all the substance gone out of them. And yet it did not occur to Jamie that they might not bear his weight.

He moved as if in an enchanted circle, as if he were freed entirely from the laws of nature. And so, he was thrown completely off balance when the weakened wood crumbled beneath his feet.

There was a strange singing in his ears, an unaccountable dizziness in his head. With no time to think, he acted instinctively. Tearing his hand from the old solicitor's grasp, he threw both arms around the unconscious child to protect him as best he could. Then he fell helplessly towards the flames.

The two girls in the windy garden were kneeling beside Tom, wiping his face with handkerchiefs damped in the dew-wet grass.

'Do you think he'll be all right?' asked Lucy, staring anxiously at his still form.

'I think so,' said Sara. 'His arm may be broken, I fear, and his ankle is badly swollen. But he breathes steadily and his face is warm.'

'And what about you?'

'Oh, I have suffered little harm,' Sara laughed shakily. 'I have a terrible headache, but that is a small price to pay for one's life.'

She moistened the handkerchief again and laid it gently

across Tom's forehead. 'We owe so much to your brother,' she went on. 'Although he is quite safe in Mr Blunden's care, yet the courage needed is very great and I think . . .'

Lucy had turned very pale. 'Mr Blunden didn't come,' she blurted out, 'Jamie went alone.'

Sara's hands were suddenly still. She turned her face slowly up and the grey eyes stared disbelievingly at Lucy.

'He has gone back alone?' she said.

Miserably Lucy nodded. 'He said he didn't think he could trust Mr Blunden after the way he treated you, that he would save you by himself. He said he would be all right,' she added lamely.

'But it is like a furnace in there! And I sent him back in again.'

Sara dropped the handkerchief and scrambled to her feet. 'I must go after him,' she said and began to run towards the house. But the drug had weakened her and before she had gone halfway, she crumpled and fell.

In a moment, Lucy was crouching beside her.

'I'm all right.' Sara's voice was shaky and uncertain, 'but my legs are weak. Oh, Lucy, we must try to help him. He is very brave, but so foolish to go alone.'

'I'll go,' said Lucy quickly. 'I'll go and see if I can find him.'

'Please hurry.' Sara clasped her hand anxiously. 'I would do anything in the world to save Georgie, but I would not sacrifice both of them.'

Lucy squeezed her hand but there was nothing she could say. She turned and ran towards the house and as she did so she heard a crashing sound from within. She forced the door open and the heat streamed out at her as if from an oven. Georgie lay a few feet inside the door, but beyond him the stairs had gone, only a mass of charred and twisted timbers remained.

Great sobs began to force their way through Lucy. 'Oh, Jamie, Jamie,' she said again and again. But even as she wept, she was gathering up the small boy who was unmarked, unharmed, and apparently sleeping.

She turned her back on the flames and went slowly out through the door, but grief was tearing her apart. She felt sick and light-headed and strangely thin, as if all that happened was no longer real.

She reached Sara and as she did, she let the limp form in her arms slip to the ground. She thought that Sara spoke to her, but she felt so ill, she could not hear or answer. Dimly she was aware of horses' hooves and carriage wheels, of voices crying out. She shook her head in an effort to clear it, and out of the darkness she saw the children's uncle running towards the house. His face was white, his round eyes staring, and he seemed to be shouting, but she could not tell whether it was for the children or for Bella that he feared. She could see no sign of the old lawyer.

She raised her voice accusingly, 'You are too late!' she shouted. 'You are always too late ...' but her words seemed to die on the passing wind.

The roaring of the fire filled her ears like the waves of the sea. Her head began to spin, faster and faster, it was like a giant whirlpool and she realized suddenly what was happening.

'Not without Jamie!' she screamed. 'I won't go back without Jamie!' But the scream was silent and everything grew dark.

When the darkness cleared, she was lying across the seat by the sundial and she was alone. The cold stone against her cheek felt very real, and, raising her head, she saw that it was a little after sunset. The last fading light in the sky caught the tops of the high trees and shone on the creeper-covered ruins of the library. It was very quiet; only a faint movement of wind among the leaves and distant owl-noises.

She felt as if she had just woken from a particularly unpleasant dream, but had forgotten the details.

Well, I don't think I want to remember, she thought, although it might have been fun to tell Jamie.

And then it all came rushing back and she knew that it had not been a dream. With a cry of fear, she sprang to her feet and ran towards the ruins. Somewhere in there Jamie must be, if he was not altogether lost in the far distances of Time.

She stumbled through the tall weeds and the all-consuming creepers. Nothing remained where the door had been but beyond there was a high decaying wall beside a broken archway. And Jamie lay still in a small, crumpled heap at the foot of the wall.

PART FOUR

Chapter 14

Lucy sat on the woodland stile, deep in thought. Bees droned and skimmed through the warm air and the scent of rotting mould was underlined by the pungent smell of bluebell leaves thrusting up towards the light. It was a good day for just sitting and breathing but Lucy's mind was on other things. She was trying to decide whether she should go on or go back.

It was Easter Sunday morning, nearly two days now. The memory of Jamie, lying still and silent against the white sheets, was like a dull pain inside her.

A bad fall, the doctor had said, difficult to tell if there was damage to the brain without a long, rough journey to the hospital ... unwilling to move him in his present state ... he may regain consciousness within the next twenty-four hours but if not ... He had peered into Jamie's eyes, shining a thin beam of light, and then frowned. Almost as though he had been drugged, he had muttered, more like a trance than a concussion ... The whole thing was very strange, very strange, not least the way the hair was singed on one side of the head.

I should have told him, thought Lucy, I should have told him that Jamie is lost somewhere in Time, somewhere we cannot reach him, and all because Mr Blunden was not there.

But what would have been the use? She sighed. Almost certainly he would not have believed her and would have thought her heartless to make a game of her brother's accident. Even if he did believe me, she thought, what could he do? I don't suppose even the most up-to-date hospitals are equipped with Time machines.

What could anyone do? Their mother had said, 'There is nothing we can do but pray,' and she had dispatched Lucy to the Easter service to say prayers for all of them. But it was really only to get me out of the house, she thought, away from all the reminders of a celebration none of us can face. She thought of the flowers she had arranged so carefully, the chocolate Easter eggs that lay untouched, the presents that no one had the heart to open.

She swung her feet idly, kicking the rail of the stile. I could have prayed at home, she thought; I could even sit here by myself and pray all morning and God might hear me better without all the others around me, praying for something different.

But she had not argued with her mother, for it had suddenly seemed that if there was any answer to be found, she would find it in the quiet grey stones of the churchyard.

For the first ten minutes she had run all the way along the footpath that switchbacked through fields of sprouting corn. But at the edge of the wood she had paused, short of breath and with a stitch in her side, and now that she had recovered, she was afraid to go on.

Suppose nothing had changed? And yet, how *could* anything be changed? Imagine the vicar's astonishment, the outcry from the sexton, if they arrived one morning to find that one of the graves had disappeared ... two really, although if Tom's was not marked, perhaps they would not notice the difference. It was just not possible to make gravestones vanish. Once in London, when she was very young, she had tried to move a mountain, though it was only a small hill really. She had sat in church listening earnestly to a sermon about faith moving mountains, and she had decided to move Highgate Hill. But though she had screwed up her eyes and covered her ears in an ecstasy of concentration, her faith had moved nothing.

I can't still be as silly as that, she thought. I'm not a child any longer. I can't really go racing up to the churchyard expecting to find an empty patch of lawn or a yawning hole surrounded by a crowd of astonished villagers.

And yet, she thought desperately, if it is all just the same, what does it mean? Did we dream it, and if so, where is Jamie? not the pale, still, silent figure in the bed at home, but the real Jamie. If only he were here, he would know what to do. But that's silly because if he were, there wouldn't be any problem. Her mind buzzed and darted as confusingly as the small striped flies which hovered around her on wings of moving air.

She tried to decide what Jamie would do if he were sitting on the stile and she were lying in bed. *He* would go straight up to the churchyard and look, she told herself, but then he is braver than I am.

Nevertheless, she climbed down from the stile and

began to walk resolutely up the hill through the trees. The steady sound of the bell flowed down to meet her and when she reached the churchyard, the last of the congregation were disappearing into the ivy-covered porch. A flapping verger came hurrying round the corner and hustled her inside. The smart hats rose in unison like a flock of startled butterflies, and the first hymn was under way.

Jesus Christ is risen today.
Alleluia!

Lucy sang instinctively, and her gloom seemed to lighten as the words and the music bore her up. She tried hard to keep her mind on the service, and though it kept drifting back to the silent bed and the grey leaning stone, yet something of the joy of Easter came through to her. She prayed hard for Jamie and when she rose from her knees she felt strangely comforted. The service drew to a close, and she was tempted to hurry home without looking at the gravestone. But it seemed like a challenge, as if by going to see it, she declared her belief that what had happened had been real, and her faith that everything might still be well.

She slipped out of her pew while the bright hats were still hesitating reverently, and hurried round to the back of the churchyard. It was very quiet and the grey stones stood above their offerings of bright daffodils as if they had been there before even the church itself. The smooth turf still lay like a vast blanket over the hummocks of the sleepers beneath. Nothing had been disturbed; nothing had changed.

Lucy tried to remember exactly where the grave had been. She knew that there was a seat opposite, and that it was somewhere on the right-hand side not far from a spreading yew-tree. It should be about here, she thought, stopping by a broken column which looked familiar. She glanced around and a carved death's head grinned up at her. It leaped up in her memory and she hurried on to the next grave only to find a tall, remarkably ugly monument in pink-veined marble.

I've obviously got it wrong, she thought. The graveyard must be full of carved skulls and broken columns. She cast about for some remembered feature that would guide her. In any case, it's no use, she told herself, it's obvious that nothing has changed, nothing is missing. Jamie was right, you can't change what is already past, just as I couldn't break the blue vase. And yet ... she hesitated, torn between going and staying, and as she did so, she noticed the inscription carved on the pink monument:

THE GOOD SHEPHERD

GIVETH HIS LIFE

FOR THE SHEEP

Her eyes blurred without warning as the words brought back the memory of Jamie. If he died, she thought, no one would ever know that he had been trying to save Sara and Georgie. No one would put up a memorial to him with a tribute carved upon pink marble. They would think he had died foolishly climbing the wall in some childish prank. She stared angrily at the over-decorated monument:

FREDERICK PERCIVAL BLUNDEN

who gave his life to save

the children in his care

Lucy's heart seemed to miss a beat. She swallowed hard and glanced nervously at the date below. Yesterday, she thought, but a hundred years ago! She looked frantically around for the children's small grey stone, but it was not there. She fought off a panicky feeling of unreality and hurried away along the gravel path. When I feel a bit better, she thought, I'll walk back and it will be the same as it was yesterday because it can't be different, it just isn't possible.

But when she had regained her composure and returned past the broken column and the carved death's head, the pink memorial was still there. Her knees felt weak. She sat down suddenly on a seat near by and stared disbelievingly. It *is* possible to change the past, she thought; Jamie did it. The children's grave had gone because they did not die, and the monument is here because Mr Blunden did. And that means that he *was* there and Jamie wasn't alone after all. She felt a glimmer of hope.

It was now perfectly clear to her what had happened, but her mind boggled at the thought of what other people would make of it. Suddenly, overnight in a small country churchyard a small grey gravestone had vanished and a massive marble monument had appeared in its place. Perhaps no one else has noticed it yet, she thought; perhaps it will cause a terrible commotion when they find out, with pictures in the papers and the churchyard full of television cameras.

She stared at the pink monstrosity with a sinking heart: she felt personally responsible for it. Suppose they should ask her to explain? She wished that Jamie were with her; he would know what to say. She rose to her feet, suddenly reluctant to be caught looking at it. She had a feeling that there were terrible penalties for tampering with gravestones.

She had once read in the paper about someone digging up a churchyard, something about sacrilege, or blasphemy, or even worse, witchcraft. Yes, that was it, something about black magic. She felt certain that whatever she and Jamie had done, it was not black magic, but would anyone believe her if she had to tell them about the ghosts and the brewing of the potion? She pictured the sour, disbelieving face of the magistrate. What would the penalties be for black magic? The boy next door in Camden Town had been sent away 'in need of care and protection' for something far less awful than spiriting away gravestones.

She glared at the hated monument and groaned. 'It's so big,' she said aloud, 'and so ugly. No one could fail to notice it.'

She jumped about a foot in the air as a hand fell on her shoulder and the vicar's pleasant voice said cheerfully,

'I'm afraid the Victorians were over-fond of the gaudier aspects of grief. Give me a simple grey headstone any day.'

Lucy took this as a personal reproach and she said apologetically, 'I suppose it must have been rather a shock to you.'

The vicar smiled. 'Well, I wouldn't put it as strongly as that, though I did wince a little when I first saw it. But during the ten years or so since I've been here, I seem to have grown rather fond of it. And you know, the old gentleman it commemorates was a rather wonderful person.

'Many years ago, there was a terrible fire up at the Old House where you are living now, and two children were trapped there. The old man was their guardian and he had been to dine at the house. As he was being driven home, the carriage broke down and looking back the old man saw the flames in the distance. He seized one of the horses and rode headlong back to the house. Rushing into the burning building, he saved the little boy, but the strain must have been too much for the old man for he collapsed and died.'

Lucy stared at the marble monument. 'Then it has always been there?' she said stupidly.

The vicar looked at her curiously. 'For about a hundred years,' he said.

Lucy thought about it. 'Perhaps I'm in the wrong place,' she said. 'I was looking for a little grey stone.'

'Well now, we have a great many of those. Do you by any chance know the inscription?'

Lucy hesitated and a strange uncertainty took hold of her. The vicar seemed to see nothing wrong with his churchyard. Her common sense told her that the monument had been there all the time, that she just hadn't noticed it before. And yet, it was so very noticeable. Then she thought, If we have really changed the past, then the monument *would* have been here all the time, and the children's grave would not have been here at all. But at the same time, she and Jamie had seen it, or rather not at the same time, but in a different time ... Her head was beginning to ache with the effort to make sense out of it all.

She said cautiously, 'It may not be here at all, but someone told us there was a grave of two children who died in the fire.'

'No, no,' said the vicar patiently. 'As I explained, the two children were saved, one by the old man and the other by the gardener's boy, or so the story goes.'

'Oh,' said Lucy, thinking hard. 'I'm afraid I didn't listen very carefully. Is that where the gardener's boy is buried, that little unmarked grave under the tree, where the forget-me-nots grow?'

'Forget-me-nots!' the vicar laughed jovially. 'Nettles and nightshade, from what my old sexton tells me. He's always complaining about them.'

Lucy frowned nervously. 'But he was the one who told us about the forget-me-nots,' she said, 'and the gardener's boy and the children.'

The vicar sighed. 'Well, my dear,' he said, a little sadly, 'he is an old man and perhaps he gets a little confused. He has always insisted to me that it was the grave of two drunken servants who died in the fire. One was the old housekeeper who was overcome by the smoke. They say she had been drinking heavily and had locked herself in her room. The other was her husband who died from a fall; some say that he was mad and that he started the fire. I don't know if there is any truth in it, I'm sure, but the old man insists that the nettles are caused by what he calls "the evil comin' up from below". He tells me that weed-killer is useless and he wages a constant battle with them.'

Lucy gave up. 'It's all beyond me,' she murmured. 'Here one minute and gone the next; first it's forget-me-nots, then it's stinging-nettles. I wonder if Jamie would understand it.'

The vicar considered this remark and decided that it was beyond him too. Children's conversation was so elliptical. He changed the subject.

'And where is your brother today? It's not often I see you alone. And your mother too? I hope the walk did not prove too much for her?'

Lucy's face darkened. 'It wasn't the walk,' she said, 'we are used to walking. It's Jamie; he . . . he had an accident, a fall, in the ruins and he's still unconscious. He's been unconscious since Friday night and . . . ' The words came tumbling headlong and then, before she could stop them, the tears followed. 'The doctor says if he doesn't come round soon, they will take him away to the hospital, and I just know he'll never come back!'

She broke off and searched for a handkerchief but in the confusion of setting out, neither she nor her mother had thought of one. She sniffed hard and wondered whether it would be worse to let her nose run or to wipe it on her sleeve.

The vicar bent down and handed her a large handkerchief of remarkable whiteness. 'My poor child,' he said. 'I had no idea! Now do dry your tears and tell me how it happened. There must be something I can do to help.'

Lucy took the handkerchief rather gingerly. It seemed almost sacrilegious to use it, like blowing her nose on the white, billowing surplice he wore. But the alternative was worse, so she snuffled gratefully among the snowy folds until she felt more presentable. Then she emerged and said, 'He was ... trying ... to save ... them.'

As soon as she had said it, she was sorry. It would be so difficult to explain and she was not absolutely sure that there was not some magic in it somewhere. The vicar could hardly approve, even if it was more white than black. But her words had been lost among her hiccuping sobs, and the vicar only said,

'Now, now! you just take things easy, while I go and take this fancy dress off. Then I'll drive you home.'

As the little car bowled jerkily along the country road, Lucy and the vicar sat in a companionable silence. There was something she badly wanted to ask him before they reached the house, but she didn't know how to put it. She couldn't think how to ask the question without having to explain it. And yet, she felt that if anyone knew the answer, the vicar might.

At last she coughed nervously once or twice and then said, 'Do you think it would be possible to die to save someone who had already died before you were born?'

The vicar took his eyes off the road to glance at her curiously. But the car promptly hit a pothole and he hastily turned his attention back to his driving.

'Well,' he began cautiously, 'that is what Our Lord did. He died to save all of us, those born before Him and those born after Him. And that is why today is a day of rejoicing for us all.'

Lucy sighed, but said nothing. He didn't even begin to understand what she was talking about. But then, why should he? She didn't understand what had happened herself, and she had been there. Jamie was the only one who might know, and he might never come back to explain it all.

What had happened after he went back into the house? The inscription on the monument seemed to prove that Mr Blunden had been there after all. But if so, what had gone wrong? The old man had promised that Jamie would come to no harm, but could she trust him?

The vicar heard her sigh and immediately regretted his tactlessness.

'You must forgive me,' he said humbly. 'I know it is not a happy day for you, but we must try to have faith.'

'To have faith,' thought Lucy; that had been one of the conditions for Jamie, perhaps it was also meant for her. In the beginning, Jamie had said, 'You must trust him too,' and she had answered, 'I will try.' Now the time had come. Maybe she couldn't move Highgate Hill, but if Jamie's faith could change the Pattern of the Wheel, then hers would bring him back from the farthest corners of Time.

She closed her eyes and concentrated very hard but it didn't seem to do any good. Perhaps faith isn't like that, she thought. Perhaps it isn't something you force yourself to, a battle that you fight in your mind, but something that comes when you stop fighting, when you admit that you can't manage it alone. And then it just grows in you, like bluebells coming up out of dark decaying despair.

She smiled at the thought, and realized with a start that the vicar had been talking all this time. She tried to look as if she had been listening.

'Somehow,' he was saying, 'I just cannot believe that anyone could come to harm on such a joyful day as this.'

Lucy stared out of the window as they went up the long drive. Everywhere the green buds were breaking, the daffodils trumpeted, and the birds sang. He was right, she thought, it was a day for living, not for dying.

A load of grief seemed to lift from her mind as the Old House came into sight, and as soon as she saw her mother in the doorway, even before she began to wave, Lucy knew that Jamie was all right.

Chapter 15

Lucy clambered out of the vicar's car before it had quite halted and running across the driveway, she threw herself into her mother's arms.

'Jamie is awake,' said Mrs Allen, and the words seemed to spin in Lucy's head. 'He just woke up, quite suddenly, about ten minutes ago, almost as if he had just been sleeping. Only, I think he was a bit confused because he said, "I'm sorry, I got held up", as if he had been on a journey instead of falling off a wall.'

'Can I go up and see him?' asked Lucy. 'Can he talk or will it tire him?'

'I don't think so,' her mother sounded puzzled. 'He seems to be full of energy and he keeps asking whether he can get up. I hate to keep him in bed when he's fretting so but I've told him he must wait until the doctor has been. I shouldn't like him to have a relapse or something and anyway the doctor will be here in half-an-hour.'

Listening to her voice chattering on, Lucy realized with a start that her mother sounded as she used to in the old days, before everything began to go wrong. Their father had always teased her for being talkative, but when the long, sad days came and she rarely spoke at all, Lucy and Jamie had come to long for her rambling sentences.

Lucy stood back a little and looked at her mother wonderingly. Her face was flushed and strangely gay. Lucy hugged her suddenly. 'Oh, Mummy,' she said, 'we do love you!'

Mrs Allen looked down at her and smiled, a rather awkward, crooked smile. 'I know,' she said, 'and I haven't been very fair to you, have I?' She hesitated a moment and then said, 'For a while, I thought I had lost Jamie too, and I suddenly realized how much I still have to be grateful for. I shan't forget again, Lucy.'

She stooped impulsively and kissed her daughter. 'Now run and see Jamie and stop him getting up, while I go and get the vicar away from his car. He's pretending to look at the engine, but I think he's just afraid of intruding.'

Lucy went scampering away up the stairs.

Jamie was sitting up and looking very normal. The bed which had been so smooth and white, was now a rumpled mess. There were rejected books all over the place, and the eiderdown was on the floor.

Lucy had pictured a touching, rather tearful reunion after all that had happened, but he only scowled at her as she came in the door and said, 'For heaven's sake, why can't I get up?'

'You have to wait until the doctor's been; Mummy said so. But he won't be long,' she added hastily seeing that he was about to argue.

Jamie snorted crossly and said nothing.

'Are you . . . all right?' asked Lucy cautiously. It seemed a vague enough question to be safe, for she sensed that she was treading upon dangerous ground. If Jamie had forgotten everything, she knew that she would never be able to explain it all, so it seemed wiser not to ask any leading questions.

'Of course I'm all right,' Jamie frowned. 'Just because I fell off a wall or something . . .' He paused, watching Lucy's face, wondering whether she had any idea what had happened to him. It was possible that he had dreamed the whole thing, including Lucy being there. Or if it was real, he could not tell how much she might, or might not, remember. He did not think he could possibly make her understand unless she already knew.

For a few minutes they sat in silence half-watching each other, like boxers looking for an opening. Then Lucy's curiosity won. She took a deep breath and said firmly,

'Well, where have you been, then?'

'Been?' asked Jamie warily.

'You know very well that we should have arrived back at the same time, but you didn't, and you couldn't have been *there*, so where were you?'

Jamie's face split open in a grin of delight. 'Then you do remember,' he said.

'Of course, *I* remember,' said Lucy indignantly. 'I didn't go rushing around in burning buildings, falling off walls and getting concussion or whatever. The question is, do *you* remember, and if so, where have you been since sunset on Friday evening? It's nearly two days, you know.'

Jamie looked surprised. 'Is it really as long as that?' he said wonderingly. 'It only seems like a few hours.'

But he did not begin to explain. He just sat there with an infuriating far-away look in his eyes.

'Well, don't go broody,' said Lucy rather acidly, 'tell me!'

'M-m-m ...?' Jamie seemed to gather his thoughts from a world away as he turned to stare at her. Then he said, 'I don't know if I can explain everything ...' and as Lucy began to protest, he went on, 'but I'll tell you as much as I remember. Only, you see, it isn't easy to sort it out in my own mind.'

He paused, with a frown of concentration, and Lucy tried hard to keep her patience.

'I remember ...' he began, 'I remember that I was with Mr Blunden, but I don't know where we were or how we came to be there. I had meant to come straight back as you did ... that was after the stairs gave way and I fell.' The awfulness of the memory caught him unawares and he had to struggle to put it out of his mind. 'Well, anyway, the old man kept saying that I must go with him and I thought, at first, that I was dead!'

He said it hesitantly as if the memory was embarrassing, and then, as if to justify his own foolishness, he went on quickly, 'I had let go of his hand, you see, I couldn't help it or I should have dropped Georgie, and he had said that I should be safe as long as I kept hold of it.'

Lucy found it very hard to follow. She wanted to interrupt, to ask a dozen questions, but she sensed that if once she broke the fine black thread of his thoughts, he might never find the broken end again in the darkness of his memory.

'So you see, when I let go, I thought perhaps I would die. But it couldn't be helped, it was just the way it happened ... And when I found I was alone with Mr Blunden in a dark empty sort of place, I didn't like to ask him whether I was dead ... in case he said "Yes". So I just said "I ought to go back to Lucy" because I knew you would be worried if you found you were alone. But the old man didn't seem to hear me. He just said, "It will not take very long, but I'm certain it will help my case if they see you."'

'Well, I had no idea what he was talking about,' Jamie sighed, 'but I went with him because I didn't know how to get back here by myself and I thought anywhere was better than being *nowhere*, which was where we seemed to be then.

'The next thing I knew was that we were in a vast room and there was a long, long, table, so long that I couldn't even see the far end of it. It was weird, Lucy, a sort of Alice-in-Wonderlandish feeling because along both sides of the table there were hundreds of lawyers, all in wigs and gowns, and they were all looking at Mr Blunden.' Jamie laughed suddenly as he remembered the scene.

Lucy stared at him anxiously. It was hardly what she had expected. She wondered if it could be the after-effects of the concussion. If he gets too excited, she thought, I shall have to call Mummy.

But he stopped laughing after a moment and went on, 'Then one of the lawyers stood up, and he began to speak as if he were in court. It was all in legal language and I didn't understand half of it, but I did gather that Mr Blunden had been accused of negligence, something about the line of inheritance being destroyed. He had been struck off, just as he told us, although seeing that he was dead anyway, I couldn't see why it mattered. I mean a lawyer couldn't practise law in Heaven, could he?'

Lucy considered. 'Oh, I don't know,' she said. 'They might let him if it was what he liked doing most. He couldn't sing hymns all the time; he might even be tone-deaf like you.'

Jamie thought this dig was beneath his notice. 'Well, who would they practise on?' he demanded.

'Each other,' said Lucy promptly.

Remembering the long table of lawyers, Jamie thought she was probably right, so he gave up the argument.

'Well, anyway,' he said, 'the fellow who was doing all the talking was asking them to put the old man's name back on the list again, because he had made amends and put everything right. They all started talking it over and I just stood there in a sort of "cloud of unknowing" because I couldn't see what it had to do with me.

'I was just asking the old man for the umpteenth time whether I could come back, and trying to explain that you would be having kittens, when a voice asked, "Is this the boy?" and I saw that they were all looking at me. I was afraid they were going to ask me to give evidence, and that I should have to tell them all about the fire ... but all they did was to ask my name. When I told them, they all nodded, and the lawyer said, "I submit these documents in evidence." He handed them some papers and they all looked at them and tut-tutted and passed them from one to the other all the way down the table. It was such a long table, I couldn't even see who was sitting at the far end and I thought it would take years for all of them to read everything. But before long, a voice came from the other end of the table; it was loud and clear and I suppose it was the judge. And it said, "Frederick Percival Blunden, we have considered the evidence before us and we are satisfied that you have restored the pattern as it was intended to be." It went on to say that Mr Blunden would be reinstated as a lawyer, and when he heard that, the old man's face lit up like a Christmas tree. He grabbed my hand and started babbling about courage and fortitude and eternal gratitude. He said a lot of other things too, but I wasn't really listening. He was getting so emotional, I was afraid he was going to kiss me at any moment, and I was racking my brains to think how I could get away.

'Then I realized that we were alone somewhere and the table and the other lawyers had all disappeared. The old man seemed to have calmed down a bit, so I tried to concentrate on what he was saying. But his words were like a loudspeaker van going past in the street; I could hear him, but I couldn't make out what he was saying.

'Everything began to grow misty and confused, my head was spinning, and the next thing I knew, I was sitting up in bed and Mother came and cried all over me and wouldn't let me get up.' He paused and shrugged his shoulders. 'And if you can make head or tail of all that,' he told Lucy, 'perhaps you'd explain it to me!'

Lucy thought about it. 'It's a pity you didn't listen more carefully to what Mr Blunden was saying.'

Jamie frowned. He could not help agreeing with her but he hated to admit it. 'You know how I hate being kissed,' he said defensively.

Lucy sniffed. 'I don't suppose he was going to; I mean, you're not exactly irresistible.'

Jamie's frown became a scowl, and Lucy realized with a sudden pang that they were on the point of quarrelling. And half-an-hour ago, she thought, I was afraid I might never be able to talk to him again. She felt a strong urge to kiss him herself, but he looked very hostile and it was more than she dared. She changed the subject.

'I went to the churchyard,' she said. 'The children's grave has gone,' and she told him about the gaudy pink monument.

Jamie was delighted though he did not seem surprised. 'Of course, I knew we had changed the pattern,' he said, 'but it's nice to have proof that things are different.'

'No one else seems to have noticed the change,' Lucy told him.

'Well, I suppose they wouldn't. After all, if we went back a hundred years to change things, then they must have been changed for as long as anyone can remember.'

Lucy found it very confusing. 'I don't think I really understand this Wheel of Time business even now,' she said.

'Oh, I don't understand it,' said Jamie cheerfully, 'but then I don't understand television either. But when you've seen it working, you can't help believing in it.'

Lucy had to admit that he was right.

'And what about Mr Blunden and the lawyers?' she asked, feeling rather put out that she had not shared this part of the adventure. 'I suppose that was just a dream, because of the concussion or something.'

Jamie considered. 'It was very like a dream,' he admitted. 'It wasn't real, like Sara and Georgie or even Bella and the Wickenses. And it didn't seem like a real place, nothing to see or touch. But I think it was real to old Blunden and the others. I mean, it wasn't as if I had dreamed it up inside my head, more as if I had stumbled upon a place where I had no right to be.' He struggled for a minute to find a better way to explain it and then gave up.

'Do you think Mr Blunden was ... well ... dead?' asked Lucy awkwardly. 'The vicar said the strain was too much for him, that he died soon after the fire.'

Jamie's face darkened as he remembered how the old man had suffered. 'I suppose he was,' he said, 'but I'd rather not talk about it.'

'The vicar said the Wickenses died too,' Lucy told him.

Jamie didn't answer. It was all very well if you thought of them as bad characters in a story, but he could only remember a hysterical old woman screaming 'Ghosts!' and a crumpled body at the foot of the stairs. But if they hadn't died, he told himself, it would have been Sara and Georgie and Tom. He made himself think of something else.

'What about Bella and Bertie?' he asked. 'Did the vicar say what happened to them?'

Lucy shook her head. 'He didn't mention them,' she said, 'and I didn't like to ask in case he wondered how I came to know about them.'

'I rather liked Bella,' said Jamie, 'she was very pretty.'

Lucy snorted. She thought Sara much prettier with her dark hair and grey eyes.

'She was a bit plump,' Jamie admitted, 'but I wouldn't have called her hair "mousy", more a sort of golden colour.'

'She probably married that pop-eyed Bertie,' said Lucy. 'She would have been an orphan after the fire, so it wouldn't matter if he didn't inherit the money or the house or anything.' She pictured them living in a tiny flat, with Bella doing her own scrubbing in a thread-bare dress like Sara's, and for a moment she was glad. Then she remembered what it was like to be poor, and it seemed mean to wish it on anyone. So to unwish it she said aloud and rather primly, 'I'm sure I hope they were very happy. Maybe Bella went back on the stage or something.'

But Jamie was not listening anyway. When she mentioned the house, Lucy had broken his dream and fragments of it came back to him. He sat up abruptly.

'Lucy,' he said, 'I've just remembered something Mr Blunden said, in between telling me how wonderful I was. It was about the house. He said, "The house will be safe; the family will go on," or something like that. And then he said, "That young fellow, what's-his-name ...?"'

'Smith,' said Lucy automatically.

Jamie ignored the interruption. '"... That young fellow, what's-his-name, will be down to explain everything." Well, that must mean that they've traced the real owners, or at least that they soon will.'

Lucy looked dismayed. 'Oh, I hope not!' she said.

Jamie was surprised. 'But why?' he said. 'It's a shame to see it empty and the gardens all neglected and the pool choked with weeds. It would be super to be able to take the dust-sheets off and get the fountain working.'

'It would be nice for the house and the new owners,' Lucy agreed, 'but what about us? They wouldn't need a caretaker any more, and we should have to go back to Camden Town.' She wondered if it was a judgement on her for wishing Bella and Bertie into poverty. Perhaps *their* descendants would come and turn them all out of the Old House. 'I'd rather it fell in ruins,' she said miserably, 'and the garden was a wilderness, than that we should have to leave it!'

Jamie's face fell. 'I hadn't thought of it like that,' he said and it was true. He felt that he had known the Old House for a hundred years, which in a way he had, and it had grown to be a part of him. It had never occurred to him that when the Latimers returned, he would have to leave it for ever. 'I suppose that if I hadn't helped the old man to put things right,' he said slowly, 'then they would never have found the rightful owners and we could have been caretakers for ever.' He sounded quite indignant, as if he had been grossly deceived.

Lucy thought it would be bad for him to get too worked up, so she said soothingly, 'Well, we had to help, anyway, because of Sara and Georgie. At least they lived to grow up and have ordinary lives instead of dying as children. That's more important than us going back to Camden Town.'

'I suppose so,' said Jamie, 'but it does seem a bit hard. After all, we are here and now, and they were a long time ago.'

'It depends what you mean by "time",' said Lucy.

'Oh, don't let's start that all over again!' Jamie sighed

and gave the whole thing up. 'The only time I want to hear about now,' he said firmly, 'is lunch-time. So go and tell Mother that I'm starving.'

But Lucy had a better idea. Forgetting all about Sara and Georgie, Bertie and Bella, she ran off downstairs, two at a time, to fetch the Easter eggs.

Chapter 16

Easter had passed. Low Sunday had come and gone, week followed week until Whitsun was upon them, and still there had been no news.

Lucy and James felt that every day brought Camden Town a little closer, and every day they loved the Old House more. And yet they were not unhappy for their mother was her old self again. When she laughed, or when the sound of her music reached them about the house, they felt that even Camden Town might be a cheerful place. But the spring days were fine and each morning the gardens seemed more beautiful as new flowers struggled up to the sun. Lucy, who had never really had a garden before, worked for hours at a time to clear the choked flower beds and her heart ached when she thought of leaving it all.

And now, at last, the lawyer had come as they had known he would, with a look of triumph on his face and a briefcase full of important documents.

Lucy had taken refuge in the attics. High up under the roof, higher even than the servants' rooms, hot and airless under the roof-tiles, were the store-rooms, silted up with the discarded jumble of several hundred years. Old clothes, old clocks, old toys, old books, which had once been swept along in the strong current of everyday life, now lay in comers like the tide-wrack along the beach, serving only to show where life had been.

All these things had been cherished once for their beauty or their usefulness, or just for the warm familiarity of their presence. Now they were cast aside and forgotten. Just as we shall be, thought Lucy, now that we have served our purpose.

Sometimes, it seemed to her that the house had brought them there for its own ends. We are like the plumbers, she thought, called in because the life-supply has dried up. So we've done all the messy work and now life will start to flow again, there will be people and children and voices, and in the excitement we shall be swept away down the nearest drain to Camden Town. The picture she had conjured up made her smile, but really, she thought, it isn't funny for us.

Down in the caretaker's cottage, the lawyer was talking to their mother. He would be explaining about the new owners, telling her that she would not be needed any longer, generously giving them a month's notice. Why did he have to take so long about it?

She looked around her at the mute, dishevelled toys, the silent clocks. They seemed not so much abandoned as resting, as if with a new generation, a change of fashion, they might find themselves called back into service. Perhaps we could retire to the attics too, she thought hopefully. It is such a big house, they would never miss a small flat up where the servants' bedrooms used to be. We could paste up the old wallpaper and make some new curtains . . . But why should the new owners bother with us? We could never explain what we have done for them, and it's not as if we are "old faithful servants", we have only been here a couple of months. How could we make them understand that in such a little time a house can take hold of your heart as surely as if you had been bound to it for hundreds of years.

'It's all very well for you,' she shouted angrily to all the voices which talked unceasingly just out of earshot. 'You will belong to someone again, but what about us? Where do we belong?'

The silence that followed was so intense that she knew the voices had stopped, and she felt as if all the ghosts were listening. When they began again, they seemed to be soothing, explaining ... But Lucy was in no mood to be soothed, in no mood to listen to explanations which she could never quite hear. She got to her feet and stamped out angrily, along the passage and down the stairs, ignoring the voices that called from the corners of the rooms.

She reached the first-floor landing where the fainting Bella had lain, charged on down the main stairs, and was on her way to the green baize door when she heard a call that was too strong. Reluctantly she turned and walked back, to the old drawing-room.

It was the blue vase that called her. It stood on its table in a pool of sunlight and Lucy flinched when she thought how close she had come to breaking it. She picked it up carefully and it was warm to touch; she saw how the light shimmered on the myriad cracks in the glaze. She did not know why the sight of the vase should comfort her, but it did. There was something about the endurance of an object so fine and so fragile that seemed to prove something. But as she did not know what it proved, she put it down gently and went off to find Jamie.

*

Jamie was lying in the long grass by the lake, trying to puzzle out in his mind what it all meant. It was not something he could discuss with Lucy. She would clutch at his vague hopes like a drowning man, and he could not bear her disappointment if he was wrong.

It was foolish to pin so many hopes upon a dream, for it had been a dream, that strange encounter with the lawyers. It had not been real and tangible like the meeting with Sara and Georgie. True, it had been clear and vivid in his mind ... But then dreams often are, he thought, like that time when I dreamed I quarrelled with Lucy and, although I knew it was a dream, I was angry with her all day for the rude things I dreamed she had said.

And yet he could not forget that the voice had said, 'Is this the boy?' Which boy? he wondered; surely any boy would have done? But if so, why had they asked his name? And why did Mr Blunden have to find me, why bring us here all the way from Camden Town unless ... But there were footsteps and Lucy was coming along the path. He sat up hastily and began to talk about nothing in particular as if she might have overheard his thoughts.

'Where have you been hiding?' he said. 'It's getting quite hot, isn't it? Has he finished yet?'

'In the attic. Yes isn't it. No, I don't think so,' answered Lucy.

She sat down on the grass beside him, and for a while they were both silent. Then she said, 'You know that blue vase?'

'The one that's cracked all over?' asked Jamie.

Lucy frowned. 'It's not exactly "cracked".'

'You know what I mean.'

'Well, anyway, I nearly smashed it ... when you were trying to get the keys from Mrs Wickens ... only I couldn't do it.'

Jamie said nothing.

'It's strange to think of it being here all this time. It was probably here before Sara and Georgie ...' She paused.

Jamie waited to see where she was leading.

'It will probably be here long after we have gone.'

'Probably,' said Jamie.

Suddenly, the endurance of the vase no longer seemed comforting, and Lucy heaved a sigh. 'It doesn't seem fair,' she said gloomily.

'Here comes Mother,' said Jamie, getting to his feet. He was relieved. He didn't feel up to a discussion about whether life was fair or not. He rather suspected that it wasn't.

Mrs Allen came walking along the path with a thin, anxious-looking man.

'It's not Mr Claverton,' Lucy sounded hopeful. 'Are you sure he's from the solicitors?'

'It's Smith, the one they keep forgetting. That's probably why he looks so nervous.'

He's like us, he doesn't feel he belongs, thought Lucy sympathetically, and resolved to be especially nice to him. She gave him her most dazzling smile and he brightened perceptibly.

'Mr Smith, these are my two older children, Lucy and James.' Mrs Allen was carrying the baby who spoiled the dignity of the introduction by blowing bubbles at his brother and sister.

'Mr Smith has brought us some very interesting news about the house,' she went on. She looked very calm and Jamie tried in vain to read some hint of their fate in her steady eyes. She sat down on an old garden seat near by, and the lawyer settled himself beside her. Lucy and Jamie sat on the grass and tried to look as if they did not care too much about the news he was bringing.

'I hope you don't mind repeating to the children all that you have told me.' Mrs Allen smiled. 'I'm sure I should never remember half the details.'

'I shall be delighted,' and indeed, Mr Smith did seem to relish finding himself the centre of attention. Even the baby was trying to wriggle across to investigate his briefcase.

When the lawyer had finished shuffling his papers, he coughed importantly. 'Well, now,' he said, 'to begin at the beginning.'

Jamie wished he would begin at the end and save a lot of suspense.

'My firm has for some time been engaged in tracing the records of the Latimer family who have owned this house for many hundreds of years. We had no difficulty with the late owner's father, Matthew, or his grandfather, George Latimer, for in each case the property passed from the father to his only child. However, with the death of Mr Michael Latimer, our late client, who was childless, this branch of the family came to an end.

'Now we found evidence that George Latimer, our late client's grandfather, had a sister, but we could find no record of her after her marriage in the year 1880. It seemed to us most likely that she had died in that year but our searches produced no death certificate. It therefore became necessary to account for her before we could go back any further in our search for heirs.

For many months we searched but it seemed that Sara Latimer, or Sara Fletcher as she was then, had vanished without trace.'

Jamie, who was politely stifling a yawn, nearly choked on it.

Lucy's eyes grew as round as a fish's. 'Sara and Georgie!' she began but she stopped short when she saw that Mr Smith was staring at her.

'Their names are familiar to you?' he asked, his voice incredulous.

Jamie thought fast. 'It was the vicar,' he said. 'He told Lucy about two children who were saved from a fire. Their names were Sara and Georgie.'

'There's a big, pink memorial in the churchyard,' added Lucy eagerly, 'to Mr Blunden, I mean his great-grandfather, because he rescued them.'

'Indeed,' the lawyer looked very despondent. 'I had not heard the story. But then, no one tells me anything. Of course, I have only been with the firm for fifteen years . . . ' He seemed to sink into gloom.

Oh Lord, thought Jamie, wishing that Lucy had never started this diversion, now he will never get to the point. 'Do tell us what you have discovered,' he said heartily, 'I'm sure it's much more interesting.'

Mr Smith brightened. 'Ah, yes,' he said. 'You may well think that it is! You see, we might never have come any closer to the truth but for a letter which arrived mysteriously in our office. It was from Sara herself,' he paused, relishing the blank disbelief on the children's faces, before adding, 'but it was not, of course, addressed to us personally. The envelope enclosing it bore our address in a fine copperplate hand, but it had no stamp or postmark, though we found it among our usual morning post. There was no covering note of explanation, no hint of who had sent it, only the old letter which I have here.

'It would seem that George Latimer quarrelled with his sister when she decided to marry a young man who had for many years been a gardener on the estate. Such a marriage would have caused a great scandal in those days when a wide gulf existed between the landed gentry and the working classes, and it seems probable from the difficulty which we had in tracing Miss Sara, that the breach between her and her brother was never healed.'

Jamie and Lucy stared at one another and it was all they could do to keep their suppressed excitement from bursting into delight. It seemed so right that Sara should have married Tom, and if Georgie didn't approve, well, he had always been a little snob. Since she had had to choose between them, it was good to know that she had chosen the faithful Tom.

Lucy thought it was the most romantic story she had ever heard. She remembered Tom's words when she had tried to stop him from climbing to the rescue: 'Happen I shall be killed, but there's some a person would gladly die for.' She wondered if anyone would ever feel like that about her.

But Mr Smith had unfolded the letter. 'We will let her speak for herself,' he was saying, and with a discreet clearing of his throat, he began to read:

My Dearest Brother,

In spite of all that has passed, I cannot bring myself to leave these shores without writing to beg you once again that we may be reconciled. Though it is hard, I know, for you to accept my marriage to Tom, yet I think you will be glad to know that we are happy, and that he is all that I would wish my husband to be. You will, perhaps, consider that to be impossible, since to you he is, and will always be, a servant, but I would remind you that he was so by accident of birth and not from any want of virtue or intelligence in himself. We sail in the morning for

America, and there I hope he may make for both of us a life in which natural talent may count for more than inherited wealth.

I need not remind you that I owe my life to his courage, yet it is not from any sense of obligation that I shall devote my future to his happiness. It is because of the great love that has grown between us since we were children together, that I shall go gladly into a new land where he may be allowed to prove his true worth.

Nevertheless, I would not have you think that in leaving you, I have ceased to love you. For so many years we had only each other, and your place in my heart can never belong to anyone else. It is a great grief to me to be estranged from you, and though you vowed upon my marriage never to acknowledge me again, yet the words were spoken in anger, and I cannot but hope that, as time passes, you will learn to forgive me.

Whether or not you reply to this letter, I shall continue to write to you and to tell you of the trials and joys that may lie ahead for us. Let me hear from you too, my dearest Georgie, so that I may be assured of your continuing health and happiness.

More I cannot write, for the mail must go ashore within the hour. Pray for us, as I shall pray for you, and believe me, in spite of all that has passed.

Your ever loving sister,

SARA LATIMER FLETCHER

As Lucy listened, the lawyer's dry tones seemed to fade and she heard Sara's level, gentle voice. She seemed almost to see her, grown up now but still dark and pretty, her wide grey eyes solemn as she sat in her tiny cabin in the gently rocking ship, writing her last appeal to Georgie before she sailed to a new land where, as Tom had once said, 'there was a fine future for a young man who could read and write and was not afraid of hard work'.

Even Mr Smith seemed moved by the letter, though he had read it many times before. He sighed before laying it aside and then returned with renewed eagerness to his story.

'This ... er ... touching document,' he said, 'directed our search to the United States of America where, I may say, inquiry agents are accustomed to moving very swiftly in these matters.'

His tone suggested that he considered such speed to

be ill-advised, and certainly, thought Jamie, his worst enemies could not have called Mr Smith 'hasty'.

'Within a very short time, we were furnished with names and dates and, er, photostat copies of documents which proved conclusively that Sara and Tom Fletcher had only one child, a daughter Georgina, who was married in due course to a young American named Allen.'

He produced the name with the satisfaction of a good conjurer who has performed a long and complicated sleight-of-hand ending in the appearance of a wriggling white rabbit. But it was all lost on Lucy.

'Alan who?' she asked blankly.

But for once Jamie's brain had raced home ahead of her. This time he knew, while Lucy was still groping in the darkness of her own confusion, exactly what Mr Smith had come to tell them. He knew, without a shadow of doubt, what the voice had meant when it asked, 'Is this the boy?'

He felt it would be cruel to spoil Mr Smith's story, but it was hard to keep his joy from breaking out on his face.

'Alan who?' tried Lucy again.

Mr Smith beamed. 'Not Alan anybody,' he said triumphantly, 'but Roderick Patterson Allen, who was your father's grandfather!'

Lucy frowned and thought hard for a moment. Then she shook her head. 'That couldn't be right,' she said firmly. 'I mean, that would make Sara our great-great-grandmother.'

Jamie seized hold of her hands and pulled her round to face him. He almost shook her in his excitement. 'That's the whole point, Lucy,' he said. 'She was, don't you see? She was! And Tom was our great-great-grandfather.'

Lucy began to say, 'But they weren't much older than ...'

Her voice died away as Jamie tightened his grip on her wrists. For a long moment they stared at each other while he willed her to understand and say nothing. Then he smiled, and his joy spread to her face like the glow of a fire.

'Oh, Jamie,' she said, 'the house and everything ... ?'

'The house and everything!' echoed Mr Smith, with a hearty boom of satisfaction. 'The entire Latimer estate will pass to your brother as the senior surviving member of the family.'

Lucy looked at Jamie, her mind working feverishly to grasp it all. 'It was because of what you did,' she said, hardly above a whisper.

'I suppose so,' said Jamie, 'and yet I never dreamed that it concerned us. I mean, not here and now.'

Mr Smith was rambling on. 'Of course, when we realized that the surviving descendants had for some time been, to use a colloquialism, "right under our noses", that they were already living, however unsuitably, in the caretaker's cottage on the estate, well, we were baffled by what seemed to us an incredible coincidence. But upon maturer reflection, it became clear to us that Mr Blunden had all along known, or at least suspected, something of this matter. Indeed, we have since come to believe that he may have been responsible for sending us the copy of Sara Latimer's letter.'

'Oh, I guessed it would be him,' said Lucy.

Mr Smith smiled indulgently. 'We have asked him, of course, but alas, he is an old man. His mind wanders and his memory has quite gone. That was why he retired,' he lowered his voice confidentially, 'it was becoming very difficult ...'

'Oh, but it wasn't that Mr Blunden,' interrupted Lucy, but she stopped abruptly at a glance from Jamie. 'I mean,' she went on, 'that he didn't seem as if his mind was wandering when he came to see us. He was, well, like a different man ...'

Mr Smith nodded. 'He has his good days and his bad days,' he agreed. 'But then, I have not come to gossip about an ex-partner of my firm. No, indeed, I came only to break the good news to Mrs Allen, that the house and the estate will pass to your son, with trustees to take care of his interests until he is of age.

'I realize, of course, that you may not wish to be troubled with a house of this size, and one so remotely situated, but we should be able to find a reliable tenant and the rents can be reinvested in some more suitable ...'

'No!' said Jamie. He said it very loudly and clearly and more authoritatively than he had ever said anything in his short life before.

Mr Smith stopped short and stared at him.

'No,' repeated Jamie. This time it was quieter, but just as firm. 'You said that the house was mine.'

'Of course' – the lawyer looked hurt – 'but you must be advised by those with more experience of business.'

'I'm sure you know more about business,' said Jamie, 'but I know more about the house. We've all been happy again since we've been here, and I shall never part with it even though we haven't got a penny beside.'

Lucy could have hugged him.

'Oh, there will be an adequate income,' said Mr Smith, 'even after duty has been paid. I'm sure I'm very pleased to find that you have become so attached to the place, though I don't know what your mother will think.'

Mrs Allen had been very quiet all this time, sitting with her face half-hidden against the baby's warm neck, watching Lucy and Jamie as they learned the good news.

Now she said gently, 'It is Jamie's house and he must do as he thinks best, but I shall be very happy if he decides we are to stay.'

Jamie felt his face glowing. He knew that this day marked a great milestone in his life, and not only because of the inheritance. He understood that in leaving the decision to him, his mother was telling him that he must now begin to take his father's place, so that life could flow on again instead of lying stagnant in a backwater of grief.

Mr Smith looked from one to the other with an attempt at a smile. He sensed that more was being said than the words that were spoken and, as an outsider, he found it a little confusing. He decided to change the subject. 'I take it then,' he said jovially, 'that there has been no trouble with the, er ... ' he put one hand in front of his mouth and turning to Mrs Allen, hissed in a loud stage-whisper ... 'ghosts?'

The children's mother laughed. 'No trouble at all,' she said, putting her head on one side to escape the baby who was poking his fist in her mouth. 'I'm afraid I don't believe in them.'

'No, no, of course not.' He beamed at Lucy and Jamie. 'No such things as ghosts, eh, children?'

Jamie said, 'It depends on your point of view.'

The lawyer looked blank.

Lucy said, 'We are all ghosts in a way.'

He began to look nervous and she grew confused. 'I mean, Jamie and I might be ghosts in a hundred years' time, and no one could be afraid of us, could they?'

Mr Smith's jaw dropped. He was already a little afraid of these rather peculiar children. But he pulled himself together and said, 'My goodness, no! Well, my dear Mrs Allen, I must really be off now, if I am to be back in London tonight.'

He shook hands with them very solemnly and Jamie and Lucy watched him as he walked with their mother across the lawn back towards his car.

'You can't explain to them, can you?' said Jamie.

Lucy shook her head. 'Not even to Mummy,' she agreed. 'They would think we were joking if we said we should love to see our ghosts again.' She hesitated a moment and then asked wistfully, 'Do you suppose we ever shall?'

Jamie sighed. 'I don't think so,' he said. 'I don't think the need will ever be great enough, but we shall know that they are here.'

There was a long silence; then Lucy said, 'Do you suppose Sara knew? I mean, that we were her great-great-grandchildren?'

Jamie laughed. Something about the idea was irresistibly funny, but he tried to take it seriously. 'I don't think she could have done,' he said at last. 'After all, if we hadn't managed to save them, then she wouldn't have been our great-great-grandmother, would she?'

They considered the implications of this possibility, but it was beyond them to make sense of it.

'Who cares anyway about what might have been?' said Jamie recklessly. 'We did and she was, and now the Old House is ours and the lake and the fountain and the gardens. And I'm going to run round the whole place without stopping, just to see what it feels like.'

And before Lucy could answer, he was off through the sunlit gardens, running and jumping with his arms spread wide as if to gather his whole inheritance to him.

Lucy watched him as he went: across the shaggy lawn where Tom had lain while Sara wiped his smoke-blackened face; along the gravel path where Georgie had stood, kicking the stones with his shadowless feet; past the pink rhododendron bush where they had crouched in hiding from the big man; across the old herb garden, trampling the musk and the madwort underfoot; until he vanished out of sight, behind the creeper-covered ruins of the library.

Then she smiled, and turning went quietly indoors on her way back to the attics. There was just a chance, she thought, now she belonged to the house, that she might be able to make out what the voices of the ghosts were saying.